Unexpectedly,

MILO

D1007162

Also by the Author

Something Missing

Unexpectedly,

MILO

A Novel

matthew dicks

Broadway Books
New York

BROADWAY

Copyright © 2010 by Matthew Dicks

All rights reserved.
Published in the United States by Broadway Books, an imprint of the Crown Publishing Group, a division of Random House, Inc., New York.
www.crownpublishing.com

BROADWAY BOOKS and the Broadway Books colophon are trademarks of Random House, Inc.

Library of Congress Cataloging-in-Publication Data

Dicks, Matthew.
    Unexpectedly, Milo : a novel / Matthew Dicks. — 1st ed.
        p. cm.
    1. Married people—Fiction.   2. Obsessive-compulsive
disorder—Fiction.   3. Psychological fiction.   I. Title.

    PS3604.I323U63 2010
    813'.6—dc22

                                        2010011082

ISBN 978-0-307-59230-9

Printed in the United States of America

10   9   8   7   6   5   4   3   2   1

First Edition

For
Jim Bengiovanni,
an only child
who became a brother

acknowledgments

This book would not have been the same without the assistance of countless friends and experts, but it would not exist at all if not for my wife, Elysha, who inspires me every day. I was recently asked by a reporter to describe what "gets me up in the morning." The answer is simple: an insatiable desire to convince my wife that I am worthy of her love and not quite the fool that I often appear to be.

Much love and appreciation to my in-laws, Barbara and Gerry Green, who have reminded me what the unwavering love and constant support of parents can feel like.

Many thanks to all of my ever-faithful readers, who continue to read each chapter with a boundless enthusiasm, a critical eye, and a generous heart. I know there are many authors who can write entire books without allowing anyone to see a single word. I do not understand these people, nor do I try. The constant audience that I enjoy is a blessing that I do not take for granted.

A special thanks to Matthew Shepard and Cindy Raynis, who never failed to read and provide insightful commentary on each chapter within twenty-four hours of distribution. Shep's analytic style, Cindy's discerning eye, and their shared affection for Milo have improved this story by leaps and bounds.

Thanks to Carole MacKenzie for her keen insight into obsessive-compulsive disorder.

Great appreciation goes to Alison Kerr Miller, the copyeditor for this book. I have begun to believe that editors' names should appear on the cover of every book, in recognition for all the work that they do in bringing a story to the finish line. Alison's expertise has spared me countless moments of literary embarrassment and has helped to craft a clearer, more cohesive narrative. Her invisible but vital imprint is hiding on every page of this book.

Thanks to Melissa Danaczko, my editor and friend, who once again has demonstrated that when an author and an editor seem to share the same brain, true collaboration can flourish. How fortunate I have been to find an editor whose opinions I respect and value without hesitation.

Lastly, thanks to Taryn Fagerness, my agent and friend, who is too humble to acknowledge how she has changed my life forever. From assuaging my flagging confidence to lending her expertise in crafting this book, Taryn has stood alongside me every step of the way. It is a strange and wondrous thing for your top-of-the-mountain, all-time heroine to be your agent and friend as well, but Taryn has been all this and more to me and my family.

prologue

The moment that Milo Slade had attempted to avoid for nearly his entire life finally arrived under the sodium glow of a parking lot florescent at a Burger King just south of Washington, D.C., along Interstate 95. His wife, Christine, about three hundred miles north of his position, was completely unaware of his present location. Though his sudden and unexplained disappearance may have been a cause of concern for her just one week ago, Milo suspected that it was significantly less so now.

Things had changed so much in such a short period of time.

The camera and the tapes, the objects that had ultimately led him to this moment, were also back in Connecticut, left there purposely lest he be unable to stop himself from watching. These items had been in his possession for less than two weeks, and he felt guilty enough for what he had seen already.

It was just after seven P.M., and his passenger and fellow traveler had expressed the need to use a restroom. Though Milo also needed to urinate, he decided to forgo nature's call and use the time alone to access some of the jars of jelly from the trunk of the Honda in order to satisfy one of the mounting demands making rational thought almost impossible. Almost an hour ago, Milo had been forced to complain to his companion about the overwhelming headache that had been plaguing him ever since the first of these demands had taken shape in his mind. Though he was loath to admit to the suffering, always wanting to keep every aspect of the demands as secretive as possible, he felt he needed to in order to limit the conversation in the car and allow him to direct all of his mental energy to the road ahead. An offer had been made to take the wheel, as he knew it would, but Milo knew that the pressure would only increase if he were sitting in a passenger seat with nothing on which to direct his attention. With each passing mile, the demands had grown stronger and louder, though that wasn't quite right since they issued no actual sound. Instead, each inexplicable demand blazed away in his mind like a small sun, a silent, unstoppable imperative that consumed all thought and reason. And as they did so, the confines of the Honda had seemed to become smaller and smaller. He had grown fidgety, his arms and legs feeling almost electrified. Even in the limited space of the driver's seat, he was unable to sit still. The fillings in his teeth had begun to ache. He was perspiring profusely. His brain felt as if it were trapped in an ever-tightening vise.

The physical toll of the demands had never been so terrible.

He had tried switching the Honda's cruise control on and off in an effort to release some of the pressure on his mind and body but found no relief. He had tried adjusting the power mirrors, and still no effect. He had pretended to accidentally lock and unlock the doors in hopes that the pop of the power locks might afford some reprieve, but it had not. Finally, he had risked snapping and unsnapping his jeans, just once, but even this had offered little in the way of respite. The demands were too many and too loud for his usual delaying strategies to work. There were four of them now, a never-before-seen number, pressing on one another like a crowd battling its way to a locked exit door in the middle of a fire.

The demand to open those jars of jelly.

The demand to replace the stale air in the Honda's tires with fresh air.

The demand to bowl a strike.

The demand to sing "99 Luftballons" to anyone who would listen.

He expected others to follow shortly, as the mounting pressure would undoubtedly force new and ever-more-challenging demands to the surface. Weebles and ice cubes and drink boxes and those goddamn words would surely follow, and maybe even some new demands not currently found in his repertoire. He wondered how much more of this he could take.

In short, Milo was a man slowly losing his mind.

But he hoped that the jars of jelly would help. The twisting of the lid, the satisfying pop of the pressure seal, and the subsequent, almost imperceptible yet supremely powerful hiss might alleviate enough of the building pressure to allow him to continue his journey.

As he feared, two jars had not been enough. He had moved a total of nine from the trunk to the front seat, the remains of his stash, and though he would've liked to have found the time to conceal them under his seat, away from the prying eyes of his passenger, he had not. Delaying their opening for even a second had become impossible.

Milo was in the midst of opening his fifth jar, having lost all track of time in the euphoric pop of the pressure seals, when the passenger door opened, the interior light came on, and the woman attempted to reenter the Honda. She paused for a moment, staring at the four opened jars of Smucker's grape jelly (Milo's preferred brand for satisfying this demand) on her seat, their lids stacked neatly in a rectangular space in the console, before asking, "Uh . . . what's this?"

Milo was sitting behind the wheel, a jar of jelly in his hand and four more sealed jars in his lap. His left hand wrapped tightly around the jar and his right gripped the lid, ready to turn. For a moment, he considered lying to the woman. After all, he'd spent the last three years of marriage, and two years of courtship before that, concealing these demands from his wife. His parents and even his friends were equally unaware, even though they consumed an enormous portion of his life. And even with the mounting pressure, greater than any he had felt before, he was still filled with shame of this secret part of him. Perhaps he could invent a story about contaminated jars of Smucker's and the desire for a peanut butter and jelly sandwich. The story would have been ridiculous (least of all because he had no bread), but the truth, he knew, would be infinitely more so. Still, he might have tried to offer up a plausible explanation for the jars of jelly strewn about the car, but it was because he was about to open the fifth jar, and because he knew that he would need at least a couple more in order to silence the demand, that Milo finally decided to forgo the lies. Though it might have eventually proven impossible, perhaps he would have been able to put off the demands a little while longer, maybe long enough to find a hotel room and satisfy enough of them to make it back to Connecticut safely. But now that he was in the midst of satisfaction— had begun the process of release—he knew that there was no stopping. He could not simply toss the remaining jars into the backseat and drive on as if nothing were wrong. And from the look on the woman's face as she placed the open jars on the floor, settled in to her seat, and turned to face him, it would've been impossible for her to ignore the jars as well.

The time for secrets had finally come to an end.

"Just give me a minute and I'll explain everything," Milo said, then turned the lid on the jar, absorbed the satisfying pop of the pressure seal, and sighed heavily.

chapter 1

When he first spotted the video camera sitting on the end of the park bench beneath the dying elm, Milo didn't take it. He had wanted to take it, to be sure. Not steal it, but claim it first in the event that it had been left behind by a careless owner who might never return. But there were still a few stragglers in the park that evening, and one of them might have left the camera behind, relying on the goodness of man to keep it safe. Though a video camera was something Milo would have liked to own, the act of approaching the bench, reaching down, and placing his hands on the device would require more daring than he could ever muster. Just stopping to take notice of it had left Milo with the feeling that a thousand eyes had been cast on him, forcing him to nudge his dog forward along the path.

Opportunity lost, he had thought as he rounded the hill in the direction of his new home.

So when he returned the following evening and found the same camera in the same location, Milo couldn't help but think that fortune was somehow smiling on him, forcing him into action. Though the north end of the park was typically deserted because of its lack of amenities (other than the single bench), the fact that the camera had lasted more than twenty-four hours without being claimed by someone, owner or otherwise, was remarkable. And although approximately the same number of stragglers was still present in the park, picnicking across the field near the gazebo and finishing up a game of basketball on the shadow-strewn court, Milo felt more emboldened this evening as he approached the shade of the elm.

Deciding to claim it for his own, he sat down beside the camera, commanding Skywalker, his newly renamed beagle, to heel while he stalled, hoping to add a perceived purpose to his stop. After what he felt was a sufficient period of time, he reached over and casually grabbed the device, which was small enough to fit in one hand, and had begun to straighten up when he noticed the nylon bag in the shadow beneath the bench.

Reflecting on the moment much later, Milo would grin, thinking how close he had come to missing the camera bag entirely. Though he had always thought that it was the camera that had changed his life, it was really the bag, filled with those fourteen numbered tapes, that had set things in motion.

Conflagration.

The word filled Milo's mind as he and Skywalker covered the mile between the park and his apartment. For the trip home, he had placed the video camera into the black bag and slung it over his shoulder, affirming his newfound ownership over the device in one single motion.

Conflagration.

For reasons that he would never understand, this was the latest in a series of hundreds, maybe thousands of words that became lodged in his mind from time to time over the course of his life, though "lodged" was perhaps an understatement. These words appeared suddenly, for no apparent reason, and though they started as a tickle in the back of his mind, they quickly grew to consume every bit of his mental processes, infiltrating the farthest corners of his brain, burning in his head to the point of physical pain until they were at last satisfied.

Conflagration.

The word had been in his thoughts for almost a week, an uncommonly long period of time in comparison to most, and so the pressure and tension building in his head was especially high. No matter what Milo did, where he went or what he thought, *conflagration* remained in the forefront, serving as an aching, insidious, and insistent distracter to all that he attempted. And as with all previous words, Milo had no idea why this particular one chose to take up residence in his mind, but as with the rest, he knew that there was only one way to rid himself of it. If things went well, he might have to endure the word for only one more day.

Milo's new home was a one-bedroom apartment on Willard Avenue in the town of Newington, Connecticut, about a mile from his real home, which was currently occupied by his wife, Christine. Milo had been separated from Christine for about three weeks, and he still had yet to completely unpack. Boxes were neatly stacked about the living room and kitchen, and his bedroom furniture consisted only of his bed and desk, both extricated from his home during the rapid departure (or what he thought of as an escape) from his house on Wilson Road.

Milo's marriage to Christine had been in decline for more than a year when she finally asked Milo for "space," and after two months of stalling, hoping that things would eventually improve, he finally began taking steps to rent an apartment close to the house in order to accommodate what he thought had been his wife's request.

Though digging through boxes for a clean pair of underwear was getting old, Milo was not anxious to finish unpacking. Part of him hoped that the separation wouldn't last long. He and Christine had been married for almost three years, and although there were clearly issues that needed to be worked out between them, he couldn't imagine permanently upending things over a few squabbles. They had a home, a dog, and a life together, and he had expected them to be discussing children soon. Making such drastic changes to his future seemed incomprehensible.

Nevertheless, for weeks prior to his departure, Milo had begun assembling the items that he thought he might need in the event that he was forced to move out. In the words of his best friend, Andy, "A woman can only ask for space for so long before she's going to tell you to get the fuck out." As much as he hated to admit it, Milo knew that his friend was right. Every time Christine broached the topic of *space*, never specifically requesting a separation but only suggesting the need for some time apart, Milo would acknowledge her comment with a dejected "I know," but he would say nothing more, waiting for his wife to press the issue. He sensed that Christine did not want to be the one to specifically tell Milo to *get the fuck out* and was hoping that her husband would instead take the hint and offer to move out on his own. At the same time, Milo was hoping that Andy was wrong and that Christine would eventually come to her senses. But even in the beginning, he feared that she would not, and so he had begun a slow but steady process of preparing to move out.

Stopping at a tag sale on the way to pick up coffee for Christine one morning, he had purchased a pair of lamps and a can opener for eight dollars, stuffing the items into the trunk of his car in the event that he suddenly found himself on his own in need of adequate lighting and a tuna fish sandwich. This was followed by more and more surreptitious Saturday-morning visits to tag sales and flea markets, where he continued to fill his trunk to the point of nearly bursting. Though it took him weeks to accept the inevitable, he wanted to be equipped to move on, knowing in his heart that he might soon be living alone with his best friend, Puggles, whose name he had changed to Skywalker during his first week in the apartment. Though his friends thought him crazy for changing the name of a dog that he had owned for two years, Milo understood that dogs reacted more to tone than words, so an excited, high-pitched *"Skywalker!"* proved to attract just as much attention from his beagle as did a similarly intoned *"Puggles!"*

Besides, he had always hated the name that Christine had given the dog.

It had been during their late-afternoon runs that the deterioration of the marriage had become obvious to Milo. Though things had apparently been going sour for some time (at least in Christine's estimation), he had never suspected real trouble until they began running together in early spring. Despite the never-ending plague of odd and inexplicable demands placed on him, Milo had managed to effectively conceal each and every one from his wife from the moment they had begun dating, and this, in addition to other, more routine efforts to keep Christine happy, should have been more than enough to keep their marriage on a sound footing. At least this is what Milo had thought when they began jogging through the neighborhood, side by side.

Christine had taken up the sport after years of relatively little physical activity, so it had come to as a surprise to Milo when he came home one day to find her doubled over and panting in the kitchen. Though she had always been in fine shape, her late-afternoon runs, seemingly initiated on a whim, had begun to take on an almost religious quality when Milo finally asked to join her. Upon reflection, he should have known that the sudden urge to exercise was a sign of trouble. He had seen married women begin intense exercise regimes before, and it usually signaled one of three things: The wife had experienced a health scare, the wife was having an affair, or the husband had been caught cheating. Though none of these was the case in Milo and Christine's marriage (as far as Milo knew), he suspected that Christine was attempting to dramatically improve her physical appearance, and he should have realized that few women (or men) are willing to do this for a spouse after three years of marriage.

Christine agreed to allow Milo to run with her, and for the first month, she finished the two-mile route through the neighborhood well ahead of her breathless, bedraggled husband. But as Milo continued to run, his high school cross-country genes began to reassert themselves, and his desire to impress his wife soon had him running stride for stride with her along the course. As Milo's endurance and speed improved, he noticed that Christine continued to push the pace, running faster and harder as Milo attempted to keep up, until one day, as they rounded a corner in a near sprint, Christine drew to a stop, threw up her hands, and shouted, "What the hell?"

Milo pulled to a stop along his wife, oblivious to the cause of her anger. Though in retrospect the cause should have been obvious, at the time it was not. "What's the matter?"

"You just keep coming, don't you? You can't let me have my own thing! You just have to be better than me!"

"Honey, I'm just trying to keep up with you," he said between breaths. "I don't need to pass you. Just keep up. I thought you wanted me to run with you?"

"I did," she snapped. She looked at her husband for a moment, eyes bulging, breathing heavily, seeming to search for more words, and for a second, Milo thought that his wife might be in the midst of a panic attack, a condition to which she was occasionally prone. Though these attacks could result in hyperventilation, a loss of equilibrium, and disorientation, Christine's primary concern had always been the public spectacle and potential embarrassment that she might suffer if one was to ever strike while outside the home, as had happened when she was younger. If Christine were to experience one of these attacks in a public location, like this street corner, Milo was under orders to remove her from the situation as best he could, as quickly as he could, in order to prevent further embarrassment.

But this was not a panic attack, Milo realized rather quickly, but simply a moment of extreme anger and a subsequent loss for words, something that did not happen often to a litigator such as Christine. For the first time that Milo could remember, his wife didn't know what to say. For a moment, he thought she might apologize. "I don't know what came over me," he half expected her to admit, which would be followed by a brief embrace and an offer of sex when they returned home.

After all, he hadn't done anything wrong.

But for almost a minute, Christine said nothing, and the protracted silence made Milo uneasy. Finally, she spoke, settling on "Never mind," and took off in another sprint. Unsure what to do, Milo broke into a sprint himself, trying to catch his wife. He understood what she had been trying to say, but at the same time, he couldn't understand the logic behind it at all. Had she hoped to always outdistance him, and if so, why bother running together at all? For Milo, who was twenty pounds overweight, the challenge had been to just keep pace with his wife, yet unknowingly and unintentionally, he had apparently stolen a source of pride from her. The expected admiration that he thought his wife might feel for his ability to match her pace couldn't have been farther from reality, and he still couldn't understand why.

Nevertheless, Milo had no intention of allowing his wife to finish ahead of him that day. To walk into the house after her would mean facing the awkward silence that comes after a couple has engaged in marital combat and is then forced to immediately resume their daily activities under the same roof. Milo hated this form of vicious, nonverbal warfare, the purposeful absence of words where there would normally be many. If Christine finished the run first, she would invariably be in the shower by the time Milo arrived home, and rather than shouting, "The shower's all yours!" when finished, she would exit the bathroom without a word, probably donning a robe rather than remaining naked as she crossed the hallway into the bedroom. Standing in front of the dresser, she would begin drying her hair, refusing to even acknowledge his presence as he made his way to the bathroom for his own shower. This stubborn unwillingness to speak, an indication of anger through a deniable lack of words, would persist throughout dinner and perhaps all night unless Milo did something about it. By forcing polite conversation on his wife and preventing a break in the action, he would give Christine no choice but to either resume hostilities with another verbal barrage or stand down. Standing down was her typical response in these circumstances, but either one was preferable to that dreadful silence.

So with a burst of speed that he didn't know he had, Milo caught his wife as she rounded the final turn and ascended the two hundred yards of hill leading to the couple's driveway. He passed his wife over the last twenty yards, then clutched his knees, gasping for breath, in front of their home as she jogged by declaring that she was going for a walk to cool down.

Whether Christine had meant to cool down from the argument or from the run was unclear, but since she had never walked before, Milo had assumed the former. Aware of the continued threat of silence if the two separated at this crucial moment, Milo adopted his cheeriest voice and replied, "Great! I'll come along."

He had always been good at pretending that nothing was wrong. Expert, in fact.

So began the tradition of a walk following their run, and what Milo considered to be the beginning of the end.

Even with the weeks of preparation, Milo couldn't help but feel a little depressed each time he entered the apartment and was faced with its spartan furnishings. The lamps that he had purchased at the tag sale were sitting on the floor, flanking a sagging futon that Milo had rescued from the basement during the move. Opposite the futon was a television perched upon one of the four wooden chairs from the battered kitchen table, which he had also removed from the basement. DVDs were stacked neatly beside the chair in alphabetical order, with Sigourney Weaver's first two *Alien* films (the rest were an abomination) on top and the *X-Files* boxed set (all nine seasons for just $124.99) on the bottom. Though he and Christine had purchased a number of movies as a couple, both had brought a collection of their own films to the marriage as well, and Milo had extricated his DVDs during the move. He had also taken about two dozen other movies that he had received as gifts or were films that he knew Christine would never want to see again, including the Matrix trilogy, *Hoosiers*, all six Star Wars films, and the first seven seasons of *The Simpsons*.

He had anticipated many lonely nights in the apartment until he and Christine settled their differences, and he had wanted to be ready to fill his time as best he could.

Milo ate a silent dinner of peanut butter and jelly sandwiches off a paper plate before taking the time to examine the camera more closely. It was a Panasonic, similar to one owned by his friend Andy, with a small fold-out display screen for recording and viewing previously recorded material. The battery attached to the camera indicated a nearly full charge, and there was no tape loaded.

In the nylon bag, Milo found an extra battery, a charger, and fourteen tapes, each conveniently numbered with a black felt-tip marker. He removed the tape marked "#1" and placed it into the camera. After a moment of fumbling for the right switch, he managed to get the tape to play. The screen was blank for several moments, and then a woman's face filled the frame and began speaking.

Things would never be the same.

chapter 2

"So you stole it?" the elderly woman in the wheelchair asked as Milo reached for the rake.

"I told you, Edith. I didn't steal it. It was sitting there for *two days*."

"My husband, Ed Marchand, used to say that if you don't earn the money, you don't get the honey. That was his way of keeping me from using my credit cards, but the rule applies here too, I think."

Milo sighed. Even though *conflagration* continued to burn in his mind at an ever-increasing rate, Edith Marchand had a way of distracting him from these inexplicable demands like no other. "Edith, gimme a break or you're going to do this yourself," he said without conviction, motioning to the rake and then to the living room carpet. "Besides, I told you that I was going to try to find the owner."

Edith laughed as Milo pulled the rake through the maroon shag that stretched across the spacious living room. Even though he knew that it was at his expense, Milo loved to listen to the old lady cackle. In fact, it was essentially what he was paid to do. Although the needs of his clients varied greatly, his ultimate responsibility was to keep each one of them as happy and as healthy as possible while their bodies and minds slowly but surely betrayed them.

"You're just trying to find the owner because you saw her on that tape," Edith said. "If you hadn't found those tapes, you wouldn't have given it a second thought."

Milo couldn't disagree. Though seeing the woman in the video had played at least a small role in his decision to seek her out, it had been the frankness and honesty in her voice that had captivated him. It had also sent a streak of guilt through his system, knowing that he had taken her camera, and more important, her apparent confessional.

> *Mira died today. This morning. God . . . like eight hours ago. So I thought I'd finally start doing this. It's as good a time as any.*
>
> *I still can't believe she's dead. It was just eight hours ago, but it feels like the whole world has changed. Like everything has been tossed in the air and completely rearranged. I can't believe that she's gone, and that there's no one to blame but me.*

She had freckles spotting her cheeks. That was what Milo had noticed first. Not the round, defined freckles that marked Christine's inner thighs, freckles that had once seemed mysterious and lusty to Milo but had since become just another part of the marital landscape. These were faint red blotches that climbed the heights of the young woman's smile. And the woman on the tape *was smiling,* despite the topic of conversation. Someone named Mira was dead, and she was to blame. And though she was upset . . . angry, really, downright pissed off, with the trails of tears still visible on her face, she had managed to smile nonetheless. She looked like the kind of woman who could always muster a smile, no matter the circumstance.

Her round face filled almost the entire frame, her auburn hair framing the image. Nothing else to distinguish time or location. Just a pretty, freckle-faced girl and her pretty voice.

"Don't forget to rake under the armchair," Edith reminded him.

"I won't," Milo replied. "But I'll never understand why I need to rake under a piece of furniture that never moves."

"My husband, Ed Marchand, used to say that it isn't what's on the surface that matters. It's what folks don't see that counts the most."

In truth, Milo had a difficult time understanding why Edith Marchand, a widow for more than two decades, saw the need to have any of her shag carpeting raked each week. Though he had to admit that the resulting effect, with the individual threads all leaning in one direction like the freshly cut grass on a professional baseball field, was strangely appealing, he wondered how she explained this oddity to the members of her weekly bridge game or her book club. Did she really tell these white-haired ladies that the nurse who was paid by her son to visit each week raked the carpet for her? Did they even notice?

"What exactly did the young lady say?" Edith asked, lifting her feet to allow Milo to rake beneath them. Edith Marchand was in a wheelchair, but she was still capable of walking short distances and raising her legs when the need demanded.

"Just what I told you. I only watched about fifteen minutes of tape before Christine called. And more than half of that was a kite. Like she was holding the camera with one hand and the string with the other."

"So she only talked about her friend dying?"

"Pretty much."

Though Milo had been tempted to fast-forward through the eight minutes of kite aerobatics, he refrained, hoping to catch a spat of unintentional dialogue during its dance in the sky. Other than a couple of gasps and a muttered *"Fuck!"* when the camera and the string nearly became entangled, Freckles hadn't said a word. When her face once again filled the frame and she resumed speaking, she was lying in the grass, the camera just inches from her nose.

> *This sounds like the worst cliché ever, but I keep expecting to wake up and find out that it's all a dream. That Mira is fine and I'm going to see her tomorrow like always. I was walking home tonight, past people who were talking and laughing, and I kept wishing that I could be them instead of me. Their lives looked so easy and good compared to mine. God, I was so happy yesterday. How can things change so quickly?*

Finished with the carpet, Milo placed the rake back on its assigned hook in the linen closet and returned to the living room, grimacing in pain as *conflagration* resumed its persistent torment. With every minute that passed, the word grew in strength and intensity, its viselike grip on his mind ever tightening. Though he had suffered through a week or more with these words before, there had not been many like this, and the pressure was becoming unbearable. He would need to execute his removal plan soon.

A cup of steaming tea was awaiting him on the coffee table. Milo didn't like tea very much, but he drank a cup each week with Edith because he knew that doing so made her happy.

Ed Marchand had once enjoyed a daily cup of tea with his wife.

"So what is your plan?" Edith asked, dropping a sugar cube in her cup.

"I dunno. I'm going to watch some more of the tape and hopefully figure out who she is. Maybe she'll say her name or I'll see an address at some point."

"I wasn't talking about your stranger. I meant Christine. What is your plan with her?"

"Oh."

Since Milo and Christine had separated, they had spoken several times on the phone, but the conversations had been awkward at best. For more than three years, the couple had lived under the same roof and slept in the same bed, oftentimes sharing the same pillow. More than one thousand days of routine and ritual, not counting the two years that they were together prior to their marriage, was now lost. Milo still occasionally awoke in the middle of the night wondering where he was. And even though they were now living only a mile apart from each other, with every day that went by the distance seemed to expand exponentially. It was almost unfathomable for Milo to envision his wife sitting at home alone while he sat equally unattended in his undecorated apartment.

Most of all, it made him feel guilty.

Though it had been Christine who initially asked for space, Milo had apparently misunderstood her request and taken things further than necessary. When he finally decided to move out, after Christine's umpteenth appeal, he had chosen an apartment close to home, hoping that the two would eventually work things out. A visit to a couples' therapist was planned in the near future, and perhaps the time apart would do them some good. In fact, Milo had begun looking at the separation as a positive step to improving their marriage. The time away might be good for them, providing them with an opportunity to appreciate what they had.

In truth, the prospect of living alone, without the need to hide the constant, unpredictable demands like *conflagration* from his wife, if even for a short period of time, appealed to Milo.

And since he had moved out of the house, Milo had also found that these demands were more easily fulfilled. Twice in the past three weeks he had climbed out of the bed, left his house in the middle of the night, and driven to Vernon's around-the-clock bowling alley in order to fulfill the sudden need to bowl a strike. Bowling a strike was a common and recurring demand for Milo, but it was one of the more logistically difficult needs to fulfill. Inexplicably, it often struck in the middle of the night, when a trip to the bowling alley would have been impossible even though the lanes were still open. Explaining to his wife that he needed to bowl a strike because something inside his head insisted on him doing so was not a conversation that Milo was willing to attempt. He knew that his entire relationship was predicated on his ability to keep his demands concealed from his wife, and during their three years of marriage, he had done this masterfully. Unfortunately, this meant that some demands had to wait longer than Milo would have liked, creating more tension and stress than he could sometimes manage. But he had always found a way of keeping them at bay until they could be fulfilled without his wife's knowledge. Much of this was accomplished thanks to the freedom of his job and his advance planning. Jars of jelly hidden in the basement in case of emergency, books with their price tags still affixed on the shelves, ice cube trays loaded with ice, and other supplies helped in times of crisis, though Milo sometimes wondered if the presence of these items in his house also caused the needs to arise more frequently than they might have normally.

Then there were the new demands, the ones that he had never experienced before, which were impossible to predict or prepare for. About six months before moving out, Milo suddenly found himself needing to acquire a Weeble, a plastic toy that was shaped like an egg with a weighted bottom, so that it would wobble when pushed, but never fall completely over. He had played with these toys as a child (*Weebles wobble, but they don't fall down!*) but could not explain their sudden reemergence in his consciousness. Nevertheless, he needed the toy, and he knew what must be done with it: Place it in the doorjamb, in the space between the hinges, so that when he slammed the door shut, it would compress the Weeble against the frame, exploding it into tiny plastic bits. He had no idea where this need came from or even if Weebles could still be purchased in toy stores, but with a weekend full of planned activities, he had found this new demand especially challenging.

Thankfully, acquiring the Weeble had proven to be easier than Milo had first imagined. He expected that he might need to purchase the toy from eBay or a similar collectible website but was surprised to find them still available in the local Toys "R" Us. But it took two days for Milo to get to the store after verifying their availability online, since he and Christine had been together for every second of the day. Even after purchasing the toy (and six others just like it in case one wasn't enough), it took another half a day before Milo could place it in the crack between the basement door and the frame, since explaining these actions to his wife would be even more difficult than the actual purchase of the toy. In the end, he had waited until she was in the shower before fulfilling this demand, and thankfully, one Weeble proved to be more than enough.

The sense of relief had been extraordinary.

Milo had been keeping secrets like these from his wife for far too long, and though revealing his secrets to Christine was not in the realm of possibility, the vacation from the lies and half-truths that their separation had afforded had been better than expected.

Christine, however, had not reacted with a similar enthusiasm.

When he arrived home on a Friday night and announced that he had signed a lease, expecting to be greeted with ironic appreciation, Christine's reaction couldn't have been more unexpected. "I didn't mean for you to get an apartment! I was thinking about a couple weeks at Andy's house! What the hell are you thinking?"

Milo stood dumbstruck in the kitchen, still dripping from the downpour outside, unsure if his wife was even telling the truth.

When a wife asks a husband for space, and when she asks for it as many times as Christine had, Milo thought that she could only be requesting a trial separation. "Are you serious?" he shot back. "Are you really serious?"

"Of course I am! I never told you to sign a lease. What in God's name are you thinking?"

Milo knew quite well what he had been thinking. He had been thinking about the dozens of requests for *space* and *time apart* from a wife who barely made an effort to speak to him anymore. He had been thinking about all the ways that he had tried to change the subject, ignore the request, appease Christine and otherwise dodge the topic altogether. He had been thinking about the fear and pain and uncertainty that came with each of Christine's requests for space and how he had finally come to terms with her appeal.

But in all honesty, he had also been thinking about a break from the secrecy and lies that his inexplicable demands demanded. A vacation from the constant vigilance and need for preparation in order to ensure that his demands and their satisfaction remained hidden from his wife. A little time alone, so he could live in peace with his oddities while simultaneously fulfilling the wishes of his angry wife.

Milo had also been thinking about the hours of walking that he and Christine had been doing, the four months of loops through their neighborhood that had started following Christine's outburst on the corner of Beachwood and Partridge. Rather than ending their run and hitting the shower, the two had continued to walk side by side since that fateful day, through what Milo had begun to think of as the Valley of the Shadow of Death of the Relationship.

Though the walking initially seemed like an opportunity for them to reconnect, the extended time that the couple spent together circling the neighborhood only served to enhance and expand a rift in their relationship that had probably been opening for longer than Milo had ever suspected. He had sensed this almost immediately and felt the strain that these walks were putting on the marriage, but to quit them would have been impossible. It would have meant admitting that the two of them were incapable of sustaining half an hour of conversation.

Instead, Milo attempted to fill the void between him and Christine with as much conversation as possible, while at the same time Christine seemed intent on perpetuating the silence, exposing the problem like the festering sore that she saw it to be. Milo would ask Christine about her day, and her responses would be short, abrupt, and she would fail to reciprocate with a similar question. Milo would then attempt to summarize his day as best he could, despite the lack of prompting. Christine's purposeful disinterest became so palpable that Milo began slowing his rate of speech, pretending to search for words or phrases in order to prolong his stories. He began to set goals for himself: *I will find a way to keep talking about work at least until we reach the corner of Garfield and East Mill Street, and only then can I mention the plans for Mother's Day.*

This cat-and-mouse game went on for more than four months. Eventually Milo developed additional strategies to combat the situation. He began creating lists of possible conversation topics while at work and would review the list on the way home. When this failed, he told stories about his childhood, seeking out visual reminders in the neighborhood to make the impetus of the stories more feasible.

"Hey, check out that crab apple tree. Did I ever tell you about the rotten apple fights that my cousin and I would get into behind my grandfather's garage?"

And though the story might go on for three or four solid minutes, Christine's purposeful lack of interest would eventually cause even these childhood tales to peter out prematurely.

Finally, Milo turned to the neighborhood for inspiration, commenting on the landscaping and overall appearance of homes in the area. It was as if he and Christine were playing chicken, waiting for the other to blink.

When Christine finally did, it wasn't pretty.

"I'm not sure what my plan with Christine is," Milo finally said to Edith. "I've never been separated before. I guess I'm just wait-ing to hear what the therapist says. He's the expert, right?" After a sip of tea, more welcome than usual, and another insistent *con-flagration* (*They're getting real close now*, he thought), Milo added, "Do you have any suggestions?"

Though he sincerely desired Edith's advice, *conflagration* made it almost impossible to focus on his client. The words were less than twenty seconds apart now, and he felt like his skin was beginning to crawl. *Antsy* is how his mother might have de-scribed the sensation racing through his body, but Milo thought that this word didn't come close to the degree of restlessness and distraction and genuine pain that he was now feeling. It had begun as a headache, the feeling that his skull was being squeezed in a vise, but now it felt as if acupuncture needles were being inserted into his brain. Before long, his entire body would be drenched in sweat. Beads of perspiration were already form-ing on his forehead, and he could barely remain still. It took all his mental effort to remain seated in front of Edith, awaiting her response to his question, and even then he wondered how long he could maintain his composure.

Edith smiled. "Listen, Milo, I don't know how this is going to turn out for you, but I know that you're young enough to survive whatever happens. You're still a young man. My husband, Ed Marchand, used to advise our son, and that's just how he would say it. *I advise you, Tony . . .*"

Edith paused for a moment, longer than she was probably

aware, and Milo knew by the look in her eyes that Edith was recalling something specific from her past, a treasured moment between a husband now dead and a son now absent.

"Anyway," she finally said, "Ed would advise Tony to make
all his mistakes before the age of thirty, because after that, they
really start to mean something. So just think of this as a bump in
a long road, my dear. You're still young. You'll be fine."

Milo didn't have the heart to tell his elderly friend that he
had turned thirty-three in February.

chapter 3

When Milo pulled his moped into the driveway of Arthur Friedman, an ever-so-slight sense of relief washed over him. The ride
to his client's house had been a difficult one, and he was happy to
still be in one piece. It had required all of his concentration just
to keep the moped on the road. But if his plan worked, *conflagration* would soon be ousted from his head. The demand would at
last be satisfied.

Arthur Friedman was one of Milo's longest-standing clients,
a seventy-eight-year old Jewish lifelong bachelor whom Milo had
met while working as a nurse in a nearby rehab hospital. He was
also the only client who paid for Milo's services without the assistance of a family member, hiring him just prior to Milo's departure from the hospital, and for that reason, Milo was grateful to
have him as a client.

There was no pretense with Arthur Friedman.

Milo chained his moped to a lamppost on the edge of the
driveway and removed a small white paper bag from a nylon
pouch behind the seat. Though he owned a car, he loved to take
his moped out on days when his appointments were local enough
to keep him off the highways, even in the middle of winter. He
found the ride in the open air exhilarating and refreshing, despite Christine's opinion on the matter. Ever since he had bought

the machine at a garage sale three years ago, she had been coaxing him to get rid of it. "It's dangerous," she would complain, and for a while, Milo found her concern touching, until last year when she suggested that the couple use their tax refund to purchase Milo "a real motorcycle."

"But how is that safer than my moped?" he had asked, genuinely confused.

"I dunno," she said. "It's bigger. It just seems safer."

It took Milo a moment to put the pieces together, but he soon realized that his wife's concern over his moped had nothing to do with safety. Christine was a woman who sent out thank-you cards the day that she received a gift, judged others on the promptness of their thank-you cards, and spent almost an hour each morning in front of the mirror. To her, image was important, and Milo tried not to begrudge her this sentiment. Image was also important to him, though he had never managed to master the right wardrobe, hairstyle, or mode of transportation. Instead, his focus remained on concealing those oddities that made him different from others, the demands that ruled his life, and for that reason, he didn't see himself as being very different than his image-conscious wife.

But still, the idea that his moped might be undesirable or embarrassing did not sit well with him. Concern over demands like the one that *conflagration* was currently imposing on him was one thing. Unease about the image that a moped projected seemed entirely different.

Milo knocked on Arthur Friedman's front door, waited for the man to shout "Come in!" and then walked through an entryway that led to the kitchen.

Conflagration.

It was becoming even more insistent now, as if the traitorous corner of his brain from which these commands were issued knew how close Milo was to finally answering its call. This wasn't the first time that the demands had grown more adamant and painful as the hour of reckoning drew near, but it never failed to unnerve him.

Though he knew that these demands emanated from some-where in his own mind—he had been living with the condition since childhood—he couldn't help but attribute them to some other force, one he often imagined as a German U-boat captain, on duty somewhere in his brain, gray uniform adorned with gold epaulets, standing ramrod straight, eyes pressed into a periscope, capable of watching Milo's every move, just waiting to twist the valves and raise the levers that would increase the pressure of the demand at the appropriate moment.

It was difficult for Milo to pinpoint a single event in his past that might have initiated the odd requirements to which he was subjected. Even in elementary school, he had experienced the pressure, the pain, and the subsequent relief that he now felt as an adult, though the requirements had been different. The tying and untying of his shoelaces, the opening and closing of the latch on his Trapper Keeper, and the puncturing of a juice box with a straw at lunchtime (a demand that still struck him from time to time). And he could still remember the anxiety and stress associ-ated with the days in which his mother had forgotten to pack a juice box or, worse, had packed a Capri-Sun drink bag in its place (a painfully inferior product in terms of straw-popping relief). He guessed that these inexplicable demands had been with him since birth to one degree or another, adapting and evolving as he grew older, but he did remember the first time they had created problems for him.

When Milo was eight years old, he had made the mistake of asking his friend Jimbo Powers if he could pop a few of the bal-loons at the end of Jimbo's birthday party. The other children had already left, and Milo was waiting for his perpetually tardy mother to pick him up. The two had been playing Breakout on Jimbo's brand-new Atari 5200 when Milo noticed the balloons in the corner and asked to pop them.

"Huh?" Jimbo had said, staring at them with obvious affection.

"I need to pop those balloons, Jimbo. You know. Pop them. Can I?"

When Jimbo said no, Milo persisted, telling his friend that they needed to be popped, that allowing them to slowly deflate would be unacceptable, and that only he, Milo Slade, could pop them and set things right. Reflecting back on the moment, Milo thought that he probably sounded a little feverish and manic in his request, because that was exactly how he had felt when contemplating the prospect of half a dozen balloons slowly deflating on their own.

Jimbo refused again, obviously confused, and perhaps a little frightened by Milo's rationale and demeanor. "They're my balloons, Milo. And it's my birthday. I get to do whatever I want with them. My mom bought them *for me*."

"I know," said Milo, becoming inexplicably worried. "But I need to pop them. Maybe just one will be fine, but I need to. Okay?"

"No," Jimbo said, rising from the sofa and taking up a position between Milo and the balloons. "Leave them alone."

Jimbo's mother had apparently heard snippets of their conversation. Seconds after Jimbo had taken his defensive stance, she had entered the living room and told Jimbo to give Milo one of his balloons. "You have plenty, honey. Let Milo take one home."

Unaware of Milo's intentions, Mrs. Powers was shocked to watch as Milo removed a red balloon from the bunch along the far wall, pulled it down to eye level by its ribbon, and pressed it against a three-foot-tall cactus plant beside the television. The cactus's spikes pierced the balloon immediately, causing a loud pop, and though it had been satisfying, Milo instantly found himself in need of another.

"Why did you do that, Milo?" Jimbo's mother asked. The confused, slightly alarmed look on her face was all that Milo needed to see to realize that what he had done was not normal. It was a slack-jawed, wide-eyed stare that made Milo no longer feel like an eight-year-old boy. In Mrs. Powers's eyes, Milo had suddenly become something else, something slightly scarier, and he instantly wanted nothing more than to immediately return to his innocent eight-year-old boyhood status.

In that moment, as Jimbo and his mother stared in utter bewilderment, Milo felt like a monster.

This incident was followed by a noticeable absence of invitations to Jimbo's home for the duration of the summer and eventually an end to their friendship as school resumed in the fall. In the classroom, on the playground, and in the cafeteria, Jimbo avoided all contact with his old friend, and within two weeks, Milo had gotten the message and stopped trying. And though Milo was certain that it was Jimbo's decision to end the friendship, he was also certain that Jimbo's mother wanted her son to keep as far away from Milo as possible. The look on her face that day, the expression of utter incomprehension, had stuck with Milo for all his life. It was this look that had first told Milo that he was not at all normal, and it had convinced Milo to keep his inexplicable needs to himself.

Milo found Arthur Friedman sitting at a small table, eating oatmeal and watching the local news. He turned down the volume on the television as Milo entered the room. "Did you bring them?" he barked.

"Of course," Milo said, removing a prescription bottle from the paper bag. "But you're going to wait until I leave before you use them."

"Then get the hell out right now," the old man barked again. Barking out orders was Arthur Friedman's primary form of communication.

"Why? You got a date?" Milo asked, removing his helmet and placing it on the countertop. He knew that his client was kidding, but he enjoyed playing along.

"That's not funny, Milo. Not funny one bit. Making fun of an old guy who helps to pay your bills ain't smart. And besides, look who's talking. You don't exactly have anything keeping you warm at night either."

"Yeah, but at least I can still get it up."

"So can I," Arthur Friedman countered. "I just need a little help from my little blue friends." Friedman gestured to the bottle that Milo had already placed alongside the platoon of prescriptions lining the backsplash of the sink.

When Milo had first filled Arthur Friedman's Viagra prescription more than a year ago, he had tried to avoid discussing the medication with his client, delivering the bottle as nonchalantly as he did every other prescription. But he had known that the old guy would not permit the subject to go unexplored. Making Milo squirm was one of Arthur Friedman's greatest sources of amusement.

"So I guess you're wondering why an old guy like me might want Viagra?" he had finally asked, waiting just long enough for Milo to think that he might escape the visit without broaching the subject.

"Viagra? I hadn't even noticed," Milo lied.

"Bullshit, young man. You noticed. And I know you noticed. So don't you want to know what's *up?*" Arthur Friedman smiled, letting Milo know that the pun had not been unintended.

"Listen, Mr. Friedman—I really don't need to know. It's fine. Honestly. If you've got some honey on the side, that's not my business. Okay?"

"A honey on the side?" the old man said, and began to laugh, more than Milo had ever heard before. Before the fit ended, Milo had begun to think that Arthur Friedman might choke to death on his own laughter. But after an interminably long period of time, he regained his composure and continued. "I can assure you, Milo, that I do not have any honey on the side. Though it may surprise you, my balding head, my expanding gut, and my flaming hemorrhoids have kept the ladies at bay for quite some time. But that doesn't mean I can't have a little fun from time to time, right?"

"You're not talking about prostitutes, are you?" Milo asked, wondering where in hell a retiree might find a hooker in a small town like Wethersfield, Connecticut.

"Not prostitutes," he said between minor aftershocks of laughter. "I'm talking about pornography, Milo. On my computer."

Less than two weeks before, Milo had installed a new desktop computer in his client's study, a suggestion that he made to many of his clients. A majority of them spent a great deal of time alone, some never leaving their homes except for weddings and funerals, so Milo had found that the Internet could provide these shut-ins with the ability to interact with other human beings, play games, and shop, all from the comforts and confines of their own living room. Edith Marchand, for example, now spent many an evening playing online Scrabble with opponents from around the world, and had even managed to establish a few friendships with these people through e-mail. But pornography had not been on Milo's mind when he first taught Arthur Friedman to open a web browser.

"Porn?" Milo asked. "Are you serious? How did you manage to find that? You can't even read the newspaper with those eyes." Though Milo had set the computer's resolution at the smallest possible, thus making the text on websites and other programs quite large, he was sure that it was still quite difficult for Mr.

Friedman to read for any length of time. He had expected the computer to be a minor diversion and nothing more for an old man with failing eyesight.

"It wasn't hard, kid," Arthur said with a grin. "It may give me a headache like you wouldn't believe, but I can still make out the print when I need to. As soon as you left, I searched for *big tits* in the Google and found more tits than I've seen in my life. Good ones too. And that was just the beginning."

"I can imagine," Milo said, thankful that Arthur Friedman didn't have children to whom he would have to answer.

"There's more sex on that Internet than you can shake a stick at. And they have videos too. I saw girls having sex with guys, girls having sex with girls. You name it and I saw it. There were even a few things that I wish I had never seen. Some of it's free, but you have to pay for the good stuff."

"You paid for porn?"

"Don't worry. I did my research. I signed up for two of them websites. Less than fifty bucks a month for the both of them. Hell, I'm spending almost that much for cable every month, and that's just for Andy Griffith reruns and Sox games. This Internet is a hell of a lot better than some black-and-white sitcoms."

Milo was afraid to ask, but since he had brought the computer into the house and introduced his elderly client to the world of online porn, he felt he must. "So how does Viagra fit in to this?"

"What do you think? After watching all this sex, I need to relieve myself. But I'm not always properly equipped to do so. So I got myself some Viagra. My doc thinks it's a great idea. *A stress reducer*, he said."

"You told your doctor about the porn?" Milo asked, dreading the details.

"Look, Milo, you can lie to your parents and your friends and even your wife if you want, but you don't lie to your doctor."

"Right."

"Do you want to see the websites that I subscribed to?" he asked.

"No, thank you," Milo said as quickly as possible. If given half a chance, he knew that his client would revel in the opportunity to have Milo watch pornography with him each week.

"Are you sure?"

"Plenty," Milo shot back. "And can we agree to never discuss this again?"

"You bet, kid," Arthur Friedman had said. But that turned out to be a lie. Ever since that day more than a year ago, his client had somehow managed to inject the subject of pornography or masturbation into every one of Milo's visits. On days like today, when Milo delivered Viagra to his client, it was especially easy.

"Want me to put that in the dishwasher?" Milo asked, gesturing to the nearly empty bowl of oatmeal. Though Milo's job did not technically require him to act as housekeeper, he never minded helping out clients who didn't expect it from him and appreciated his efforts.

"Thanks. What's on tap for today?"

"Something a little different, if you don't mind," Milo answered. "I just came from the ophthalmologist, and I'm not supposed to strain my eyes for at least six hours. So I was wondering if you could read to me today."

"What's wrong with your eyes?"

"Hopefully nothing, but they've been dry lately. The doctor wanted to be sure that I was producing enough tears, so he ran some tests. He put some chemicals in my eyes, so I'm supposed to take it easy."

"Well, you know how bad my eyes are," Arthur Friedman said. "Hell, why did you bother coming over today if you knew you couldn't read? That's the whole reason for you coming over. You know I can't read to you."

While Milo knew that one of the reasons that he visited

Arthur Friedman was to read to the old man, he also knew that it was the company that his client also craved. Otherwise Milo would have simply dropped off an audiobook or two each week and been done with it. "I thought I might not be able to read today, so I came prepared." Milo extracted several sheets of neatly folded paper from the inner pocket of his jacket and handed them over to Friedman, just as *conflagration* once again flared in his mind. "It's 'The Black Cat' by Edgar Allan Poe. A classic. And it's a short story, so you can read it in one sitting. I copied it from the Internet and increased the font size. I thought you might be able to read it. I know we've tried those books with large type before, but I made this printing even bigger."

Arthur Friedman unfolded the sheaf of paper and examined the front page. The title of the story was centered in bolded type at the top of the page. The nearly four-thousand-word story filled fifteen sheets of paper, double-sided, with the margins on each page reduced to the narrowest possible. Just to be sure that his client would be able to read the story, Milo had chosen thirty-point font, almost twice the size of a standard book set in large type, making the story look like it had been written for a child.

A legally blind child.

"Look at this," Arthur Friedman said in near astonishment. "You said that you could make the words larger on the Internet?"

"Sort of," Milo replied, pleased with his client's unexpected interest in the topic. He thought that he'd be pulling teeth to get him to read the story. "I could show you how to do it if you want. But it takes up a lot of ink and paper, even for a story this short. But I could show you. That is, if you can pull yourself away from the porn for long enough."

"Not funny," he said, his eyes transfixed on the page. "Let's go into living room and give this a shot, huh?"

"You head on in," Milo said. "Let me clean up in here and I'll be along in a second. All right?"

"Sure."

Milo couldn't have been more pleased. The old man hadn't been able to read for almost a decade, and suddenly the words were jumping off the page at him. Though the extreme size of the font made it unrealistic to print longer stories and novels, he thought that he might be able to find shorter pieces like "The Black Cat" for his client to enjoy.

As Arthur Friedman exited the kitchen, Milo turned on the top burner of the stove, watched it glow a fearsome red, and sighed with relief. In the matter of minutes, perhaps less, the viselike grip on his mind would finally be released. The pounding, incessant headache and his inability to concentrate or focus would instantly be washed away in a torrent of relief.

Conflagration was about to be satisfied at last.

chapter 4

When Milo was young, he and his father built model airplanes in
their garage, though it was never Milo's idea to spend hour upon
hour in a dusty garage, gluing together bits of wood until they
resembled miniature flying machines. Even at his young age, he
was fully aware of the toxic chemicals involved in shellacking
these fragile models and knew that there were little boys and
girls in sweatshops around the world doing similar work for a pal-
try paycheck, so why emulate them for free?

But it was something that his father had done when he was a
boy, so Milo had made allowances, knowing how much it meant
to his dad.

The most troublesome part of the process was that Milo was
not at all adept at building model airplanes. Lacking attention for
detail when it came to things like building, he would often forgo
the use of the tweezers, X-Acto knives, and grip pins that littered
the workbench and would simply stick the minuscule parts together with his clumsy oversized fingers. As a result, the model
would fail to meet his father's specifications for perfection and
would inevitably engender a look of disappointment.

All of this never bothered Milo much, because the process of
building model airplanes was simply a means by which father

and son could spend time together. Whether or not Milo ever achieved the model-building status of his father, the two of them could have found relative happiness together under that single ninety-watt bulb had it not been for Milo's unexplainable and pressing need to snap the wooden parts of his models in two.

The planes that Milo and his father constructed were made from balsa, a lightweight wood optimal for model building because of its versatility and flexibility. Milo's father would purchase kits for the two of them to build and they would occasionally dabble in scratch builds of their own design, but in either case, these designs invariably called for the builder to bend the balsa wood in varying degrees in order for it to take on the shape of a wing, fuselage, or tail section.

For Milo, this process seemed inexplicably wrong. Regardless of the time that was spent cutting, sanding, and treating a piece of wood, Milo found it nearly unbearable to bend the wood to the correct specifications without applying just enough additional pressure to make the wood snap in half. He couldn't explain his need to snap it, and neither did he feel he needed to. It made perfect sense to him, and he couldn't understand why anyone wouldn't feel exactly the same way. To Milo, balsa was like the thin, pale sheets of ice that he would sometimes find at the end of the driveway while waiting for the school bus, the kind with no water beneath that crackled like Styrofoam when broken.

The kind of ice that was *impossible* not to break.

When the wood finally snapped beneath his unyielding pressure, Milo would suddenly be consumed with a sense of euphoria, the gratifying combination of satisfaction and relief. The increasing pressure on the wood seemed to build equally increasing pressure on his mind, persisting until the wood had to be broken. With its satisfying snap, Milo would shiver in delight.

Unfortunately, his father's reaction was anything but delight.

Though normally a patient man, he could not understand why his son was incapable of bending the wood without snapping it. Again and again he would demonstrate the process to Milo, modeling the technique and providing ample time for his son to practice, but as soon as he as he turned his back to affix a propeller or assemble a fuselage, his son would invariably break some piece of balsa that had required the smallest degree of bending. At the sound of the snap, his father would spin, hands balled into fists, eyes wide, lips pursed. Exclamations like "For God's sake!" or "What in hell is wrong with you?" would follow, and Milo would invariably be shuffled over to the staining table where he could do no more damage.

There were times when Milo thought that it took all his father's strength and self-control not to lose his temper and scream at him.

Even when it was his father who bent the balsa into place, the process still felt terribly wrong to Milo, and the thought of the pressure that the wood was under would plague his mind for days. It made model building maddening for Milo, as he struggled to find new ways to snap pieces of wood that he should have been able to bend into place with relative ease.

This phenomenon was remarkably similar to Milo's feelings when words like *conflagration* took up residence in his mind. When he finally answered their call, it was like the satisfying snap of balsa in his hands.

Euphoria.

When that snap came this time, Milo's sense of relief was greater than usual. *Conflagration* had proven to be an especially difficult demand, particularly now that he was living on his own. Though many of his other demands benefited from the absence of Christine, finding a means of answering the demand of a word like *conflagration* had proven to be more challenging than usual.

In the end, Milo had turned to the Internet to help satisfy the call, a resource that he'd started using several years before. Prior to the Internet, answering these inexplicable demands had been incredibly difficult and had required a great deal of creativity and luck. But thanks to *the Google*, as Arthur Friedman referred to it, solutions to even the most challenging of words could often be found.

Edgar Allan Poe had been his savior on this particular occasion.

As Milo sat in a recliner beside Arthur Friedman, drinking hot chocolate and listening to his client read the story of a black cat and its alcoholic owner, Milo reveled in the now constant, cacophonous call of *conflagration*, knowing it would soon be satisfied. The word was now searing his brain, the acupuncture needles heated before insertion, the intervals between words now less than ten seconds—but somehow, knowing that the moment of liberation was upon him made the pain almost bearable. Thrilling, even. The combined pressure of the word and the anticipation of fulfillment exerted itself throughout his entire body, forcing his hands to ball into fists, his toes to curl inside his sneakers, and his mouth to clench shut. He found himself unconsciously holding his breath and had to force oxygen into his lungs. All other thoughts ceased as he braced himself for the moment of release. Though he had dreaded the initial demands of the word as he did all others before it, these final moments, when relief was so close, often made the struggle seem almost worthwhile.

Thankfully, the demand for words like *conflagration* took up residence in Milo's mind half a dozen times a year or less, so following the completion of today's mission, he would likely be issued a reprieve of several weeks or even months, though on one or two occasions, the time between words had been considerably shorter. The last word to assume a place in Milo's mind prior to *conflagration* had been *garner*, and that had been more than four months before. In that case, Milo had circumvented what he thought to be the U-boat captain's original intent and had used James Garner, the television and movie actor, as his solution. He had learned long ago that simply asking a person to repeat the word or read it out of context would never satisfy the demand, and attempting to do this would often cause the demand to become more insistent and more painful. Instead, the word needed to come naturally, in the course of normal conversation, its ultimate significance unbeknownst to the person actually speaking the word. In the case of *garner*, for example, the solution had been a simple question about *The Rockford Files*, a crime drama that James Garner had starred in during the late 1970s, asked to the right person at the right time.

Other demands would arise in the time between words. Jelly jars. Ice cubes. Bowling. But at least these demands, as equally insistent and inexplicable as the words like *conflagration*, could be resolved without the assistance of others.

As the moment of *conflagration* approached, Milo straightened in his chair, anticipating its arrival. In Poe's short story "The Black Cat," the unreliable narrator had already gouged out the eye of his cat in a fit of alcoholic rage and, unable to bear the guilt and shame of his actions, had just hung the poor creature from a tree by the neck.

> On the night of the day on which this cruel deed was done,
> I was aroused from sleep by the cry of fire. The curtains of
> my bed were in flames. The whole house was blazing. It was
> with great difficulty that my wife, a servant, and myself,
> made our escape from the conflagration. The destruction
> was complete.

Milo had read the story more than a dozen times before arriving at his client's home and knew the paragraph containing *conflagration* by heart. Poe's prose seemed to hum in the air as the magic word drew near, full of energy and heat, and when it finally came, the breaking of the tension, the satisfaction of the demand, the utterance of *conflagration* by someone other than himself, Milo sighed so audibly that Arthur Friedman stopped reading for a moment and looked up, wondering what might be wrong with his audience of one, before returning his attention to the page and finishing the story.

It turned out that Milo had done more than simply fulfill his own need by placing Poe's story of irreconcilable guilt in his client's hands. Arthur Friedman had given up on reading a decade ago, the small print taking too great a toll on his aging eyes. But the ability to increase the font size of text thrilled the man, and before Milo left for home, Friedman insisted that he deliver a quick lesson on the magic of cut and paste. As Milo prepared to leave the house, Arthur Friedman was printing out a Raymond Chandler story and was already reading the first page of thirty-six-point font.

Better than porn, Milo thought, though he knew that his client probably would disagree. He was feeling good about himself, confident that he had made a difference in the old man's life while finally ridding himself of *conflagration*.

Perhaps this new sense of purpose would make up for the guilt that he continued to feel about watching Freckles's tapes, and the knowledge that despite his guilt, he would be watching them again soon. By spending a little extra time with Arthur Friedman, perhaps he could get the universe to forgive his indiscretion when it came to Freckles. He only hoped that the extra fifteen minutes with his client wouldn't make him late for his first session of couples' therapy.

Christine hated it when Milo was late for anything.

chapter 5

Things were not going well for Milo, because things were going well for Milo.

He had allowed Christine to choose the marriage counselor, assuming that one therapist would be just as good as another and thinking that the ability to choose might make his wife happy. So Christine had chosen Dr. Dana Teagan of Hartford, Connecticut, and having only spoken to the therapist's secretary, was visibly surprised to see a middle-aged man enter the waiting room and invite the couple inside.

Dr. Dana Teagan was a short, thin man with a full head of hair and a well-groomed goatee, making him look decidedly younger than his fifty-plus years. His voice was soft and warm, and as he shook Milo's hand, he held it a second longer than necessary, somehow assuring Milo in this subtle gesture that everything would be all right. He wore the type of clothing that actors donned in holiday commercials, connoting tradition and family: a soft patterned sweater, a pair of dark corduroys, and well-worn brown loafers. The appearance of the man had made Milo suddenly feel as if he were in a Hallmark Hall of Fame Christmas special, and he half expected to find a group of uncommonly good-looking people sitting around a stone fireplace as he entered the doctor's office instead of the three chairs, an assortment of indoor plants, and the desk he found instead.

After the formalities of insurance coverage and scheduling were complete, Dr. Teagan suggested that he spend some time meeting with Christine and Milo separately, in order to get to know them on a more personal level before moving forward with them as a couple. They agreed, and Christine eagerly volunteered to take the first twenty minutes while Milo retreated to the waiting room.

Though Milo embraced the idea of meeting with a therapist in order to find a solution to his troubled marriage, the thought of sitting across from a mental health professional scared him to death. He had no intention of mentioning the demands that plagued his life, but he worried that a psychologist might see right through him, picking up on things he said or even physical symptoms of which he was completely unaware. These were, after all, professionals who were trained to diagnose and treat mental illness. Perhaps there were indicators that Milo exhibited each day without even knowing.

Worse still, what if a demand arose while he was meeting with Dr. Teagan? What if *conflagration* had still been pounding away in his mind when he entered the doctor's office? What if the need to pop a balloon or shake and open a can of Canada Dry diet ginger ale struck while he was sitting on what he thought was going to be the kind of leather couch that Freud might have used? Would a doctor be able to detect the amalgamation of signs indicating that his patient was under an unusual amount of *unusual* stress? The clenching of teeth, the nearly imperceptible (but not nearly imperceptible enough) shaking of the hands, the inability to focus, the tightening in the chest, the occasional bouts of flatulence, the beads of sweat that would eventually sprout on his forehead, and the inevitable piercing, searing pain that came with his inability to satisfy a demand?

All of these concerns made the prospect of entering Dr. Teagan's office daunting and unnerving. If he weren't so concerned that his refusal to attend these sessions might arouse suspicion in Christine's mind and raise questions that he could not answer, Milo might have forgone the counseling process entirely. But this, he feared, was their only solution, the only means of reconciling and continuing on with their comfortable life. He would have to hold the line, maintain his composure, and do everything he could to avoid entering the doctor's office with a demand already weighing him down. And if a new one arose in the midst of a session, Milo hoped that its onset and initial symptoms would be too small for even a professional such as Dr. Teagan to notice.

Dr. Teagan's office was located in a building that housed several other therapists, family counselors, and similar *head doctors*, as Milo's father would have referred to them. Therefore, the waiting room contained an odd collection of reading material, differentiated enough for the wide variety of patients that the room serviced. Included in the pile was the innocuous *Highlights* magazine, which Milo recognized as a children's magazine though he had no memory of ever seeing a child actually reading it. Without a conscious thought, he began thumbing through the most recent copy, stopping to read the three-page spread of children's poetry. The poems weren't very good, but they were amusing just the same, including his favorite:

My Hurt Elbow
My school nurse is the smartest adult person I know.
I went to her office because I had a rash on my elbow
That hurt when I scratched.
My mom put smelly cream on it that just made it smell.
But Nurse Mancuso found the cure.
She told me not to scratch.
And it worked.
It didn't hurt anymore.

Milo was reading this poem for the third time, beginning to commit it to memory, when Christine emerged from the hallway connecting Dr. Teagan's office with the waiting room. "Your turn," she said, avoiding eye contact as she passed him, or so he thought. Milo couldn't be sure. It was easy to read too much into Christine's facial expressions at a time like this, but still, it made him uneasy as he commenced the short walk down the hall into Dr. Teagan's office.

"Hello, Milo. Take a seat, please."

The doctor's informal use of Milo's first name surprised him. During their preliminary encounter, the doctor had referred to him as Mr. Slade, but after fifteen or twenty minutes with Christine, it seemed that he was already on a first-name basis with Milo.

He wondered what she might have said.

Milo crossed the rectangular office and took a seat in a cushioned chair positioned between two large indoor plants, noting a small table with a digital clock placed just to the left and behind him, affording the doctor a clear view of the time while presenting Milo with none.

"So Milo, I know that you and Christine are having some trouble, and I'm here to listen and help as much as possible. Can you tell me what goals you have in mind for our sessions?"

Milo breathed a sigh of relief. He was concerned that the doctor's first question might be something like "So what secrets are you keeping from Christine?" He worried that he might be asked to talk about his odd and inexplicable demands: the bowling or the Weebles or those persistent, inescapable words in his head.

Most of all, he was terrified that this head doctor might ask if Milo thought that he was crazy.

Instead, the doc had opened up with a softball.

"I guess I'd like to get our marriage back on track," Milo said, pleased with his response.

"What do you see as the problem with your marriage?"

"Honestly, I'm not sure." He waited for the doctor to respond, but when he continued to sit there, staring, Milo went on, almost surprised that he had more to say. "I may not be the happiest guy in the world, but I thought that we were doing okay. Then Christine started to get angry over the littlest things. I felt like everything I did upset her. Then she started asking for some space. Some time apart to think things over. But when I finally got an apartment, she went ballistic. Told me that she had never expected me to sign a lease. I guess that she just wanted me to stay with a friend for a couple weeks while she thought things over, but when your wife asks for time apart, I didn't think that meant a sleepover. So now I don't know what to think."

"Did you want to move out?"

"Not at first. When she first asked for space, it scared the hell out of me. I felt like she was trying to throw me out. But after a while, I started to think that some time apart would be good for us. So when she tried to get me to stay, I refused. It had taken me so long to accept the separation that I couldn't just turn back on it without giving it a try. If that makes any sense."

"It's been about a month now, right? How has it felt living apart?"

"It's odd," Milo said, unsure how to express the mixture of so many emotions and concerned about saying too much. Arthur Friedman had warned Milo not to lie to doctors (and had ironically expressed his tacit approval of lying to one's wife), but he didn't think that his client was referring to a therapist.

Arthur Friedman likely despised the notion of therapy altogether.

"I mean, it seems crazy to think that Christine is in our house, only a mile away, and I'm stuck in a crummy little apartment, waiting for her to figure things out. But I have to admit that it didn't feel wrong either. Moving out, I mean. And even when she didn't want me to take the apartment, I did, because I thought it would be a good thing for us."

He didn't mention that the absence of Christine had also made it exceedingly easier to deal with most of his demands, and that he had found this to be remarkably liberating.

"You said that Christine's trying to figure things out," Dr. Teagan said. "Are you figuring things out too?"

"Honestly, I don't know what there is to figure out. I don't know what has changed. Like I said, I don't think we were the happiest people in the world, but I thought we were doing all right."

"When did you know that there was a problem? Was there a moment when you knew for sure?"

Milo knew the moment. Would never forget it. Though Christine's eruption on the corner of Beachwood and Partridge had represented the opening salvo in their martial combat, it wasn't until an afternoon in January when he knew that the marriage was in serious jeopardy.

They had just completed the outer lap of their neighborhood walk and were heading for home. Milo had exhausted his list of conversation topics generated earlier that day and had been filling the last fifteen minutes of silence with comments on the neighbors' choice of landscaping, which amounted to little considering the season. They were just a block away from the house when Milo proposed the enormous value of grass that was genetically engineered to grow to a predetermined height (an idea that had spontaneously come to Milo but one that he still liked a lot) and their game of chicken finally ended.

Christine blinked.

"Goddamn it, Milo! Is that all you've got? Grass? Goddamn motherfucking grass!"

Milo remained silent for a moment, hoping that the outburst might be followed by an apology, the rapid retraction of Christine's acknowledgment that there was trouble. As much as he had hoped for months to confront the issue head-on, he now found himself wanting to make it go away as quickly as possible and resume détente. Instead of offering an apology, Christine held her ground and stared at her husband, cheeks flushed, breathing heavily.

"I don't know what you mean," Milo said, hoping for a conciliatory *Never mind* or *Forget it.*

Christine pressed on. "Don't lie to me, Milo," she shot back. "We walk together every single day but don't have a goddamn thing to say to each other. Do you think that's normal?"

"Well, you don't help the situation," Milo said, surprised by his willingness to fight back. "The sky could be falling and you wouldn't have a word to say about it."

"I hardly think that genetically engineered grass constitutes the sky falling, Milo. The problem is that nothing you say interests me anymore. I wish the goddamn sky would fall. At least I would have something to get excited about. Because right now, I've got nothing. *Nothing.*"

Even though he had known all of this on some level already, these words had stung Milo the most. Had silenced him.

And despite the sting, he couldn't help but note Christine's dramatic repetition of the word *nothing,* with its resolute emphasis and intended finality. Milo wanted to ask if this bit of drama was really necessary considering their lack of an audience, but as he always did in these circumstances, he refrained.

Christine waited for a response from her husband, and when nothing came, she turned and began walking, not waiting to see if Milo would follow. After a moment, he did, and the two were walking side by side again as they climbed the concrete steps into their home. As Christine crossed through the kitchen toward the bathroom, where she would shower with the door closed for the first time during their relationship, she turned and said, "I think I need some space, Milo. I think we need some time apart."

The way in which she made this request, followed by the immediate closing of the bathroom door, left the conversation in limbo, where it would remain. She would continue to ask for this space but without giving specifics or demanding a response for another three months until he finally obliged.

Milo related this story as succinctly as possible to Dr. Teagan, who seemed to nod at precisely the right moments, just enough to encourage him to continue without appearing to pander. His affection for the man grew with each passing minute.

When finished, Milo had wanted to ask the doctor if it was normal to assume that *time apart* and *space* meant a trial separation, but he was afraid to even mention the word *normal* to the doctor, as if entering the word into the record might expose a considerable chink in his armor.

Instead, Milo waited, and after ten interminable seconds, Dr. Teagan spoke again. "Do you still want to be married to Christine?"

"Yes," Milo answered quickly, and meant it, though the reasons that he desired to remain married to Christine were unclear. Milo thought that he and Christine were fairly compatible, and they were fortunate enough to share some excellent friends. They owned a home in which they had invested a great deal of time and money, and it was finally starting to look like the house of their dreams. Milo also adored Christine's family, particularly her mother and father, and the thought of throwing all that away for a shortage of conversational topics befuddled him.

When Dr. Teagan failed to respond to his one-word answer, Milo reasserted his affirmative response and waited, determined to force the doc into the next move. After a moment, the doctor suggested that they ask Christine to join them.

When Christine sat down in the chair beside Milo, she could not have felt farther away from him. He thought about the information that he had just shared with the doctor, information that he didn't think Christine would have wanted shared, and he shuddered to think about what she might have said during her time alone in the office. Milo turned and looked at Christine, hoping to flash a smile or take her hand, which would have been second nature less than a year ago, but Christine's eyes remained forward despite Milo's certainty that she knew he was looking in her direction.

"So, Christine, why don't we start with you? I know that you're not happy with Milo's decision to move out. But you also told me that you had been asking for time apart prior to Milo's decision to move. What was it that you wanted from Milo when you asked for space?"

"I didn't want him to move out," Christine said, a razorlike quality to her voice. "I didn't expect him to take furniture and pillows and canned goods, for Christ's sake. I just wanted a week or two apart, to think things over."

"Christine," Milo said. "I didn't know that. I really didn't. When you asked for space, I thought you were talking about separation. I really did."

"But when I told you what I really wanted, you moved out anyway. Not only that, but you waited until I was in Chicago to move out. You couldn't have waited until I came home?"

Milo knew that if they had been alone and she had been angry enough, Christine might have thrown the word *coward* into the last statement, and perhaps justifiably so.

"I thought it would be easier on you if I moved out while you were gone. But I told you I was going."

"And it was easier on you too, Milo?" Teagan suggested.

"Yes," Milo said, once again admiring the doc's sense of timing. "It was easier on me too. You knew I was moving out. I just didn't want to have to do it under your nose."

"But why did you move at all? After I asked you to stay, you still left. Why?"

"Look, Christine. It took me three months to come to terms with it, but in the end, I thought that it would good for us. I know you didn't mean to, but you convinced me that time apart would be for the best."

"So you went out and got a lease without even telling me? Without even consulting me?"

"I know it sounds stupid now, but I thought it would make you happy. I thought it would be a nice surprise for you."

"In fairness, Christine," Dr. Teagan added, "when a spouse suggests for a couple to spend some time apart, they aren't typically referring to a week or two in a hotel or at a friend's house. They are usually referring to a trial separation of some kind. I know it hurt you that Milo moved out, and I think that Milo made a mistake in not consulting you in the process, but I don't think he intended on hurting your feelings. In his mind, he was doing what was best for both of you. And to be honest, it might end up helping your relationship a great deal. Can you see that?"

The words came forth from Dr. Teagan like liquid sugar. They weren't said in judgment or condemnation, but rather like the cooing whisper of a mother's voice in a baby's ear. At least that's how they sounded to Milo. But he was sure that they were not being received as well by Christine.

"So you think this separation is a good idea?" Christine asked, turning her anger on the doctor.

"It may be," Teagan said, his casual tone unwavering. "It might give the two of you a chance to appreciate what you may have forgotten. It could give you a chance to become acquainted with each other all over again."

"What do you suggest?" Milo asked, trying to cut off any more potentially charged remarks from Christine. He knew that his wife's temper was like a freight train: slow, nearly impossible to get started, but thundering and unstoppable if given ample momentum.

"I think the two of you should try to get to know each other again. Go out on some dates. See how that feels. It's obvious that we have some work to do here as well. Communication seems to have broken down between the two of you, and we may be able to do some of that work here. But I think it's important that the two of you begin reconnecting. And maybe that process can start with dinner and a movie. Or maybe just a coffee. What do you think?"

Milo looked back to Christine, hoping for some cue. The idea seemed a little ridiculous, but if Christine approved, he would as well. After a moment, Christine sighed and said, "We can give it a try," and Milo agreed. They set a time to reconvene with the doctor in a week and committed to at least one date before that time.

Milo felt that the meeting had gone well, but he knew that Christine would feel otherwise.

As they exited the building together into the uncommonly bright sunshine, Christine turned to Milo and said, "That went well for you, didn't it?"

"I don't know what you mean," Milo lied.

"I bet you just love him, don't you?"

"If he can help us fix our marriage, you're right. I'll love him. But it's not about who wins or loses. It's not a contest. It's about us. Right?"

"Did you know that he was going to be a man?"

"Christine, you made the appointment. I just showed up. I had no idea who the doctor was until I saw him. But who cares if he's a man or a woman as long as he can help us? Right?"

"Yeah, right." Christine turned and walked to her car without saying another word.

Milo had the urge to shout at his wife, remind her that there were no cameras rolling, no histrionic music playing in the background. "We're not in a movie!" he wanted to bellow. "We've got no audience!" He wanted to remind his wife that her dramatic exit would only serve to make their next conversation more awkward and difficult, whereas a simple exchange of farewells would have made things so much easier.

Instead, he played his own clichéd role in her melodrama, turning with head down back toward his car. Better to keep the train from thundering down the track any faster than necessary.

Once he was sure that Christine was well on her way home, Milo reentered the doctor's office and tore from the magazine the poem that he had been reading and memorizing.

He had no idea why. ˆ

chapter 6

Milo stopped at a RadioShack on the way home from Dr. Teagan's office, provided his credit card and zip code to a middle-aged clerk who seemed under the illusion that he was a genuine electronics expert, and purchased a cable that would allow him to watch Freckles on his television rather than the tiny camcorder screen. Milo had intended to pay cash for the item, but after seeing the silver pen in the clerk's pocket protector, the kind that required the user to click a button on the end in order to eject the ink point, he switched to a credit card, suddenly consumed with the demand to click the man's pen at least once, but probably many more times.

When the clerk pointed to the pen already on the counter, one without an alluring retractable point, Milo was forced to pretend that this pen wasn't working by pressing down with diminished force on the sales receipt. "I'm sorry. This is out of ink. Can I use yours?" he asked, making sure to point to the pen in the clerk's pocket lest he offer another pen behind the counter.

Milo was forced to click the pen a dozen times before the demand was satisfied. In order to maintain possession of it long enough to do so, he asked the clerk about purchasing a warranty and service contract on the cable, even though he knew that such a request was absurd.

On his drive home, he reflected back on his session with Dr. Teagan. Though he was happy and relieved to discover that his understanding of the concepts of *space* and *time apart* had been normal, he wasn't sure if it was worth the anger that the meeting had engendered in Christine. Though the two had committed themselves to at least one date before next Wednesday, they had hardly parted on good terms. Milo wondered how long he should wait before calling his wife.

Then, as if on cue, the phone rang. Milo answered, expecting to hear Christine's voice. Instead, it was Andy, informing Milo to bring his laptop to the Wednesday-night meet-up.

"I've got a new game for us to try out. It runs online, so bring your machine. There's a thirty-day free trial that we'll all sign up for and play. I think we're going to like it. A lot like D and D online."

Andy was one of a foursome of guys, Milo included, who got together every Wednesday night for what Christine referred to as Nerd Time. Though she had initially intended the moniker to be endearing, she had begun to use it more acrimoniously in the past year. Milo never told his friends what Christine thought of their get-togethers, but he couldn't disagree with her estimation. Among the many activities in which he and his friends would engage were video games, Sabermetric baseball, Dungeons & Dragons, and the occasional game of setback or poker. They rotated homes each week, with the host choosing the activity and supplying the food. Video games and D&D often vied for the top spot, with Dungeons & Dragons, a game Milo and Andy had played since they were kids, usually winning out.

Milo looked forward to Wednesday nights with great excitement and loved the time that he spent with his friends. He and Andy had been friends since high school, and Danny had joined their group several years back. Since then, the three of them had been inseparable, and rarely did they miss a Wednesday meet-up.

Andy owned a comic book store in Bristol (where he and Danny had met) and Danny worked as a dog trainer and part-time landscaper and gardener. Both were in their early thirties, living alone as bachelors, and occasionally involved with women, though not nearly as often as either would prefer. They reminded Milo (and Christine) of a couple of grown-up teenagers, and Milo loved them for it.

Christine's opinion of *the boys* was somewhat less appreciative.

Eric Cushman had recently joined them on Wednesday nights, and since then, the group dynamic had suffered terribly. Cushman was a tall, pale-faced, balding blackjack dealer who worked afternoons at Foxwoods and routinely gambled his paycheck away ten minutes after receiving it. He still lived with his mother (making Wednesday nights at his place especially nerdy), mooched beer off his friends, and insisted on getting his D&D party killed by bursting through doors without checking for traps or taking on monsters well above the party's level. Worse still, Cushman insisted on dressing up as his Dungeons & Dragons character regardless of their activity or locale, so in the past six months, Milo had found himself eating burgers in Applebee's, playing basketball at the Churchill Park courts, and attending the latest Spiderman film at the Berlin Cinemas with a guy dressed like Dumbledore from the Harry Potter novels, complete with a crimson robe, tiny spectacles, a wooden staff (*ironwood*, Cushman insisted), and a four-inch-thick spell book in which he actually wrote down the spells that his Dungeons & Dragons character had learned.

Cushman had also met Andy at the comic book store, and though he had seemed likable at first, he quickly managed to embarrass and annoy Milo to no end. Though there was a great deal not to like, Milo's greatest problem with Cushman was the flaunting of his eccentricities. While Andy, Danny, and Milo attempted to conceal their love for Dungeons & Dragons from the rest of the world, aware of the stigma that came attached to it, Cushman flaunted his affection and utter devotion of the game wherever he went. As someone very intent on appearing normal despite his many abnormalities, Milo could not abide this kind of behavior, and as a result, he had been looking for a way to get rid of Cushman for some time.

It was also equally clear to Milo that Cushman did not like him and had not liked him from the start, and though he wasn't sure why this was the case, it made Milo nervous. Though he despised the man, Milo had made every effort to conceal his feelings from Cushman, ever cognizant of the danger associated with an enemy. When one had as many secrets as he did, the best course of action was to maintain friendly relations with all parties, regardless of their stupidity or selfishness, and Milo managed to do this surprisingly well. Though it sometimes required a great deal of effort on his part, Milo tried to ensure that his friends, his clients, Christine's family, and even the annoying blackjack dealer whose primary form of sustenance was Hot Pockets and Dr Pepper approved of him and liked him, and almost always he had found success in this endeavor. This occasionally meant compromising a belief or ideal, but more often than not, Milo found that if he simply remained silent when the opportunity to debate or disagree arose, friendships and goodwill could be forged, maintained, and even strengthened over time.

To voice an opinion might invite disagreement, strife, anger, and genuine hatred. This would simply not do for a man who tried to avoid confrontation at all costs. Milo knew how unlikely it would be for someone (even Christine or the ever-accepting Andy) to like him if they knew about his secrets, and worse still, he knew what kind of ammunition an enemy might have upon learning these secrets. Avoiding enemies altogether helped to mitigate this concern. Therefore, Cushman's reciprocating dislike for Milo concerned him a great deal.

After all, it was more difficult to deceive an enemy than a friend.

Milo assured Andy that he would not forget his laptop and hung up the phone. After a long walk with Skywalker and another dinner of peanut butter and jelly sandwiches, he settled down on the couch to finish the first of the fourteen tapes he had found in the bag. Unlike during his previous viewing, he now had a purpose. While watching Freckles's video diary, he would be looking for clues to this mystery woman's identity. For this purpose, a legal pad and a pencil sat on the futon beside him and the dog.

Milo debated watching the fifteen minutes of footage from the previous day, concerned that he may have missed an important clue. But, anxious to see more of the tape, he vowed to review the first fifteen minutes in the event that he found no other means of identifying the woman. Connecting the camera to the television via the cable that he had purchased, Milo pressed the play button and watched the last few moments of kite flying before Freckles appeared on the screen.

This time she was indoors, sitting on a patterned sofa of beige and blue. The camera appeared to have been placed on a coffee table; the frame cut off the very top of Freckles's head. She was wearing a gray sweatshirt with a Champion label, blue sweatpants, and ankle-high white socks. She was sitting cross-legged, and behind her, on the wall above the couch, hung what appeared to be a metallic sculpture of twists and curves, though most of it, like the top of her head, was not within the frame. It appeared as if she had pressed the record button and sat down on the couch, for she was still settling in as the recording started. A moment later, she began to speak.

> *I just got back from Mira's wake and it was awful.*
> *Dreadful and horrible and so goddamn sad. Her poor*
> *mother. And all those people crying and crying, and*
> *all of them there because of me. Mira and her*

mother and her friends and even those funeral home
guys, standing outside in their black suits, trying to
look sad while getting paid, all there because of me,
and they didn't even know it.

Freckles stopped for a moment, sighed, and craned her neck
back as if she were looking at something on the ceiling (Milo
knew that she was only pausing to collect her thoughts). Then
she resumed.

I felt so guilty standing there. And I never know
when to leave. And why do the guys all stand in line
with their heads bowed, staring at their shoes, their
hands folded in front of them like they're trying to
cover up their dicks? Are they afraid that the Grim
Reaper is going to come along and try to castrate
them with his goddamn sickle?

Milo paused the tape and stood up, then folded his hands in
front of his body as Freckles had described, and smiled with the
realization that she was right. He could actually picture himself
assuming this pose in the past while waiting to shake the hands
of grieving loved ones at his father's funeral, perhaps adding an
embrace when appropriate, and even one of those manly, back-
slapping hugs that guys often perform as a public assertion of
their heterosexuality.

Before resuming the tape, Milo picked up the legal pad and
jotted down the words *Mira? Dead? Obits? Surviving mother.*
Father?

He thought that he might be able to locate a recently deceased girl named Mira (a thankfully uncommon name), and
that doing so might lead him to someone who knew Freckles.
With that thought, he added *Need a photo* to his legal pad, think-

ing that he could print a still frame of her face from the video in order to help identify her. Then he pressed play again.

> *We're all just standing there, waiting for the awful-*
> *ness to happen so that it could finally end. Waiting for*
> *the moment when we could say hello, sometimes to*
> *people we don't even know, and offer some standard*
> *bullshit to someone who's barely able to listen. It's*
> *like the scoliosis screening we did back in junior high.*
> *We all stood in line, waiting to take our shirts off be-*
> *hind the screen so that Doctor Big Eyes could stare at*
> *our backs and breasts and tell us we were fine. I hated*
> *the wait, I hated the moment when I had to take off*
> *my shirt, but I couldn't wait to get it over with just the*
> *same. Like you couldn't decide which was worse,*
> *waiting for the screening or the screening itself.*
> *That's how I felt today.*

Milo considered writing down *No scoliosis* but decided against it.

> *And then if we're lucky, like we were today, we get to*
> *view the goddamn corpse. Why the fuck does anyone*
> *want to do this?*

Freckles began to cry, had started to as she described her friend's body, but now it was genuine weeping: nose running, cheeks reddening, tears streaming down her face. Milo felt like an intruder, trapped in a place that he didn't belong, a Peeping Tom, a pervert in a Good Samaritan suit. As he watched the woman on screen bury her face in her hands and sob uncontrol-lably, he wondered how he could ever return the camera and tapes to her now. She would know that Milo had witnessed this private moment, and he didn't think he could bear this unspoken awareness between the two of them if they were to ever meet.

She cried for almost five full minutes as Milo watched helplessly from his perch on the futon. Unlike the actors in a movie or television show, who Milo knew were only pretending to be distraught (probably doing cartwheels on the inside over the amount of money they were making with each phony tear), this woman was in genuine despair, and there was no one to comfort her. He had the sudden desire to comfort her himself, a yearning that almost took the shape of one of his demands, even though this moment of sadness had probably occurred weeks or months ago, and it pained him that he could not do so.

This desire led Milo to think about Christine, probably back in their home, finished with dinner, watching television or reading at this very moment. How many tears had Milo caused her to shed by moving out? Did she cry at night while climbing into their empty bed? The thought of Christine weeping every night like this brought tears to Milo's eyes, and for a moment, Milo and Freckles were crying together.

Milo managed to compose himself before Freckles did, but not much sooner. He thought about stopping the tape to call Christine, to check on her, see how she was doing and perhaps set a time and day for their first date. But then he remembered how angry she had been outside Dr. Teagan's office just hours before and decided against it. Her fury was probably keeping sadness at bay this evening, he thought.

A moment later, Freckles wiped away the last of her tears and began speaking again.

> *Well, I guess I'm going to have to edit these tapes after all. I can't let the world see that disgusting display of snot.*

Freckles stood up and exited the view of the camera for a moment, giving Milo his first, albeit brief, view of her lower torso. Even though she was concealed by bulky sweatpants, he thought Freckles probably had a good figure. Lean and athletic. A second later, Milo heard the sounds of her blowing her nose, and when she returned to the frame, Freckles had a box of tissues in her hand, which she placed on the sofa beside her.

> *Anyway, tomorrow's the funeral, which means that Mira's last gift to me is a day off from work. Maybe two or three if I decide I'm too upset to finish the week. I should be, right? I mean, one of my best friends is dead.*
>
> *God, just saying those words is incomprehensible.*

Milo continued to watch as Freckles blew her nose one more time, stood up, and exited the frame. A second later the screen went black. Milo fast-forwarded the tape to the end and found the last twelve minutes blank.

Freckles had moved on to another tape. He hoped.

Milo picked up his legal pad and made some final notes. *The wake was probably on a Tuesday or Wednesday, because she said two or three extra days off.* Milo waited another minute before placing the legal pad down, trying to think of anything else that he might have missed. Satisfied that he had recorded everything of importance, he removed the tape from the camera, returned it to its plastic case, and loaded in the tape marked 2. Though he had hoped to start the next tape before he went to bed, he had been suddenly consumed with the need to go to the grocery store.

He had just opened his last jar of jelly earlier that evening, and he was in need of many more.

chapter 7

Five jars of Smucker's grape jelly would probably be enough, he thought, but he bought ten just in case. It didn't hurt to have extra jars stacked in the cupboard in the event that the demand arose again, as it undoubtedly would. Though new demands were not uncommon, old standbys such as the pressure seals on jelly jars could always be depended on to return again and again. Had he still been living with Christine, bringing home ten jars of grape jelly would require an explanation, but now that he was living in the apartment, he had to explain the purchase to no one.

A decade ago, Milo might have been embarrassed to bring ten jars of jelly to a cashier, and so in order to reduce his level of mortification, he might have purchased several other items as well in order to camouflage the abundance of jelly in his cart, much the same way as a teenage boy might pile candy bars, magazines, and soda atop a box of condoms in order to conceal the true reason for his purchase. But now, though he was still not completely comfortable with the oddity of this purchase, Milo no longer felt the need to fill his cart with other items. Cashiers, in his experience, just didn't care.

Milo had found that cashiers came in two varieties. The first and more prevalent kind were nearly robotic individuals who barely took notice of the customer, the items being purchased, or what they themselves were even doing. For these employees, ringing up customers' orders had become equivalent to turning a screw on Henry Ford's assembly line.

Just another customer in an endless line of customers.

This, Milo thought, was probably why they appeared so mindless. Unlike many occupations, in which one assignment or task could be finished and another one started, the career cashier faced a lifetime of incompletion. Their purpose was to service a line of customers that would never end, and if it ever did, this would mean the end of their employment. Even in Milo's line of work there were small accomplishments and notable milestones. Training a client to use the Internet. Convincing another to adopt a pet. Assisting another through the difficult process of dying. These were all accomplishments from which Milo derived great pride. For the cashier, these moments did not exist, and so most eventually became mechanical in their actions.

There was a minority of cashiers, however, who insisted on engaging their customers in meaningful exchanges of dialogue during every possible transaction. These people were typically new to the job (and therefore didn't understand the monotony of their future) or were those constantly upbeat and cheery people whom Milo never understood. If Milo were to run into one of these cashiers, questions about his inordinate amount of jelly might arise (*That's one big peanut butter and jelly sandwich you're making, mister—hardy har har!*), and though a query like this might infringe on Milo's sense of normalcy, he had learned to combat this reaction with the same detachment of those cashiers who understood the truth about their occupation and their future.

The cashier manning the express lane in the Stop & Shop this evening was an older woman named Lauren (or so claimed her name tag) whose shoulders appeared to be bearing the weight of a thousand jelly jars. She was short, hunched, and frowning, the archetype of what Milo imagined an older Russian woman would have looked like living through the siege of Stalingrad: hopeless and defeated. Her green smock bore a pin (*flair*, Milo mused) with the incongruous phrase *Can I help you?* written in a shade of yellow that bespoke of a happiness and whimsy to which this woman did not seem capable.

Clearly the type of cashier who would not question Milo's purchase.

Once money had exchanged hands, Milo made his way back to his car. He had hoped to wait until he was home to begin opening the jars, but, as it was with most of his demands, the proximity to its fulfillment increased the immediacy of the need. His head was aching badly by the time he opened the car door.

Sitting in the front seat underneath the yellow glow of the parking lot's sodium fluorescent bulbs, Milo took the first jar in his hand, fingering the round metallic depression in the lid that indicated the pressurized seal. So close to fulfillment, the need was excruciating now, but he waited a few seconds longer, as long as he could possibly bear, in order to heighten the anticipation. Like those insistent words in his head, the time leading up to the moment of completion was torturous, but the instant of fulfillment, and the seconds just before, were ecstasy.

Grasping the lid around the edge and bringing the jar close to his ear, Milo exerted adequate force in order to move the lid a quarter turn, releasing the pressurized safety seal in the process. The satisfying hiss and pop of the jar caused Milo's tightened muscles to relax with a shudder. A second later he released a sigh, barely audible despite the quiet of the car.

Milo remained still for a moment, waiting to see if the one jar would be enough to satisfy the demand. Though rare, there had been times when a single jar would do the trick. As he waited, he thought about how different things would be if he and

Christine had still been living together. He might have not been able to sneak away to make the necessary purchase, and as a result, more than a day could have gone by before meeting the need. During a delay like this, it was as if that German submariner residing in his head, possibly an admiral based on the power he wielded, would continue to watch through his periscope, slowly and steadily increasing the pressure on the dials and valves before him. The need would linger in the back of Milo's mind, always present and ever nagging, and at times dangerously distracting and even painful, building until the needles were redlining, steam was venting from the complex web of pipes and hoses within the submariner's vessel, and ignoring the demand became almost impossible.

Thankfully, his job offered him ample freedom during the day to meet these needs without much trouble.

Though Christine didn't know about Milo's demands, she knew that her husband was odd and had said as much to Milo in the past. He wasn't surprised. Milo knew that it would be impossible to fulfill these demands on a regular basis without appearing a little neurotic and strange, but he had managed to convince his wife that his behavior was the result of his personality and not the demands placed upon him. When necessary, Milo even fostered and encouraged this belief about his peculiar personality. For example, he would sometimes find himself with the need to watch a movie that he had already seen a hundred times before, in hopes that the end of the film might turn out differently. Even though he knew on a cognitive level that this could never happen, something inside his head (that damn U-boat captain, he suspected, jonesing for a little entertainment) demanded that he watch the movie again, and regardless of what his practical side told him, Milo found himself on the edge of his seat every time, half believing that this might be the one time when things finally and miraculously changed for the better.

There were several films that Milo found himself rewatching over and over again, but one of the most common was episode 3 of the Star Wars saga, in which Darth Vader rises from the ruins of Anakin Skywalker. At several key points in this film, the fate of the galaxy rests on the actions of a single character, and in each of these instances, Milo would tense with unrealistic expectation, hoping that things might turn out better than expected. His muscles would bunch into knots, his fists would clench, and he would bite down on his lip until the moment passed, always unchanged and unfulfilled. The worst was the scene in which Mace Windu confronts Palpatine in order to arrest him and end his plot to take over the galaxy. A lightsaber battle ensues between the two, and Windu ultimately disarms Palpatine. Just as he is about to end the reign of the Sith with a killing blow, Anakin Skywalker arrives and interferes, insisting that Palpatine be spared. "It's not the Jedi way!" he shouts to his comrade.

At this point in the film, Milo often found himself screaming at the television, reminding Skywalker that he had no problem with execution when it came to Count Dooku. And part of Milo, the part that demanded that he watch, truly believed that Anakin might listen to him and stand down, allowing Mace Windu to kill Palpatine and prevent all that was to follow. Instead, Sky-walker provides Palpatine with the opening he needs to kill Windu (although Milo would also wait with great anticipation to see if Windu would return by the end of the film, since his ulti-mate demise takes place off-screen) and take control of the galaxy.

When the film finally ends and Darth Vader is born (after Obi Won foolishly leaves Anakin alive by the river of lava for Pal-patine to find him), Milo would invariably experience a sense of relief, a release from the demand, though this feeling of fulfill-ment hardly provided the euphoric sensation that bowling a strike or popping open a jar of Smucker's would.

Had Windu killed Palpatine or had Obi Wan tossed his apprentice into the river of lava like he should have, Milo imagined that the feeling of fulfillment would be indescribable. And if it actually happened someday, part of him wouldn't be surprised one bit.

So as he watched the same dozen or so films over and over again, played Dungeons & Dragons with his thirty-year-old buddies, and hung out with what appeared to be a genuine wizard, Christine thought her husband was a little odd, but these oddities were nothing compared to the genuine demands that ruled his life. Opening jars of Smucker's jelly (which he sometimes did inside the store without ever purchasing the jars, when he and Christine split up in order to expedite the shopping) might not seem simply odd to his wife. It might appear downright insane. So this demand, along with many, many others, was kept secret from her.

Milo opened three more jars of jelly before the demand was satisfied and he was able to head home. But before pulling out of his parking spot, he removed the page from the *Highlights* magazine that he had acquired earlier that day and read through the poem once again. He hadn't thought much of it at first, but he found that it was growing on him.

chapter 8

Milo had intended on spending part of the evening conducting research online in hopes of identifying and locating Freckles's now deceased friend Mira. But a combination of curiosity over the next tape and his desire to immerse his mind in auditory and visual stimuli in order to stop thinking about Christine persuaded him to put the research aside for another day.

Ever since their parting outside Dr. Teagan's office, Milo had been wondering how he might resume contact with his wife. More than twenty-four hours had passed without communication between the two, and the weekend was nearly upon them. If they were going to squeeze in at least one date this week, it would probably need to take place over the next couple of days. Christine's caseload, combined with her aerobics and art classes and volunteer work, kept her extremely busy during the week.

Asking his wife on an official date was something that Milo had never imagined having to do again, and he wasn't sure how to proceed. Should he treat it as if it were a first date, or would a simple dinner be enough? He wasn't sure. The rules for dating one's wife had not been explained to him, and he doubted that there was a book available on the subject. Instead, he was playing things by ear.

Their actual first date had been bad enough.

Milo had been nervous from the start. Milo and Christine's initial meeting had been a brief encounter outside of a Japanese restaurant in West Hartford Center. Christine had been with one of Milo's coworkers at the time, a nurse at Hartford Hospital who had been working the same shift as Milo, and for the brief moment that the two of them conversed, Christine had sized up Milo and deemed him "cute." The next day, his coworker, a woman named Nina, had passed on the favorable estimation as well as Christine's phone number. "She wants you to call."

"What? I'm just supposed to dial her number and start talking? What am I supposed to say?"

"I dunno. Ask her out, silly."

This type of interaction seemed all well and good on the silver screen, but in real life, calling a strange girl and asking her on a date based on a split-second impression was not easy.

Hello, Christine?
Yes?
Hi, this is Milo.
Oh, hi, Milo. How are you?
Good. And you?
Fine.

Then what?

If the conversation proceeded thusly, Milo would be on the hook for the first meaningful statement of the phone call. He would have to proffer the next thought or idea. What might it be?

So, I hear that you think I'm cute. I barely remember what you look like from the minute that we spent together, but I figured I'd give it a shot. I don't exactly have a stable of girls to call upon.

Milo spent hours trying to find a foolproof way to be the last one in the conversation to indicate his current state of being, thus placing the onus of the first meaningful statement of the conversation on Christine, but there was no getting around it. If he placed the call, he would eventually need to express something other than pleasantries.

In the end, he managed to make the call after a three-day cocktail of rehearsal, rescripting, and avoidance, and thankfully, Christine had made the conversation easy on him. Milo led by saying that Nina thought they might have a lot in common, including a love for hiking and the movies, and Christine essentially took it from there.

Three nights later, they were back in West Hartford Center, enjoying a candlelit dinner at Arugula. It was his first date in a long time, so Milo was feeling uncommonly normal as he sat down at the table by the window. No longer relegated to the role of the Dungeons & Dragons nerd, he was sitting across from a beautiful woman who had greeted him on the sidewalk outside the restaurant with a warm and genuine smile. Her hair was short and dark, and she appeared to be wearing little if any makeup, and it didn't appear as if she needed any. She possessed the kind of natural beauty that seemed to require little effort. She was short, barely five feet tall, which was fine with Milo, who was only five feet, seven inches tall. She wore small diamond studs in her ears and was otherwise unadorned. *Simple but beautiful,* Milo had thought as she approached him on that warm spring evening. He was also pleased to see that the shirt, pants, and sport jacket had been a good choice of attire. Christine was wearing a short black dress and heels. Not too formal, yet not too casual either.

The trouble began just after they had finished ordering. In the short time that they had spent together in the restaurant,

Milo had finally begun to relax at bit. The pressure of the near-blind date had been wearing on him, but after just fifteen minutes together, it was clear that he and Christine were going to get along just fine. With the relaxation came the sudden need to use the restroom for what Milo feared would be more than just a couple of minutes. Apparently the release of tension had sent a signal to his body that the time had come for him to have a seat and take care of business.

Milo realized this almost immediately after handing the menu back to the waiter, and hoped for a moment that he might suppress the need. Abdominal discomfort indicated otherwise. So with hopes of accomplishing the task quicker than usual, he excused himself from the table and made his way to the men's room, where he took a seat in one of the two stalls.

As with many things, the need to complete a task quickly caused the process to become exponentially more difficult, as the relaxation he felt moments ago was replaced by muscle-wrenching tension. For a minute, Milo thought that he might abandon the process altogether, his body offering him a last-minute reprieve, but as he rose from the commode, his body reminded him of what must be done.

Milo was in the restroom for twelve minutes (he watched the minutes pass on his cell phone) and had no idea what to say when he returned to the table. He had been gone excessively long. The salads had probably arrived five minutes ago. Christine might already be on her second glass of wine. He could attempt to pretend that the time that he was away did not warrant mention, but then he feared that the specter of his absence would linger over the night.

He thought about telling his date that he had met an old friend in the restroom and had chatted with the guy for a few minutes, but Arugula was a small restaurant with no more than a dozen tables, all in clear view of one another. Christine would surely ask Milo to point out his friend, which he would be incapable of doing.

Unable to come up with a reasonable excuse for his delay, Milo resigned himself to returning to the table and hoping for the best. But as he exited the restroom into the narrow corridor that connected the dining room with the restrooms and the kitchen, Milo noticed that the rear door to the restaurant, one that appeared to be for employees only, was ajar.

Suddenly, he had an idea.

Four minutes later, a total of sixteen minutes after he had stepped away from the table, Milo reentered the restaurant through the front door, slowing and deepening his breathing in order to mask the effects of the sprint that he had just made around the building and down the alley between the restaurant and the adjacent gourmet dog bakery.

"Huh?" Christine said, startled to see Milo walk through the front door and across the restaurant to his seat.

"Sorry," he said, sitting and placing his cloth napkin back in his lap. "It was stupid. There's a door at the back of the restaurant. In the back hall. It was open a crack, and I heard some shouting coming through it as I came out of the restroom. Coming from the back parking lot. So I went to take a peek. A couple of teenagers with skateboards were picking on another kid, a smaller kid, calling him fag and queer, so I chased them off and made sure the smaller kid was okay. But I got locked out in the process."

"Oh," Christine said, eyes widening in surprise. "Are you all right?"

"Yeah. I'm fine. I mean, they were just kids. No big deal."

"God . . . I feel bad," she said, a grin forming on the corners of her lips. "I was sitting here thinking that you were *indisposed*. Or worse. You were gone so long, and it was getting a little awkward, just sitting here alone, sipping wine. I was starting to get a little annoyed. But I didn't know that you were out saving someone's life."

"I didn't save anyone's life. I just told the kids that I'd call the cops if they didn't get lost."

"It sounds pretty heroic to me," she said, reaching her hand across the table to squeeze his. "A lot of people would have ignored the whole situation. And I bet the kid thinks you're a hero too."

"Maybe," Milo said. "But honestly, it was nothing."

The rest of the date had gone exceptionally well. Transforming a potentially negative moment into a positive one, Milo had managed to relax and gain a measure of poise, shedding the nervousness and apprehension that he had felt ever since asking Christine out. She had found his actions, albeit fictitious, heroic, and that had set the stage for an unexpectedly positive first impression.

It had also been the first time that Milo had lied to his future wife, and though he sometimes wished that he could have been more honest with her at the beginning of their relationship rather than starting off on fraudulent terms, this minor act of subterfuge had helped to provide Milo with the belief and the confidence that he might be able to keep his non-bathroom-related demands a secret as well.

Now Milo was feeling the same anxiety that had consumed him at the onset of their first dinner, and he wondered how he might deal with it this time. Calling his wife and asking her on a date seemed like both the easiest and most difficult thing that he could ever do, so in hopes of avoiding it for one more night, he chose to sit on his futon, watch tape number two, and look for clues as to Freckles's identity instead.

The screen was black for about ten seconds, and when it resumed, her face filled it. The picture was wobbly, indicating that she was holding the camera this time, and her clothing had changed, though Milo realized that shouldn't have been a surprise. A week or a month could have passed without him being able to tell.

It appeared that she was wearing blue and yellow flannel pajamas, the kind that always seemed uncomfortably warm to men but just right for a woman. She was sitting on a bed. Her bed, Milo guessed, based on appearances. White and yellow pillows were piled against a headboard behind her. She looked much better. Not as tired or worn out as she had previously.

Milo found surprising relief in her renewed appearance.

> *Hi. I know it's been a few days, but I've been in a bit of a funk and haven't had much to say. Actually, I don't know how these people do it, recording their thoughts every day. I just don't think I'm going to have enough ideas and stories to make this interesting. But today I saw something that I thought I should share. I was in the supermarket parking lot after work, pushing my carriage back to my car, and this man was getting out of his truck and coming toward me. He was wearing a black knit cap and a leather jacket and boots, with one of those ridiculous barb wire tattoos on his wrist, like some kind of mean-ass biker dude, except he was driving a pickup. Just as he passes me, another man, an old guy in a silver minivan, starts shouting at the biker.*
>
> *"Hey! You're parked in a handicapped spot!" the old guy says. But louder than that, and angrier. Really pissed off. His van is in the lane with its blinker flashing, waiting to pull into the space where the biker dude had parked. So Biker Dude flips the old guy off and just goes into the store. Doesn't even*

bother to look back. Doesn't even flinch. Then I watch
as the old guy puts the van in park right in the mid-
dle of the lane, jumps out, goes to the back of the
van, and opens the hatch. That's when I see his wife
in the passenger seat, or who I assume was his wife,
just sitting there, waiting. An older lady with gray
hair and the kind of fuzzy sweater that my grand-
mother used to wear. She's just sitting there, not a
worry in the world. We make eye contact for a second
and she smiles at me, like what's about to happen is
completely normal. Then the old guy comes back
around the van with a tire iron in his hand. He walks
over to Biker Dude's pickup and puts the tire iron
right through the windshield. Bam! Just like that.
Then he walks back over to his van, gets in, and
drives away. Like nothing happened.
  It was unbelievable.

Freckles stopped for a moment and shook her head, and in
those few seconds, Milo knew that she was envisioning the scene
all over again. Reliving it in her mind. The biker. The old man.
The wife. The tire iron. He found himself doing the same. Visu-
alizing the moment. Seeing it through Freckles's eyes.
  She was right. It was unbelievable.

The whole scene was surreal. I couldn't believe what
the old guy had done, but that asshole deserved it. I
give the old guy a lot of credit. It's one of those
things that I wish I had the guts to do myself. God,
that old guy had balls.
  But you know what? It's the old guy's wife who I
can't stop thinking about. She just sat there, watching
her husband bash in another guy's windshield. The

kind of guy who could've kicked her husband's ass
twice over. But she just sat there and didn't say a
word. Smiled at me, in fact. It wasn't like she was
afraid to say anything to her husband either. There
wasn't a drop of fear on her. And I think that if she
had wanted to, she could've stopped the old guy right
in his tracks. Convinced him to get back in the van
and drive away. But she just sat there. Sat there and
let her husband teach that asshole a lesson.

  That old guy is one lucky man. I hope he knows it.

Milo thought that he understood the scene better than most.
He knew that as people become older, many begin to feel a loss
of control over their lives. Their mind and body begins to fail
them and their families stop relying on them as they once did. In
response, they try to find ways to reassert the control that they
once possessed. It was entirely possible that taking a crowbar to
Biker Dude's pickup truck had been a way for that old guy to
remind the world that he wasn't in the grave just yet.

And Milo suspected that Freckles was right about the wife
too. Understanding and supporting her husband in a moment
like that was unusual. Special. The kind of relationship that few
couples enjoyed. Milo suddenly found himself envious of this
man whom he had never met.

The screen went black once again, and when Freckles returned, she was still on the bed, pillows piled in the same moun-
tainous formation as before. Milo marveled at the number of
decorative pillows that women seemed to require on a bed.

  You know what? I think this needs to be for me. My
  visions of posting this diary online might have been
  a little crazy. I've been sitting here for the last fifteen

minutes, thinking of all the things that I'd like to
share on this video but can't because I plan to let other
people watch. Maybe that's not what I should be
doing. Maybe this should just be for me. At least for
now. I can't keep a diary that excludes all of my se-
crets, my own windshield-bashing moments that I
don't want the world to know about. It wouldn't be
worth my time. So I think that for now, this will be
for my eyes only. Maybe someday, when I'm good
and dead, someone can watch this.

Freckles paused for a moment, let out a deep sigh of relief, smiled, and then added:

You know what else? I suddenly have a lot to say.

Milo pressed the stop button on the camera and set it down on the coffee table. In a single moment, things had drastically changed. Prior to Freckles's decision to start recording just for herself, Milo had justified his eavesdropping with the expectation that the videos were intended to be made public someday. But now the rules had changed. Who knew what Freckles would share next?

> The color of her underwear (Milo couldn't bring
> himself to use the word *panties* without feeling
> stupid)?
> Her bra size (Milo guessed a 34B or C)?
> Her voting record?
> Bizarre bathroom rituals?
> Secret sexual fantasies?
> Incidents of undertipping waitresses?

The list of secrets that Milo kept from his closest friends and wife was long, and the idea that someone might come along and have access to all of them made him shudder. Could he now violate Freckles's privacy in the same way?

Fortunately, in the midst of his thoughts, the phone rang. Milo picked it up and saw the phone number that had been his for more than three years. Christine was calling.

His decision on Freckles would have to wait.

chapter 9

Milo didn't expect that his second first date with Christine would take place in his apartment, and neither did he expect it to end with sex against the kitchen wall. But his wife had requested the location for the date, apparently curious about how her husband was living, and before Milo had time to serve dinner, the two were half naked and trying desperately to stay upright while remaining effectively engaged in the task at hand. This was not Milo's choice of position, to be sure. Had it been up to him, the two would have been in bed with the lights off, enjoying any of the more easily achieved positions that did not require the balance and agility that Milo was now mustering. Contrary to what was often displayed in movies, sex standing up was not at all simple. On the big screen, burly men lifted petite women with effortless grace, and, without so much as a drop of lubricant or a guiding hand, instantly connected penis and vagina in a mystical embrace. Several thrusts would ensue, typically followed by a simultaneous orgasm that would impress the finest of Olympic synchronized swimmers.

These fantasy moments made no sense to Milo. Though they seemed delightfully spontaneous and blisteringly sexy on screen, the reality of the situation was that the human body was not designed to engage in upright sexual relations. The mere positioning of the penis and vagina on their respective owners made certain positions much simpler to accomplish, so why the upright version of sex was admired by so many was baffling to Milo.

Furthermore, this was not a position that anyone should attempt past the age of thirty, as one's strength and agility diminished. Attempting it past that age would only serve to emphasize the debilitating effects of advancing years on the couple.

Milo should have known better and avoided this trap.

In addition, Milo doubted that he had any chance of achieving orgasm in this ridiculous position. The strength required to support his wife's entire body, as well as the concentration and balance necessary to remain connected made any hope of orgasm seem pointless. Even in the standard missionary position, Milo found that it took him longer to achieve orgasm than it once did, and contrary to commonly held beliefs about men and women and sex, this did not always sit well with his wife. Though he took pride in his stamina, there were many nights when Christine wanted the action to end quickly, something that Milo found increasingly difficult to accomplish as he got older. It simply took longer to climax since he'd entered his thirties, and in Milo's estimation, this was not a bad thing. Sex felt good, so the more time he spent doing it, the better. Yet many times Christine would encourage Milo to orgasm before he was good and ready (and even able), and this added pressure for speed, much like the pressure for speed that he had felt in the Arugula restroom, made it nearly impossible to accomplish something that he could once manage in twenty seconds or less as a teenager.

As a result, Milo frequently faked orgasms with his wife, which he intended to do this evening.

He often wondered if other men faked orgasms, but he could never bring himself to ask. In fact, Milo's understanding of sex in general had come along slowly and at times painfully. The extent of his parents' instruction on copulation came one night after Milo had moved in to a partially finished basement bedroom as a teenager.

"You can do whatever you'd like with girls down here," his father had advised. "Just don't get them pregnant."

That was the first and last time that his parents spoke to him about the birds and the bees.

As a result, Milo's initial understanding of sex was limited. Growing up in a small town prior to the advent of the Internet didn't help, and his lack of knowledge occasionally caused problems. It wasn't until a few years ago, for example, that Milo could say for certain that he was circumcised. He was aware of the two types of penis, had seen both varieties in the locker room at the gym, and knew that his penis did not resemble the ones that appeared to be wrapped like German sausages. But he did not know if his penis, the type which he was inclined to prefer, was circumcised or uncircumcised and was therefore never confident enough to declare his penile status until finally finding definitive photos of each online. Mistakes such as misidentifying his own penis were ones that Milo had tried desperately to avoid since childhood.

When he was thirteen, a bunch of older kids in his Boy Scout troop questioned Milo on his knowledge of sex on the way to a campfire jamboree. In the back of his scoutmaster's van, bench seats and no seat belts in those days, Brian Dean, Eddy Lindo, and several other brutes had asked Milo if he knew what a rubber was. Milo was certain that the item was sexual in nature but had no idea what it looked like or what it even was. In a panic, he claimed to know the answer to their question but refused to give them the satisfaction of a definition, and so began an hour-long berating that would continue to resurface within his Boy Scout troop for years to come.

At the time, Milo suspected that he knew what a rubber was, but he didn't want to risk being wrong, knowing it was better to feign knowledge than to confirm ignorance. Once, while retrieving a book for his mother from her nightstand, he had spotted a long, penis-shaped slab of silicone peeking out from underneath her pillow, and he guessed that this might have been a rubber. He envisioned a slit on the end in which the man would insert his penis, thus providing it with protection as well as increased length and girth.

Obviously, he had been mistaken.

But without understanding it completely, Milo was too afraid to venture a guess, so he allowed Brian Dean, whose older brother, Michael, would commit suicide later that year, to belittle him to the point of tears. Still, it was better than mistaking your mother's dildo for a condom.

Milo often thought about Michael Dean, wondering what secrets this seemingly normal and well-liked boy had that caused him to blow his head off with his father's hunting rifle. Milo had secrets, to be sure, and though they seemed exceedingly strange at times, none of them had been awful enough to cause him to contemplate suicide. Michael Dean's secrets, Milo thought, must have been terrible.

So Milo found himself attempting to fornicate with his wife just a foot and a half from Skywalker's (whose name had reverted to Puggles for the evening) water dish and the kitchen garbage can. Though Christine's insistence on sex had been initially thrilling, the combination of the awkward position, the water dish, and the faint odor of garbage had quickly eliminated any hope for excitement.

In fact, if it had been Milo's decision, he and Christine would not be having sex at all. He had something more pressing on his mind at the moment.

Breaking ice cubes from their plastic trays was one of those recurring demands by which Milo was occasionally plagued.

Thankfully, this demand was easily met so long as there were filled trays in the freezer. This had meant talking Christine out of a refrigerator with an automatic ice maker, which hadn't been easy, but the need to run a water line under the kitchen floor in order for the appliance to produce ice had convinced her that the convenience wouldn't be worth the hassle. But when Milo had moved in to the apartment, he had failed to notice a lack of ice cube trays in the freezer. Why the previous tenant would take the ice cube trays when every freezer on the planet was already equipped with them was beyond Milo's understanding, but when the need to crack the cubes from the trays arose less than two hours before his date with Christine, Milo made a mad dash for the supermarket, where he purchased the trays, along with five extra jars of grape jelly. Once home, he filled the trays with water, decreased the temperature inside the freezer to its lowest setting, and placed them inside.

Milo had actually been exceedingly pleased with the purchase. The trays were the type with an extra-tall ridge around the outer edge, allowing the user to fill the bucket-like containers for each cube as well as add a layer of water over all the cubes. Once frozen, this additional layer of water would form a sheet of ice across the top of the tray, making the cubes infinitely more satisfying to snap out.

However, Christine had arrived before the water had finished freezing, so now he found himself just five feet from the freezer, the water likely frozen, ready to go. Yet instead of popping the cubes from their frozen perches, Milo was forced to engage in a nearly impossible sexual position with his wife. Had they taken the passion to the bedroom, Milo might have been able to silence the demand for a time, but listening to the hum of the refrigerator's compressor comingling with Christine's whines and pants made the ice cubes an immediate necessity and an orgasm an absolute impossibility.

Milo found himself wishing that he could explain this predicament to his wife, and he thought that if he could, he might be able to save the marriage right there and then. The truth might destroy any hope of reconciliation, but perhaps there was the slimmest of chances that his honesty would open new doors for them.

But to bring it up for discussion would be like risking a guess at the definition of a rubber and confusing it with a dildo. If he didn't get it right, there would be no turning back.

Milo waited until Christine achieved orgasm, a small miracle in Milo's mind considering the circumstances, before he began his feigned escalation of pants and grunts that would culminate in his own climax. Under normal circumstances, even when orgasm was possible, Milo attempted to time his release as close to Christine's as possible, uncertain and doubtful of the degree of pleasure that a woman experienced when she continued having sex after achieving orgasm. So less than a minute after Christine's shuddering climax, Milo followed with a faux orgasm of his own, thrusting deeply and forcefully and declaring his enthusiasm loud enough for the neighbors to hear.

In the world of fake orgasms, Milo thought that it was impossible to be over the top.

Another problem with upright sex was the awkwardness of the moments that immediately followed. Had the couple been in bed, Milo would have rolled off his wife and remained beside her for a time, allowing his heart rate to return to normal. The two might hold hands, or if chilly, they might embrace, Christine resting her head on his chest while they engaged in postcoital small talk. But from a standing position, there was nowhere that the couple could go. Milo stepped away from Christine's body, feeling cold and sticky in the middle of the kitchen floor as his wife peeled her backside from the wall in a motion that was anything but sexy.

Moments like these were absent from the movies too, Milo noted.

"Do you mind if I use the bathroom first?" Christine asked, standing directly over the dog's water dish, attempting to reposition her breasts inside her bra. During the first frenzied moments of the encounter, Milo had managed to remove his wife's top but was unable to negotiate the fastener on the bra, opting to push it down to her belly rather than fighting to remove it.

"Of course," he said, having hoped she would ask. "The bathroom is just around the corner."

Milo waited for his wife to leave the kitchen before shouting, "Would you like a cold drink?"

"That sounds great. Thanks." A moment later Milo heard the bathroom door close and felt his spirits drop a bit. Christine could have sex with him while standing in the kitchen but still felt the need to close the bathroom door, even though it was around the corner and out of view.

Nevertheless, with excuse in hand, Milo went into action. First, he grabbed a dish towel and used it to wipe his penis clean of the stickiness that the sex had left behind. As with all his fake orgasms, the cleanup was minimal. Nevertheless, he tossed the dish towel into the cabinet below the sink, lest he accidentally use it before washing it. He then retrieved two mismatched glasses from his collection of three in the cupboard and placed them on the counter beside the sink. Finally, he opened the freezer and removed the first of four ice cube trays from the stack.

To his delight, the water was completely frozen.

Milo took the tray in both hands and held it over the sink, examining its contents closely. As expected, the individual cubes were covered by a satisfying layer of ice that reached to the lip of the tray on all four sides. Minuscule air bubbles had been trapped under the water during the freezing process, giving the ice a white, opaque appearance.

It looked perfect.

Gripping both ends of the tray, Milo began twisting slowly, back and forth, watching cracks spontaneously erupt throughout the upper layer of ice, throwing tiny shards out as the crevices grew larger. As he continued to twist, bending the plastic to a greater and greater degree, more substantial cracks forced chunks of the ice to break free and tumble into the stainless-steel sink with a thrilling clang. A moment later Milo heard and felt the first popping of actual cubes as they were released from their plastic compartments. He was careful not to allow the cubes to dislodge from the tray just yet, wanting to be sure that every cube was free before tipping the tray over and watching them spill out all at once. If just one cube remained trapped in the tray after he had turned it upside down, or if a cube managed to escape prematurely, the anticipated feeling of relief and satisfaction would be greatly diminished, necessitating the freeing of more cubes from more trays.

There would be no time for a second tray tonight. Though he had never been certain about what Christine did in the bathroom following sex, he knew that whatever it was, it didn't take long. One tray would have to be enough.

Fearful of waiting a second more, Milo held his breath and turned the tray over in his hands, catching flashes of cubes as they dropped and clanged into the sink as the tray instantly lightened in his hand. It was this combination of sensory input, the amalgamation of sound and sight and touch, that sent a wave of relief washing over him, causing Milo to issue an audible sigh.

Thankfully, one tray had been more than enough.

Milo took a moment to compose himself before moving on. The fact that his pants were still around his ankles didn't help matters, but within a few seconds, he was removing four ice cubes from the sink and splitting them between the two glasses. He was reaching for the bottle of soda when he heard the bathroom door open. Forgoing the drink, he quickly reached down and yanked up his pants.

"All set," Christine said, her disheveled hair already back in place, her postcoital glow nearly gone. "When you get out of the bathroom, we should really talk."

Milo didn't like the sound of that one bit.

chapter 10

"You bought a video camera?"

When Milo reentered the kitchen, he found Christine at the table with Freckles's video camera and nylon bag sitting in front of her. The plate and cutlery he had set out for her had been pushed back into the center of the table and several tapes had been removed from the bag. Christine was holding the camera in one hand and tape number six in the other.

A lump formed in the back of Milo's throat. He had placed the camera behind a row of unopened boxes in the living room, not planning to show it to Christine. Apparently she had made a brief inspection of the apartment while Milo was in the bathroom, probably looking around to see how her husband was living. Milo could envision his wife scanning the room, examining piles of books, wondering at the origin of the black and gold lamps that Milo had purchased at a garage sale, and taking mental inventory of the items that he had removed from their home during his move. Had she opened any of the boxes that were concealing the video camera, Christine would have also seen his Dungeons & Dragons paraphernalia: books with archaic covers, multisided dice, an assortment of die-cast creatures, and stacks of notes representing an adventure that he had been guiding his friends on for more than three years. Though she had never spoken in opposition to his role-playing hobby, Milo knew from the persistent absence of commentary that she did not approve.

"No," Milo said, moving closer in hopes of somehow casually removing the camera from her possession. "I didn't buy it. I found it in the park a few days ago. I'm trying to find its owner." Milo knew that he had already said too much. Milo lied to his wife frequently, of course, in order to conceal the demands of the ice cubes and Weebles and the words that became trapped in his head. But, feeling perpetually guilty about the lies that he told his wife, Milo made every effort to minimize his lying in all other situations, and he had managed to adhere to this policy with few exceptions during their marriage. Telling his wife the truth about the camera had been almost instinctive.

"How do you plan on finding the owner?"

"Well, there are a bunch of tapes in the bag." In truth, Milo knew exactly how many tapes were in the bag but had learned through experience that people found his constant, exacting precision to be unnerving. Casual was cool, he had discovered long ago, and though Milo knew that he would never be cool in the conventional sense of the word, he still converted exactitude to generalization for the benefit of those around him. Even a little bit of cool was better than none at all.

"Yes, I can see the tapes, Milo. So what?"

"Well, I started watching them to see if I could figure out who the owner was. You know, hoping that she might say her name or something."

Christine smiled. "But the problem is, the owner probably doesn't appear on camera, right? She's always behind the camera?"

"Actually, no. It turns out that she was recording a video diary. So she's the only one on film. At least so far."

"So who is she? What do you know about her?"

"Not much. She hasn't said her name yet." Milo purposely avoided telling his wife that he had assigned Freckles a nickname, thinking it might sound too familiar for his wife's liking. He wanted to find a way off this topic as quickly as possible. In an effort to change the subject, he moved into the kitchen to make himself busy, hoping his wife would offer her assistance. The unexpected sex had given the food that Milo had prepared time to cool, so he began picking out the pots and pans needed to reheat the meal. In truth, he had purchased prepared meals at Whole Foods earlier that evening (prior to his mad dash for ice cube trays) and had plated the food (stuffed pork chops, garlic mashed potatoes, and baby carrots) on dinnerware that he had extricated from the attic during his move.

"So what's she like?" Christine asked.

"I don't know. She's probably in her early thirties. A friend of hers just died. In video time, I mean. There are no dates on the tapes, so I don't know if I'm watching something three weeks old or three years old."

"Have you watched all the tapes yet?"

"No, just the first couple," Milo replied, attempting to determine if the stove was gas or electric. He had yet to use the appliance and wasn't entirely sure. "They're kind of boring, to be honest."

"Can I watch some?"

Milo feared that this question might come and wasn't sure how to answer. Though he knew what his response would be, he had no idea of how to convey the answer to his wife without offending her. So he said the first thing that came to his mind. "I wish you could, but to be honest, I'm not sure if I'm going to keep watching. The tapes are getting kind of private." He took a moment to explain Freckles's decision to stop recording for broadcast and his resulting hesitancy to watch any more of the tapes.

"Well, can I watch some of the first couple tapes? The ones you've already seen?"

"If you don't mind, Christine, I'd rather you didn't. I feel weird enough having watched the first couple hours. Like I've invaded this girl's privacy. If I let you watch too, I'd feel like I'm violating her privacy even more."

Milo knew that this wasn't the entire truth, but he liked the way it sounded. It was a decent explanation, he thought, and he had fleeting hopes that his wife might accept it. In reality, Milo oddly treasured his relationship with Freckles, and considered it a private one. And in an equally odd sort of way, he cherished the secrecy of it. The tapes had been left behind for reasons Milo didn't understand, but as the temporary owner of them, he felt an obligation to protect Freckles from prying eyes. Even those of his wife.

"You really don't want me watching the tapes?"

"No, I don't. Please don't be upset."

"Fine," Christine said, but he knew that Christine was anything but fine.

Milo had managed to coax a flame on the stovetop (a gas stove, he had determined) and remained silent as he stirred the carrots in an overheated skillet. He was certain that his wife would have more to say momentarily, and from experience, he knew that it was better to wait until she began speaking again on her own. Prompting never made things better.

Less than a minute later, Christine broke the silence. "Let me ask you this: If you were living at home with me and had found the camera, would you still feel the need to protect this girl's privacy?"

"I don't know," Milo said. "I mean, if I were still living in the house, we probably would've watched the tapes together. It wouldn't be an issue."

"Exactly. So why don't you want me to see them now?"

"Well, now I know what's on the tapes, and if I were Freck-les, I would want as few people to see them as possible."

"Freckles?"

"Oh, yeah. She has freckles on her cheeks, so that's what I've been calling her. In my head, I mean."

"I don't get it, Milo. I'm your wife. We've been married for three years. You find a camera and some tapes in the park and won't let me watch them, even though you admit that if we were living together, I would've already seen them. What the hell is going on here?" She was still holding tape number six in her hand and shaking it at him. "What's so special about Freckles that prevents me, *your wife*, from watching?"

"Look, Christine. This has nothing to do with Freckles. If I had found the camera with you, we probably would've watched the tapes together. But we didn't. And now that I've seen them, I know that she wouldn't want you to watch. Wouldn't want any-one to watch. Not even me."

"*Not even you?*"

"Yes, not even me. Look. I can't take back what I've seen. I can't go back in time. But I can keep others from watching. Keep her tapes as private as possible until I find her. It's what she would want."

"You think you know what this girl wants? You don't even know what the hell *I* want. How are you supposed to know what a stranger on a tape wants after watching . . . what? Two hours?"

"It doesn't take long to see . . ."

"Bullshit. You don't know anything. I asked for a little space and you got yourself an apartment and a six-month lease. I needed some time to think and you emptied out the attic of fur-niture and dishes. I wanted a chance to work on our marriage, and you've started decorating a new home. How the hell would you know what this girl wants when you don't have a goddamn clue what your own wife wants?"

With that, Christine threw the tape that she had been holding (still tape six, Milo noted) at her husband, missing badly and striking the hood above the oven with a metallic clang. She was breathing heavily and on the verge of crying, struggling mightily to hold herself together.

Milo decided to wait another moment before speaking. Allow her to calm down before responding. Oddly enough, he was pleased with the direction that the conversation had taken. He didn't want his wife to be angry with him, but since she had become so, the topic had shifted away from Freckles and her tapes and onto their relationship, which is where Milo thought their attention should be focused anyway. Finally, when he thought she had dipped below the boiling point, he spoke. "I'm sorry, Christine. I know that I misunderstood you about getting the apartment, but I honestly thought that this is what you wanted from me. You heard what Dr. Teagan said. Most people would've thought the same thing."

"Fuck Dr. Teagan! Fuck you! Fuck this whole goddamn thing." Now Christine was crying. Tears streamed from her eyes, and her nose was beginning to run. Milo moved forward in an attempt to comfort her.

"No!" Christine said, rising from her chair and backing away. "I can't believe this. I come over here thinking that we'd have dinner, fool around, and talk about things. Maybe get back on track. But now I find out that you're keeping secrets from me. Can't even trust me to watch a tape of a girl that you've already seen. Did you plan on ever telling me about her? Did you?"

Once again, Milo wished that he could lie to his wife, but could not. "I don't know. Probably not. Maybe after I found her and returned the camera and the tapes, I would've told you. I knew that you would want to see the video, and I knew that I couldn't let you. Christine, I'm just doing what I think is right."

"Fine. I'll do the same." She then turned and left the apartment, slamming the door behind her.

Milo considered following her for a moment, desperate to avoid the awkwardness of his wife's latest dramatic exit, not wanting to endure the suspense over when she might call again. But instead he turned off the burner, removed the skillet from the stove, and retrieved tape number six from the floor and replaced it in the nylon bag.

Tape number three was the one that he needed.

chapter 11

Had Christine not found the camera and tapes, Milo might have stood by his decision to stop watching completely. But a wave of indignation and loneliness rose up in him as the door slammed behind Christine, and before he had given it any conscious thought, the camera was reconnected to the television and tape three was playing.

> *Okay. First secret. I like to eat in hospital cafeterias. Not a huge secret, and I know it sounds ridiculous, but it's true. The food is usually good and cheap as hell, and there's something about hospitals that I like. Knowing that I'm there for some reason other than being sick or dying—knowing that there is a reason to be there other than dying makes me feel... I don't know. Better about things.*
>
> *And it's just easier to eat in a cafeteria. No waitress to deal with. No tipping. You get to choose your seat. I hate walking into a restaurant full of empty tables and not being allowed to choose the one I want.*
>
> *And I love Jell-O. Not the unrefrigerated crap that they put in snack packs. I like the kind that requires boiling water and a saucepan. I love the stuff*

but I've never made it once in my life. Single people
just don't make Jell-O. But hospital cafeterias do.
When I was a kid, I thought Jell-O was some kind of
magical food. What other food needs to chill in the
refrigerator but starts out at a boil? Reminds me of
that fire and ice poem by whoever that was.

Freckles was back on the couch, wearing a hooded sweatshirt
and a pair of jeans. She sounded conversational and relaxed.
More relaxed than any previous recording. It was clear that she
was now recording for herself. No more audience to consider.

So there you have it. My first secret. I like to eat in
hospital cafeterias. When I say it out loud like that, it
doesn't sound like such a big deal after all.

Milo paused the tape, catching it in the moment of blackness
between frames, attempting to determine if there was any information worth writing down. She said that she was single, but he
had already assumed that. Not that it mattered. Despite promises
to himself to begin searching for Freckles's identity with the information that he had gathered so far, he hadn't so much as
turned on the computer. When the choice was between searching
online for the identity of Mira, Freckles's deceased friend, or
watching more of the tapes, the tapes won out.

And perhaps he also knew that if he was able to identify and
locate Freckles, then he wouldn't be able to watch the tapes anymore. While he wanted to find Freckles and return the camera
and tapes, he was admittedly not in a rush.

Deciding that Freckles hadn't revealed anything else of
value, Milo pressed play again.

When her image returned to the screen, she was no longer sitting on the couch. Pillows and the fuzzy corner of a blanket indi-

cated that she was in bed again. Her face filled the screen, looking down on the lens this time, as if the camera was resting in her lap, pointing up. A dim yellow glow to her left was the only source of illumination in the room. Probably a bedside lamp, Milo thought.

Despite the limited lighting, Milo could tell by the look on Freckles's face that something was wrong. There was a fierceness in her eyes that he had not seen before. It caused Milo to lean forward and grip his pen with unconscious force.

> *I couldn't sleep. Either I'm going to do this right or not at all. Fine. I eat in hospital cafeterias. But if that's the kind of secret that I'm going to tell, I might as well post this online after all. Except that no one would care. That I like hospital Jell-O hardly constitutes a secret. If I'm going to do this, I'm going to do it right. Here goes.*

Milo was holding his breath now, leaning so far forward that he was in danger of toppling headfirst off the couch. Freckles took a deep breath, almost as if she were reminding Milo to do the same, and repositioned the camera a bit, bringing her face closer to the screen. Milo didn't know how he knew, but he was certain that she was stalling, still debating about whether or not to take the plunge.

For a moment, he feared that she wouldn't. Then she began speaking again.

> *I wasn't a popular kid in school. I wasn't exactly un-popular, and that was part of the problem. When I was in elementary school, I was in the top group of kids. Back then, we were all sorted by ability, so the smartest kids were in Group One and we all knew it. The teachers even called us Group One. A notch*

below us were the kids in Group Two, then Group Three, and so on. The bottom group of kids didn't even get a number. They were the T Group. T stood for transitional, I think, but I never understood what the hell that meant. We used to say that the T stood for 'tards, but it should've stood for tough, because that's the kind of life that most of those kids had.

Anyway, in elementary school, I was friends with most of the kids in my class. We were still little kids, so none of the middle school bullshit had started yet. There were no popular and unpopular kids. Just smart kids and not-so-smart kids. I was with the same twenty or so classmates starting in first grade, and they were all basically my friends. The girls at least, and some of the boys too. All the smartest kids in my grade. All the kids who were going to be popular in high school. All the goddamn prom kings and queens stuffed into one classroom.

But once we hit middle school, things changed. Clothes, makeup, and jewelry started to matter, and my family didn't have a lot of money. Hell, I didn't think we had any money. I was wearing worn-out sneakers in January and eating macaroni and cheese for dinner every night. Try walking home in pink Keds through three feet of snow. Not fun, and not easy to hide from the other kids.

I was clueless about a lot of things too, and all of a sudden the right clothes and the right haircut and the right number of jelly bracelets made all the difference in the world. It seemed like overnight I went from a girl with lots of friends to someone on the outside looking in. Probably not true, but that's how it seemed at the time. I thought the other girls hated me, *but the truth was probably worse: They just stopped noticing me. A few of them kept inviting me to birthday parties out of habit, or maybe because their parents forced them to, but to me, things seemed fine until middle school. And the funny thing is, if I hadn't been in Group One, things might have been different. I could've been friends with girls in Group Two or Three. Even some of the T Group kids wouldn't have been bad. I might've been a little smarter than them, but a lot of those girls dressed just like me. Keds and Kmart specials. Funny how our tests scores seemed to almost always match the amount of money our parents made. Except for a handful of kids, like me. For us, life sucked. I was smart enough for Group One but poor enough for Group Three.*

But by then, I had the Group One stink about me. The other kids saw us as brains. And at the same time, my friends started seeing me as slightly beneath them. The wrong clothes, the wrong shoes, the wrong hairstyle, and a serious lack of makeup. I was caught in the middle, smart enough to be in Group One for the forty-five minutes of class but useless when the bell rang. Me and a couple other girls in my boat, Meghan Phelps, or Phillips, and Kristen Sloane, clung to those Group One friends like our lives depended on it, doing almost anything to remain in their good graces, but by the time we reached eighth grade, the birthday party invitations had stopped and the lunch tables had gotten emptier and emptier. Halfway through eighth grade, there were days when I was eating alone. Eight kids to a table, and depending on who was absent that day, I was often the odd girl out. You can't imagine the embarrassment of sitting in a school cafeteria all by

*yourself. In high school, I'd actually skip lunch and go
to the library just so that I wouldn't be seen sitting by
myself. Better to be not seen at all.*

*And here's the saddest part. I liked Meghan and
Kristen a lot. Lisa Palumbo too. Another tweener like
me. Smart but no money and terrible skin. The four
of us could've been friends. Good friends. Me and
Lisa and Kristen and Meghan. But to become their
friends and be seen hanging out with those girls
would've meant admitting to my second-tier status.
Instead of getting closer to those girls, I tried to distance myself from them, as if that would make it
clear to everyone that I was better than them.*

*There were only a couple times after elementary
school that I felt in the good graces of my old Group
One friends. Kim Maynard. Melissa Davis. Annette
Ryler. Charity Dumars. All those girls who I admired and hated at the same time. The first time was
in the fall of eighth grade. Mrs. Walker's language
arts class. First floor. Harry Truman Middle School.
I was sitting in the back row one day when I was
called on to diagram a sentence on the board. I think
I was the only kid in the fucking world who liked to
diagram sentences. No wonder I had no friends.*

*On the way back to my seat, I noticed Sherry Fer-
roni, a fellow Group One reject but a hell of a lot
worse than me. She was a girl who had started out cute
in first grade but was fat by seventh grade. Poor was
bad enough. Fat and poor was a killer. Anyway, she
was sitting in the third or fourth row, and a red blotch
was clearly visible on the crotch of her shorts. Yellow
shorts too. Like three sizes too small. The worst. She
had gotten her period and didn't know it. Probably the*

first time the poor girl had gotten it, and in that moment, I saw my opening. A chance to increase my status at Sherry's expense. I went back to my seat, leaned over to Kim Maynard, and told her the news. She got up immediately and went to the front of the room to throw something away and caught her own view of Sherry's growing stain on the way back to her seat. Kim sat down, looked at me, and mouthed the words "Oh my God!" And in that moment, in those three little words, I was back in the Group One fold. Buddies with Kim, just like we were in second grade again.

I spread the news around the class as best as I could, and before long, everyone was finding a reason to get out of their seat and walk by Sherry. Pencils needed sharpening. Bathroom passes were being asked for left and right. Every boy in the class was suddenly coughing and needing a drink from the water fountain. Every excuse in the book to get up and take a peek. Kids started giggling, the whispering got louder, and finally Mrs. Walker stopped the class and demanded to know what the hell was going on. Asshole extraordinaire Glenn Trudel then announced the news to the class, even though almost all of them already knew.

"Sherry needs a rag, Mrs. Walker. She needs one bad!" he said.

God. I'll never forget it.

Sherry looked lost for a minute, clueless about the asshole's comment, and then I saw her begin to figure things out. She looked around the room, saw the kids giggling and whispering and staring, and then she looked down and saw. Then she put her hands over her crotch like a three-year-old that's pissed her pants and ran out of the room.

She was out of school for the rest of the week,
and when she came back on Monday, kids had a nick-
name ready for her: Ragamuffin. The popular kids
used it behind her back and the scumbags said it to
her face. I think it stuck all the way through high
school.

Of course, Kim and Melissa and Charity didn't
like me any better after that. I don't know what I was
thinking. I guess it's sometimes nice to see someone
other than yourself put down. In some twisted way, I
thought that bringing down someone like Sherry
would automatically increase my standing, like there
was a pecking order and my meanness would move
me up a couple spots. But it didn't matter if I was
above or below Sherry, because I was never going to
crack that top group again. No matter what I did, I
wasn't going to get back into that pack of popular
Group One girls.

Freckles paused for a moment, and Milo used the opportunity to stop the tape, consumed by an odd blend of emotions.
Though he felt genuine sorrow for Freckles, who was clearly
plagued by childhood cruelty, he also couldn't help but feel a
sense of camaraderie in her confession, knowing full well how
difficult childhood could be, especially as an outsider. Though
Milo also wasn't a popular kid in school, he had found a niche of
friends through his participation on the cross-country team and
the chess club (which eventually morphed into his first Dungeons
& Dragons group). He didn't have many friends, but he had a few
good ones and had never been forced to endure a lunch period
alone. But he remembered the kids who did and suddenly felt as
cruel to them as Freckles had been to Sherry Ferroni that day in
Mrs. Walker's language arts class.

Not that high school had been easy for Milo. Even with his modicum of social standing, he had been a late bloomer in terms of dating, though initially he had thought it would be otherwise. Milo could remember with remarkable clarity the day in Mrs. Shultz's sixth grade math class when he noticed Amy McDonald's breasts for the first time. In Milo's mind (and perhaps it was true), it was as if one day her chest was as flat as his own and the next day it wasn't. Small round orbs were suddenly protruding from Amy's yellow and peach sweater, and Milo could barely take his eyes off them. Forget her blue eyes, her high cheekbones, or her impossibly wide smile. It was all about the boobs. And sure, he had seen breasts under sweaters before (and had even seen the bare breasts of a neighborhood mom as she passed by her picture window one evening), but he had never understood their magnificence and allure until he had seen them on a girl his own age. And in that moment of recognition, any possibility of a homosexual future was erased with the startling launch of an erection from beneath his corduroy hand-me-downs. The unconscious and damn near traitorous act of his penis had forced him to conceal its exuberance beneath *Principles of Mathematics,* the textbook that had rarely served Milo as well as it did at that particular moment.

Despite the awkwardness of sporting a boner in math class, Milo had felt nearly euphoric that day. It was as if the universe had opened and revealed one of its greatest secrets to him, and like Gollum's hoarding of the Ring, he was determined to keep this precious treasure to himself, revealing his revelation to no one.

Of course, Milo later learned that he was probably already behind the curve in terms of noticing Amy McDonald's breasts. His innate shyness and desire to keep certain aspects of his life private (even back then he struggled with inexplicable demands) prevented him from dating until late in his junior year, when a sophomore named Jennifer Ray showed interest in him despite his awkwardness and verbal incapacity around girls. Before that,

Milo had doubted that any girl would ever like him and had already resigned himself to that fate. As a member of the cross-country team, he could remember passing through Boston one autumn afternoon on his way to the state championships in Lynn, Massachusetts. As the bus drove past the exit for Chinatown, one of his teammates announced, "If you ever need a hooker, that's the neighborhood for you!" Milo had filed this information away, determined to remember it, certain that the only sex he would ever have would be with a prostitute, when he was old enough to venture into the seedy parts of Boston and find one for himself.

He had never told anyone that story but wished in this moment that he could tell Freckles. Let her know she wasn't alone in her childhood secrets.

He might not be willing to tell her about the submariner and his demands, but suddenly Milo's childhood secrets didn't seem so bad after all. If only he could help Freckles understand this. He knew it was ridiculous to think this way. Freckles was, after all, a complete stranger. For all he knew, these tapes were ten years old and she had long since overcome the specter of her adolescent indiscretions, but still, he couldn't help but feel a need to come to her aid and relieve this unnecessary sense of guilt that was burdening her. And the more he watched the tapes and learned about her life, the greater this need to help her intensified.

Milo took a moment to jot down several bits of information gleaned from the tape.

Mrs. Walker
Harry Truman Middle School
Sherry Ferroni

Freckles had mentioned other names too, but he would have to rewind the tape if he needed them. In his fixation on the footage, he had forgotten to write down a single word. He would go back and get the names later, if needed. For now he reached over and pressed play.

> *Well, that took longer than I thought. Damn, it's almost two A.M. But at least it was something. More than hospital cafeterias and Jell-O. God. I haven't thought about some of those people for years. I wonder where Sherry Ferroni is today.*
>
> *Anyway, I'm going to try to go to sleep now. I have a fight at ten tomorrow and need some sleep if I'm not going to lose in the first three minutes.*

Milo saw Freckles's hand reach for the camera, probably motioning to turn it off, but then it stopped in midair. She paused for a moment then brought the camera up to her face, so close that only the center features of her face—her short nose, her blue eyes, and those large brown freckles—appeared on screen. Her next words were said in a whisper.

> *I'm sorry, Sherry. I really, really am sorry. I hope you can forgive me.*

Milo thought that she might cry had the tape continued a second longer, but instead the screen went black, then blue, indicating that tape number three had reached its end. Had it been a second or two longer, Milo thought that he might've cried too.

Instead, he picked up his pencil one more time and added the word *Fight* to the list, followed by a question mark. Though he desperately wanted to pop in tape number four, he resisted the urge and turned off the television and the camera.

Finally, he would keep his promise and do a little research.

chapter 12

Timothy Coger reached out and shook Milo's hand, something he did quite often, usually at the conclusion of some minor piece of business. At first it unnerved Milo, but he had grown accustomed to the odd habit after a while.

Milo would assist his client in paying some bills. Mr. Coger would extend his hand after the envelopes had been sealed.

Milo would replace the screens on the front and back doors with glass for the winter. Timothy Coger would vigorously shake his hand upon the task's completion.

Milo would set the VCR to record a PBS documentary or a rerun of *Newhart*, and his client would offer his hand in thanks.

There were days when Milo shook Timothy Coger's hand a dozen times, and once he shook the man's hand three times in the span of a minute, after Milo had dispatched with a pair of Jehovah's Witnesses on the doorstep (handshake), watered the geraniums on the same doorstep (another handshake), and retrieved the mail from the box on the corner (a third handshake). In Timothy Coger's estimation, the completion of any chore represented the conclusion of a business transaction, and as such, a handshake was required.

Though shopping was something that Timothy Coger no longer did alone (lifting the bags had become too difficult for him, and Milo suspected that he was becoming more and more anxious about being outside his home), his client had no desire to march around the supermarket with a babysitter either, so he and Milo always shopped separately, with Mr. Coger starting at the front of the store in the produce section and Milo moving to the rear of the store to begin in dairy. They would typically pass each other at some point in the course of their shopping, in the cereal or cookie and cracker aisle, and Mr. Coger would say hello to Milo as if they hadn't seen each other in a week, only to meet at the front of the store by the cash registers minutes later in order to check out together.

Milo never ceased to find this amusing.

On days like today, when Milo had no shopping of his own, he would browse the magazine and book aisle while waiting for his client to fill his shopping cart with necessities, for Timothy Coger bought nothing else. Bread and cereal but never a Pop-Tart. Orange juice and milk but never a beer. The man owned a dishwasher but had washed every dish by hand since his wife died, declaring dish detergent to be a waste of money. Milo wondered if his client might ask him to purchase a washboard soon, forgoing the expense of laundry detergent and fabric softener for a bucket and some soap.

Only the essentials for Timothy Coger.

Milo was skimming the cover article in the latest *Scientific American* magazine, trying to rid his mind of Freckles, Christine, and all the drama that seemed to recently be dominating his life, when Bruce Springsteen's "The Rising" began filtering from the speakers in the ceiling, filling the store with the Boss's song about the despair and hope in the aftermath of 9/11. Standing in the supermarket on a Sunday morning, amid the ordinariness of linoleum floors, rack-mounted magazines, and fluorescent lighting, Milo cringed at the way a song that had come to symbolize one of the most tragic events in American history was suddenly infusing the drone of consumerism.

He and Christine had been in New York City on September 11, 2001, walking through Central Park on their way to a conference on elderly housing alternatives in Midtown when the planes struck the towers. It was still the dawn of their relationship. Year two. They had just moved in together prior to the trip, and Milo was still giddy over the prospect of any woman becoming his wife. So far, he had managed to conceal his inexplicable demands from his future bride, rapidly developing coping mechanisms that allowed him to satisfy them without detection, and he couldn't have been more pleased. Most of it had simply involved preparation and forethought.

A stash of jelly jars in the basement, as well as an emergency supply in the trunk of his car.

The twenty-four-hour bowling alley in Vernon, a coup in terms of his ability to handle this demand on a timely basis.

And most important, his planned shift from the hourly grind of the hospital to a schedule that was more flexible and accommodating to his unexpected yet insistent demands.

Things were truly falling into place.

Milo had wished that his future wife was a little less concerned about her appearance, a little more accepting of his friends and their hobbies, and a little less interested in network television and tabloid magazines, but in Milo's view, at least on the day that they were crossing Central Park, beggars couldn't be choosers. After all, he was once a teenage boy who had thought that the only sex he'd ever have would be with a prostitute. The acceptance and love that he had already received from Christine, albeit under somewhat false pretenses, was more than he had ever hoped for.

And there was plenty about Christine that he did love. She had a sense of humor that was smart, sarcastic, and sharp, and she placed no limits on whom she might attack. Milo loved to listen to her rant about the inequities in her office, the ineffectiveness of government officials, and the stupidity of her brother and his wife. Milo would sometimes come home to find her shouting at the television, enraged by something said by a talking head on MSNBC or a senator on C-SPAN or even the local weatherman.

It was quite a sight to see.

Yet she was equally passionate in a positive way about causes in which she believed. She spent a great deal of time volunteering for the Red Cross: organizing blood drives, educating people on the importance of blood donation, and donating her own blood every six weeks without fail. She also served as a Junior Achievement mentor in an impoverished Hartford school and spent several weekends a year building homes with the local Habitat for Humanity chapter.

Milo couldn't help but find this dichotomy in her personality, the sarcastic shark and the compassionate caregiver, compelling.

But most of all, Christine had been the first woman to make him feel normal. Unlike the girls from high school or college or even his fellow nurses, Christine had met Milo with no preconceptions. No backstory. Their first date had been only their second meeting, so he had felt as if he wasn't saddled with any preexisting conditions. He had not been thrown into an ocean of testosterone and forced to swim to the surface. When Milo had met Christine, there were no jocks, geniuses, or well-dressed future attorneys and stockbrokers standing to his left and right. It was simply Milo, solo and incomparable, and as such, she treated him like a man devoid of oddity and idiosyncrasy. And while this dearth of comparison may have helped his standing in Christine's eyes, he suspected that it had actually done more for him. Absent competition, he found himself with a level of self-confidence that he had rarely possessed in the presence of a beautiful woman. It had allowed Milo to be at ease with Christine, and most important, it had allowed him to be as close to himself as he had ever been before.

Of course, as true to himself as he was with Christine, he knew that he still wasn't even close, and though he suspected even then that this might eventually be a problem, he refused to acknowledge it. For once, he had found a woman with whom he could be happy, even if it came at a price.

As the two were exiting Central Park, turning the corner toward the conference center where Christine would leave Milo and proceed uptown to meet a college friend for a day of shopping, an ashen-faced woman stepped out from a taxi on the curb, turned to them, and said, "Did you hear? A second plane just hit the other tower?"

"Huh?"

"The World Trade Center. Both towers have been hit now." The woman then pointed to the south, where a trail of smoke could already be seen drifting above the Manhattan skyline.

"I don't understand," Christine said, reaching for Milo's hand. "What happened?"

"Two planes crashed into the World Trade Center. *Look*." The woman pointed again, this time more impatiently, and as if on cue, the first of what would prove to be an endless wail of sirens that day suddenly filled the air.

"How could two planes hit the same building?" Christine asked, squeezing Milo's hand now.

"They didn't hit the same building. They hit *both towers*." The woman was dressed like she meant business, a stereotypical New Yorker in a suit and heels, eyes shaded by a pair of Gucci sunglasses, but Milo could see that her hands were trembling as she forced them into her jacket.

A fire engine came roaring down Eighth Avenue, heading south. Milo, Christine, and their unnamed informant stood on the corner, staring at the red truck as it passed, filled with firefighters already in their helmets and gear. The driver blared a siren as the vehicle passed through the intersection, short blasts warning pedestrians that they no longer had rights to the crosswalk. Milo turned to ask the woman what kind of planes had hit the towers, but she was already halfway up the street, heading north.

"Let's find out what's happening," Milo said, pulling his wife in the same direction.

They were standing inside a coffee shop, staring at the television mounted over the counter when the first tower fell. At least thirty people had crowded inside the tiny café in order to listen to the news coverage, but rarely was a word spoken as reporters described the scene and video footage from helicopters and adjacent buildings showed the buildings on fire and replays of the planes slamming into them again and again. News of the attack on the Pentagon had already been reported, and Milo could sense the fear that had gripped this band of impromptu onlookers.

Their country was under attack.

As the south tower began to collapse just before ten A.M., someone behind him shouted. "It's falling. Jesus Christ Almighty, it's falling!" Gasps, shouts, and a muffled scream filled the space as the building disappeared from the sky, replaced by an enormous cloud of smoke and ash. Christine buried her head into Milo's chest and began to cry. A middle-aged woman standing beside Milo dropped to her knees in prayer. Several people pushed their way out of the shop, suddenly fearing for the safety of loved ones in the city. A man in a business suit advised everyone to head for Central Park. "It's the only place where a building can't fall on you!" he shouted as he pushed through the crowd and out onto the street. An older Jewish man sitting on a stool at the counter dropped his head into his hands and began to weep.

They remained in the shop until almost two P.M., eventually finding stools at the counter as the crowd began to disperse. The quiet and reverence of the first few hours of that morning was slowly replaced with the sharing of news as people came in and out of the coffee shop with stories to tell. An Indian cabdriver who helped transport police officers to Ground Zero. A high school English teacher who had watched the towers fall with his class on CNN before school was canceled for the day. A thin man in his twenties, white dust still trapped in his hair and goatee, who stumbled in around noon, the only eyewitness that Christine and Milo would meet that day. He had been four blocks from the World Trade Center when the south tower fell and couldn't stop talking about the sound of the building as it collapsed. "It was just so fucking loud. Like you couldn't even think, it was so loud. I can't even describe it. Have you ever heard something so loud that you couldn't even think straight? That's what it was like. It was just so goddamn loud."

Though the U-boat captain in Milo's head was never loud per se (the only auditory component of his demands were the repetition of words and that damn song), Milo understood the concept of something in your head being so powerful and omnipotent that it prevented you from thinking straight.

Others came into the shop throughout the day, regulars who knew the waitresses by name and strangers looking for a cup of coffee and a place to watch the news. Some arrived bearing information that had already been reported on television while others carried rumors of additional impending attacks. A pipe bomb outside police headquarters, a truck bomb on the Brooklyn Bridge, and one more plane circling above Washington, searching for a target.

The day was especially difficult for Christine, who didn't stop trembling until well into the evening. She had suffered from a serious case of claustrophobia since childhood, the result of being accidentally locked in a closet for more than six hours as a toddler, and though she loved the city, it always made her feel a little uneasy. "Too many people squeezed onto one tiny island," she had told Milo more than once. Whenever the couple was visiting New York, they did their best to avoid Times Square and other places where large crowds gathered, and they never, ever took the subway. Even the lower level of Grand Central Station and the ten minutes that their Metro-North train traveled underground before emerging in the outskirts of the city could send Christine into a near panic.

The attacks on the World Trade Center and the subsequent bridge and road closings only served to heighten her sense of feeling closed in and trapped and so increased the chance of a panic attack as well. Six hours after the second tower had fallen, Christine was still pale and sweaty, her dark hair matted against her forehead. Her breathing was rapid and shallow, and her grip on Milo's hand, which she latched on to with every opportunity, was strong and unyielding, as if to let go would be to allow the panic to consume her. Her condition prior to one of these panic attacks reminded Milo of that of an improperly medicated patient. Jittery. Unfocused. Withdrawn.

Similar to how he reacted when one of his demands went unsatisfied for a long period of time.

Layered on top of Christine's symptoms was fear. Not the claustrophobic fear that was the cause of the problem, but an added layer of fear of what others might think of her if she experienced an actual panic attack in public, which had happened on several occasions over the course of her life. As difficult as it was for Milo to understand, it seemed as if Christine worried more about the spectacle that she might create as a result of her panic attack rather than the cause of the panic attack itself. During the actual attack, this fear of embarrassment dissipated, dominated by actual claustrophobic fear, but prior to its onset and almost immediately afterward, the concern for her public image consumed her and probably made it exponentially more difficult to regain control. Despite the frequency of Milo's assurances that her claustrophobia was not her fault, Christine would not listen, convinced her embarrassment and shame were justified.

Though Milo recognized the similarity between her condition and his own, as well as their similar feelings of shame and embarrassment, he also thought that the two conditions were entirely incongruous. Christine's claustrophobia was a condition that people understood and accepted, akin to a fear of heights or public speaking. It did not result in the need to pop the pressure seal on a jelly jar or a similarly bizarre behavior; therefore the embarrassment that his wife felt was, in his mind, unwarranted and silly. Just like an epileptic has no reason to feel embarrassed about a seizure, a claustrophobic has no need to feel the same about an anxiety attack.

Milo's condition, on the other hand, was not the kind that anyone would ever understand or accept. Therefore, his concern over keeping it hidden was legitimate.

Additionally, Christine's admitted embarrassment over her condition had served to reinforce Milo's need to keep the U-boat captain and his demands a secret from his wife. If she found a panic attack to be the greatest source of shame in her life, how would she feel if Milo described his need to smash a Weeble in a doorjamb, or his fixation on ice cubes as the two were having sex the day before? On those rare days when Milo began to wonder if telling Christine the truth about his life might bring them closer together, he thought about the shame that his wife felt over a legitimate psychological condition, and quickly decided otherwise.

Better to enjoy a tenuous, less than genuine relationship than none at all.

As the couple made their way back to their hotel on the Upper West Side later that afternoon, American flags had already begun to appear, hanging from the windows of apartment buildings. Cars and trucks covered in a thick gray dust could occasionally be seen moving through the streets, joining what little traffic there was.

Milo had been in the city many times in his life and had never heard such silence.

Though the buses were running and transporting New Yorkers free of charge that day, Milo and Christine walked the three dozen blocks back to their hotel. The streets weren't entirely empty, but a hush had fallen over them.

It took them two days to get out of the city, and in that time Milo had seen the reaction of New Yorkers to the attacks evolve and had become consumed with the same blend of sorrow and anger and disbelief and patriotism that had filled so many American hearts. Milo loved Springsteen's album *The Rising*, particularly its signature song, for all the truth and hope that it possessed. He had teared up the first time he heard it, playing over the radio in his car on his way to work, and to hear it playing now, less than a decade after the towers had fallen, serving as a background tune to help pass the time while customers debated a cereal choice or waited for a deli order, made him want to find the office from where this song was being broadcast and stop the irreverence immediately. It seemed as if the gods of commerce were attempting to turn the page on that tragic day by adding this song to the grocery store and elevator lexicon alongside Barry Manilow and Billy Joel, in much the same way that Milo felt like Christine was attempting to turn the page on their marriage, run away from it, move on as if those moments on that September morning and the vows they had later made on their wedding day had become little more than the dismissible background noise of one's life.

Milo hated the man or woman who had added this song to their playlist, but he listened in reverence anyway, trying to diminish the diminishment of the song and its meaning.

Had he been wearing a hat, he would have removed it out of respect.

As Springsteen was singing the final verse of his song, Milo spotted Timothy Coger rounding the front of the aisle and heading his way. As he passed by, the large man lifted his meaty hand and offered a hearty "Good morning, Milo!" It managed to return a smile to Milo's face.

Milo could always depend on the oddities of people like Mr. Coger to keep him happy. Amusing, unapologetic, and, most important, odd, these were the people in his life that helped him to feel normal. Timothy Coger, Edith Marchand, and even Arthur Friedman had all reached a point in their lives, and in their relationships with Milo, at which they could be themselves, as strange and bizárre as they may be. Arriving to the grocery store with him but pretending otherwise. Masturbating to Internet porn with the help of Viagra. Raking shag carpets in preparation for guests. Not all, but most of his clients had been willing to reveal secrets like these to Milo, and in turn, he never judged them for their oddities, knowing full well how difficult a secret is to bear, and of course having his own oddities with which to compare. Oftentimes his clients were the people whose company and friendship he valued the most, for he felt that these relationships were more honest than those he had with his wife and friends.

Though in truth, Timothy Coger wasn't Milo's choice of company at this particular moment. Freckles was still firmly on his mind, and after a night of fruitless research, he desperately wanted to review the situation with someone who might offer a varying perspective. Though he had known Timothy Coger for quite a while, he did not have the same kind of casual, friendly relationship as he did with a client like Arthur Friedman or Edith Marchand. Formality ruled the roost in the Coger household, so the unnecessary exchange of personal anecdotes and information did not occur. There were others more willing to listen and dispense advice.

Milo had spent more than two hours researching online the previous evening, beginning with Freckles's deceased friend, Mira. He had expected to find a bounty of information on the dead woman, particularly because of the way that Freckles had alluded to her friend's death as less than ordinary, but regardless of his query, he could find nothing related to a recently or otherwise deceased woman named Mira formerly living in or around Connecticut.

His search on the name Sherry Ferroni, a.k.a. Ragamuffin, provided no matches whatsoever, which both surprised and frustrated Milo. Though he had never known anyone with the last name of Ferroni, it didn't sound unusual enough to be absent from the Internet entirely. After reviewing the tape again and recording the names of the seven other girls that Freckles mentioned, he searched for information on them as well and was marginally more successful.

Searches on Melissa Davis, Kim Maynard, Meghan Phelps, and even Lisa Palumbo produced many results, too many in fact, but Milo was unable to connect any of these names to Harry Truman Middle School, the state of Connecticut, or even one another, and sorting through the hundreds of possible hits was nearly impossible. Searching with the names Charity Dumars and Annette Ryler produced no results (Milo was less surprised with these more unusual-sounding names), and though hits on the name Kristen Sloane were abundant, the number of ways in which the name could be spelled made it impossible for Milo to know which Kristen Sloane or Sloan or Slone once attended school with Freckles.

In all, trying to find information on the correct girl was like trying to find a suspected needle in a possible haystack.

Milo had no better luck researching Harry Truman Middle School. There were more than a dozen such schools in the United States (almost all including the letter S from Truman's full name), stretching from California to Louisiana to Ohio, but there was no record of a Harry Truman Middle School or a Harry S. Truman Middle School anywhere in the Northeast, and neither could he find a Mrs. Walker employed at any of these schools. Milo wasn't certain that Freckles had grown up in the Northeast or even east of the Mississippi for that matter, but her lack of any discernible accent and a gut feeling told him that she had. Either way, finding a dozen schools with the same name as Freckles's middle school didn't get him any closer to ascertaining her real name.

But Freckles's mention of a ten o'clock fight had intrigued him a great deal (he actually replayed the tape three times to ensure that he hadn't mistaken the word *flight* for *fight*) and sent him searching websites on women's boxing, wrestling, kickboxing, karate, and other forms of hand-to-hand combat. Though Freckles did not appear to be the boxing or wrestling type, in either build or demeanor, one never knew. So he searched for almost an hour on these websites in hopes of finding a clue or lead.

None materialized.

He learned that women's boxing had become more popular and mainstream in the past decade, with the World Boxing League, the North America Boxing League, and many statewide and regional tournaments dominating the scene. But looking at images of the female boxers, kickboxers, and wrestlers online showed clearly that Freckles was not built like a female fighter. Furthermore, he wasn't even able to find a woman's boxing or wrestling league anywhere in Connecticut.

Even if one existed, what kind of league would hold its fights at ten in the morning?

Milo was sure that he was missing something. He desperately wanted to discuss the matter with someone like Edith Marchand, or perhaps Andy. These were people who might see or think of something that he was overlooking. And though he didn't want to violate Freckles's privacy any more than necessary, he needed to speak to someone who he could trust.

Sadly, Christine did not currently occupy this short list.

chapter 13

Milo couldn't remember the last time he heard Edith Marchand come close to swearing, so when she told him to "watch the god-damn tapes!" he decided to take her advice seriously. After finishing his morning visit with Mr. Coger, Milo had spent the afternoon with Edith, a rare Sunday visit. Edith was hosting a book club that evening and had asked Milo to come over and rake out the rug (a phrase he always found to be a little dirty) and discuss the book with her prior to her friends' arrival. Though Edith Marchand was a confident and intelligent woman, the members of her monthly book club included a retired high school English teacher, a University of Connecticut biophysicist, and a poet of some local renown, so she constantly worried about the impression that she might make on them during the discussion. In order to compensate, Milo and Edith had an arrangement in which he would read the assigned book and provide a warm-up discussion for her, during which she could try out observations and criticisms for the first time and co-opt some of Milo's as well.

The biophysicist had chosen this month's book, and though Milo didn't usually mind reading the chosen texts, the months in which the biophysicist chose the book tended to be the exception. In the past, the guy had forced the group to read *Finnegan's Wake*, *To the Lighthouse*, and *The House of Mirth*, as well as this month's gem, José Saramago's *Blindness*, which in Milo's estimation was the single most depressing book ever published. Had he not liked Edith Marchand as much as he did, Milo would've stopped reading the book by the eighth chapter and faked his way through their discussion.

But out of friendship and obligation, he had finished reading the book three nights ago, and was pleased to hear that Edith despised the book as much as he. In fact, according to her, the book had made her cry on several occasions. Though Milo hadn't come close to tears, he wasn't surprised at Edith's admission. Based on the horrific way that Saramago treated his characters, he wouldn't have been surprised to discover that the author despised each and every one of them.

After discussing the book with her for nearly an hour (to his credit, the biophysicist at least chose books that promoted conversation), Milo rose to rake out the shag and Edith finally asked about Christine and then Freckles. Though Milo had wanted to bring up these topics as soon as he entered the house, he knew that Edith would eventually find time for his concerns.

"So she doesn't want to go back to therapy?" Edith asked as Milo finished raking under the final chair.

"I'm not sure. The message that she left on my machine last night was strange. She asked if I thought that therapy was still a good idea. Then she asked if I'd like to have coffee on Wednesday morning, before she goes to work and before we see the doctor. Then she reminded me not to be late for our appointment."

"Was that it?"

"Yeah. She asked me to call back, but I had to leave early this morning, so I'll call her back tonight. What could she be thinking?"

"I have no idea, Milo," Edith said. "But Ed Marchand used to say that there are no incomprehensible women. Only ignorant men."

"Thanks, Edith. That's really helpful."

"Don't get snippy with me. I have no idea what your wife is thinking. I've never even met the girl. But here's what I do know: You'd better find out what's wrong. That girl used to adore you, but from what you tell me, that's no longer the case. You need to know why. I can't imagine why that fool doctor hasn't asked her that question yet."

Edith had a point. Though Milo knew that Christine was unhappy and that the two of them were struggling to communicate (and seemed to have run out of things to say to each other), he had no idea what had precipitated the change in their relationship and, more specifically, what had caused Christine's feelings to change so dramatically. "Maybe Dr. Teagan asked her the question when they were alone."

"Maybe Dr. Teagan should pass that information on to you, then, because it seems to me that it would be more helpful in your hands than his. Don't you think?"

Milo thought Edith was right, but he also wondered how much he cared anymore. Did he want to repair his marriage because of a love he had for Christine or because of a desire to return to the convenience and steadiness of the relationship? He had begun to wonder.

Edith finished her last sip of tea, and when Milo didn't respond, she continued. "Now, what about that girl on the videotape? Have you found her yet?"

Milo related the events of the previous evening pertaining to his search, including his fruitless attempts at researching Freckles's identity. He added in the new information that he had gathered since he had last seen Edith, including the name of Freckles's middle school and her mysterious morning fight, but he left out the part about Sherry Ferroni and cruelty in Mrs. Walker's language arts class.

He thought that Freckles would've wanted it that way.

"Milo, why are you fooling around with the computer? Watch the goddamn tapes!"

"Yeah, I know. But I thought it might be pretty easy to find some information on her dead friend, and from there, I thought I might be able to find her."

"You don't know if those tapes are three weeks old or three years old. You could be watching video from ten years ago, right? What if this girl's friend died in 1998? Will you still be able to find her obituary on the Internet?"

"Probably not, but the tapes don't look that old. And the camera is in good condition. In fact, I might be able to figure out the year that the camera was sold, since the models change almost every year. That might give me an idea about how old the . . ."

"Milo, just watch the goddamn tapes. Save all this other nonsense for later. If she doesn't say her name by the end of the last tape, then you can start looking on the Internet."

Edith's advice made sense, but part of Milo had hoped to discover Freckles's identity by watching as little of the tapes as possible. The footage was becoming more personal with each recorded minute, especially since she had decided to keep the recordings for herself. This decision, combined with her growing comfort with the camera, had led to her revelation about Sherry Ferroni and her act of childhood cruelty. Milo was hoping to avoid any more personal moments like these, out of respect for Freckles's privacy, but Edith was probably right. If he wanted to return the camera and the tapes to their owner, his best chance would be to finish watching the tapes.

Besides, a part of Milo found comfort in Freckles's admissions of imperfections. He wished that he had the courage to do the same.

"You're right, Edith. I'll go home and watch the tapes tonight."

"Good. And call that wife of yours too. Don't forget that she's more important than your video girl, okay?"

He wondered if this was still true but said, "Of course. Do you think I'm losing my mind?"

"No. But sometimes I wonder if you don't have a crush on this girl, Milo. You've got a look in your eye when you talk about her that I don't much like."

"Don't be ridiculous. I don't even know the girl. How could I have feelings for a complete stranger?"

"I don't know, but just keep it that way. At least until you have this Christine business settled, one way or the other. Okay, my boy?"

Milo smiled. "You bet. Now tell me: Do you feel ready for your book club tonight?"

"As ready as I can be. They all speak so fast, and Charles makes me so nervous. Just stares at me with a blank face when I'm speaking. I can't tell what he's thinking. I wish I were twenty years younger. My mind was so much sharper back then."

"Edith, you're smarter than people half your age."

"That's nice to say, but you know it isn't true; otherwise you wouldn't be here. Don't get old, Milo. It's not nice. Old age is the last dirty trick."

Milo returned the rake to the closet and left as Edith was starting to roll curlers in her gray hair. Her notebook was propped against the mirror, and she was frantically reviewing her notes from their book discussion as she worked. She had more than three hours before her guests arrived, but she was still worried that there wouldn't be enough time to pull herself together.

Of all his clients, Milo loved Edith Marchand the most.

The idea to surprise Christine with flowers occurred to Milo as he exited Route 9 in Newington on his way home. Though "99

Luftballons" had begun to consume his thoughts during his visit with Edith, the sign for Central Connecticut State University, surrounded by flowers that had just begun to bloom, had given Milo the idea to surprise his wife with a bouquet. Though there was an outside chance that the gesture might be perceived as overkill, he thought it was more likely that Christine would receive the flowers with excitement and appreciation. It had been at least a year, and probably more, since Milo had sent roses to his wife, and perhaps this was the kind of gesture that Dr. Teagan had meant when he suggested that they begin dating.

His plan was to purchase flowers and drive them over to the house, handing them off in person on the front stoop or leaving them on the dining room table for his wife to find when she arrived home. Christine was often volunteering with the Red Cross on the weekend, so many Sunday afternoons were spent in gymnasiums, malls, and town halls, ensuring that these events went off without a hitch. Whether or not she was home didn't matter much to Milo, since the flowers would be a surprise either way.

Even though Milo had moved out of the house, he had kept his house key on his key ring, so he let himself in after pulling into the driveway and finding it void of automobiles. Visiting his house for the first time since the separation, he couldn't help but think about all that he might lose if he and Christine were unable to settle their differences and resume their marriage as previously scheduled. The house, a spacious ranch on the corner of Wilson and Taft, had required a great deal of work when they first moved in, and Milo had done most of it himself. Rosebushes had been growing wild around the foundation of the house, and after attempts to prune them back, he finally decided to tear them out completely and replace them with plants that were more manageable. This process had taken more than a week to accomplish, and he could still remember the subsequent nightmares of rosebushes creeping into the house at night to enact their thorny revenge. Those hours of work and hundreds of tiny cuts on his hands, arms, and legs would all go for naught if he and Christine did not repair their relationship.

It was a small thing, he knew. The elimination of some rosebushes hardly constituted a marriage. But it was the accumulation of small things: the roses, their DVD collection, his relationship with Christine's parents, the new lawn mower, the wedding photos, the flat-screen television, the plans for finishing the basement and replacing the windows, and the trip to Martha's Vineyard later that summer. All of these small things were the stuff of their marriage, and combined, this stuff made up their relationship. Held it together. Made it tangible. Certainly there was more at stake than lawn mowers and DVDs and vacation plans, but Milo was beginning to realize that these things had become important to him, perhaps because Christine no longer was. The part of him that had always known that Christine was not right for him had jumped at the chance to move out and grant Christine her space, even when the part of Milo that loved his marriage struggled to hold on. And perhaps that was the crux of the matter: Though Milo was still unwilling to fully embrace the idea, he thought that he might have loved his marriage more than his wife. The home, the companionship, the family, and, most important, the comfort in knowing that his oddities were safely hidden away. That after more than three years of marriage and five years together, his wife did not have even an inkling of the U-boat captain who sometimes insisted he open a jar of jelly or smash a Weeble.

Though this was good, Milo found himself wanting more. Part of him believed that he could still find the joy and excitement and genuine love that he had felt for Christine in the beginning. This hope is what had led him to the idea to do something romantic for Christine, and how he found himself, a dozen roses in his hands, on the doorstep of the house they once shared.

Milo entered through the side door facing the driveway, feeling like an intruder upon setting foot in the kitchen. It had been just over a month since he had left, yet in that time the house had begun to feel foreign to him. At any moment, he half expected a police cruiser to pull into the driveway, officers piling out in order to arrest him for breaking and entering. Nevertheless, things inside the house looked as they always had. The kitchen was spotless, with uncluttered countertops, clean appliances, and an empty drying rack by the sink. Christine insisted on cleanliness in the kitchen.

Milo placed the glass vase on the small kitchen table and was turning to leave when he remembered the need for clean sheets in his apartment and instead passed through the kitchen, heading for the bathroom. Multiple sets of bed linens had been one of the many things that Milo had not thought about in his attempt to exit the house as quickly as possible.

In the linen closet adjacent to the master bedroom he found several clean sets, most of which were given to him and Christine as wedding gifts. He took a set that had not been a wedding gift, as well a few extra towels, as they were also in short supply at his apartment.

Needing to relive himself, Milo took a few more steps down the hall into the bathroom, noting the empty slot where his toothbrush had once resided and the disappearance of the magazine rack, which had sat underneath the pedestal sink opposite the toilet. Christine had never been a fan of the reading material that Milo kept on hand and had apparently eliminated it in his absence.

Several pairs of bras and panties hung over the shower rod to dry, and, once again, Milo was consumed with the feeling that he was an intruder in his own home. Even though he had seen Christine's underwear a million times and had just had sex with his wife a few days ago, standing in the small room, staring at her dangling straps and cups and the lacy panties, made him feel both uncomfortable and . . . devious? Sneaky?

Yes, sneaky.

He had lived with Christine for more than three years, but in that time, he had never stood in such wonder over her underwear, so surprisingly and unaccountably curious about her bra size. He pulled down a teal bra from the rod and examined the tag inside the cup.

32C.

Gathering the towels and linens, Milo exited the bathroom, noticing a new piece of furniture across the hall in the bedroom. *My bedroom*, he reminded himself. In the corner beside the bed was a portable playpen of some sort, the type that parents use to reconfigure the environment when invading the homes of friends and relatives with babies in tow. Milo stepped into the room and examined this latest addition, assuming that one of Christine's friends had recently visited with her newborn, but unable to think of any of her friends who might have a baby. The Pack and Play, as it was labeled, contained several stuffed animals, a tiny pink blanket, and a plastic book that looked ideal for chewing. Perfect for chewing, in fact, though it appeared to be void of any teeth marks. And just like that, what began as a simple observation had instantly blossomed into a sudden need, a demand to chew on this book that had been specifically designed for chewing, ignored by some baby, a girl, Milo surmised, who was probably too clever for her own good. Milo would have liked to be able to say that he tried to resist this new and especially odd demand, but he did not. Already consumed by the impulse, he chose to chew rather than wait for the demand to explode into an all-encompassing, pain-inducing, brain-busting imperative that would send him to the infant section of the toy store in frantic search of a plastic book.

And so he chewed, and with each gnawing grind, demand was replaced with satisfaction. A feeling of relief. A sense that the world was once again in order and as it should be, much like the broken balsa wood airplanes and the smashed Weebles. It was as if these items, the plastic book, the balsa wood, and the Weebles, had all been created for the express purpose of chewing, snapping, and smashing, and to do otherwise with them would have been wrong. The demands were simply the cry of the universe to make things right again.

Chew on the book, for that is why it exists.

And so he chewed.

As he chewed, Milo wondered who Christine knew who had a baby girl. His wife had more than a dozen friends from the office, paralegals and fellow attorneys for the most part, and though Milo knew some of them well, others were characters whom he heard about only in stories about the office or happy hour escapades.

Probably one of them, he thought.

The rhythm of the "99 Luftballons" once again filled Milo's mind, almost as if a radio had been switched on in the next room, reminding him of its increasing persistence. Milo knew that the song would continue to fill his mind, eventually encroaching on all other thought, until it became so loud and pressure-inducing that its sheer size and weight would become a hindrance to its fulfillment. Milo thought of it as the Point of No Return, the moment at which a demand ceased to be an impetus for fulfillment and transformed itself into an impediment.

He tried to avoid these situations at all costs.

In response, Milo placed the well-chewed book into his coat pocket before heading for the door. Better for Christine's friend to think that she misplaced the book than to have her wondering who had chewed it up. He wanted to leave before Christine returned home, in hopes of preserving the surprise.

A card sticking from the bouquet read:

> *Christine,*
> *Dating you the first time was unforgettable.*
> *Let's make this second go-round the same.*

Milo was locking the door, his back to the driveway, when he heard a car pull in behind him. His heart sank. The surprise that he planned for his wife would be muted at best if she found him skulking away. He turned, expecting to see Christine's blue Jetta, but instead saw a black Jeep Wrangler coming to a halt. The top was down and Christine was sitting in the passenger seat beside a man Milo didn't recognize. Tall, with dark hair and a goatee, and wearing mirrored sunglasses, he was the kind of guy who outweighed Milo by fifty pounds but was still in better shape than he was. He was thick in the neck, the arms, and the chest, with an indeterminable tattoo emerging from underneath the collar of his polo shirt, his face remained expressionless as he engaged the emergency brake and turned the vehicle off.

Milo didn't like the look of him one bit.

A baby was sleeping in a car seat behind the man, dressed in a pink and white jumper.

chapter 14

"You fucking son of a bitch! How dare you accuse me of cheating!" Christine was shouting into the phone so loudly that her voice was distorted, forcing Milo to position the receiver a good six inches from his ear.

"Well, what am I supposed to think? You pull into the driveway in another guy's car, and I saw the playpen in the bedroom. What did you expect?"

"How about a little trust, Milo? How about a little faith in your own wife?"

Admittedly, Milo wasn't pleased with his response after seeing Christine pull into the driveway with the stranger, but he also felt that the deck had been stacked against him from the start. All the details in the scene had pointed to something shady and illicit, as if the universe had been plotting his overreaction.

The good-looking guy with the goatee and the tattoo.

The mirrored sunglasses.

The standard transmission.

Christine's windblown hair.

The playpen in the bedroom.

Even the Jeep made things appear less than innocent. Had the guy been driving a Honda Accord or even a Subaru Forrester, Milo might not have jumped to the same conclusions and lost his temper. But there was something about a Jeep, jet black, top down, mud on the tires, padded roll bars, Nirvana on the radio. It all screamed, *Sex! Sex! Sex!*

And there had been the sudden burst of jealousy that had caught him off guard as well. Though Christine had her fair share of male friends from the office, many of them high-powered attorneys with luxury automobiles and personal trainers, Milo had never felt a hint of jealousy about his wife's relationship with these men.

But this time, standing on his front stoop, staring down on this scene, things were different.

Already his face was flushing, his hands balling into fists, his mind instantly running through possible scenarios that would place Christine and this man in these circumstances.

None of them proved to be very innocent.

Without a moment of thought or reflection, Milo had turned back into the kitchen, snatched the roses from the table, and exited the house, doing his best to ignore his wife and her companion even though he had to walk directly in front of the Jeep and along the passenger side in order to reach his car on the other side of the driveway.

"Milo? What the hell are you doing?" Christine asked, still seated and buckled in the Jeep. The two vehicles were parked side by side, the driver's side door of Milo's car and the passenger side door of the Jeep almost perfectly aligned, making it impossible to avoid his wife.

"What do you mean?" Milo asked, trying to avoid eye contact while reaching for the door to his car. He just wanted to get in his car and leave as quickly as possible.

"What do I mean? How about starting with what you were doing in the house? And what's with the flowers? Could you look at me, for Christ's sake?"

Milo turned and faced his wife, stealing a glance past her to the man sitting in the driver's seat. Despite the awkwardness of the situation, he appeared completely at ease, impossibly relaxed, as if this type of situation happened every day in his life.

"Can we just talk about this later?" Milo asked, wishing now that he had left the flowers on the kitchen table and exited the house with a smile and a lie. Not only did he feel awkward, but in the presence of this stranger, he felt cowardly and petty too.

"Can't you just tell me what the hell is going on? What were you doing in the house?"

"It's still my house," Milo countered, feeling jealousy mix with anger. "I'm still paying half the mortgage. Remember?"

"That doesn't mean you can just barge in whenever you want."

"Why? Are you afraid that I might interrupt something?"

"What are you talking about?"

"You know what the fuck I'm talking about!" Milo shouted, motioning to her male companion.

Swearing wasn't a normal part of Milo's repertoire. In fact, his infrequent use of obscenity rivaled that of Edith Marchand, so he had regretted his choice of language, particularly in light of the sleeping child strapped into the backseat and the sideways glance of the man behind the wheel from beneath his sunglasses. He seemed to be growing larger and handsomer with each passing minute.

"What's your problem, Milo?" Christine countered with controlled rage. "This is Phil from work. You met him last year at the picnic. This is Ashley. His daughter. Remember?"

He did remember. Phil was one of the new attorneys who had been hired the previous spring. Christine had been on the hiring committee, and he remembered that she had liked the guy a lot. He had interviewed well. Made everyone laugh at the right moments, if Milo was recalling the right guy. And though he didn't specifically remember meeting Phil at the picnic, Milo had

met a number of new faces that day and could've easily forgotten the introduction.

But still, why was Phil driving around on a Sunday with his wife, and why was his daughter's playpen set up in his bedroom? "I don't care where I met him," Milo shot back, using these unanswered questions to gather steam. "Why the hell are you driving around with him, and where the fuck is his wife?"

Rather than responding in anger, which is what Milo had expected, Christine stole a nervous glance over to Phil and then leaned in. "Milo, go home. Now. I'll call you in an hour."

Milo knew at that moment, with absolute and undeniable certainty, that the correct decision would have been to follow his wife's advice and get into his car. It's what he had wanted to do all along. Something was wrong here. He was missing something. Milo sensed that a large piece of the puzzle was absent from the picture. An important piece. The sudden change in Christine's voice and the evaporation of anger from her eyes had convinced Milo that he should go back to the apartment and wait for the call. But to turn tail and run in front of this man, this thick-necked, tattooed usurper who refused to speak, did not fit the script that Milo was following. It simply would not do. For once in his life, Milo was facing confrontation head-on, unafraid and undeterred.

"Please," Christine repeated. "Just go home. I'll call you soon."

"I am home, goddamn it! This is my house. And I have a right to know what he's doing here and why his daughter's playpen is sitting in my bedroom."

At this, Phil finally spoke, barely turning his head to do so. "Chrissy, maybe I should just leave and let the two of you sort this out." His voice was ridiculously calm, increasing Milo's rage. And he had called her Chrissy, a nickname that even Milo didn't use.

"Yeah, maybe you should leave, *Phil*," Milo said.

"Milo, please go home," Christine insisted, reaching out and squeezing his forearm. Again, he sensed that missing puzzle piece looming over them, waiting to fall into place like a hand grenade, but still he pressed on.

"I am home. Why don't you tell Phil to go home to *his wife*."

"Milo, you asshole. Phil's wife died last year in a car accident. Don't you fucking remember?"

He remembered. It had been just after Christmas. Phil (he had been Philip back then), his wife (Mary Liz or Mary Claire or Mary something-or-other), and their daughter had been on their way to Vermont when a truck jumped the median and side-swiped their car. Milo had forgotten the names of the people involved, at least until now, but he remembered the accident, the phone call in the middle of the night, and the argument that had ensued when Milo refused to cancel a trip with Arthur Friedman to a diabetes specialist in Albany in order to attend the funeral.

"Oh . . . Jesus," he stuttered. For the first time since he had approached the Jeep, Milo realized how crazy he sounded. "I'm so sorry."

"It's all right," Phil said, turning to check on his daughter, who was still sound asleep.

"I saw the two of you together and the playpen in the bedroom and . . . I don't know. I just sort of went a little crazy. God, I'm sorry, man."

Phil nodded behind his mirrored glasses and said nothing more.

"Go home, Milo," Christine said, finally releasing his arm. "I'll call you later."

He did.

Two hours later, Christine called as promised, not wasting a second before screaming obscenities.

"Look, I'm sorry, Christine. You're right. I should've trusted you. But I didn't know what to think. I'm sorry, okay?"

"No, it's not okay. It was embarrassing and ridiculous, Milo. I work with Phil every day. How the hell am I going to show my face in the conference room tomorrow? Jesus, Milo. You acted like a lunatic."

"I know, but I'm sure he understands, Christine. We're not the first people to have trouble with their marriage. Do you want me to talk to him? To apologize again? I will if that's what you want."

"Forget it. There's nothing that you can do. I'll clean up this mess myself."

Then she hung up.

Despite his desire to continue the conversation with Christine, to avoid another three days of awkward silence, wondering when and if he should call, he was relieved when she hung up the phone.

He had been waiting at home for more than two hours, the pressure of "99 Luftballons" building with each passing minute. He had attempted to release some of it by opening a jar of jelly and popping some ice cubes, but as expected, this had failed to achieve any noticeable results. At times, there were things that Milo could do to alleviate the pressure of a demand when satisfaction was impossible, but these strategies did not always work. Milo suspected that the anticipation of Christine's call only compounded the mounting pressure, making any temporary relief impossible.

Eventually he had removed the *Highlights* poem from his pocket and had begun reciting it again and again, unsure of why this might help but doing so nonetheless. It just felt right.

But Nurse Mancuso found the cure.
She told me not to scratch.
And it worked.
It didn't hurt anymore.

Though he hadn't understood his initial fascination with the poem, the repeated recitation, more than a hundred times in total, had caused Milo to develop a newfound admiration for the author. If only he had the same self-restraint as the boy who was able to resist scratching his rash. Milo thought that the demands of the jelly jars, the ice cube trays, and the incessant pounding of "99 Luftballons" in his head were similar to the author's rash. They also required scratching, but unlike the author, Milo couldn't ignore his demands. Doing so would only increase their intensity to the point of debilitation.

Yet he recited the poem anyway, hoping to somehow discover the child author's inner strength. With nothing left in his bag of tricks, it was all that he could do.

Like the Borg, Milo thought, resistance is futile.

This was why Milo was secretly pleased when Christine hung up on him. The pressure of the demand had increased to a boiling point. The Point of No Return was fast approaching. In short order, Milo's ability to focus would be compromised by blinding pain in the center of his head, a blurring of his vision, and a simple yet inexplicable inability to think.

It was time to go to Jenny's.

On his drive up the Berlin Turnpike, into the south end of Hartford, thoughts about his driveway encounter with Christine continued to filter through his mind.

Yes, he had made a mistake in accusing Christine of infidelity.

Yes, he had told a widower to go home to his dead wife.

Yes, he had jumped to conclusions and lost his temper like never before, and in front of a stranger and his infant daughter, no less.

Yes, he had cursed like a sailor for all the neighbors to hear.

But questions still remained. Why was Christine driving around with Thick-Neck Phil in the first place? Why was the kid's playpen set up in their bedroom? How did Philip become Phil and Christine become Chrissy? Though he had admittedly made a spectacle of himself, Christine had never really answered any of his questions.

Most pressing, was Thick-Neck Phil still in the company of Christine? Was he inside their house? If so, what were they doing right now?

Milo brought his car to a halt outside of Jenny's and spent several minutes behind the wheel, trying to clear his mind of these thoughts and compose himself. He took several deep breaths and tried to relax his hands and face. He closed his eyes and turned his neck and head in circles, working out the kinks. When he felt his nerves were as calm as they could be considering the circumstances, he went inside. As many times as he had done this before, and the number was probably in the hundreds, he was still a little nervous every time he took the stage.

Jenny's was a bar on Brainard Road in Hartford. Small, dim, and adjacent to a movie theater, the bar was a bit of a dive that catered to pilots and mechanics who used the small airport at the end of the road, as well as the after-movie crowd. The food was good, the restrooms clean, and the atmosphere friendly. The bar also had its share of regulars, though Milo did not include himself in this group.

He had chosen the bar for two reasons. First, the owner, Jenny Glover, a busty blond pushing forty but trying desperately to cling to her twenties, was almost always working, and she liked Milo. She probably found him to be a little odd, but he was always polite and made a point of buying a beer before a performance and chasing it with a couple of Cokes afterward. The regulars liked Milo as well. Probably found him equally strange, but men and women who spent enough time in a bar to assume ownership of a stool were likely to be less than normal as well.

More important, the bar was also equipped for karaoke, and

though Thursdays and Fridays were Jenny's advertised karaoke nights, she left the system set up throughout the week and allowed customers to use it from time to time if the desire to sing grabbed hold of someone.

"How's it cooking, Milo?" a large man with an Italian accent shouted as Milo passed through the doors and made his way inside. Several leather-backed stools surrounded a horseshoe-shaped bar, which was attached to a fairly large, rectangular stage on the open end.

"Just fine, Carmine," Milo said, commandeering a stool close to the stage. "How about you?"

"My foot's still giving me hell, but as long as I sit here and drink, it keeps its damn mouth shut. Know what I mean?"

"Yeah, I know. But you really should see a doctor."

"Yeah, yeah, yeah. You sound like my wife. I already got one of those and don't need another, thank you very much. Unless you're offering, Jenny?"

"Forget it, old man," the blond behind the bar said, tossing a towel in his direction. She was dressed in a yellow tank top and jean shorts, and she had several tattoos covering her shoulders and back, including a large one across the back of her neck— *Fred* written in red ink. Milo had yet to find the courage to ask her about that one.

"You gonna belt out a good one, Milo?" asked a pear-shaped man, catching Milo's eye from across the bar. From the neck up, the man, an airplane mechanic and a Jenny's regular, looked as if he might be in decent shape, with a thin face and a strong jaw. But below the neck, an almost impossible quantity of fat and cellulose had collected between the man's chest and thighs, making the man look like one of the Weebles that Milo occasionally crushed in a doorjamb.

"Don't I always, Pete?"

"You must certainly do, Milo. Ain't that the truth."

A second later, Jenny slid a beer in front of Milo. "How you doing?" she asked, taking a moment to look him in the eye. Though Milo had never discussed the trouble in his marriage with anyone in the bar, it seemed as if Jenny knew something was wrong.

"I'm good. Thanks. In a rush tonight, though. Got to get home soon."

"Whenever you're ready, then."

Milo's need to sing karaoke had actually begun in a bowling alley several years ago. Having stopped in on a Saturday night to fulfill the pressing need to bowl a strike, Milo had noticed that a DJ had set up a karaoke machine in the alley's adjacent bar and was inviting patrons to perform on the small dance floor. Through the glass door that theoretically separated the bowlers from the drunks, Milo could see and hear a threesome, a guy and two girls, all young and drunk, singing "Love Shack" to a small and inattentive audience of drinkers at the bar.

Milo had managed to bowl his strike in the first frame and was finishing his game when the thought of singing first entered his mind. Though he had never sung karaoke before and had never felt the desire to do so, the idea quickly lodged itself in his mind, where it began to take hold. The thought grew into a possibility, and the possibility blossomed into a genuine demand. By the time he had returned his rental shoes and collected his deposit, the need to sing had consumed him, a flashing, incessant beacon that droned out all other thought. It wasn't a genuine desire to perform or the sudden need for applause. Rather, it was a demanding insistence, an assertion of unknown origin, the building of pressure not unlike the strain exerted on him by his other demands. Based on experience, Milo knew that he could leave the bowling alley and head home without singing, but that the pressure would not alleviate, and would assuredly increase, until he had sung.

A decade before, he might have tried to avoid singing altogether, ignoring the enigmatic demand in his head. But after years of trying to disregard these demands, he now knew better. Never in his life had any of them simply faded away. Each and every one had demanded and ultimately received satisfaction.

Karaoke would be no different.

Thankfully, the audience had been as lackluster and disinterested in him as they were in the previous performers. Scanning the DJ's list, he had chosen George Thorogood's "Bad to the Bone," singing it out of key and at times terribly out of tempo, unable to keep up with the multiple B sounds in lines containing "B-B-B-Bad." Despite his poor performance, the pressure lifted as he sang, word by word, until he had reached a state of glorious equilibrium by the end of his performance.

Milo had hoped that karaoke would be a onetime demand, a spur of the moment requirement based more on availability than anything else, but less than a week later he had awoken on a rainy Sunday morning with the need again and was soon frantically searching for a bar or nightclub that offered the service. He had been forced to wait three days before singing at a country-and-western bar in Granby and had thought his head would explode by the time he took the stage with his rendition of Van Morrison's "Brown Eyed Girl." For months, whenever the need arose, he would scramble to find a bar or nightclub with the next available karaoke night, inventing excuses usually pertaining to clients in order to slip away from Christine, until one day he stumbled upon Jenny's and her open-mike policy. From then on, whenever the need struck, he would make his way here.

As Milo took the stage, Carmine, Pete, and a rail-thin woman named Rosy at the end of the bar all turned to watch the performance. Though Milo had initially sung a variety of songs to meet the demand, the choice of song was taken away from him a couple years ago when he heard the song "99 Luftballons" on the radio during the station's Way Back Weekend. The German version of the song had made it to number two on the Billboard charts in the summer of 1984, even before the English remix was released, and Milo remembered the song well. Like most Americans, he had not memorized the German lyrics of the song (or even the English ones for that matter), but after hearing Nena's song that day in the car, he suddenly felt the need not only to memorize the words but to perform the song as well, the first time a specific song had been associated with the demand for karaoke.

That association had yet to cease, so for the last two years, each time he performed on Jenny's stage, it was in German, singing the one-hit wonder that was emblematic of the cold war of the 1980s. He often wondered if the image of the German U-boat commander in his mind, or his preference for German pop music, had somehow influenced the choice of song.

He carried three extra copies of the song in the glove compartment of his car (and had taped one to the bottom of the passenger seat in Christine's Jetta) in case the one that he had given to Jenny two years ago became scratched or he found himself out of town and suddenly in need of the music.

If it had to be just one song, Milo didn't think "99 Luftballons" was a bad choice. Since the song was sung in German, few people understood the words (including Milo, who had memorized the pronunciation but not the meaning), and certainly no one in Jenny's. Therefore, expectations were low. As he opened with the somewhat dramatic line—

> *Hast Du etwas Zeit für mich*
> *Dann singe ich ein Lied für Dich*
> *Von 99 Luftballons*

—he was often greeted with curious and amused smiles but little more. Milo had visited many karaoke bars and had seen the people who took their performances to heart, closing their eyes and belting out a Mariah Carey or Whitney Houston tune as if performing in Giants Stadium. No one enjoyed watching a hack posing as a professional, failing to reach the high notes and missing many of the others as well. But when Milo sang "99 Luftballons," people might laugh at the oddity of the choice, but more often than not they would simply ignore his performance, finding it difficult to invest themselves in a song sung in a foreign language.

After his fourth or fifth performance of the song, the regulars at Jenny's had come to expect it. They teased him at first for choosing the same song over and over again, and a guy named Dick had threatened to "pop him one" if he sang it again, but Jenny stepped in, threatening to cut Dick off, and eventually Milo's performance had become a staple in the bar. It saddened Milo to know that this was a world from which Christine was excluded. Though he would hardly characterize any of the Jenny's regulars as friends, he had gotten to know these people over the years and had shared in their life stories.

Pete was the New England backgammon champion who collected soda bottles in his spare time. He had lost almost twenty-five pounds over the past year but still weighed more than three hundred and fifty pounds. He spit when he laughed and had a bum knee, and, not surprisingly, he had been a bachelor his entire life.

Carmine was a retired barber who now spent his days gardening and watching Italian television by satellite. His wife was a fine cook who would sometimes send her husband to the bar with meatballs for Jenny, though she herself had never set foot in the place.

Rosy was a down-on-her-luck divorcée with an eating disorder and an affinity for vanilla vodka. She looked much older than her forty-one years and worked part-time as a cashier at the sex shop down the street. Of all the regulars, she was the one who Milo knew the least. Speaking to Rosy always made him sad.

These people, and the half dozen others who inhabited the bar on a regular basis, had seen Milo sing hundreds of times, had shared untold numbers of drinks with him, and had become fixtures in one another's lives. They knew that Milo was a Yankees fan, that he liked soda better than beer, and that his hands always shook during the first few bars of "99 Luftballons," no matter the audience. They knew a little about Christine, even less about his clients, and nothing about the demands that often ruled his world, but they were in his life nonetheless. They were people occupying the space and time of his existence, and yet Christine knew nothing about them or this place.

She had never even heard him sing.

Though they had been together for years, Milo never felt as if he was finished with his attempts to impress Christine. Though they were husband and wife, part of Milo always felt as if he was still trying to earn her love and respect, and as such, he kept the more embarrassing parts of his existence away from her. In short, Milo had never felt cool enough for Christine. Between his job as a home health aide, his Wednesday-night role-playing games, his moped, and the incessant demands in his head, he had never felt like he measured up to men like Thick-Neck Phil and their prestigious jobs and mirrored sunglasses and top-down Jeeps. He wasn't sure if this was Christine's fault or his own, but he was certain that his wife would not find his karaoke pastime amusing, and for that reason, more than any other, he had kept it a secret from her, like so many other things.

No one danced during Milo's performance. With only three regulars around the bar and a couple eating lunch at a table by the door, he hadn't expected anyone to. If there were people dancing, Rosy might occasionally join in the fun, but Carmine and Pete left the dancing for others.

This didn't bother Milo a bit. As he sang the song, the pressure gradually decreased until his mind was clear again. And for the short time that he was onstage, he was happy. He sang because he had to, but Milo also sang because he loved to.

Once finished, he downed his two sodas quickly and headed for the door, saying goodbye to Jenny as he left.

"You take care of yourself, Milo," she said, turning to refill Carmine's mug.

"Always do," he assured her.

Two thoughts filled his mind as he crossed the parking lot to his car:

> Follow Edith Marchand's advice and watch the tapes.
> Find out if Thick-Neck Phil was spending the evening with Christine.

He thought that he could do both without much difficulty.

chapter 15

Thick-Neck Phil's Jeep was still sitting in the driveway when Milo returned.

It was nearly eight o'clock when he rolled his Honda Civic down Wilson and parked on the street, four doors down from his home. The Hires were hosting another Sunday-night cocktail party, so Wilson Road was lined with vehicles. By parallel parking between a minivan and a station wagon, Milo hoped that his car would blend in nicely. The sun had officially set just moments ago, dipping the tree-lined street into a dusky twilight.

From his vantage point, he had a full view of the driveway (including the Jeep) and side door to the house. Two kitchen windows, a family room window, and a single upstairs window were also visible from his spot on the road. The kitchen and family room lights were on but the second floor appeared dark.

Before driving over to Wilson, Milo had stopped by the apartment to walk Skywalker and pick up the video camera. Grabbing the last of the tapes, his notepad, and an extra battery, he planned on spending the evening in his car, watching Freckles on the camera while ascertaining the nature of Christine and Thick-Neck Phil's relationship.

Admittedly, Milo felt a bit like a stalker, sitting in the dark, keeping watch over his wife's movements, but he felt he had no choice. Unlike the demands of jelly jars and karaoke machines, this was a self-imposed need. If Christine was involved with another man, he had to know.

Most important, he had to know why.

Milo had begun to wonder if the care and planning that had gone into keeping his demands hidden had not been as effective as he had once hoped. Perhaps Christine had finally seen through his layers of concealment and discovered the truth about the man to whom she was married. Maybe not the specifics—the karaoke, the jelly jars, and the bowling—but the overall package of abnormality and strangeness that he couldn't help but be.

When Milo first considered marrying Christine, after several less-than-casual hints from Christine and her friends, he had been worried, terrified really, that the closeness and intimacy of a marriage would eventually lead to the uncovering of his secrets. With friends and even his family, Milo had been able to maintain a safe distance, creating a cushion of privacy that kept his secrets safe and secure. But in moving in with Christine and ultimately marrying her, he feared that this would no longer be possible, and in short order, she would come to realize the oddities and idiosyncrasies of the man whom she had once thought of as normal. It had only been through the process of dating Christine, the development of strategies to deal with the demands, and especially the freedom associated with his job that had allowed him to risk the closeness of matrimony. But maybe now all that planning and preparation and concealment was unraveling, and as a result, Christine had been drawn to a new man, one who did not need to chew on plastic baby toys or pop open pressure seals.

Knowing if Thick-Neck Phil was in the house was necessary to Milo in the sense that any man would want to know if his wife was fucking another guy, but even more important, Milo wanted to know how and why this man had managed to infiltrate his life.

He was happy to have the video camera sitting in his lap. Had he not brought it along, he might have been tempted to creep up to the house and peer in a window. Even with the prospect of Freckles waiting, he was tempted.

Instead, he inserted tape number four and hit play. A pale glow filled the interior of the Civic as a blue screen flickered to the image of Freckles's face. Milo knew immediately that something was wrong. The camera was in her lap again, wobbly and slightly out of focus. Her cheeks were red, her eyes wet, and she was sniffling. It appeared as if she had stopped crying just moments before.

> *I tried to tell them tonight. I went to Mira's mother's house for dinner and thought I could do it. But I just couldn't. Mrs. Singh lost her husband two years ago, and now she's lost Mira. How could I tell her that it was my fault?*
>
> *And it was my fault. I don't give a damn what anyone tries to say. I know that I didn't push her off that horse, but I was supposed to be riding that day. I was supposed to be riding Scarlet the day that Mira died. There. I said it.*
>
> *It was supposed to be my training session that morning, but I had stayed out late the night before. I knew I had to get to the barn early the next morning, but I knew that Mira would cover for me if I called. That was Mira. God, if she had only ignored my phone call. So now what? How am I going to tell Mrs. Singh that I was supposed to be on that horse? That I was supposed to be running Scarlet through those jumps. That I was supposed to be in the saddle when he refused on the last turn. It's me who should be dead right now. I know it's not my fault that she died,*

but it was my fault that she was on that horse, and
that's close enough. I didn't do the killing, but I threw
her in front of the train.

Freckles began crying again, and before the tears had time to
run down her cheeks, her hand reached out and stopped the tape.
When it resumed, it appeared that little time had passed.
Freckles had regained her composure, but the camera was still in
her lap, and she was still wearing what appeared to be a simple
yellow dress or perhaps a tank top. Eyes still red, but not as teary
as before, and it appeared that she had blown her nose.

I haven't been able to set foot in the barn since that day.
Josh keeps calling, asking if he can do anything and
wondering when I'll be back, but what am I supposed
to tell him? Does he think that I'm going to just climb
back onto a horse after my best friend was killed?

Tears came again, but this time Freckles didn't switch off the
camera. Milo watched them cascade down her cheeks and splash
somewhere off screen. She was weeping now. Just pouring out
tears and staring past the camera, at some place in the distance.
Milo wanted to take this moment, this break in dialogue, to jot
down a few notes, but he couldn't take his eyes off the woman on
the screen. His mind was screaming with details, from Mira's last
name (Singh) to Freckles's occupation (horse trainer). All of
these thoughts flooded his mind, yet he held them off, consumed
by the desire to make things better for Freckles, to assure her that
her friend's death was an accident. He wanted to tell her that life
is full of those *what if* moments, and that we have no control over
them. That it's okay to take a day off. People stay out late. Friends
cover shifts. Bad things happen. More than anything, Milo
wanted to reach out and take Freckles by the shoulders, stare into

her blue eyes, and say, "Listen to me. It's not your fault, damn it," throwing in the *damn it* because he knew it's how Freckles would've said it. Then he would pull her close and let her cry until she could cry no more, even if it took until morning.

Unable to do all these things, he sat in the dim light of his car and watched her weep.

Finally, Freckles reached up, releasing the camera from her grasp and momentarily shifting it off her face in order to wipe her eyes again and take a few deep breaths. In that moment, Milo could see that she was in her bedroom. The quick blur of a bureau topped with a mirror, a chair strewn with clothing, and a partially opened closet door reminded Milo to refocus on the task at hand. The still frames of that five-second glimpse into her bedroom might provide clues to Freckles's identity. As the camera returned to her face, Milo noted the tape number and time on his legal pad, finishing just as Freckles started speaking again.

> *Thank God I have someone to talk to. Honestly, I've had my doubts, and more than once, I've thought about quitting this whole damn thing. Starting a video diary on the day that your best friend dies seemed a little crazy at the time, but talking about things has helped. It sounds crazy ... there's no way I'll be posting this online now, but still, it's as if someone has been listening. Constant Listener. Always there when I press record.*

The screen went blue and Milo pressed pause, leaving him with the remarkable feeling that Freckles had been speaking directly to him. He knew it wasn't possible. She couldn't have known that someone would ever find and watch her tapes, but still, it was as if she had been addressing him, as if he were her Constant Listener.

Before resuming the tape, Milo took a moment to check the house again. Thick-Neck Phil's Jeep was still in the same place, and the downstairs lights remained on. No shadows moved within the home and there was still no sign of his wife. Content as he could be that things remained status quo, he returned his gaze to the camera and pressed play.

When Freckles returned to the screen, she was no longer on the bed. She was *in the bed*. Monkey pajamas, hair pulled back, pillows set behind her, a single lamp providing a shadow-filled illumination of the bed. She had assumed a similar pose one time before, when relating the story of Sherry Ferroni. This made Milo hopeful that she was about to share something equally important.

He was not disappointed.

chapter 16

I can't sleep. I can't stop thinking about Tess.
  Tess Bryson.

Freckles released the camera for a moment, dipping the lens into a pillow, and when she retrieved it, she was sitting up straighter, with an indefinable purpose to her posture, as if she was readying herself for something important. Something official.

> *Tess Bryson. I think about her a lot, usually more than once a day, but ever since Mira died, she's been on my mind constantly. I've never told anyone about Tess. Not one single person. Not her parents. Not my friends. Not the police. I don't think I've ever spoken about her out loud.*
> *God. Tess Bryson.*
> *Me and Tess were in sixth grade together. Best friends since first grade, when Mrs. Laverne sat us next to each other. It was our last year in elementary school, the year before I stopped being cool. It was the year that Mrs. Dubois went out on maternity leave with a few months to go in the semester and Mrs. Lavallee had taken over the class. So the last few*

months of school were a complete waste of time. We would work on art projects all day while Kim Maynard and Charity Dumars played tapes of Blondie and Joan Jett. I can still sing all the words to "The Tide Is High" to this day. They must've played that fucking song a thousand times.

In May, Tess asked me to help her run away from home. It wasn't as big a deal as it sounds. Tess was like a professional runaway, always disappearing from home for a night or two. She'd only go as far as the tree house on Farm Street or the little island in the middle of Harris Pond or maybe the sand pits, but it would still send her parents into fits. Her mom would show up at my house, telling my parents that Tess had run off again, and I'd end up sitting in the back of Mr. Bryson's pickup, taking them to all our regular spots. Eventually we'd find her with a box of Ritz crackers and a blanket and her parents would take her home. She never told me why she ran away so much, and I don't think I ever asked. It was just Tess's thing. Some kids play guitar. Some kids go fishing every Saturday. Tess liked to run away. She'd been doing it for years.

But in May she asked me for help. It was the first time she even talked about running away ahead of time, at least to me. She wanted to go to her aunt's house in North Carolina, and she needed some help with maps and planning. Since we were learning almost nothing by then, except for fucking Blondie songs, Tess and I would sit in the back of the classroom with atlases and maps from the AAA and plot her course. My family was always taking car trips around the country, to Florida, New Hampshire,

Chicago...all over. Mom hated to fly. So the station wagon's glove compartment was stuffed with old maps. I found one for New England and one for the southern United States, starting around Maryland I think, and we filled in the rest of the trip, New York and New Jersey mostly, with an atlas from the library. Today we'd just use MapQuest and have our route in seconds, but back then, things were harder.

At the time, it was exciting to think about Tess running away to a place as far as North Carolina, even if it was just Chisholm, a tiny little town that no one had ever heard of. God, I still remember the town's name after all these years. Chisholm. I can still picture where it is on the map. But I never thought that Tess would really do it. I guess I figured that she'd eventually end up in the tree house or the sand pits or under the bridge near Getchell's Stream. Not hundreds of miles away.

Not that she ever made it that far.

We spent about three weeks planning her trip, writing down directions, calculating how far she might be able to walk each day, and finding roads off the beaten path. We knew that she wouldn't be able to walk down I-95 without being picked up, so we found back roads and good spots to pitch her tent for the night. Campgrounds. State parks. Not bad for a couple of thirteen-year-olds with no Internet.

The night before she left, she was over my house for dinner, and before she went home, she asked me if I could loan her any money. I gave her forty dollars. Almost all of my savings at the time. I know that makes it sound like I knew that she was really going, but in my heart, I never really believed it. I figured *that Tess would be back in a day or two, the money would make it back to my piggy bank, and Tess would be grounded like always. But before she left my house that night, she took my hands and made me promise not to tell anyone where she was going, no matter what. She was so serious, standing there in the moonlight in front of my house, more serious than I thought possible from a thirteen-year-old, and she wouldn't let go of my hands until I swore on my mother's someday-grave that I wouldn't tell. I remember thinking that her parents already knew about all her good hiding spots anyway, and that they'd find her with or without my help. Promise or no promise.*

I can still remember the day that she ran away like it was yesterday. It was a Friday, and Tess didn't show up to school that day. I remember sitting at my desk, listening to Mrs. Lavallee take attendance, knowing all about Tess's plans and feeling so superior to everyone in the room, like I was the only one who could be trusted with the biggest secret of the year. I knew something so important that no one else knew. It took all my willpower to keep my mouth shut.

Then the weekend came and my family went to stay with Aunt Nancy on the Cape. This was long before cell phones and pagers, so the Brysons had no way of getting in touch with us during those two days. And with the beach and the sun and the two cute boys in the house next door to ours, Noah and Ewan Wola-something, I forgot all about Tess and her plans. Besides, I wasn't really worried. Like I said, Tess ran away all the time. I guess if I had taken the time to think about it in between all the swimming and flirt-

ing, I would've assumed that Tess was already home, stuck in her room for the weekend without TV.

We got back late Sunday night and my parents found a note on our door from the Brysons asking for us to call as soon as we got home. I knew that it was about Tess, and so did my mom, but it was nearly midnight when we pulled in, so she decided to wait until the next day to call. Tess running away was just a regular part of life back then. No big deal. I know it sounds crazy, but it's true.

I was in class the next morning, Monday morning, and Tess wasn't there. At first I thought, Wow, she must've caught a cold hiding under the bridge all night. *But then I started to think that maybe she had really done it. Maybe she really had packed up our maps and directions and my forty dollars and taken off for North Carolina. That's when I started to get scared. Not for Tess, but for me. What if my parents found out? What would they say if they knew that I had helped Tess run away for real this time?*

I was sitting at my desk in the back of the classroom, thinking about how much trouble I would be in if my parents found out, when two police officers walked right into our class like they owned the place and started talking, without an introduction or anything. They said that Tess Bryson was missing and her parents thought that she might have runned away. "Runned away," the older cop said, and I remember that it made a few kids around me giggle. But not me. I was thirteen years old and suddenly understood what it meant to be fucked.

They said that they wanted to know if anyone had information about Tess and would be asking

each one of us to come across the hall to the music
room to answer a few questions. "No big deal," the
older guy said, but I didn't believe him for a second.
Then the one with the Yosemite Sam mustache said,
"We'd like to start with Cassidy Glenn." God, my
stomach felt like it had dropped right out of my
body. It took me like a minute to say anything, and in
that time, everyone had turned and was staring right
at me. Then Yosemite said, "Are you Cassidy Glenn?"
and he pointed at me. I nodded. I couldn't have said a
word even if I had wanted to. Then he asked me to
follow him.

Milo understood the importance of the information that he had just heard. Freckles's real name was Cassidy Glenn. But he almost didn't care, completely transfixed by the woman in the tiny screen on his lap. Unlike with previous stories, Freckles (using Cassidy would take some getting used to) was not exhibiting any emotion despite the content of her narrative. She had become a storyteller, conveying the emotion of the time without the emotion of the present interfering. And he noticed that she was speaking slower and with more of a cadence, as if the woman on the screen were suddenly thirteen years old again and telling the story in a long-forgotten pubescent voice.

If Tess's parents had shown up at my house, Mrs.
Bryson crying like she always did when Tess ran
away, I probably would've cracked in three minutes
and told them everything. But those cops scared the
hell out of me. I was absolutely positive that I was
going to prison. I had helped a girl run away from
home, had given her money for the road, and now I
was in the biggest trouble of my life. We went into the

music room, the older cop in front of me and Yosemite behind me. The older guy, the clean-shaven one, told me to sit and asked me if I knew where Tess was.

I said no.

Then they asked me if Tess had mentioned anything about running away from home.

I said no.

Then they asked me if Tess had a reason to run away. A fight with her parents? Trouble in school? A bad breakup with a boyfriend? I didn't really understand the questions at the time, because Tess never had a reason. And it's not like either of us had boyfriends. She just liked to run away.

So I said no.

Then they asked me about Tess's parents ... if I thought they were good parents, and they asked me a lot of questions about Mr. Bryson. Did Tess get along with him? How did Mr. Bryson treat me? Did I like Mr. Bryson? I realized that they thought that maybe Mr. Bryson did something to Tess, chopped her up in a wood chipper or threw her down a well, which I knew he didn't do, and this scared me too. I thought, Oh my God. Now Mr. Bryson is going to be in trouble too. Because of me. And this made me want to keep my secret even more. It was like one of those snowballs in the cartoons that keep getting bigger and bigger as it moves down the mountain. The whole thing felt impossibly huge and just getting huger. The old guy asking the questions was sitting next to Danny Pollock's tuba and I remember looking at my reflection in it, all blurry and twisted, and I thought to myself that the person looking back at me had made a promise to Tess and I was going to *keep it. But that was just an excuse. It felt good and sanctimonious and righteous, but it was all bullshit. Nothing more than a good reason to keep my mouth shut and not feel guilty or responsible. Something to hang my coward's hat on. The truth was that I was scared out of my mind and ashamed and couldn't bear the thought of everyone knowing what I did.*

I think the police believed me, because they only came back to class once more after that day, and that time, they didn't meet with us individually. They just explained how serious the situation was and asked us to think hard about anything that might help them find Tess. Then Mrs. Lavallee put the phone number to the police station on the board, just in case anyone thought of something. By then, things in town were crazy. No one knew if Tess had run away or been abducted, so parents were keeping their kids at home after dinner. There was talk about canceling the Little League playoffs for a while, but that didn't happen. It was a small town, still is, and people weren't accustomed to kids disappearing in the night. I remember hearing rumors about Mr. Bryson, but I think that was later on, after people had pretty much given up hope on finding Tess. People wondered if he had something to do with it, and I think it got pretty uncomfortable for him for quite a while. But I was off the hook. My parents asked me some questions a few times, mostly trying to find out if I knew something that I didn't realize was important, and Mrs. Bryson called once and asked if I could think of anything that might help, but I said no.

I just kept saying no, no, no all spring and summer, waiting, praying for Tess to come home or show

*up at her aunt's place. I'd ask Mrs. Bryson if she
heard anything when I'd see her at the grocery store
or the laundromat, but my mother finally told me to
stop. That it was too painful for Mrs. Bryson to talk
about. So I just waited for word that she had come
back or shown up in North Carolina like we had
planned.*

*She never did. For all I know, she was picked up
on the highway by some sick fuck half a mile from
town and was raped and killed in the back of a
pickup truck. That's what I think about most often.
What might have happened. I can't help it.*

*Whatever happened to Tess, it couldn't have been
good or she would've eventually called me or her parents or someone else in town. But no one ever saw her
again. And thirteen-year-old girls just don't disappear
into the night and start new lives. When thirteen-
year-old girls disappear forever, something bad happened. Something sick and twisted and fucked up. You
find yourself lying in bed at night, praying to God
that whoever killed her did it quick and didn't make
her suffer. Think about that. You go from praying that
she'll just come home to praying that maybe she was
smothered in her sleep or shot in the back of the head
when she wasn't looking or something else quick and
painless. This is the kind of stuff that occupies my
mind. I used to try to think of all the best ways to be
murdered. The least painful ways. The ways where
you don't know it's coming. I'd make a list in my head
and then pray to God that whoever killed Tess used
one of them instead of cutting her throat or throwing
her into the bottom of a well to drown or starve to
death. And I still find myself wondering if Mrs.*

Bryson thought the same thing in her bed at night. If she still does.

And just like with Mira, it was my fault. Maybe if I had told the police the truth that day in the music room, they might've found her somewhere in Connecticut or New Jersey. Hell, I could've shown them her exact route. The places we planned for her to stop and pitch her tent, the parks, the campgrounds, the rest areas. I knew everything about her trip and didn't say a goddamn word. I can say that I was keeping a promise, but honestly, I was just a scared little girl who didn't have the courage to help her friend. I didn't put Tess on that road, and I didn't give her the idea to run away, but I sat in the back of that classroom and planned the whole damn thing with her, excited about being a part of something so big. And when the time came to speak up and make a difference, I decided to save my own skin and leave Tess on her own.

God help me. I let her die somewhere on the road, alone and probably scared out of her wits.

That's two on me now. First Tess and now Mira.

Freckles was finally crying, the final words coming forth between sniffles and sobs before the tape ended, and in the dim light of the Civic, Milo found himself crying too, not for Tess Bryson, but for Freckles and the secret that she had kept inside for so long. As much as she wished that she could change her past, alter her decisions from so long ago, she could not, and as a result, the disappearance of Tess Bryson had become a part of her. A secret part that she could never remove.

In listening to her story, Milo realized that he too understood what it was like to feel this way, to live every day of your life in constant fear that someone might discover your secret life. He knew what it was like to live with never-ending tension and worry. Though there were moments in the day when Milo's secrets might fade into the landscape of work and daily routines, they were never far off, and they never, ever faded away for long. Always pushing forward, demanding action, requiring vigilance, and occupying most of his mental processes, his secrets were inescapable, and as such, they required constant attention. In the dim light of his car, sitting outside the house that no longer seemed like his own, Milo realized that these inexplicable demands were his single most defining characteristic, the part of him that consumed the most time and energy and the part that had insinuated itself into every aspect of his life, yet he had never shared this enormous chunk of his soul with another human being.

Milo suddenly felt lonelier than he had ever felt before. The loneliness was almost palpable, a leaden weight bearing down on his shoulders. He realized that even worse than this fear of discovery was the isolation that came with not being able to share the most important parts of himself with another person. Because so much of his life was hidden from others, Milo now understood with deepening sadness that no one truly knew him. They might have known small parts of him, the parts that he carefully vetted and willingly disseminated for public consumption, but no one, his friends, his wife, or even his parents, had ever truly known the man that Milo had become.

In essence, Milo was a fraud to all who knew him, an actor playing a role for his audience, yet he was the only one who knew there was a performance going on.

He had been thrilled to discover that Christine was in love with him and eager to spend the rest of her life with him, but in looking back on those days now, he realized that perhaps he should have instead been thrilled with his ability to deceive a woman so effectively, beginning with that first night in Arugula and continuing through his marriage and separation. Though he was reticent to admit it, even to himself, Milo had come to the realization that he had tricked Christine into loving him by playing a role, when in truth he was someone whom she barely knew.

Until Milo was willing to share his secrets with someone, he would remain a stranger to all, and as a result, he would always be alone to some degree. He knew this with certainty now, but also knew that there was nothing he could do to change it.

Milo thought that Freckles was probably suffering with the same kind of burden, the same inability to open up to another human being, and while he understood why she felt this way, he also thought that Freckles's circumstances were far different than his own. The secret part of Freckles, the part that had kept Tess Bryson's disappearance hidden for twenty years, could be exorcised. Milo suspected that Freckles's burden, unlike his own secrets, could be easily lifted from her shoulders. Even if Tess Bryson was dead (and he suspected she probably was), no reasonable person would ever blame a thirteen-year-old for the role that she played in the tragedy, save the woman who the thirteen-year-old had become. By being forced into immediate secrecy, the teenage version of Freckles had locked away an ample supply of shame and guilt that had continued to plague her well beyond her teenage years. Had she simply been able to share her secret with someone, as a child or even as an adult, she might have been convinced that she deserved no blame and should therefore feel no guilt about the disappearance of her friend. Tess was running away with or without Freckles's help. As an adult, Freckles might have realized this immediately, but as a kid, facing interrogation by police officers, she automatically had placed all the blame on herself, and there it had remained.

For Milo, the revealing of his demands would do nothing to erase them from his being. They were a part of him now, an inextricable component to the man he had become. Sharing his secrets would only serve to push others away and heighten his degree of strangeness, but he was now convinced that if someone could persuade Freckles to share her secret, she might come to the realization that, while tragic, the disappearance of Tess Bryson was not a burden that she was required to carry, and that her life could be exponentially better.

Milo sat in his car, lit by the glow of the video display, and watched Freckles cry. And he cried too, for all the years that he and Freckles had lost to their secrets, for all the friendship and love that they had sacrificed for subterfuge, but through his tears, he also felt hope, not for himself, but for Freckles. He felt a new and even deeper connection to this woman, Cassidy Glenn, whose secret life was in many ways like his own. He may never be able to save himself, but he thought that he might surely be able to save her.

The sobs hadn't quite subsided when the police officer tapped his flashlight on Milo's passenger window, motioning for him to roll it down.

chapter 17

Milo opted for honesty. Still in the throes of Freckles's over-whelming outburst of candor, it seemed like the right decision. And for the first few questions, the truth served him well.

Yes, he could place his hands on the wheel.

No, there weren't any weapons in the vehicle.

No, there were no drugs in the car.

Yes, he could present his license and registration.

No, he had not been drinking.

Yes, he could step out of the car.

This is where honesty stopped being easy.

Complicating the situation was a second police officer, a red-faced, blond-haired man at least six inches taller than Milo who had been standing opposite his partner on the passenger side of the Civic. Milo hadn't seen the man until he had climbed from his driver's seat and was standing outside the car, trying to keep his back to the house in case Christine or Thick-Neck Phil emerged from within. It was then that he also noticed the police cruiser parked about four feet behind his car, its lights thankfully off.

Yes, he told the officer closest to him, a short, wiry man with what Milo thought were the hairiest knuckles he had ever seen. He had been sitting in his car, watching a video on his camera's view screen.

Yes, he told the second officer, whom Milo now liked decidedly less than the first. He had been crying.

Yes, according to his driver's license, which he had not changed since moving out, he lived on this street, just four houses down from his present location.

"Do you still live at home, sir?" Hairy Knuckles asked. The man was wearing a badge displaying his name, but in the dim light, Milo could not read it.

"No," Milo said, surprised at how quickly the cop seemed to be catching on. "I'm separated from my wife right now. We're working on getting back together."

"What's on the tape?" the second cop asked, still on the opposite side of the car and behind Milo. Suddenly sandwiched between two cops, Milo flashed back to Freckles and her own interrogation back in sixth grade. She must have been terrified that day.

"Sir? Did you hear me?"

Milo turned to answer. Holding on to the truth like a life preserver, he said, "It's a video diary. Like a confessional."

"Is your wife on the tape?"

"No. It's another girl." Milo tried to sound as nonchalant as possible, which wasn't very.

"Sir, does your wife know that you're sitting here, outside the house?" Hairy Knuckles had asked this question, forcing Milo to turn again. He was starting to become unnerved by the barrage of questions from both sides.

"Not unless she's the one who called you guys."

"Nope. A neighbor called. Reported seeing a guy sitting in his car. You can imagine how nervous you might make someone, just sitting here, right Mr. . . . Slade?" The cop had looked back at Milo's driver's license in order to recall his last name.

"Sure, but I wasn't doing anything wrong."

"Just keeping an eye on your ex-wife. Right, Mr. Slade?" The second officer again. Officer Unfriendly, Milo dubbed him in his mind.

"She's not my ex-wife," Milo said, the most forceful words out of his mouth so far. "We're separated, but we're getting back together."

"Right. But that's what you're doing. Keeping an eye on her. Correct?" This was Hairy Knuckles, smiling in way that Milo did not entirely trust.

"Sort of. She had a guy over the house today. It was probably nothing, but she . . . I wasn't sure. She wasn't clear about who he was and why he was over the house. I just wanted to find out what was going on."

"Mr. Slade, I need you to turn around and put your hands on the hood of your car, so I can pat you down for weapons. Okay?"

"I don't . . ." Milo said uncertainly, but before he could protest, his body had turned and his hands had planted themselves as instructed in what seemed to be an act of conspiracy.

"Mind if we take a peek in your car, Mr. Slade?" Officer Unfriendly asked while his partner finished checking Milo for weapons.

"I guess not."

The peek in the car turned into a full search of the vehicle, including the trunk, which led to an awkward question about the half dozen jars of jelly nestled in a box on top of the spare tire. Unable to honestly explain their presence, Milo was finally forced to abandon the truth.

"They were on sale," he explained, which he realized was actually true. They had been on sale when he bought them. "I'm in a second-floor apartment and haven't brought them up yet." Milo hoped that the cops hadn't noticed that each jar had already been opened.

The search complete, Hairy Knuckles returned to his squad car, presumably to run Milo's name through their computer. This left Milo standing alone with the redhead, Officer Unfriendly, while still trying to keep his back to the house. Even with the fear and dread that had consumed him, Milo's mind continued to stray back to Freckles and Tess Bryson and the events surrounding her disappearance. Despite his desire to find out what was going on with his wife, and an equally strong desire to rid himself of these police officers, an even more urgent need to get home as soon as possible and start his research was forcing its way into the corners of Milo's consciousness, not unlike many of his other demands.

Cassidy Glenn. Her full name, at last.

"So what did you plan on doing tonight, Mr. Slade, if you found your wife with this other guy?"

"I don't know," Milo said, back to honesty. "Probably nothing. I just had to know the truth. Know what I mean?"

"Sure. But then what's up with the video camera? Who's the woman on the tape? A girlfriend of yours?"

Milo was saved from answering this question by Hairy Knuckles, who had returned with Milo's driver's license. "Okay, Mr. Slade. Here's what we're going to do. You're going to wait with Officer Eblen and I'm going to have a chat with your wife. Get some information. Then we'll take it from there."

"I don't understand," Milo said, already feeling the mortification of Christine finding out what he was doing. "I didn't do anything wrong. Can't I just go home?"

"Of course. But let me talk to your wife first. If this is a one-time thing, it won't constitute stalking. And your record is clean, which is good. But I don't know for certain that you've never done this kind of thing before."

"I haven't. Honestly. I'm not a stalker." The sentence sounded ridiculous to Milo.

"I'm just going to confirm that with your wife while you wait here. Is your wife's last name Slade too?"

"No, she uses her maiden name. Turcotte. But officer, do we really have to do this? I swear. I've never done anything like this before."

"Then you have nothing to worry about, Mr. Slade. Just wait here with my partner. I'll be right back."

Milo watched as the cop crossed the street and headed in the direction of his house. He couldn't believe this was happening. What would Christine think? What would she say? What would she tell Dr. Teagan when they met next week?

"You know," Officer Eblen said, still sounding unfriendly. "If you've done this before, it's better to tell me now before we hear about it from your wife."

"I've never done anything like this before. I swear. I saw the guy today for the first time. That's his Jeep right there. I just wanted to know if my wife was dating another guy. That's all."

At that moment, two thoughts materialized in Milo's mind.

The first was to the need to strike a match or two, or maybe ten. Not the flimsy kind you would find in a book of matches, but one of those blue-tipped wooden kitchen matches that Christine kept in the drawer beside the dishwasher. The kind with the match head mounted on an honest-to-goodness block of wood. He had never experienced this need before, but he knew immediately that it was no different than the demand that had forced him to open the jars of jelly in his trunk, except that it was growing in intensity with surprising speed. Perhaps the tension of the situation in which Milo found himself was stoking the flame, both literally and figuratively.

The second thought was that he might end up in a jail cell this evening, unable to satisfy this and any other demand that might appear, and unable to research the street address and hometown of Cassidy Glenn. The possibility that he might find himself locked up in an small concrete room, with no access to kitchen matches or jelly jars or the Internet, sent Milo's heart rate skyrocketing. His muscles tensed, his felt his face and neck flush, and in moments, he knew he would be sweating.

He could not allow himself to be arrested.

Milo watched as the door to his house opened and Christine appeared in the entranceway. She looked nervous and scared at first, but then seemed to relax a bit as Hairy Knuckles began to speak. After a minute, the officer motioned in Milo's direction and he saw Christine look around the cop to see her husband standing by his car in quasi police custody. She did not look pleased.

"Mind if I ask who did the separating, Mr. Slade? Was it you or your wife?"

"Depends on who you ask," Milo said, fixated on the scene at the front door of the house. The conversation between Christine and the cop went on for almost three minutes, and with each passing minute, Milo grew more and more nervous. He wondered how long it could take to confirm that he was not stalking his wife. What the hell could they be talking about?

Just as Milo thought that the discussion was ending, Thick-Neck Phil appeared in the doorway beside Christine, and after a moment, he seemed to be answering questions from Hairy Knuckles as well. Even though Milo suspected all along that Phil was inside the house, the sight of the man and the resulting confirmation that he was with Christine, in their home, after nine, made Milo angrier than ever before.

"Is that the guy?" Officer Eblen asked.

"Yes," Milo said, afraid to say more. He was seething inside.

Finally, Christine and Thick-Neck stepped back into the house and closed the door and Hairy Knuckles made his way back to Milo and his partner.

"Okay, Mr. Slade. Just a couple more questions. Your wife said that you were in the house today when she wasn't home. Is that true?"

"Huh?"

"Is that true, Mr. Slade. Were you——"

"Yes, it's true. I stopped by to give her some flowers. When I saw that she wasn't home, I left. Did Christine complain about me going into the house?"

"Did you and your wife have an agreement about when and how you might enter the home?"

"No," Milo said. "Did she say we did? It's my house too." Hairy Knuckles just stared, so after a moment, Milo continued. "She never even asked me for the key. We're only separated, for Christ's sake. I'm still paying half the mortgage. I didn't do anything wrong."

"No, but you can see how it might make a woman nervous. Right? Finding out that someone has been inside the house while she was gone. Especially after she finds out that the same man is sitting in a car outside her house."

"Did you want her to feel nervous, Mr. Slade?" Officer Eblen asked.

"Of course not! I'm not just *some man*. I'm her husband. All I did was bring my wife some flowers. I had a key. She wasn't home. That's it."

"What about the confrontation between you and your wife in the driveway? She said that you seemed very angry this afternoon. Angrier than she has ever seen you before."

"Of course I was angry. I found my wife with another guy. I found his kid's playpen in my bedroom. I didn't know what the hell was going on, and she wouldn't tell me anything. But that doesn't make me a stalker."

"So you didn't just drop off the flowers? You went into the bedroom too?"

"Yes, I did. It's my house. I went to use the bathroom and I noticed the playpen next to the bed. I went into the bedroom to check it out. It's my house, damn it."

Milo left out the part about examining Christine's lingerie and chewing on the plastic book. He didn't think that would go over so well.

"No need to get excited, Mr. Slade," Officer Eblen said. "We're just making sure that things are okay here. Just doing our job."

"Fine. Can I go now?" He couldn't believe how quickly the need to strike a match, a whole box of them perhaps, had filled his mind.

"Yes, you can, Mr. Slade. You've done nothing wrong. But you should keep in mind that sitting here in the street like this can make people nervous. You may want to reconsider that decision in the future."

"But that's just our opinion, Mr. Slade," Officer Eblen added, already turning toward the squad car.

A minute later Milo was standing alone by his car on the darkened street. Terrified of a possible encounter between him and Christine (and Thick-Neck Phil), he climbed into his car and headed home.

He had matches to strike and a woman to find, and finally, he knew her name.

chapter 18

Cassidy Glenn, who might always be Freckles in Milo's mind, was older than Milo had expected. Perhaps as old as he was. With more than a hundred feet still separating them, Milo couldn't be sure. He was standing on the edge of the Mill Pond Park in Newington, his shadow long in the late-afternoon sun. Just moments ago, he had solved the final mystery of Cassidy Glenn, the one that had proven elusive during his Internet search the day before. Milo now understood what Freckles had meant when she spoke of a morning fight on tape number three, and with that final piece of the puzzle in place, he felt ready to return the camera and the tapes to the woman whom he thought he might know better than almost anyone else in the world.

Less than twenty hours had passed since Milo's encounter with Officer Eblen and his hairy-knuckled partner, and during that time, he had placed eight unreturned phone calls to Christine, on both the home phone and her cell. Though this seemingly purposeful disconnect by his wife and the continued uncertainty surrounding Thick-Neck Phil left him uneasy, the free time that it had afforded had allowed him to locate Freckles and piece together much of her life.

Once he had the full names of Freckles and Mira, it had been easy.

To start, Mira had turned out to be Meera, an Indian or Pakistani name with which Milo had not been familiar. Combined with the last name Singh and his knowledge of the circumstances of her death, he had found several news reports of her accident with relative ease. Last October, Meera had been training at Bartolini Farm and Stables in Glastonbury, Connecticut, when the horse that she was riding refused to jump over a routine obstacle on an indoor equestrian course, throwing Meera from the saddle and onto the turf. The fall had broken Meera's neck, killing her almost instantly; an incident that Milo discovered is not so uncommon in the equestrian world. This indicated that Freckles had begun her diary just six months ago, which thrilled Milo. It meant that in getting to know her through the tapes, he had gotten to know the Freckles of now, of today, and not some decade-old version of the woman.

Though the story about Meera's death had not included any reference to Freckles, Milo had managed to find her the old-fashioned way: through the phone book. Searching through the listings of Newington (the town in which he had found the camera) and surrounding towns, he had found a Cassidy Glenn, the only one in the book, living about twenty minutes from his apartment, in the town of Berlin.

He was confident that he had his girl.

Milo had also managed to find information on Freckles's runaway friend, Tess Bryson, or more specifically on her father, Sean Bryson. Milo hadn't expected to find anything on Tess, given that she had disappeared more than a decade before the Internet had become ubiquitous, but in searching on her name, Milo turned up a story about Sean Bryson in which his daughter, Tess, was referenced. Sean Bryson, formerly of Millville, Massachusetts, was in year eight of a fifteen-year sentence at Walpole State Penitentiary, convicted for the sexual assault of his ten-year-old niece during a camping trip to the Berkshires. Though the writer of the story was professional enough not to explicitly link the possible disappearance of his daughter ten years earlier to his apparent predilection for familial pedophilia, she had included a short paragraph on Tess's disappearance, trusting the reader to make the obvious connection.

Milo wondered if Freckles knew about Mr. Bryson's current place of residence and thought not. Had she known, she too might have suspected that Tess had run away from more than just an unsatisfying social life or a failing grade in math, and that maybe her disappearance was intentional and not at the hands of "some sick fuck" with a pickup truck. Maybe Tess Bryson had wanted to disappear.

Maybe the sick fuck that Freckles suspected in her friend's disappearance had been Tess Bryson's own father.

Most important, maybe Tess Bryson remained missing on purpose, in order to hide from an abusive father.

Maybe she was still alive.

Finished with his final client of the day, a widow named Grace Bedford who obsessed over a backyard herb garden and wore a necklace made from her daughter's baby teeth, Milo had headed to Berlin to take a peek at Freckles's home, hoping to confirm that the Cassidy Glenn of 19 Cynthia Drive was the same girl who had appeared on the tapes. He had no doubt, but confirming this information, as well as the opportunity to see her in person, was too much to resist. Sitting outside her home, feeling like the stalker that Hairy Knuckles had all but accused him of being the night before, Milo watched as Freckles arrived home shortly after five. Though he was across the street, parked two houses down from Freckles's home, there was no doubt in Milo's mind that he had found his girl. Stepping out of her Ford pickup, she had the same look, the same gait, and the same glow of the woman in the video. He watched her enter the house and disappear behind curtains, and for a moment, he thought he might walk right up to the house, ring the doorbell, and introduce himself as the man who had found her video camera and tapes. Get it over right now and head home with a clean conscience.

A blend of curiosity and fear stopped him.

Though he managed to find the name, address, and phone number of the woman whom he had sought, Milo still had questions. Had she gone back to training horses yet? Was she still blaming herself for Meera's death? What was her middle name, and did she even have one? Most pressing, what was the meaning behind her reference to a morning fight?

But more than curious, Milo was afraid. Planning his first conversation with Christine years ago had been difficult enough, but this exchange would be infinitely more challenging.

Christine had been expecting his call. She had even been looking forward to it.

Freckles was not.

Christine had known something about Milo prior to the call. She'd had some familiarity with her future husband.

Freckles didn't know that Milo existed.

Christine had possessed no reason to hate Milo, though she had apparently found ample opportunity in the past year.

There were already plenty of reasons for Freckles to hate Milo, even though the two had never met.

The camera.

The tapes.

The removal of the nylon bag and its contents from the park that night.

Milo's decision to watch the tapes, even after it was clear that the footage contained a private confessional of sorts.

The fact that Milo knew about Freckles and her deepest, darkest secrets made the impending conversation between them almost impossible to imagine. Her possible range of emotions was limitless.

Appreciation

Embarrassment

Shame

Disbelief

Shock

Anger

Rage

He wondered if she might be happier if he never returned the camera to her, but then he thought about how it might feel to know that the record of one's most private thoughts were somewhere in the world, ready to be posted online at any time. Milo reasoned that knowing that one person had viewed the tapes was better than worrying that the world might someday have access to the recordings. Even though he would not be able to explain his ability to identify and locate her without admitting to watching the tapes, Milo could at least assure Freckles that he had been the only one to see them and that no copies had been made.

But that was a conversation that would require some planning.

What Milo did decide in that moment outside her home was not to watch the rest of the tapes. When he finally returned them to Freckles, he wanted to be able to assure her that he watched the recordings only until she mentioned her full name. Though this unfortunately occurred during the telling of her darkest secret, he could at least present himself as an honorable man.

Fooling himself into believing that curiosity trumped fear, Milo decided to return to Cynthia Drive the next morning, early enough to follow Freckles to work and wherever else she may go. He told himself that by filling in the blanks of her life, he could better prepare for their eventual encounter. In truth, he was simply delaying the inevitable, afraid to face a woman whom he liked and admired but who would probably end up hating him.

The following morning, Milo had followed Freckles to the neighboring town of New Britain, to an ugly rectangular box of brick and glass, where she apparently spent her days working. Horse training was not Freckles's only gig, or at least it wasn't anymore. Knowing that she had arrived home around five o'clock the previous day, Milo met with two clients during the morning and early afternoon (including Arthur Friedman) before returning to New Britain at four to resume his tail. Freckles left work at four forty-five and had made her way straight to Mill Pond Park, where she had joined a group of a dozen friends and a small horde of children on the far field.

As Milo watched her across the open field, he thought about the possibility that his entire future with Freckles might comprise a single, uncomfortable three-minute encounter. Despite his effort to do the right thing, it was likely that after returning the camera and tapes, he would never see Freckles again. Though he knew it made no sense, it still broke his heart to think of such a future.

He closed the distance between them to less than fifty feet and then remained in place, continuing to watch. This is when one of the final pieces of the puzzle, the explanation of Freckles's morning fight, finally fell into place.

A middle-aged Indian man in wire-rimmed glasses was standing about twenty feet from Freckles, grappling a spool of kite string. Freckles was standing to his left, spinning out string of her own. High above them, their kites were engaged in a form of aerial combat that Milo had once read about in a novel set in Afghanistan.

Kite fighting.

The two kites, one purple and white and the other various shades of green, were spinning, looping, climbing, and diving around each other at impossible speeds. Milo watched in amazement as Freckles and her opponent made their kites act more like small planes than simple toys on string. In fact, the kites were moving so quickly that Milo couldn't determine which kite belonged to Freckles and which was controlled by her opponent. Regardless, he was in awe of the performance taking place overhead.

He wondered if Meera had introduced her to the sport.

The battle went on over the contestants' heads for more than ten minutes, the gathering crowd watching the sky intently as several small children followed the kites on foot, running back and forth across the field, attempting to stay directly below them. Several other kites were scattered around the field, all of various designs and colors, appearing ready for flight. Just as Milo was ready to venture over to the crowd to inquire about the status of the fight, two girls standing near Freckles leapt into the air, screaming in delight. Though he assumed that Freckles had won, Milo wasn't sure what constituted a victory until he saw the green kite gliding gently to the ground, pursued by the pack of screaming children. Its line had been cut.

The two women, one wearing jeans and a T-shirt and the other a teal sari, ran over to congratulate Freckles, whose purple and white kite still soared high overhead. They were followed by a smaller group of men and women, older and less enthusiastic than the first two but seemingly happy for her nonetheless. Freckles smiled as she shook their hands and listened to them speak, but she seemed uncomfortable with the attention that she was receiving, turning attempts to hug and even lift her off the ground into brief, awkward embraces. Once each member of the group had offered his or her congratulations, she turned and took several steps toward her opponent, who appeared to be waiting patiently for her. She reached out and shook his hand, exchanging words that Milo could not hear; the two appeared to be cordial and maybe even friendly. Then with a brief nod, she stepped away, taking several steps in Milo's direction, away from the rest of the crowd, before beginning the process of reeling in her kite. Only when the attention of her friends was directed at the launch of two new kites into the air on the other side of the field did Freckles dare a surreptitious fist pump of celebration, her long shadow stretching close enough to Milo that he could've reached out and touched it if he had wanted.

Milo had seen Freckles in many private moments like this. Exclusively private moments, in fact. But this was the first time that he had seen her happy, if only for a second. Milo also experienced similar flashes of happiness, moments when his secrets faded away from consciousness for a time, replaced by the normal, everyday pleasures of a normal, everyday person. But for Milo, and likely for Freckles, these moments were brief and fleeting, and regardless of the happiness that he might have felt, there was always a pall cast over his joy, a constant, unwavering awareness that there was something much bigger looming overhead. There was the fear of discovery, of course, but more than that, there was the knowledge that a lifetime of isolation lay ahead. Like the cashier with an endless line of unsatisfied customers, Milo felt his existence stretched out before him like a line of brief and fragmentary moments of joy amid a lifetime of tiring, unending vigilance and loneliness.

In this singular moment, Milo was certain that Freckles was happy, but more important, he knew like no other that she too faced a lifetime marked by fitful, solitary moments of delight. He knew that regardless of the joy in this victory, Freckles would eventually find herself in her brown and blue colonial later that night, burdened with thoughts of Meera Singh and Tess Bryson.

Secrets that only he knew.

There was nothing that Milo could do for himself, no way of eliminating the persistence and weight of his inexplicable demands (he was, in fact, in need of a jelly jar at this very moment). Even if he had found the courage to share his secrets with Christine or Andy or even Freckles, nothing would ever change for him. The relentless submariner in his head who issued forth his demands would remain, undaunted and unchallenged, regardless of his confession. Milo knew in that moment, with absolute certainty, that the truth would never set him free. The subterfuge and stratagem could perhaps end, but to reveal his secret would risk the loss of people who he cared about most, and it would likely cost him his dignity as well. Even if he found the courage to tell his friends or family about the karaoke or the bowling or the pressure seals, he didn't think he could ever face them again afterward.

But he thought that there might be a chance for Freckles, an opportunity for her to be unburdened by her secrets. By telling someone about Tess Bryson, Freckles might be made to realize that she was not to blame, and perhaps Milo could be that person for her.

In that moment, Milo realized that there was something else that he might do for Freckles, something more powerful and convincing than simply telling her that she was not to blame. Like the need to pop a pressure seal or sing karaoke, this idea came on him unexpectedly, a dim light glimmering in a dark room, but in moments, the idea overwhelmed him, expanding to fill every corner and crevice of his mind, the Big Bang of his brain, so large and consuming that it nearly replaced his current need for a jar of jelly.

Yes, he would eventually return the camera and the tapes to her.

Yes, he could be the confidant that Freckles needed.

And yes, he could be the one to convince her that Meera Singh's death and Tess Bryson's disappearance were not her fault.

But first, there was something else he must do. An idea that emerged in his head, fully formed. And as outrageous and ridiculous and unlikely a plan as it already seemed, it also would be impossible to ignore. In that instant, Milo realized that he might have stumbled upon a way of unburdening Freckles of her demons forever.

chapter 19

Milo wasn't sure if Christine would show up to their next appointment. He was sitting in Dr. Teagan's waiting room on
Wednesday afternoon, holding the same *Highlights* magazine
from which he had removed the poem a week before, wondering
if his wife would even call if she planned on not showing. They
had not spoken since the incident outside the house two days ago,
and his half dozen phone calls over the last twenty-four hours to
the house and her cell phone had gone unanswered.

Though he couldn't imagine leaving the state without telling
Christine of his plans, a small part of him, the part that dreaded
confrontation, hoped that Christine would not show. Any discussion of Freckles, and especially an explanation of his intent to
help her, would undoubtedly anger her to an even greater degree. And an hour to talk to Dr. Teagan about his plans, confirm
his suspicions, and attempt to obtain his therapist's approval of
his impending journey appealed to Milo a great deal. He had
called Andy the night before to tell him about Freckles and Tess
Bryson, but about thirty seconds into their conversation, he had
decided against it. To discuss Freckles, even with his best friend,
felt like violating a trust that he had established with the woman.
Andy would ask for details, would want to know everything, and
would be annoyed when Milo refused. His frustration would not

reach the level of Christine's, Milo was sure, but it would be enough to make things uncomfortable between the two men for at least a while. Milo reasoned that unless they had watched the tapes, it was impossible for most people to understand the level of privacy involved in the situation.

He thought, however, that Dr. Teagan might.

It was almost ten minutes after their assigned appointment time, and Milo's hopes that Christine would not show were growing when Dr. Teagan emerged from behind the waiting room door, smiled, and asked for Milo to step in. He followed the doctor down a short hallway and then turned left into the office that he and Christine had occupied a week ago, a time when things seemed simpler and more hopeful than they did now.

Sitting beside Dr. Teagan's indoor plants, in the same seat that she had been sitting in a week ago, was Christine, arms crossed, glaring at Milo.

Milo stood for a moment in shock, trying to process the meaning of the situation.

How long had she been sitting there?

Had she come in a back door?

Why hadn't she met Milo in the waiting room?

Something, perhaps Christine's posture, the arch of her eyebrows, or maybe the way her right foot was gently but impatiently tapping on the carpet, told him that she had been there for a while. But why?

Milo had been standing in the doorway, staring at his wife for half a minute, before Dr. Teagan finally suggested that he take a seat beside Christine. He did, finding the position of the chair in relationship to his wife frustrating in that it did not allow him to see the look on her face without turning and staring. He suddenly felt ambushed and unable to gather information. Alone and outnumbered. To calm himself, he focused on the doctor, who took a seat beside his desk and began.

"Milo, I know you're surprised to see Christine here, but she called me on Monday morning and asked to talk before we all got together this afternoon. It's not uncommon, and given the circumstances involved, I thought it was a good idea. Christine, would you like to explain what we've been talking about to Milo?"

"I don't understand," Milo interjected. "What circumstances?"

"You scared the shit out of me, Milo. How did you think I would feel, having cops come to my door and tell me that my husband is sitting in his car outside the house, watching me?"

"C'mon, Christine. You know me. Do you really think I'm some kind of stalker? You know why I was there."

"No, I don't," Christine shot back. "How long have you been watching me, for Christ's sake? Were you out there every night?"

Milo was still too stunned to answer, unable to formulate a reasonable response to Christine's accusation. After a moment, Dr. Teagan spoke up. "Milo, that's not an unreasonable question. How many times have you done something like that prior to Sunday night?"

"That was the first and only time. I swear." He was still trying to recover from the shock of seeing Christine already in the office, and the barrage of questions wasn't allowing for him to even catch his breath.

"Can I ask why you chose that night to sit outside the house?"

The house, Milo noted. Not *your house*, which it still was. He chose to ignore the doctor's word choice for the moment. "You want to know why I chose that night? Did she tell you about Phil?"

"Just tell me your story, Milo," Dr. Teagan said. "What were you thinking at the time?"

"Fine. I stopped by in the afternoon to drop off some flowers for Christine. I thought it would be nice. She wasn't home, so I left. As I was leaving the house, she pulled in the driveway in this guy's Jeep. Phil. Some guy from her office."

"A man you had met before. Correct?"

"Yes, but like a year ago for half a second. I didn't remember who he was until Christine reminded me."

"Christine says that you became very angry in the driveway. What happened there?"

"This is ridiculous," Milo said, and immediately regretted it. The situation *was* ridiculous, but he understood that the doctor was just looking for Milo's side of the story, and that on its face value, the whole thing seemed ridiculous and stupid. Despite the justification for his anger, he could imagine how easy it had been for Christine to paint him like a jealous lunatic, and it appeared that she had done exactly that. He also knew that Dr. Teagan wanted to understand what had happened, but he couldn't help but feel that these questions were coming directly from Christine. Nevertheless, he had to try to make the doctor understand the truth of the situation. "When I saw Christine in that guy's Jeep, someone who I didn't know, I got jealous. And I had noticed a crib in our bedroom, and Phil had a baby in the backseat, so it just all looked bad to me."

"It wasn't a crib. It was a Pack and Play," Christine said.

"Whatever. It was something for the kid and it was in our bedroom."

"It wasn't like Phil and his daughter had moved in. They were visiting for the day and Phil needed a place for Penny to lie down. What the hell did you think was going on? Did you think he had moved in? That we were having sex while his daughter slept next to the bed?"

Milo didn't know what to say. He still couldn't believe that Dr. Teagan would allow him to be ambushed this way. Every word from the doctor's and Christine's mouths sounded planned,

186

plotted, and purposefully impossible to answer without sounding like a crazy person.

Finally, Dr. Teagan broke the silence. "Milo, I think that any reasonable person could see how you might have felt jealous after seeing your wife and this man pull into your driveway. I think Christine understands that too. But what concerns me is your decision to sit outside the house late at night, watching her. I don't think you're a stalker, but this is the kind of thing that a stalker does. Can you see how this might frighten your wife?"

"Yes, I do. And I'm sorry about it. It's just that I still didn't know what was going on between her and Phil. And I wanted to know. It was killing me not to know."

"*I told you.* I work with Phil. His wife died last year. He's been having a tough time lately and I offered to spend the day with him and his daughter. What more did you want to know?"

"I don't know. It just looked bad. You guys in the Jeep. The top down. The music that was playing. I don't know. It just looked like more than a couple friends spending the day together. And even if I had met Phil last year, you've never invited him over the house before. It just looked bad. It looked like a date."

"And what if it was a date, Milo? It was your brilliant idea to start dating again. Isn't this what you wanted?"

"In fairness, Christine," Dr. Teagan interjected. "I had suggested the idea of dating again."

"Fine, but you agreed, Milo. How do you think I feel, telling people that my husband and I are dating again? Oh, sure, he moved out, got his own goddamn apartment, but we're still having dinner and sex from time to time. We're hoping that dating again would make it all better. Isn't this what you wanted?"

"I didn't think we'd be dating other people. I thought this was supposed to be about me and you."

"You and me, huh? Then what about your mystery girl on the tapes? The cop told me that you had been watching a video on that goddamn camcorder. Are you going to try to tell me that it wasn't her on the tape?"

"I don't even know that girl. I've never met her. You know that. I'm just trying to find out who she is so I can return her camera." Milo was lying now, and he didn't like it. Too easy to get tripped up.

"Then why couldn't I watch the tapes too? And why in hell are you watching them outside the house, sitting in the car?"

Milo had no answer. No reasonable answer. He could try to explain the pressing need that he had felt, in terms of both watching the tapes and uncovering Christine's possible relationship with Thick-Neck Phil, but no matter how he tried to make Christine and Dr. Teagan understand, he knew it would come out wrong. He felt like he was trapped in one of those movies in which a perfectly sane protagonist cannot help but appear insane to the surrounding cast of characters.

At last, Dr. Teagan broke the silence. "Milo, I think that Christine's concern is reasonable, considering how important these tapes seem to have become to you and how little she knows about them or the woman who appears on them."

"I know that it looks bad, but if you had just seen the tapes, you would understand how wrong it would be to violate this woman's privacy. I feel awful doing it myself. But I started watching without knowing what I was getting into. I feel like I have to finish what I started, but letting someone else watch them seems . . . wrong. I can't do it."

"Can I ask why you were watching the tapes outside the house?" Dr. Teagan asked. "It seems an odd and almost purposefully risky decision to me."

"I know. I understand. But I just had to know what was going on with Christine. I couldn't just sit at home all night wondering if Christine was on a date with that guy."

"It wasn't a date, goddamn it!"

"Maybe we should——" But before Dr. Teagan could finish, Christine was heading for the door. "Christine, do you need a minute?" he asked.

"I need a hell of a lot more than a minute. Two nights ago the cops found my husband sitting outside my house in his car, watching another woman on videotape, and now he's accusing me of screwing around on him!"

Milo started to speak but was stopped by Dr. Teagan's voice. "Why don't we take ten minutes to cool down and then——"

"Not today," Christine said in a calmer tone. She had turned and was speaking directly to Dr. Teagan, avoiding eye contact with Milo entirely. "Okay? I just can't do this anymore today. I'm sorry."

Without even a glance in Milo's direction, she turned again and was out the door.

There was a protracted moment of silence in the small office before Dr. Teagan finally spoke. "You have to understand, Milo, that as innocent as your actions may have been, they were very disconcerting to Christine."

Dr. Teagan waited a moment, perhaps hoping that Milo would speak, but when Milo remained silent, he continued.

"And I can understand your wanting to know about the nature of her relationship with this man Phil, but unless she's given you reason to doubt her, accusing her of anything nefarious is probably out of line."

It was true that Christine had never given Milo a reason to not trust her, but even still, he knew that there was something going on between Thick-Neck Phil and his wife. Perhaps it was just a minor flirtation, but it wasn't as innocent as she made it seem. Even in the doctor's presence, she hadn't made it seem very innocent. *So what if it was a date?* she had asked. Though the question seemed to be hypothetical, Milo wondered if she hadn't been revealing some version of the truth.

The Jeep, the song on the radio, the mirrored sunglasses, the way that Christine had been wearing her hair that day, out of the customary ponytail that she favored, despite the wind that the topless vehicle would have generated. It would be impossible for Milo to convince Dr. Teagan that his intuition was undoubtedly accurate, but he knew that it was.

"Well, Milo, we have some time left if you'd like to talk."

This was exactly what Milo had hoped for. An opportunity to explain his plan and receive his therapist's seal of approval. He had played the conversation in his mind a hundred times over the past two days.

He would start by describing his plan to drive to Chisholm, North Carolina, in search of Tess Bryson. He would elaborate on his suspicions about the real reason that Tess Bryson had run away from home, using the information that he had uncovered about her father, Sean Bryson, and the time that he was serving in prison for molesting his niece, to support his claim. Dr. Teagan's eyebrows would rise in approval, and he would compliment Milo for his powers of deduction. *Though we can't be certain*, he would say, his hand stroking his chin, *I think it's a fair bet that you are correct. It's likely that Tess Bryson ran away from her father rather than from her home.*

Milo would then explain his goal: to find Tess Bryson and persuade her to call Freckles and tell her childhood friend that she was alive and well, thus relieving her friend of this ancient burden. Dr. Teagan would find this idea to be excellent in that it would serve the needs of both women. Tess Bryson, who had undoubtedly changed her name in order to hide from her father and the authorities, would be thrilled with the opportunity to thank her friend, and Freckles would finally be able to let go of the guilt and remorse that she had lived with for years. Milo suspected that Dr. Teagan would find the symmetry of the plan as beautiful as he did.

But how do you intend on finding her? he would ask.

Milo would admit that finding Tess Bryson would be a long shot, but he had a couple things going for him. First, Chisholm was a tiny mountain town with a population of fewer than five thousand people. If she was still in Chisholm, finding her would be considerably easier than finding the proverbial needle in a haystack. Also, according to what she had told Freckles years ago, Tess Bryson had family in the town, which made sense. Perhaps they also knew of Sean Bryson's predilections and had assisted Tess in disappearing. If Milo could locate one of these relatives and convince them of his sincerity, they might be willing to lead him right to her.

Dr. Teagan would undoubtedly mull this over a bit, warning Milo not to raise his hopes too much. A great deal of time had passed since Tess Bryson disappeared, and many things could have happened in that time. She could have moved. Any family living in the area could have also moved. She could be dead. He would warn Milo that while his intentions were noble, his probability of success was extremely low. Ultimately, he would offer Milo his blessing, declaring the journey to North Carolina an act of remarkable kindness and charity. One of which Christine would ultimately approve.

But Milo said nothing when Dr. Teagan asked if he'd like to talk. Instead, he sat there, staring at his shoes, imagining how easily their conversation could veer off Milo's projected course. As certain as he was that Dr. Teagan would find merit in his plan, he was afraid to face the possibility that the doctor would declare Milo's intentions to be ludicrous and foolish, and he felt crazy enough already after his conversation with Christine.

With such a long journey ahead, he could hardly bear the thought. Even if Milo also decided that his plan was foolish, turning back was now incomprehensible. The idea had taken on a life of its own, not unlike the demands that constantly plagued him. And though this demand had not originated from the same source as the demands for pressure seals and words like *conflagration*, it was no less pressing or insistent.

It had become impossible to ignore.

Besides, his bags were packed and loaded in the car. Half a dozen Weebles, two ice cube trays, twelve jars of Smucker's grape jelly, his bowling ball, and his entire DVD collection were piled in the backseat. The CDs were burned and loaded into the player, the engine oil had been changed, and the tank was filled with gasoline. The *Highlights* poem was safely in his pocket, along with Freckles's address and phone number.

He felt as ready as he ever would be.

All he had to do was drop off Skywalker with Andy and he would be on his way. He had four days to make it to North Carolina, find Tess Bryson, persuade her to call her grade school friend, and return home before his clients would need him. Though Dr. Teagan's words might serve as encouragement, he couldn't risk them doing otherwise. Not with so many miles that lay ahead.

And though he was loath to admit it, it had taken only seconds to realize that Dr. Teagan would never endorse his plan. As much as it had made sense to him, he once again felt like that perfectly sane protagonist armed with a perfectly insane idea. "No thanks, doc," Milo finally answered, rising to his feet. "There's something I've got to do."

chapter 20

The CDs hadn't worked out as well as Milo had planned. In the spirit of every movie character who had ever embarked on a road trip, Milo had prepared a playlist of classic road trip songs to carry him on his journey.

Taken from films such as *Forrest Gump*, *Garden State*, and *Jerry Maguire*, the songs on the two CDs Milo had burned included such classics as Bob Seger's "Against the Wind," Bob Dylan's "Blowin' in the Wind," Poison's "Ride the Wind," and less gusty numbers such as Peter Gabriel's "Solsbury Hill," Tom Petty's "Free Fallin'," and Springsteen's "Born to Run." But unlike in a film, when a three-minute montage can carry a character halfway across the country, Milo's playlist of more than thirty songs ran out before he even crossed the Connecticut state line, leaving him with the option of playing the same songs again or switching to a significantly less thematic soundtrack.

Either way, it was a less than auspicious start to his adventure.

Milo opted for Supertramp's *Greatest Hits*, an album that he wouldn't normally play in Christine's presence but one that he enjoyed a great deal when she was not around. Bands like Supertramp, Wham, and Abba weren't exactly the trendiest musical acts on the planet, so to play their songs in Christine's presence, as much as he liked them, risked appearing even less cool to her than he already feared he was. The album included Supertramp's minor hit "Take the Long Way Home," which wasn't such a good song for the beginning leg of a journey, but Milo made a mental note to add it to his return-trip playlist.

Milo rarely traveled far from home, and almost never farther than New York City. In fact, he had only left the Northeast once in his life, and that was during his honeymoon to Disney World, a trip that had been difficult to say the least. As he and Christine had boarded the flight to Orlando, the word *catatonic* had lodged itself in his head, eventually repeating with the pulsating monotony of a nuclear-powered metronome. It was three days later, while in the line for the Tower of Terror (a ride that Milo thought was aptly named), that he had managed to trick the mother of two disinterested teenagers into saying the word as a means of describing her sons' state of being after a three-hour wait under the hot Florida sun.

The entire trip had required more patience, endurance, and ingenuity than Milo could normally muster. Jelly jars had been nearly impossible to locate (a gift shop in Epcot Center sold miniature jars of souvenir jam, supposedly from various countries around the world, but none was nearly as satisfying to open as a twenty-ounce jar of Smucker's grape), and the ice cube trays in their hotel room were equally miniaturized, providing minimal relief when the need to pop cubes consumed him.

Though his needs made it nearly impossible to travel anywhere without undue stress, Milo had hoped that this trip would be different. He was alone and therefore better prepared for travel than ever before. Though he might have difficulty finding a bowling alley if the need to bowl a strike arose, he knew that his GPS would eventually help him locate one. After all, bowling was hardly an activity relegated to New England (though he had checked the Internet prior to leaving, just to be sure).

It was the intense need for secrecy that had always prevented him from being as prepared as he was for this trip. Stocking the trunk of the car with jelly jars, ice cube trays, Weebles, and a karaoke version of "99 Luftballons" on CD (among other things) had not been possible when Christine was accompanying him, and explaining the sudden need to stop at a bowling alley or a karaoke bar would have proven equally difficult. This time, there was no one from whom he would need to keep his secrets, and Milo found this freedom remarkably liberating.

After stopping for a fast food dinner at the Molly Pitcher rest area along the Jersey Turnpike, Milo continued on through southern New Jersey, hoping to reach the Washington, D.C., suburbs before finding a place to rest for the night. He had identified College Park, a town just north of the city, as a possible stopping point. Since the University of Maryland was situated in the center of this suburb, Milo presumed that accommodations would be easy to find.

It was around the time that he crossed the New Jersey–Delaware border that the word *placebo* suddenly lit up in Milo's head like a flashing detour sign on a rain-soaked highway.

One minute it wasn't there. The next minute it was.

He had suspected that it might be coming, had felt the characteristic building of pressure between his temples, but he had hoped that the symptoms would not culminate in a word. The discharging of ice cubes from a plastic tray perhaps, or even the bowling of a strike, would have been be easier to accomplish than finding a stranger in a strange land to utter a word as infrequently used as *placebo*, but somehow he had known it would be a word. Though impossible to fully describe, it was the texture of the ever-building pressure, its inexplicable nuance and flavor, that often allowed Milo to predict the requirement before it arrived. He had guessed that a word might be coming ever since crossing over the George Washington Bridge, and had been dreading it, knowing how difficult it would be to fulfill.

But still, there it was, pulsating in his head, a quiet hum now that would only grow more forceful as the hours passed.

Loquacious had been the first word to lodge itself in Milo's twelve-year-old mind, and when it did, he had assumed that his fixation had more to do with the desire for a definition rather than the need to hear another human being speak it aloud. Though he had experienced similar fixations in the past, he couldn't begin to understand how this word had suddenly taken up residence in his mind. He had been sitting on the school bus, third seat from the front as always, staring out the window at nothing in particular, when the word began its monotonous, unrelenting incantation in his mind. Milo had no idea what the word meant at the time, or where he had first heard it. In truth, he doubted that such a word even existed, but as the morning bus ride turned into American history with Mrs. Allen, math with Mrs. Schultz, band rehearsal (Milo had been a flutist), and recess, it became clear that the word was going nowhere fast.

It was after lunch, in the midst of science class, that he had finally found the time to look up the word in a dictionary and discover that it actually existed. He and his science partner, Taylor Thumma (lamentably not the newly breasted Amy McDonald), had been rolling steel spheres down varying degrees of slope and recording their trajectories on carbon paper for reasons that Milo still did not understand to this day. In between rolls, he had stolen off to the back of the room and had found the definition of the word in one of the *Webster's* dictionaries piled in a corner:

Loquacious: Talkative or chatty, full of excessive talk.

He had hoped that satisfying his curiosity would eliminate the unending repetition in his head, but it had not. Not that he was surprised. Though he had been praying that this was a mere instance of uncontrollable curiosity, he feared, and nearly expected, that it was more. Something in his gut had told Milo that this would be another of the many demands that were routinely placed upon him by some unknown force.

Demands that served no purpose other than to plague him.

As Mr. Morin, the science teacher with the floral bow tie and Hitler-like mustache who required his students to raise their dominant hand when asking a question, described the next series of experiments (which amounted to the rolling of more steel spheres), Milo came to understand what he must do in order to free himself of *loquacious*. It wasn't a sudden inspiration or a miraculous realization. It wasn't a brilliant moment of insight or the dawning of self-awareness. The solution had been there all along, out in the open, if you will, just waiting for Milo to confirm that a problem existed in need of it. Once Milo had determined that the demand of this word wasn't the result of curiosity or happenstance, he knew what must be done.

How he might achieve satisfaction had been another thing entirely.

As Milo turned off Route 95 onto Baltimore Avenue in the direction of the University of Maryland, *placebo* grew more persistent in his mind. It was nearly ten P.M., and he was ready to find a place to sleep for the night. Despite the new word having taken up residence in his head, Milo felt good. He had made it to College Park before having to stop for the night and could expect to be in North Carolina by the next afternoon. *Placebo* might slow him down a bit, but it wouldn't prevent him from getting a good night's sleep or making it to his destination on time or close to it. Thankfully, he had learned to assume some degree of control over these words long ago.

Twenty-one years before, a word like *placebo* would have already been careening throughout his brain, gaining volume and intensity without restraint. Part of the escalation, Milo had come to understand, was a result of his own fear that he would be unable to rid himself of the word. Anxiety and the strict secrecy that he maintained had fed the need, causing it to become more and more debilitating. But as Milo had found a means to alleviate each word, hundreds and perhaps thousands over the years, he had learned that the ability to remain confident and calm kept the demand temporarily at bay. Kept it manageable.

Loquacious had been anything but manageable.

By the end of the first day, *loquacious* was ruling Milo's middle school life. He found it impossible to concentrate on anything else for any length of time, and even *Dr. Who*, his favorite television program of the time, could not provide an escape from its echoing call. His sleep that first night had been fitful and broken as his fear that the word might consume him grew exponentially. For a time, he considered speaking to his parents about the problem, but, having successfully hidden his other oddities from them for years, he wasn't ready to let them in on this embarrassing secret.

His experience with Jimbo Powers and his mother had taught him better. There were parts of a person, of his person, at least, that were better left hidden, and from the moment that he had popped that red balloon up until *loquacious* entered his mind, he had managed to do so with surprising effectiveness. He wasn't about to start embarrassing himself now by telling his parents about this word trapped in his head. No matter what, he would not give anyone else, especially his mother and father, the chance to view him as some kind of monster.

But by the third day, Milo was in a near panic. Though he knew it wouldn't work, he had asked friends to repeat the word, not even bothering to create a backstory for the request. He had also written the word down on paper and asked Mrs. Allen to pronounce it for him, but still the word would not abate. He knew that the only way to rid himself of the word was to find a person who was speaking the word normally, as part of an unadulterated, uncontrived conversation, but that, he feared, might never happen.

Mr. Compopiano, Milo's short, perpetually sarcastic English teacher, finally presented Milo with a possible solution.

On the third day of *loquacious*, Mr. Compo, who Milo had always liked and found amusing, had assigned his students the task of writing an essay about any member of their family. Though Milo loved writing and often achieved high marks in his English classes, he doubted that he could get fifty words down on paper before accidentally writing *loquacious* at least a dozen times. It had become that omnipresent in his mind. This thought had provided Milo with his solution. Or at least the possibility of a solution.

Milo immediately put pen to paper, writing about a make-believe uncle named Jeremiah who lived in the make-believe town of Creedance, Kentucky. Uncle Jeremiah was the pariah of the family (the rhyme not lost on Milo) because of his excessive need to talk, regardless of the circumstances.

Stifled by a mouth filled with peanut butter and jelly, Milo wrote, Jeremiah would still manage to squeeze in a word or two between each chew.

During a sermon on Christmas Eve, Jeremiah's voice could be heard just beneath that of the minister.

Even while observing a moment of silence, Milo mused, Jeremiah would somehow find a way to get a few words in.

Throughout his essay, Milo did little more than describe Uncle Jeremiah's obsessive need to talk, using the words *chatty* and *talkative* twenty-nine times in the first 250 words, twice separating the two adjectives by a single comma. Once he had filled the front and back of a lined sheet of notebook paper, he brought his unfinished draft to Mr. Compo for a critique.

As Mr. Compo had done for every previous writing conference, he read the entire piece through once before saying a word.

"I must gauge the piece in its entirety," he would tell his students, who would be asked to sit on a short stool beside his desk, waiting for the would-be editor to finish. After reading, he would then sit quietly for up to a minute before speaking. That day was no different.

"Well, Milo," he finally began. "Your Uncle Jeremiah is quite an interesting guy."

"Yup," Milo agreed. "He talks a lot. Wicked chatty."

"Yes, I certainly got that from your essay. But isn't there more that you could say about your uncle? Other than his chattiness?"

"Yeah, and I still might, but that's the one thing that makes him unique. He's really talkative, Mr. Compo. And chatty too."

"Sure," Mr. Compo said. "But I think you might want to dig a little deeper for this essay. Show us other parts of his character. A man isn't made from a single part. You know what I'm saying?"

"Yup," Milo answered, feeling a surge of both anxiety and anticipation rise up in him. If his plan was to succeed, it would happen in any moment, and he could barely contain himself. He felt flush with excitement. His feet tapped involuntarily on the tiles beneath him, and his hands were folded tightly in his lap in order to minimize their trembling. If it was going to happen, it would happen now. Milo knew this in his heart.

"Now, as for the nitty-gritty . . ."

This is it, Milo had thought. *My chance. Please. Please, let it be my chance.* And at the same time, he wondered if the wait might have been worth it—if the enormous relief that he was about to experience was worth the three days of agonizing and distraction and worry. As foolish as it seemed, he thought it might be.

Mr. Compopiano was a fanatic when it came to increasing a student's vocabulary and believed in passing new words on to his class at every opportunity. Each week he assigned his students twenty new vocabulary words, each more archaic and multisyllabic than the last. Students were required to memorize the spelling and definition of each word for a quiz on Friday. Milo would not have been surprised to discover that *loquacious* had been on one of those lists, though he didn't remember ever studying it. "The greater your vocabulary," Mr. Compo routinely said, "the greater your ability to communicate."

Milo also suspected that Mr. Compo enjoyed using large and unusual words, and that he took great pride in hearing his students use them as well. As he finished critiquing a story or essay, he would routinely affix a Post-it note to the piece and begin a list of editing suggestions. Though this process often included suggestions related to punctuation and sentence structure, it invariably included a list of new vocabulary that the writer might consider adding to his or her piece.

Sometimes a writer would leave Mr. Compo's desk with a dozen Post-it notes covering his or her paper. If only Milo could be so lucky this time.

As many times as he used them, Milo had no doubt that Mr. Compo would provide alternatives for *chatty* and *talkative*. He just hoped that *loquacious* would be one of them.

"Obviously you didn't reread your piece, Milo," Mr. Compo began. "Or else you would've noticed that you used words like *talkative* quite a bit. I mean, they're all over the page."

"Yeah, I was so anxious to have you read the piece that I didn't really do any editing yet."

"Well, you could start by limiting the repetition in the piece and making some better word choices."

And then it happened. Like a thousand juice boxes punctured at once, *loquacious* burst forth from the lips of Marvin Compopiano, three syllables spoken at an ordinary volume but echoing vociferously in Milo's head. In that moment, all the tension and pressure of three days of agony were released. Milo's muscles instantly relaxed, his jaw, which he hadn't even realized was clenched, went slack, and his mind suddenly felt open, clear, and uncluttered for the first time in days. Most of the relief was the result of the actual word, but Milo also felt a small degree of pleasure and satisfaction with his plan coming together.

"*Loquacious* might be an excellent word choice for this piece, Milo. Have you ever heard it before?" Mr. Compo said, and in Milo's mind, angels sang.

There was no telling how long Milo sat beside his teacher, silent and unmoving, reveling in the moment, before Mr. Compo finally broke the silence.

"Milo? Are you all right?"

He was.

In fact, Milo was great. Better than he had been in days. Though there would be many words after *loquacious*, and for years, each of these words would carry a burden of anxiety and pressure that would weigh greatly on him, Milo could always look back on that first word and the challenges that it had presented and know that relief was possible.

After years of facing the challenge of words like *loquacious*, Milo had learned to manage their demands well. Though they were still accompanied by pressure, distraction, pain, and occasional anxiety depending on the difficulty of the word, he was usually able to remain composed and focused in the face of their monotonous calls.

And Milo was now beginning to understand how this ability to maintain a secret life might have doomed his marriage from the start. In many ways, he had lived through his three years of marriage on the edge, fearful that the wrong decision might cause him to lose Christine forever. For much of his life, beginning years ago with his teenage resignation to prostitutes in Chinatown, Milo had assumed that his future would be a solitary one. His inexplicable, indescribable demands, coupled with his nervousness around women and his garden-variety oddities, made the possibility of a long-term girlfriend, let alone a wife, incomprehensible. So when Christine, a fledgling attorney at a large practice in downtown Hartford, continued to show interest in him after three dates, Milo could hardly believe his good fortune, and so he did everything in his power to foster the relationship: flowers once a week, candlelit dinners at the finest restaurants in town, and the concealment of every quirk and idiosyncrasy in his formidable arsenal. He hid the bowling, the jelly jars, the ice cubes, the karaoke, and every other demand that his inner submariner placed upon him, rapidly building coping strategies to accommodate the new person in his life.

And thanks to Christine's presence, these coping strategies became more refined and easier to employ over the years. Simply put, her presence had required him to establish a life of subterfuge and quasi independence. By setting his own schedule, he could easily find thirty minutes in a day to sing karaoke, bowl a strike, or smash a Weeble. And when new demands arouse, these were also more easily managed. For example, Milo recently found himself needing to peel off half a dozen price tags from books at Borders Books and Music, a surprisingly persistent demand that had begun after finding several books during his move with the price tags still affixed. The removal of those tags from the books he already owned had been unexpectedly satisfying, the adhesive peeling off cleanly and with relative ease, but the need to remove more tags three days later had caught Milo off guard. Initially he considered purchasing books in order to satisfy the demand but realized upon entering the store that he could simply find a section unoccupied by customers and peel off as many price tags as he wanted. During his first visit, he found himself in the religion section, relieving fourteen King James Bibles of their $119.95 price tags.

Even though he wasn't a religious man, charging that much for Bibles seemed ludicrous to Milo. And rather than removing the tags from the store or stuffing them in a shelf, he layered them, one atop another, onto a fifteenth Bible, trying to limit his negative impact on the store.

This had taken place on a Tuesday afternoon, something that would have been impossible had he still been working at the hospital. As a result of his career shift and newfound scheduling freedom, the levels of stress and tension in Milo's life had reduced dramatically. Living with Christine had also taught him the value of preparedness and forethought, since his ability to leave the home at any hour without explanation was impossible once he and Christine decided to cohabitate.

Most important, in living with and marrying Christine, Milo had developed a degree of control over his demands that had not existed when he was younger. A year before meeting Christine, the idea of waiting twenty-four hours or more to visit the bowling alley after the demand for a strike lit up in his mind would have been unthinkable. But being forced to put these demands off for a time, even if doing so caused their intensity to increase, had allowed Milo to build the stamina required to hold back their surge. He could now go to sleep in a hotel room in Maryland with a word like *placebo* still ringing in his head, knowing that the next twenty-four hours would be difficult if he found no way to relieve himself of the word, but they would not be unbearable.

Thanks to Christine, Milo was now able to drive to North Carolina without much trepidation, knowing that his preparedness, his coping strategies, and his stamina would allow him to survive.

And it was this ability to better deal with his demands that had allowed him to move out in the first place, evacuating the insulating cushion of his home and routines when the opportunity had presented itself. The Milo of three years ago would have never responded to Christine's demands for space. Reliant on routine, comfortable in a passionless but convenient marriage, and secure in the sanctity of his secrets, Milo would have fought like a dog to remain in his home and would have likely made greater efforts to meet Christine's needs. But as he became better able to manage the demands placed on him, his need for Christine had waned.

Perhaps, Milo thought, he had been confusing need with love. As he lay in his hotel bed under the intermittent glow of passing headlights, Milo considered this for the first time and was surprised by the resonance of truth in the idea.

Had he loved Christine, or had he simply needed her? Needed someone to steady him, stabilize his life, and force him to adjust to the demands that had ruled his existence since that day with Jimbo Powers's red balloon.

But there had been love, Milo knew. He had loved the idea of the marriage and all that it brought to his life, and he still did. It was this love that had him trying to resurrect his relationship with Christine, or perhaps, more accurately, to establish a relationship based on more than just need and dependence. Milo had needed Christine in order to feel normal and safe, but now he found himself in a hotel room, alone, with *placebo* blazing away in his mind like the crimson Vacancy sign outside the hotel. At any moment, the need to crush a Weeble or pop a straw into a juice box or peel a price tag could strike, and yet he was relatively relaxed.

At ease, even.

This would all soon change.

chapter 21

In the film *My Cousin Vinny*, Vincent Gambini and Mona Lisa
Vito arrive in Beechum County, Alabama, to find the town set
around a main square, with the courthouse, hotel, diner, and the
rest of the town's businesses all essentially positioned within view
of one another, a slightly updated or seriously downgraded version of the town square in the *Back to the Future* films (depending on the film and Marty's position on the space-time
continuum). Though there are undoubtedly other parts of
Beechum County that remain unseen in the film, a visitor to this
fictitious town could conceivably park his car in the town square
and walk for the duration of his stay. This is how Milo had envisioned Chisholm, North Carolina, population 4,833: a small
southern town with a centralized square. But as it had with his
road trip playlists, the real-life version of Milo's cinematic imagi-
nation had proven to be quite different.

Though Chisholm had a Main Street populated with many
of the town's businesses, this street stretched for more than five
miles from end to end, making a walk from the Kroger's grocery
store on the south end of town to the post office on the north end
a lengthy trip. The entire town was larger and more spread out
than Milo could have ever imagined, with more than a dozen
restaurants, fast food joints, and diners along Main Street and its

immediate vicinity. Milo's vision of walking into the town's only diner, chatting it up with the busty, redheaded waitress who knew everyone in the place by his or her first name, and determining the location of Tess Bryson with a couple of cleverly framed questions had all but disappeared.

Adding to the difficulty of the situation was time. Though he had hoped to arrive in Chisholm by noon, several barriers had been placed in his way. The first had been *Butch Cassidy and the Sundance Kid*.

Rising with the sun, Milo had moved quickly, hoping to get an early start. He showered, dressed, and packed his clothing and toiletries, all while listening to Meredith Vieira and Matt Lauer juggle the incongruence of an interview with the secretary of defense alongside a story about a cat that had supposedly befriended a mouse in a West Virginia medical laboratory.

After a complimentary continental breakfast in the hotel lobby, he was on his way out the door, just after seven A.M., when he passed by a video rental kiosk near the hotel's entrance. Displayed at eye level were six films, one of which was *Butch Cassidy and the Sundance Kid*, a movie that held the same allure for Milo as episode 3 of the Star Wars prequels. It was the story of two bank robbers and their rise and fall from grace after seeming to tempt fate one too many times. Milo had seen the movie dozens, perhaps hundreds, of times, at first simply because he loved the film, despite its utterly bizarre musical sequence featuring B. J. Thomas singing "Rain Drops Keep Falling on My Head." But later on, Milo had found himself needing to watch the film, one of those insatiable demands linked to a hope, an expectation, that the end of the film, in which Butch and Sundance are gunned down by Bolivian law enforcement officials, might somehow change if he watched it often enough. Though Butch Cassidy and the Sundance Kid had fallen off in terms of cinematic demands of late, replaced by films like episode 3 (*Star Wars: Revenge of the*

Sith), *Saving Private Ryan*, *Jaws*, and *Titanic* (*Climb on the god-damn door, Jack!*), Milo was not surprised that his chance encounter with the DVD had reignited the demand.

Many of his demands were precipitated by outside stimuli.

Neither was he surprised that these movies continued to have this same attraction despite their persistently static endings. When the demand rose in Milo's mind, he simply answered the call. It was what he did. And when the need to watch one of these films struck, it was difficult for Milo to do anything else.

Already saddled with *placebo*, he had little choice.

Swiping his credit card, Milo paid the one-dollar rental fee and extracted the film from the tray along the bottom of the machine. He then returned to the hotel desk, where he asked the young woman who had just processed his bill moments ago if he could return to the same room for a couple of hours.

"You want to check back in?" she asked.

"No, I just want to keep my room for a couple more hours. I didn't need to check out until noon, so I just want to keep using the room. I'll still be out well before checkout time. Probably before ten."

"So you want to undo your checkout? Use the same room you stayed in last night for a while? Is that right?"

"Yes," Milo said.

"So you can watch that movie?" the woman asked, pointing at the DVD case under Milo's arm. The amused but friendly grin that had formed on the corners of her mouth, in combination with her slight southern drawl, made Milo feel at ease.

"Well, yes," he said. "Would that be all right?"

"Then why did you check out in the first place?"

Milo thought for a moment about lying, telling the woman that an early-morning meeting with a client had been pushed back until after lunch and he needed to kill some time, but he did not want to lie when it was not necessary. So he answered as honestly as possible. "I didn't know you had *Butch Cassidy and the Sundance Kid.* I saw it as I was walking out and decided that I just had to watch it. It's a classic, you know."

The use of the word *decided* made his explanation not entirely true, Milo knew, since he decided nothing when it came to his demands. Some unseen force always determined his next course of action, and he simply answered as best he could. Still, this answer was closer to honesty than even he had expected.

"Yeah, I like it too," the woman answered, still smiling. "I had to watch it in a film class a few years ago. In college. But its ending is so sad. It seems like a rotten way to start the day."

"I know," Milo said, relaxing a bit. Despite her beauty, the woman behind the counter seemed surprisingly down to earth. "But the rest of the movie is so good. Whenever I watch it, I try to imagine a different ending for Butch and Sundance, and sometimes, I secretly hope that it might happen. That if I watch it often enough, it might actually change someday. It never does, of course, but there's always hoping. Right?"

Milo was stunned by the level of honesty in his statement. He wasn't sure if he had ever been so honest about any of the demands placed on him with Christine, but he doubted it.

"Yeah. It would be nice if Butch and Sundance could live. I know they were bank robbers, but still. Not every thief is a bad guy. Right? Some are downright angels."

"I'm not sure if Butch and Sundance are angels," Milo said. "But they're all right in my book. They deserved a better fate, I think."

"All because of that stupid kid," she said, leaning in closer, almost conspiratorially. "Right? The one that sees the brand on their stolen horse, I mean. You know?"

Milo knew. What he didn't tell this woman, whose name, according to the gold badge on her chest, was Lily, was that he had screamed at this boy dozens of times, urging him, *to mind your own goddamn business and leave Butch and Sundance's horses alone.* It was this boy, who noticed that Butch and Sundance were riding a stolen horse, who ultimately led half the Bolivian army to the square where Butch and Sundance were gunned down.

"Yeah, I know," said Milo, also leaning in. "I hate that kid. I really do. He might be the worst character in all of movie history. But maybe today he'll mind his own business and let Butch and Sundance ride off into the sunset."

"There's always hoping."

Milo knew that all too well.

"Listen," said Lily. "I can't let you back in the room. Once I've checked you out, that's it. The cleaning crew is probably already in there, getting it ready for the next guest. You could pay for another night and I could put you in a different room, but that seems silly. Just to watch a movie, I mean."

"Yeah, it does," Milo said, thinking this might be his only solution.

"But what I can do is let you use the employee break room, just around the corner. There's a TV and DVD player in there, and the room should be empty this morning."

"I don't know," Milo said. "Won't you get in trouble for letting me use it?" In truth, Milo wasn't worried about possible disciplinary action against Lily. He thought that watching the movie among the other hotel employees would be awkward and uncomfortable, and he didn't want to spend the next two hours explaining himself to a bunch of curious strangers on a coffee break.

"The managers don't even go into that room. Last week one of the bartenders locked the door and had sex with her boyfriend on the lunch table. At least she said she did. I don't know her too well, so who knows? But I hardly think the boss would mind me allowing a guest to use the DVD player for a couple hours. Good customer service, right? And besides, the break room is down that hall, just past the restrooms. It's not like you need to come behind the counter or go through the kitchen."

"What about the other employees?" Milo asked. "Won't I be bothering them?"

"Not at all. There's only two or three of us left on duty from the night shift, and we all get off in less than an hour. The rest of the staff just came on at seven, so no one will go on break until later this morning. You'll probably have the room to yourself the whole time. Trust me. It's perfect."

Though Milo still wanted to decline the offer, finding the idea of using the break room too unorthodox and unpredictable, no alternatives were coming to mind. He had no choice but to watch the film, and soon. Lily's proposed solution only served to heighten the demand by creating an expectation of satisfaction. Rejecting this solution, as much as he might want to, was no longer possible. By the time he left the hotel and reached his car, the pain would have started, beginning with the viselike pressure on his brain, followed by the piercing of those imaginary acupuncture needles and accompanied by an inability to focus and even see clearly. Driving would become impossible, and on top of the need to watch the film, *placebo* would likely resume its thunderous call. Already, he could feel stirrings inside his head, threatening pain and discomfort if he did not act quickly. As with most of his demands, the proximity to their fulfillment only served to increase the pressure.

"Okay," Milo said, relenting to Lily and the growing threat in his mind. "But only if you're sure that you won't get in trouble."

"Don't be silly," Lily said. "Meet me by the restrooms down that hallway. I'll get someone to watch the desk and be right there."

Milo strode across the lobby in the direction that Lily had indicated, carrying his suitcase in one hand and the DVD in the other, and thinking that Lily's suggestion might not be so bad after all.

chapter 22

A short time later, Milo was sitting on a wooden bench, staring at a flat-screen television hanging at the far end of the room. The employee break room turned out to be a small, dimly lit rectangle consisting of a large wooden table surrounded by four sets of benches, a wall of ancient lime green lockers, a battered microwave and coffeemaker, and a small refrigerator tucked into a corner beneath a bulletin board full of OSHA notices, employee newsletters, and handwritten For Sale flyers. A Honda motorcycle, a hair dryer (*Like NEW!*), a three-legged lamp—and something in particular that caught Milo's eye:

For Sale: Unopened pancake mix.
Powdered or refridgeratored kind. I got both.
$2 each. No credit cards.

Below these two lines of text was a phone number.

Milo pointed to it as Lily removed the DVD player's remote control from a drawer beneath the coffeemaker. Now that she had come out from behind the counter, he had a better view of her. She was short, with a compact athlete's body. He wondered if she might have been standing on a box or a pile of phone books behind the counter but didn't dare ask.

"Oh," she said, examining the flyer. "That's Linda. Linda Errickson. She works down in the laundry, but she works part-time at Safeway too. Somehow she gets her hands on food from time to time and tries to sell it here. I don't know if the store manager gives it to her or she steals it or picks it out of the dumpster after it's expired, but sometimes she's got extra, and when she does, she tacks up a notice like that."

"Does it work?"

"Sometimes. Depends on what she's got, I think."

"And the *no credit cards* part?" Milo asked. "Does she really expect people to hand her a Visa?"

"I dunno. Just Linda being Linda I guess. Weird, huh?"

Milo nodded in agreement.

"But wait," she added. "Did you see the other flyer?" Lily was indicating a flyer on the far end of the bulletin board, which had initially escaped Milo's attention. It read:

For Sale: Pancake mix. Unopened. Refridgeratored or powdered. Both for sale. Only $1.75. Cash only. I can make change. Email me if you want to buy some. goodpricefood@gmail.com or you can ask Linda Errickson in Laundry about it.

"I don't get it," Milo said, stepping forward to take a better look at the second flyer.

"It's Linda. The same Linda as the first flyer. She says that people are more likely to buy her food if they think they're getting a deal. So she competes with herself."

"Does it work?"

"Who knows? Linda says she sells more food when she posts two flyers, but I think it's just because people are more likely to the see the sale if she has two flyers posted. Either way, she's an odd duck."

"Sounds like it," Milo agreed, though he couldn't help but marvel at the way that this woman was willing to publicize her oddity on a break room bulletin board for all to see. Perhaps she was unaware of her strangeness and was oblivious to the impression that she was making, but Milo didn't think so. It would be difficult for Linda to compare her flyers to the rest on the bulletin board and not recognize them as at least a little bizarre, and yet she posted them nevertheless.

He couldn't imagine why.

"So listen," Lily said. "Here's the remote. The DVD player is in that cabinet under the TV. Can you figure it out yourself, or do I need to show you how to get it working?"

"No, I'll be fine."

Lily told Milo that she would pop her head in to check on him before her shift ended, and then left the room. Before setting up the DVD, Milo pushed the table to one side of the room and placed a bench in front of the television in its place. Though he had no intention of sitting at the table, just the thought that it had been used as a platform for sex a week ago had made him cringe.

Despite the unusual location, Milo was feeling better as he loaded the disc into the player and waiting for the customary FBI warning and movie trailers to finish. Though *placebo* continued its monotonous call in his mind, it had migrated to the background ever since Milo had seen Butch and Sundance in the kiosk and ignited this new demand. He had no doubt that when the movie was over, *placebo* would reassert itself in his mind, but for now, it seemed content to allow Milo to complete this task without too much interference.

The film, which has a running time of one hour and fifty minutes, was just getting started when a large, dark-skinned Latino, dressed in blue coveralls, head covered by a red bandanna, entered the room and turned toward the wall of lockers. "Hey," he grumbled, casually taking note of Milo's presence.

"Hello," Milo answered, instantly wishing he had answered less formally. When the newcomer failed to respond or question his presence in the break room, Milo realized that the man had probably assumed he was just another employee. With a hotel this size, it was unlikely all the employees would know one another.

"What's that?" the man asked, slamming his locker shut and pointing at the television screen. He looked to be in his mid-thirties, wrapped in thick cords of muscle around his arms and neck. His face lacked any discernible emotion, and his eyes, brown and topped with a mass of bushy eyebrows, seemed to be trapped in a perpetual squint, as if someone were holding a flashlight to his face at all times.

"*Butch Cassidy and the Sundance Kid,*" Milo said, wondering if he should pause the film to respond. He didn't want to miss too much while conversing with this man, but he worried that pausing the film might invite additional conversation. After waiting a moment for him to respond, Milo added, "It's a classic."

The man said nothing.

Milo turned back toward the television and tried to refocus on the film, but, unsure of what the stranger was doing behind him, he found it difficult. No sound of the door opening or closing. No shuffling of footfalls. No scrape of bench against tile floor. Just silence, as if the man were standing directly behind Milo, eyes fixed on the television screen, or on him.

Milo was ready to turn and check on the man's position again when the overhead lights switched off and the man plopped down on the bench beside him. At this proximity, Milo could smell the aroma of bleach and sweat.

"Is it any good?" the man asked.

"What? The movie?"

"Yeah. The movie. Is it any good?"

"Yeah, it is," Milo said. "One of my favorites."

"Cool."

Assuming that the man was finished speaking, Milo returned his attention to the television. Though he would prefer to watch alone, he couldn't envision any means of extricating this large man from the break room, so he tried to make the best of an awkward situation. At least the guy had thought to shut off the lights. He had to admit that it made for a much better viewing experience.

The two men had been watching together for about ten minutes (Milo had just begun to forget about the man sitting beside him and get absorbed in the film) when the door to the break room opened again and the lights came on.

It was Lily.

"Hi. How's the movie?"

"It's good," Milo said, turning on the bench to face her. "The same as always, but good."

"I know this sounds weird, but I just got off my shift and I was wondering, if you're still watching the movie, would you mind if I joined you?"

"Hey. Pause it," the man said, pointing at the remote control in Milo's hand.

"Sorry." Milo fumbled for the pause button, finally managing to freeze the action on screen.

"I see you met Eugene," Lily said with a smile.

"We sort of skipped the introductions," Milo said.

"Hey, don't start the movie yet. Let me use the can. Okay?"

"No problem," Milo assured Eugene as he left the room.

Lily waited for the door to close before speaking. "Sorry about Eugene. He works nights and usually goes home right after work. I didn't think he'd stay and watch."

"It's no problem. I don't mind."

"So do you mind if I watch? I was going to ask you down in the lobby if you wanted some company, but I didn't want to sound crazy or make you think that I was coming on to you. You're married, I know. I saw the ring. But I've got to meet my mother at the hair salon around ten, so I thought I might watch the rest of *Butch and Sundance* with you, if you're still watching. And if you don't mind."

Lily had changed out of her maroon jacket and matching slacks and was now wearing a pink T-shirt, a pair of blue jeans, and sneakers. Her auburn hair was now down, falling over her shoulders, and the makeup that Milo hadn't noticed before was gone. For the first time, Milo noticed her green eyes and freckled cheeks. *Freckles, freckles, everywhere,* he thought.

"I'm sorry," Lily began, backing toward the door when Milo failed to respond. "I didn't mean . . ."

"No. I mean, no, you should. I mean, it's fine. Please. Sit down."

"Thanks. I'm Lily, by the way."

"Yeah, I saw your badge. Nice to meet you. I'm Milo."

Lily took up a position on the other side of the bench from where Eugene had been sitting, and a moment later, Eugene reentered the room, cutting off any further discussion. He switched off the lights and resumed his position on the bench, sandwiching Milo between him and Lily.

"I hope this isn't too weird," Lily said as Milo raised the remote control and pointed it at the DVD player. "I just thought it would be fun."

"Not weird at all," Milo said, thinking otherwise. "We've been watching for a little while, though. Do you want me to rewind?"

"You didn't ask me if I wanted to rewind," Eugene said.

"No. Don't be silly. I've seen the movie before. Go ahead and hit play."

Milo did. On screen, Butch Cassidy, played by Paul Newman, and the Sundance Kid, played by Robert Redford, were lounging

on a balcony above their favorite saloon, basking in their presumed invulnerability. None of the men gathered in the street
below was willing to answer the sheriff's call for a posse, meaning there would be no pursuit after the outlaws' recent train
heist. Milo knew that this was the high point of the film for
Butch and Sundance, the moment at which everything seemed
good and right. In less than fifteen minutes, things would drastically change for his beloved bank robbers.

Moments later, the voice of the sheriff was replaced by that
of a bicycle salesman, who was taking advantage of the gathering
crowd to pitch his new device.

"Who would buy a bicycle when the streets are all dirt and
stuff?" Eugene asked.

"Be quiet!" Lily said, raising her finger to her lips.

On screen, the scene had shifted to a small farmhouse outside
of town. Sundance and his lover, Etta Place, were sharing a moment together in bed. Though the scene was hardly racy by
today's Hollywood standards, the mere implication of sex, in
combination with his companion and their current seating
arrangement, made Milo think again of Christine. What would
she think of all this? He was sitting in a darkened room with a
beautiful woman whom he had known less than an hour, watching two people on television roll around in bed together. Regardless of the innocence of his intentions, he couldn't help but feel
guilty, and he was certain that Christine would see it this way,
and probably worse. If so, Milo could hardly blame her. He had
thought that Thick-Neck Phil and his top-down Jeep and mirrored sunglasses had been bad. But this was downright illicit,
even with Eugene sitting to his right. In response to these
thoughts, Milo leaned closer to Eugene, increasing the distance
between him and Lily. He straightened his back, pulled his knees
together (considered crossing his legs for a moment but then
thought otherwise), and folded his hands on his lap, in the hopes

that this position would somehow enhance the visual purity of the situation in the event that anyone else walked in.

He knew it was crazy, but it nevertheless made him feel better.

Seconds later, the on-screen action shifted again to the infamous "Raindrops Keep Falling on My Head" scene, in which Butch takes Etta on an early-morning, dialogue-free bicycle ride around the farm.

"Did you know that Paul Newman did all the bicycle stunts himself?" Milo asked, taking advantage of the absence of dialogue. "The stuntman couldn't stay on the bike, so Newman did everything except for one fall. A cinematographer had to do that one."

"No, I didn't know that," Lily said, eyes still locked on the screen. Milo had hoped that his knowledge of the film might impress her, but Lily seemed utterly uninterested in this cinematic tidbit. A moment later, she spoke again, this time turning to face him. "The thing is, Etta wants to be with Butch. Or at least part of her does. The sensible part."

"Huh?"

"Etta," she said, turning back to the screen. "She wants to be with Butch. See her on the bike with him? You can tell. Sundance might be the good-looking guy, the fastest draw in the West, the guy that every girl wants to sleep with, but Butch is the guy who every girl wants to marry. Or the guy who every girl should marry, at least. He's the kind of guy who reminds you of your father. He's safe. For a bank robber, I mean. He's safe and dependable and loyal. You can trust Butch. And that's the sticky part. Sticky for Etta and sticky for the rest of us too."

Milo waited for Lily to continue. On screen, Etta was hanging her feet out of a hayloft, throwing hay down at Butch as he rode in circles in front of the barn. Finally, when it was clear that Lily wasn't going to continue, he said, "I don't get it. What's the sticky part?"

"Who a girl chooses to marry. A girl has to decide whether she wants the dangerous guy or the safe guy. Marry the dangerous one and your life may be exciting, but you're just as likely to end up pregnant and alone, or even worse. Marry the safe guy and you'll always have your man beside you, but you risk a lifetime of boredom. That's what Etta's problem is. Her dilemma. Butch or Sundance? Safe or dangerous? Like most girls, she chooses dangerous. But you can tell that part of her wants to choose Butch. Just look at her. Even Sundance knows it."

"You're crazy, Lily," Eugene said in a whisper, as if the three were sitting in an actual movie theater. "All girls care about is money. Who got the biggest paycheck."

"Shut up, Eugene," Lily whispered back. "You don't know what the hell you're talking about. When was the last time you even had a girlfriend?"

"I don't want a girlfriend," Eugene countered. "Too damn expensive."

Milo couldn't help but wonder if Christine saw things the same way Lily (and perhaps Etta Place) did. Did she equate her husband to a law-abiding, exponentially safer version of Butch Cassidy? Was Christine suffering from a lifetime of boredom?

And if so, was Thick-Neck Phil currently starring in the role of Sundance?

Milo tried to push those thoughts out of his mind and focus on the film. "Well, at least that makes this scene a little more bearable. The way you describe it, I mean."

"You don't like it?"

"I hate this scene. It nearly ruins the movie. Sticks out like a sore thumb. It's like one minute I'm watching a Western and the next I'm watching some ridiculous musical. I have no idea what the director"—who Milo knew was George Roy Hill, Academy Award winner and two-time nominee who died in December of 2002—"could have been thinking when he included this scene."

"Oh, but I love it," Lily said. "I think it says so much, and without any words. Without any dialogue, at least. The song isn't so important. I could take it or leave it. That doesn't matter so much. Just the way Butch and Etta are together. They way they want to be together but can't. The scene says it all, but without a single word. It's perfect." She paused a moment before adding, "But a couple of people in my film class felt the way you do, so you're not alone, Milo."

"I'm with you, man," Eugene said, still whispering. "This scene sucks."

Milo, Lily, and Eugene sat silently on their wooden bench as Butch and Sundance botched the second robbery of the Union Pacific Flyer, blowing up the safe and the money in the process. They laughed at the conversation between Butch and Woodcock, the man assigned to guard the safe, and especially at Woodcock, the spectacled, mousy, unlikely protector of anything precious.

> Butch, you know that if it were my money, there is nobody that I would rather have steal it than you.

A minute later, the second train, loaded with a posse specially trained to hunt and kill Butch and Sundance, arrived on the scene and the chase was on.

"Oh, shit," Eugene murmured to himself. "This ain't good."

Eugene was right, Milo knew. Across miles and miles of desert and scrubland, the posse, led by a man in a white hat, followed Butch and Sundance, undeterred.

The three sat nearly silently for the next hour, watching Butch and Sundance and Etta make their way to Bolivia, where the duo, aided by Etta's lessons in Spanish, resumed their bank robbing ways. As Milo sat and looked on, the desire to see the film end differently and the resulting pressure of anticipation grew as Butch and Sundance drew closer and closer to their fate.

But even if the universe had wanted to change the ending of the movie, allowing Butch and Sundance to survive *this one time*, he doubted that it would happen on this day, when he was in the presence of two other people. To witness a miracle alone seemed entirely possible to Milo. It *had to be possible* for the incessant demands to watch these films over and over again to make any sense. Though it ran contrary to everything he believed, Milo was certain that someday, his persistence would pay off. Butch and Sundance would survive, Mace Windu would strike down Palpatine, Quint would dodge the jaws of the great white shark, and Jack would climb on that goddamn door with Rose. But to witness one of these miracles in the company of another seemed highly unlikely.

In Milo's mind, one of the key components of a miracle was the ability of the majority to discount its having ever taken place.

Nevertheless, as Butch and Sundance took jobs as payroll guards in an attempt to go legit, Milo felt the pressure building more and more, knowing that if they could just save the mining boss, Percy Gather, and protect the payroll that he was transporting up the mountain, they could have a chance at a normal life. Milo had argued more than once with Andy, another fan of the film, over the merits of a normal life for Butch and Sundance. Andy's contention was that Butch Cassidy and the Sundance Kid were not meant to live a normal life, and that they should instead be admired for their chosen path. "Butch and the Sundance Kid were bank robbers," Andy had said. "Both the real and fictional versions of them. And they were damn good ones at that. That's more than most of us can ever claim of ourselves."

But for someone who craved normalcy as much as Milo did and understood the difficulty in being anything but normal, he suspected that if given a chance, even the Sundance Kid would've taken a wife, three kids, and the life of a rancher over his chosen profession.

Normalcy, in Milo's mind, was consistently underrated by the normal.

"I love this guy," Lily whispered, seeming to unconsciously adopt the same movie-house etiquette as Eugene. She was referencing the mine boss, Percy Gather, who was seconds away from being shot in the chest by Bolivian bandits—unless the universe decided to intervene.

"That old guy?" Eugene asked. "Are you crazy?"

"I love him too," Milo said, and he meant it. Percy Gather was someone to whom Edith Marchand might refer as *a character* and whom Arthur Friedman would surely call *a goddamn idiot;* a wild-eyed expatriate who couldn't spit tobacco straight but never stopped trying and who described himself to Butch and Sundance with six words that Milo had clung to during his darkest moments:

I'm not crazy; I'm just colorful.

It was easy for Milo to fear that the demands placed upon him were a symptom of insanity, and though he had learned to live with them and almost accept them as part of his life, his greatest fear was that they were simply the tip of the iceberg, the beginning of something more, the first steps in his descent into madness. So far, this had not been the case. The demands had changed over the years, some falling by the wayside while others took their place. Overall, the demands had increased in variety and frequency, but they had remained the extent of his insanity, its only symptom. And whenever Milo began to think of it as insanity, he would think of the old expatriate prospector Percy Gather, who was not crazy.

Just colorful.

The universe did not choose to intervene in Percy Gather's fate today, and so he was once again shot in the chest and the movie went on. Perhaps because Lily and Eugene were sitting beside him and the chances that the ending might change seemed even slimmer than usual, Milo did not feel the usual level of tension building as Butch and Sundance's stolen horse was spotted by that nosy little boy, or when dozens of Bolivian soldiers surrounded the marketplace.

"Damn," Eugene said, leaning in toward Milo. "That little son of a bitch. Don't tell me how it's gonna end, but are those boys gonna die?"

"Just watch," Milo suggested, unable to suppress a grin at Eugene's contradictory request.

"This was stupid," Lily said, her voice sounding even softer than before. "Why did I do this to myself? I was right when I said that this is lousy way to start off the day."

"Do you want me to stop the movie?" Milo asked, knowing she would decline. To stop now would leave the demand unsatisfied and even more potent.

"Hell, no!" Eugene said, and Milo noticed for the first time that the large man was sitting on the edge of his seat.

"Don't be ridiculous," Lily added. "It's sad, but it's the right ending too. I mean, how else could it end?"

"They could ride off into the sunset," Milo suggested, envisioning the ending that he hoped for each time he watched the film, including today. "Or maybe they could go legit. Start a little business together. Sundance could marry Etta, and Butch could find a girl of his own."

"Good Lord, Milo. Thank goodness you weren't in charge of the script. That would've just about killed the movie."

"But I thought you said that you wished the ending were different too."

"Of course I do," Lily said. "I don't want Butch and Sundance to die."

"They're gonna die?" Eugene nearly shouted. "Damn. Why did you tell me?"

"You just asked Milo to tell you."

"I know, but he was smart enough not to tell me. Damn, Lily. You just ruined it for me."

"They have to die," Lily said. "That's what makes the movie so great. Just look." She was pointing at the screen, where Butch and Sundance were reloading their guns. "Even in the end, as they are getting ready to charge out into the town square and face all those soldiers, they're chatting away like it's just another ordinary afternoon together. They're both shot, probably bleeding to death already, and they talk about going to Australia like it might actually happen. Have you ever seen two braver men?"

Milo wanted to assure Lily that it might happen someday, regardless of how hopeless their situation appeared. Butch and Sundance might make it to Australia, if Milo watched often enough. Instead he asked, "But why do they have to die? Why can't they slip out the back and end their lives as cattle ranchers in Australia?"

"Yeah," Eugene said, sounding genuinely emotional. "Why can't they?"

"Because sometimes bravery requires death. Butch and Sundance have to die so that we can love them."

"That's bullshit," Eugene said. "Bullshit."

"It's all right, Eugene," Lily said, reaching across Milo's lap in order to squeeze his hand.

As Lily said these final words, almost in a whisper, Butch and Sundance launched themselves into the open square, guns drawn. A second later the image of the two men froze, turned sepia, and the sound of a thousand gunshots filled the break room.

Lily, Milo and Eugene sat silent for almost a minute as the credits began to roll. As expected, the ending had satisfied the demand placed on Milo, but the relief that he typically felt was muted. He didn't mind. He had enjoyed watching the film with Lily and Eugene. But before he even had time to stand up, *placebo* had returned to the foreground of his mind, as persistent as ever.

"Well, thanks for letting me watch that with you, Milo," Lily said, rising from the bench and switching on the lights. "Eugene, are you crying?"

"Fuck you, Lily. I ain't crying. I might be crying 'cause I just wasted two hours of my life, but I ain't crying." He rose from the bench and exited the room, head down.

"He cried when the Giants won the Super Bowl too. He'll be fine."

"He's a nice guy, huh?"

"Yup. Most big lugs are. I've worked with him for five years now. You know, a couple months ago, he walked me to my classes after a girl was attacked on campus. Not hitting on me or anything. Just being nice."

"It's good to have friends like that," Milo said.

"Yes, it is. Listen, Milo. I've got to run if I'm going to be on time for my mom. But this was great. Thanks for . . . I don't know. For letting me watch the movie with you and not thinking I was crazy."

"Hey, I was the one who wanted my room back to watch a movie I've seen a dozen times," Milo said, knowing the number was much higher. "If anyone acted crazy today, it was me."

"I don't think so, Milo. You may be a little sentimental, but you're certainly not crazy. It's a damn good movie. Worth watching again and again." Lily extended a hand and Milo reached out to shake it, but before he could clasp her palm, she had converted the handshake into a brief, somewhat awkward hug. Then she turned, said one final "Bye," and was off.

Before Lily had even disappeared from view, the ring of *placebo* forced him get moving once again.

Chisholm, North Carolina, waited.

Before Milo could resume his journey south, however, *placebo* would need to be satisfied. Milo's solution had come to him while brushing his teeth earlier that morning, and for that bit of seemingly divine inspiration, he had been thankful. So far away from home and without his customary resources, he had started to worry about how he might meet this demand. But in the end, the solution had actually been easier than most. Ten miles south of the hotel, Milo stopped at his third pharmacy that morning and finally found success.

"Good morning," he said to the pharmacist, a middle-aged man wearing glasses and a yellow bow tie, looking a little bit like a modern-day Woodcock, Milo thought. "I have an odd request. I'm traveling with my daughter, who gets car sick anytime we're on the road more than an hour. We used to give her Dramamine, but about a year ago, our doctor prescribed . . . What do you call it? A fake pill? The one that makes her think that she's taking real medicine?"

"Oh, you need a placebo?"

"Yes," Milo said, trying to mask the wave of relief washing over his body on hearing the word spoken. "A placebo." The first two pharmacists had failed to use the word, referring to them instead as sugar pills. But the modern-day Woodcock had come through.

"So the placebo helps her with the motion sickness?" the pharmacist asked.

Milo said yes, answered a few more questions, laughed at a bad joke, and finally left the pharmacy with a dozen sugar pills, free of charge. There were twenty more already in the car from his previous two stops.

Finally, after all these distractions—*Butch and Sundance,* Lily and Eugene, and *placebo*—Milo pulled into Chisholm, North Carolina. By the time he brought the car to a halt in the gravel parking lot of the Town Chef, a diner on Main Street, it was after five o'clock. He was tired, hungry, and once again in need of the restroom.

As he entered the restaurant to the sound of bells ringing above the door, he was pleased to see a redheaded waitress behind the counter, chewing gum, drying a plate, and welcoming him with a smile.

Town square or not, maybe things were looking up.

chapter 23

Prior to leaving for North Carolina, Milo had acquired several
bits of information that he thought might assist him with his
search of Tess Bryson.

In reading additional news reports of Sean Bryson's arrest
and conviction, he found that the niece whom Bryson had mo-
lested had been on his wife's side and that his wife's maiden
name was Plante. He also found that Sean Bryson's wife, Tess
Bryson's mother, had died of pancreatic cancer a year before her
husband had been arrested.

Milo wondered if Tess Bryson had ever returned to Massachusetts to attend the funeral or visit her mother's grave. Probably not the funeral, but maybe the cemetery, he thought. That is,
if she was still alive.

Next, he conducted a search on WhitePages.com for the last
names Plante and Bryson in Chisholm, North Carolina, and
found two Brysons and one Plante within the town's limits. He
had the addresses and phone numbers for all three of them.

Emily and Michael Bryson, presumably married, lived at 107
Federal Street.

Kelly Plante lived at 9 Summer Street.

Milo had no way of knowing if any of these people were related to Tess Bryson, or even to one another, but he thought it

was a good start, and based on the size of the town, he thought his chances were excellent that at least one was related to Tess. In truth, he hadn't expected to find a single Plante or a Bryson in the entire town, so he considered finding three an absolute boon.

Most surprising, Milo spent less than thirty minutes gathering this information, and with little expertise on his part. As he sat in traffic on the George Washington Bridge, he had begun wondering how much more he could have uncovered with the help of a private investigator. Probably a lot.

In the twenty years since Tess Bryson disappeared, the Internet had made information of this kind readily accessible to any novice researcher, and he couldn't help but feel bad for Freckles, who probably could've acquired this same information at the time of Tess Bryson's disappearance had the Internet existed in its present form.

In the same vein, did Tess Bryson even know that her mother was dead?

So much pain and uncertainty simply because of a lack of information. Still, there was no telling if these names, addresses, and phone numbers would prove to be fruitful, or if, once again, Milo's hunch was right and Tess Bryson was still alive.

Milo chose the Town Chef over the half a dozen or so diners and restaurants that lined the five miles of Main Street because it had the fewest cars in its dirt parking lot (just two). His hope was to engage in conversation with one of the waitresses and he thought that if there weren't many customers, his chances of speaking at any length with the waitress would be better.

"Sit wherever you'd like," the redheaded woman said in a distinct southern drawl, motioning to the right, where the restaurant extended thirty feet like a greasy finger. The Town Chef consisted of a tiled counter wrapping around the far end of the restaurant (where Milo had entered) and extending halfway down the length of the side wall, where it gave way to an area of booths and tables. Behind the counter were coffeemakers, a soda dispenser, stacks of white plates and racks of glasses, and a swinging door that presumably led to the kitchen. Short, vinyl-covered stools were spaced along the counter, which was cluttered with napkin dispensers, sugar bowls, paper place mats advertising local businesses, and (much to Milo's horror) ashtrays. Two men were sitting at the counter, both silent and drinking coffee. The rest of the restaurant was empty.

Milo chose the booth closest to the end of the counter. Though sitting at the counter would've been ideal, allowing for more frequent contact with the waitress, he feared that the waitress would be less willing to speak about private matters in the presence of others. Distance between him and the two men at the counter would be important if a meaningful conversation were to take place.

The waitress approached a moment later with a menu, which amounted to a single sheet of paper, printed on both sides and laminated. It appeared to be about a thousand years old, and Milo tried desperately to disguise his disgust as the filthy thing was dropped into his hands. It was still sticky around the corners with pancake syrup from the morning's breakfast, or perhaps from a breakfast served on the morning of Kennedy's assassination.

There was simply no telling, and neither did Milo really want to know.

"Hi. I'm Macy," the woman said, bending at the knees to bring her nearly six-foot frame into better view. "It's you and me tonight, hon. Can I get you something to drink?"

"Water, please. Thanks. I'm Milo, by the way."

"Nice to meet you, Milo."

Macy departed, leaving Milo to plot his next move. In the films, this busty redhead, who couldn't have fit the bill any better, would undoubtedly be the town gossip, knowledgeable about all of Chisholm's deepest, darkest secrets. But Milo suspected that this real-life version might not live up to her fictional counterpart.

Even so, the fact that Macy was the picture of the gossip-driven, small-town waitress, right down to her peach-colored uniform, white sneakers, and voluptuous figure, gave Milo hope that she would prove to be as helpful and obliging as her image betrayed. The way she chewed her gum, tucked her pencil into the bun in her hair, and spoke with that deep-fried southern accent gave every indication that this woman might just be the real deal. The lady with all the answers.

How to extract the necessary information from Macy would be the challenge.

A moment later, she returned with water and asked if she could take Milo's order. Though Milo had yet to look at the menu, he wanted Macy to like him and believe him to be competent, so he ordered a cheeseburger and fries, assuming both were on the menu in some form.

"Will that be all?"

"Actually, I was wondering if you could suggest a hotel close by. I'm from Connecticut and need a place to stay the night."

"Connecticut, huh? What brings you here?"

"I'm hoping to look up an old friend who moved down here years ago." Milo couldn't be more pleased with Macy's question. It provided the opening that he would need.

"Well," she said, gnawing on the eraser of her pencil as she considered the question. "The nearest hotel that I can think of is in Taylorsville, but that's about twenty minutes south of here. There are a couple motels in town, though. The closest, probably the best, is about a mile down Lincoln Road, which is right off Main. Pineview or Pinehurst. Pine something-or-other. It'll be on the right, just past the church."

"That's great. Thanks."

Milo decided not to push his inquiries too hard at first. Better to space out his questions throughout the meal so as to not seem desperate. As he was plotting his next move, his cell phone rang. Not recognizing the number, he answered on the second ring.

"Milo Slade?" the voice asked, one with which Milo was familiar but could not place.

"Yes?"

"Hello, Mr. Slade. It's Officer Eblen of the Newington Police."

Unsure of what to say, Milo said nothing, suddenly feeling both angry and frightened.

"Mr. Slade, can I ask where you are at this moment?"

"Why do you want to know?" Milo asked, regretting the words as soon as he had said them.

"You won't answer the question?" Officer Eblen asked.

"No, I just want to know why you're asking."

"Mr. Slade, your wife thinks that she saw your car sitting outside the house about fifteen minutes ago. Is that true?"

"No. It's not. In fact, it's impossible. I'm in North Carolina right now. And I brought my car with me. I mean, I drove here. With my car. In my car, I mean. It couldn't be in Newington." Milo could never understand how he could be so composed around his clients and so useless around everyone else in life, and especially men like Officer Eblen.

"So you haven't seen your wife all day?"

"No," Milo said, fearing that he sounded like a petulant child.

"Have you seen your wife since we last spoke?"

"Yes," Milo said. "Once in the therapist's office, but that was it."

"No more late-night stakeouts outside the house?"

"I told you. That was the only time. I'm not a stalker."

"Listen, Mr. Slade. Separation and divorce can be tough on folks. I've seen too many people do too many stupid things because someone stopping loving them. I just don't want you to do anything stupid."

"Don't worry. I won't."

"Most people don't think they will," Officer Eblen said, his voice softening a bit. "They think they're handling things just fine, and then boom. They realize that their marriage might be ending and they lose their head. Men more often than women. Remember that, Mr. Slade. You never know how you might react. So don't be stupid."

"That won't happen to me."

"I've heard that before," Officer Eblen said. "What makes you so sure?"

"I don't know. I don't think I care anymore, to be honest. I don't think I love her anymore." Milo paused a moment, checking to see how this last statement felt. Checking to see if there was truth in these words. "You know what? I don't think I do. Wow. Can you believe it? I think my marriage is over, and I'm okay with that. And you were the first one to know. I don't even think I knew it myself until just now."

"My condolences, Mr. Slade. Let's just keep the divorce as friendly as possible, okay?"

"Thanks," Milo said, appreciating the sincerity in Eblen's voice. "I will."

"Okay. And listen. I hope this all works out for you. I really do. But don't screw it up, no matter what happens. You're feeling fine now, but when she tries to take the house or demands alimony, it might not be so easy anymore. Guys can get stupid. Don't do anything that will bring me and Officer Heyer back out to see you. All right?"

"I know you're just doing your job, but you've got nothing to worry about."

"Good. Have a good night, Mr. Slade. Oh, one more thing.

You never answered my question. Why are you in North Carolina?"

Milo thought about explaining his plan to Officer Eblen, even requesting his advice in terms of finding Tess Bryson, but he quickly thought otherwise. Less than forty-eight hours before, Eblen had thought that Milo was a stalker, and he still might be thinking it. No need to tell him that he traveled almost seven hundred miles to find a girl who he had never met before.

"Visiting a friend," Milo said.

The two men said goodbye, and just as Milo was tucking his cell phone back into his coat pocket, Macy returned with dinner. There was mayonnaise on the burger, a condiment that Milo despised with every fiber of his being, but, wanting to remain in Macy's good graces, he accepted the burger with a smile and then tried to scrape off as much of the vile substance as he could before eating.

Milo had finished off most of the burger and about half of the fries when Macy returned to check on him.

"Will there be anything else, hon?"

"No, thanks. I've got to get a move on."

Macy placed the check upside down on the table in a gesture that Milo had always appreciated. It somehow conveyed the idea that the waitress and the customer had a secret between them, a secret that the public could see and accept without needing to know the details. It was an acknowledgment by all of society that certain things are better kept unknown. Hidden away. He liked that and wished the gesture extended to more aspects of his life.

"I'll take this at the counter whenever you're ready," Macy said, pointing to the cash register at the far end of the restaurant. In following her gesture, Milo noted that the two coffee drinkers had exited the restaurant, leaving them alone. Just the two of them. Better than he had hoped.

"Actually, can I ask you a question, Macy?"

"Sure. Shoot."

The woman bent her knees again, this time leaning forward on the end of the table, bringing her ample bosom into full view and causing Milo to pause for a moment as he attempted to maintain eye contact with her. He never understood women when it came to their breasts. He knew that it was considered impolite to stare at them, and yet women so often wore clothing specifically designed to expose their breasts and the valley between them. *If you don't want me staring at your chest, why do you literally hang your boobs out of your shirt?* he had often wanted to ask women like Macy, but not today.

"Like I said before, I'm in Chisholm to look up an old friend, but I don't know where she lives exactly. Her last name was Bryson, but she might have gotten married since I last saw her. It's been twenty years. But I know that there are a couple Brysons living in town. Possibly relatives of Tess. And she may be related to people with the last name Plante as well. I was wondering if you knew them. Or if you knew anything about them."

"Sorry, hon. I don't even live in Chisholm. I live in Stony Point, a couple towns over. I went to high school with the fella who owns the Chef, and he gave me the job. Says I'm the only person he's ever trusted, and that includes his wife."

"Oh." Just like that, Milo's hope that Macy would be his guiding angel had disappeared.

"But I got a phone book in back," she added. "If you want to look up their phone numbers, we could do that."

"No, I have their numbers and addresses. I just didn't want to start asking questions to strangers, right out of the blue, especially if they don't know who Tess is." Milo paused for a moment, thought about how honest he could be with this woman, and then continued. "Truthfully, Tess might not want to be found. She disappeared a long time ago. Ran away from home as a kid.

I'm trying to find her to let her know that it's okay to come home. If she wants to."

The rosy expression on Macy's face quickly shifted to one of disapproval, making Milo wish he had said nothing. "People usually disappear for a reason," she said. "If your friend wanted to be found, don't you think she would've popped her head up out of the sand by now?"

"Maybe. But she doesn't know everything that's happened. Back home, I mean. I think she'd like to hear what's going on."

"Well, I don't like it," Macy said. "Not one bit. If she wanted to know, she'd check things out for herself. But if you're going to get in touch with those people, I suggest you do it face-to-face. If they know where your girl is, they ain't gonna say so over the phone. No way in hell. I don't think they'll tell you anyway, to be honest, but you got a better chance if you do it face-to-face. That's what I think."

Milo thought Macy was probably right. He checked his watch.

Six thirty.

Still time to knock on a couple doors if he hurried.

chapter 24

There were many reasons Milo did not want to knock on Kelly Plante's front door. First and foremost, he was afraid of the reaction that he might receive from this stranger and had no desire to become engaged in a verbal confrontation. Just finding a way to start off the conversation would be difficult enough. If she was a relative of Tess Bryson and had been complicit in her disappearance, she might still be protective of Tess, fearful that Sean Bryson or someone working for him might be looking for his long-lost daughter. If so, their conversation could quickly become heated.

But Milo also did not like the business of going door to door and presenting himself to strangers. The last time he had done such a thing, events had not turned out well.

He had been fourteen years old at the time, working on a door-to-door campaign with his Boy Scout troop. He and his fellow scouts were canvassing the neighborhoods of his hometown of Vernon, Connecticut, on a bottle and can collection drive. This was an annual event for his troop. The money earned from the deposits on the collected recyclables would help fund the troop's upcoming trip to Camp Yawgoog, a Boy Scout camp in southern Rhode Island and one of Milo's favorite places on the planet. Though the boys were instructed to remain in pairs while knocking on doors, Milo's partner, Scotty Gould, had suggested that they could cover more ground if they split up and worked opposite sides of the street. Thinking it a good idea, Milo had agreed.

Things had started off fine. Between the two of them, Scotty and Milo had managed to cover four blocks in the time that it would've taken them to cover two. And for the most part, they were always in sight of each other. Milo might turn the corner just ahead of Scotty, or vice versa, but if so, the boys were out of each other's view for no more than a couple of minutes. Eventually, the plastic bags that they filled were placed on the corners of each block, tied to a street sign or telephone pole, and adult leaders in cars would drive by and pick them up. The system, perfected over the years, was working well, and Milo and Scotty were carrying more than their share of the load thanks to their slight violation of the rules. But as the afternoon progressed, they grew complacent, a condition that success often breeds, so by the time they had started their second hour of work, the two were hardly looking for each other anymore.

It was Milo's last block of the day. He was on Skinner Road, about half a mile down from the elementary school where he had spent his kindergarten through fifth grade years. The house was a green cape with white shutters. Number 324. A rusting Ford Pinto with a dangling muffler was parked in the driveway. No cans or bottles were on the stoop.

The weekend prior to the collection, Milo and his troop had canvassed the same area, passing out leaflets that informed residents of their bottle and can drive and inviting them to leave the empties by their front doors to be picked up. Though many residents had done just that, others had not. Milo's scoutmaster, Mr. Daniels, a meticulous man who folded and reused the aluminum foil in which the troop's burgers and hot dogs were wrapped, had asked the boys to knock on every one of these doors in the event that the resident had simply forgotten the day of the collection. And this request had paid off. More than half of the doors that Milo and Scotty had knocked on that afternoon had residents behind them who were more than willing to donate bottles and cans to the drive. When Milo knocked at 324 Skinner Road, Scotty was a quarter-mile away, canvassing a cul-de-sac off his side of the main road, though Milo didn't know it at the time.

The woman who answered the door did not look well. There were many aspects of her appearance that were askew: oily hair, fuzzy pink headband (the kind a little girl might wear), and her outfit, which seemed to amount to a man's white tank top, a teal bra (clearly visible through the larger-than-necessary holes for her arms), an apron wrapped around her waist, a pair of checkered boxer shorts, and pink slippers. But it had been her hands, one trembling as it cracked open the door and the other stuffed into an apron pocket, pressed up against her body as if she were in danger of having it taken away, that told Milo that something was not right. His eyes made contact with the woman's, and for a moment, he nearly turned and walked away, the silent warning in those gray irises nearly enough to convince him to go. Instead, he spoke.

"Hi. My name is Milo. I'm with Boy Scout Troop Twelve and we're collecting bottles and cans for recycling. We use the money to help us go to camp. Do you have any empties that we could have?"

The woman remained silent for a moment, maintaining her gaze on Milo as if offering a last chance at escape, before finally looking back into the house and calling out, "Louis?" A moment later, without any response that Milo could hear, the woman invited Milo to enter.

The door opened up onto a dimly lit living room carpeted in a thinning olive green shag. Though Milo hadn't noticed from the outside, the shades were drawn and the only illumination was coming from a lamp that was positioned on an end table adjacent to a patchwork couch, and from a large console television to the far right.

Both sources of illumination startled Milo.

The lamp, a three foot tall replica of a woman's leg, adorned in a stiletto and garter belt and topped with a lampshade tasseled with purple and red fringe. The lamp looked remarkably similar to the one featured in the classic movie *A Christmas Story*, a film that had failed miserably in theaters only to gain popularity once it was syndicated for television. At the time, the movie was just becoming a holiday staple on network television, but Milo hadn't seen it yet. If he had, it might have reduced his shock on noticing this highly suggestive lighting fixture.

Of course, this lamp paled in comparison to what was showing on the television: four naked muscular men having sex with a petite blond female modeling an outfit surprisingly similar to the lamp's. The performers, writhing on a bed large enough to fill the living room in which Milo was now standing, were moaning, whimpering, and panting in ways that Milo had never heard before.

Reclining in front of the television, in a La-Z-Boy that was comically large in comparison to his size, was a rail-thin man in dark horn-rimmed glasses, a white tank top, camouflage pants, and black combat boots. His receding hairline exposed a wrinkled, pale forehead, and a bald patch had formed in the back as well, making it seem as though his scalp were waging a two-front war on baldness, without much success.

"Louis," the woman said. "This kid wants empty bottles for the Boy Scouts. They're recycling."

"Cans too," Milo added, hoping the normalcy of his words would somehow compensate for the insanity of the rest of the living room scene.

"You know where they are. Go get 'em," Louis said in a voice that was nasally, authoritative, and disinterested. He waved his hand in a dismissive gesture, eyes still affixed to the television screen, where the writhing continued.

"Wait here," the woman said. "The bottles are in the basement. I'll be back in a sec."

Please don't leave me here, Milo wanted to say as the woman disappeared through a short hall into a kitchen and beyond. Instead, he stood his ground as instructed, desperately searching for something in the room on which to affix his own gaze while he waited. Anything but the television.

Unfortunately, the room was lacking of anything else of interest. Stairs to Milo's left ascended to the second floor. An identical recliner stood about three feet to the left of Louis's recliner, both pieces of furniture filling the center of the room, with a folding tray occupying the narrow space between the two. The top of the tray was littered with Chinese food containers, opened cans of Tab and Fresca, and half a bag of miniature marshmallows. Several marshmallows had fallen onto the floor beneath the tray, alongside a discarded pair of chopsticks and a plastic container of dental floss.

"Come over here, kid," Louis said, finally turning away from the television long enough to make eye contact with Milo. As he lifted himself from the cushions of the recliner in order to pivot, Milo could see that his body barely filled the tank top that he was wearing. The twin strips of cotton holding it up were struggling to maintain their purchase on the man's measly shoulders.

"Thanks," Milo said. "But I'll just wait by the door. I don't want to be a bother. I'll be out of here in just a minute."

"Come over here, kid," Louis repeated with authority that did not match his insubstantial frame. "Annie's gonna be a minute. I just toss my empties down the cellar stairs. She's gonna have to pick 'em up and stick 'em in a bag. And get the ones in the garage too."

Milo had no desire to close the distance between himself and the pornography on the screen, but he also couldn't ignore this man's request. Though Milo suspected that the man was a loon, he did not appear dangerous or even rude. So moving as slowly as possible, all the while praying that Annie would return with the recyclables, Milo crossed the living room until he was adjacent to the empty recliner.

"Take a seat," the man said, this time not bothering to look up at his guest. At this distance, Milo could see a name badge stuck to his tank top that read:

Hello, my name is:

Below these preprinted words, written in red ink, was

Louis, AKA Hot Potato

"Take a seat, man," Louis repeated, now breaking away from the pornography long enough to make eye contact with Milo and motion to the empty recliner. Unable to resist, Milo sat, sinking into the chair further than he had expected. He suddenly felt trapped.

"Want a marshmallow?" Louis asked, pushing the bag in Milo's direction. Several marshmallows tumbled to the floor, joining their compatriots in surrounding the chopsticks.

"No, thank you," Milo said, watching three more marshmallows plummet from their perch as Louis returned the bag to the tray.

"Your loss."

The man's eyes returned to the screen, where the moans and pants were increasing in frequency and intensity, but Milo remained turned toward the second recliner. "Thank you for donating the bottles and cans," he said, not wanting to stare at the man without trying to make conversation.

Louis nodded.

"We're going to use the money to go to camp this summer."

"Just gimme a second, kid. This is almost done."

Milo was perfectly willing to give the man a minute, but he wanted to avoid the television screen at all costs. Anything but the writhing images of the naked people illuminated five feet away. But this left him staring at the man.

A second later, probably sensing the eyes upon him, Louis turned. "Kid, just gimme a second. Okay? You're giving me the creeps."

Giving you the creeps? Milo wanted to say. *Are you insane? A Boy Scout comes into your house and you can't find the decency to turn off the porn that you and your wife were watching—in the middle of the day, mind you—for what? Two minutes? Not only that, but you invite me to sit down next to you and watch this stuff like it's something I do every day. What the hell?*

Instead, Milo turned his gaze onto his hands, which he had folded on his lap in an unconscious attempt at innocence.

Thirty seconds later, the moaning reached a high point and began to wind down. Milo noticed movement to his right and turned to see Louis lifting a remote control from the floor. It was attached to the VCR on top of the television by a wire, a setup that Milo had seen once before in his uncle's home when video cassette recorders first hit the market, but not since.

"The wire, right?" Louis asked. "Ain't seen one like this before, huh?"

"No, my uncle had one. But I haven't seen one in a long time."

Louis had thankfully stopped the movie during what Milo thought had been the credits (he never dared to look). Without the moans and pants filling the room, conversation with the man was supremely easier.

"I could get a new one," Louis said. "A VCR, I mean. I got

the money. Money ain't the problem. But the wire is so goddamn fun. When my sister brings her two little brats over here, I trip them with it. And I caught Annie once or twice too. When she's not looking."

"Oh."

"Don't worry. I don't hurt the kids or nothing. They're still little, so they don't got far to fall. It's just that my sister's got something against me. She don't approve of my lifestyle. Makes me turn off the porn and hide my videos when the kids come over. She tells me to put on a shirt and lock the bedroom door too, so her kids don't sneak in and see my stuff when they're visiting. Like she's embarrassed of me. But a guy's got a right to be himself."

"Yup," Milo said, listening and praying for Annie's footsteps.

"You know what I mean, right? It's like when you're a kid, everyone says to be yourself. Forget all the other assholes and peer pressure and shit like that. Be yourself, everyone says. So you grow up and decide that you want to work at a video store and watch a little porn at home and suddenly everyone's got a beef with you. Why do you work at that video store? Why do you got porn all over your house? But I thought I was supposed to be myself. You know? And I like porn. Hell, even Annie's into it now. Never trust a man who don't watch porn. That's what I always say. You didn't mind me finishing my movie. Right?"

"Not at all," Milo said, relieved to hear a door somewhere in the house slam shut. The basement door, he hoped. Perhaps Annie was back.

"See. You know. You get it. But even Annie gave me that look. You know, that *do you want to turn that off?* look. When you knocked, I mean. But I figured, What the hell. He's a Boy Scout, for Christ's sake. It's not like you're in grade school. And what boy don't like porn?"

Certainly not me, Milo might have said, hoping to placate the lunatic Louis, but Annie's voice interjected. "I'm just grabbing the empties on the back porch. Two seconds!"

In truth, the brief glimpses of the television before the screen had gone blue had been Milo's first encounter with pornography, so noting his appreciation for the genre would have been disingenuous. In the years before the Internet, he had no way of acquiring video pornography, even if he had wanted to. And not understanding everything that he had seen on the television, he felt like he was right back in that van, being questioned about what a rubber was by boys who knew damn well that he did not know.

"You sure you don't want a couple marshmallows for the road?" Louis asked, stuffing a handful into his mouth.

"No, thank you," Mio said, using the mention of *the road* as an opportunity to extract himself from the La-Z-Boy and begin sidling toward the front door.

"Your loss," Louis said between cheek-filled bites.

A moment later Annie returned, dragging two plastic garbage bags full of empty bottles and cans. Less than a minute later, he was out the door and back on the street.

Memories of those ten minutes spent in the living room of Louis and Annie ran through Milo's mind as he drove over to 9 Summer Street, the home of Kelly Bryson. He had never told the story to anyone, choosing to bury it like so many other things that he had kept to himself, even as far back as childhood. The words. The drink boxes. The balsa wood. The confusion between a rubber and a dildo. He had nearly told the story to Arthur Friedman when the old man began watching pornography, but even Arthur had the good sense to keep his new hobby between Milo and himself.

Porn fiend Louis had lacked all discretion.

Yet Louis had said something that day that had resonated long after Milo had left the glow of the garter belt lamp and the aroma of Chinese food. As crazy as Milo thought Louis had been, he also thought that the man had been right about a lot of things. It was true that Milo's teachers, beginning as early as kindergarten, had assured their students that it was okay to be different. They had encouraged Milo and his classmates to take the road less traveled, find their true colors, and be themselves. They had read books to their students in which characters such as Rudolph the Red-Nosed Reindeer and Dumbo had found acceptance by embracing their obvious differences, and deservedly so.

Throughout much of his childhood, all manner of adults had warned Milo about the dangers of peer pressure and trying to fit in no matter the cost. They had encouraged him to find his own way in life, develop a personal sense of style, and to be true to his heart. Qualities such as individuality and uniqueness were prized by his elders and fostered within him and his peers. Milo had even taken a peer leadership class as a junior in high school, where he learned about how to mediate disputes among his classmates and promote tolerance and acceptance in the school community. Milo had come to the assistance of younger students who were being bullied, had encouraged middle-schoolers to Just Say No, and had helped a freshman boy who was almost certainly gay find a modicum of acceptance by his peers. He did all this with great enthusiasm and pleasure, even with a locker full of juice boxes waiting to be popped open and words like *catatonic* and *delectable* (one that had proven to be especially difficult to rid himself of) pounding away in his head and secret after secret piling up around him.

All of this encouragement to be yourself and find your own way was meaningless to those beyond the curve of normality. For the compulsive karaoke singers with the need to bowl strikes and pop open jelly jars and the unapologetic porn fiends with a fondness for miniature marshmallows, there was no red-nosed reindeer acceptance, no aerodynamic elephant ears, and no duckling-to-swan future for them. As much as Louis the Porn

Fiend had unabashedly embraced his individuality, and as much as his wife may have even accepted it as well (though Milo still doubted it all these years later), Milo knew that society would never accept these people for who they were, despite the constant, insistent messages indicating otherwise.

Though Milo doubted that he would find a ninety-pound porn fiend behind Kelly Plante's door, he wasn't sure what he would find, and this made him nervous beyond measure. The last time he had knocked on a stranger's door, he had found Louis and Annie, shameless and surreal but otherwise harmless. But that was not all. He had also found someone so strikingly different than himself; forthright, unashamed, and quite possibly courageous, and yet someone with seemingly so much in common with him as well. Louis the Porn Fiend was a man full of oddities and peculiarities, only he was willing to share them with the world. For Milo, it had been like looking in a mirror and seeing what he could have been (and could still be) and not knowing whether he should loathe or admire the image.

He had no time for this debate. All he wanted to do was find Tess Bryson, fill her in on Freckles's story, and go home.

It began with three firm knocks on Kelly Plante's yellow door.

chapter 25

Kelly Plante was not a porn fiend.

Nervous was the best way to describe the woman, who couldn't have been more than thirty years old, if that. When she opened the door and saw a strange man standing before her, Milo saw a flash of uneasiness in the woman's brown eyes, indicating, at least to him, that she was probably home alone. He quickly tried to put her mind at ease, and in doing so, put his own at ease.

"Hi, my name is Milo. I'm sorry to bother you. You don't know me, but I'm trying to find an old friend. Someone who I think might be related to you. I'd like to ask you a few questions, but if this isn't a good time, or you'd prefer to chat in a more public place, or over the phone, that's fine." As he spoke, he began backing up across the porch toward the steps in an effort to punctuate his purposeful timidity.

"You're looking for a friend?" she asked.

Milo paused before descending the first of three steps to the brick walkway. "Yes, an old friend from grade school."

"You're not from around here," she said.

"No, I'm from Connecticut. Would you like me to come back at another time? Or maybe talk over the phone instead?"

"No," she said, seeming to relax a bit. "That's okay. But how 'bout we sit out here, on the porch." She was tall, at least as tall as

Milo, with a short, dark, somewhat messy hairstyle and the muscular build of a woman who worked out seven days a week. Milo wondered why she might be nervous around someone like him, since he was relatively certain that she could kick his ass if need be.

"Sure," Milo said. "It's a nice night. My first night in North Carolina. Sitting out here would be great."

"I'm Kelly, by the way," she said, motioning to a pair of wicker chairs a few feet down the screened porch.

"I know," Milo said, taking a seat. "Kelly Plante. I looked you up online. That's why I'm here."

"I don't understand," she said, looking nervous again.

"I'm looking for a girl named Tess Bryson. She may have come to Chisholm about twenty years ago. She'd be about thirty-two years old today."

"Why do you think I would know her."

"Your last name is Plante," Milo answered. "Tess Bryson's mother's maiden name was Plante."

"And since we have the same last name, you thought we might be related?"

"I was hoping. I mean, Chisholm is a small town. I thought there was a chance that you might be her cousin, or a distant relative."

"I'm afraid not. At least not that I know of. I'm the only Plante in town, I think. There was a Bryson family living in town for a while. A husband and wife. And they had kids. Two, I think. But the kids grew up and moved away a while ago. And they weren't related to me. But you're right. Chisholm is a small town, so I knew them. Well, I didn't know them. I knew *of them*. But she's moved away too. The kids' mother, I mean, about two years ago. I think the husband might've died. At least that's what I heard."

"Do you know where she might have gone? Or where the kids went?"

"No idea."

"Do you know where they lived?"

"Somewhere on the south side of town, I think. Near Milk Pond. But like I said, I didn't really know them."

"Do you have any other relatives in the area?" Milo asked, hoping to find another lead.

"Afraid not. I went to school at Chapel Hill and stayed down here after I graduated. I'm originally from upstate New York."

"What about Emily and Michael Bryson?" Milo asked. "They live over on Federal Street. Do you know them?"

"No, I don't," she said. But maybe they can help you out better than I can. Sorry I couldn't help out." Kelly Plante was rising, attempting to end the conversation.

Milo held his hand out, motioning her to stop. "Just one more minute, if you don't mind?"

"Sure," Kelly Plante said, resuming her position in the chair. Though her voice remained friendly, her eyes indicated otherwise. It was clear that she wanted the conversation to be over.

"Listen," Milo said, leaning forward in his chair. "I know this probably won't make any sense to you, but there's a chance that Tess Bryson doesn't want to be found. She might even be afraid to be found. If that's the case and you know her, you might be protecting her, and I understand that. You don't know me."

"Look, I really don't . . ."

"Please. Let me finish. If you know where Tess is and can get a message to her, please just tell her this: I'm a friend of Cassidy. I know how Cassidy helped her run away, and I know why. Cassidy isn't doing well. She thinks Tess is dead, and she blames herself. She's blamed herself for the past twenty years. I'm hoping that Tess could just give Cassidy a call. Tell her that she's still alive and well. That she made it to Chisholm in one piece. Just to put Cassidy's mind at ease."

"I'm sorry, but I really don't know who she is. I'd help you out if I could, but I just don't know the girl."

"I know," Milo said, and he meant it. It was clear that Kelly Plante did not know Tess Bryson. But he continued. "But just in case you do, take this." He passed a slip of paper over to Kelly Plante with his name and cell phone number written on it. "Like I said, I'm sure that you don't know her, but I just want to play it safe. Okay?"

"All right," Kelly Plante said, rising from her seat and stuffing the slip of paper into her jeans. "But I mean it. I don't know the girl."

"I know. But thanks anyway."

Once he was back in his car, Milo checked his watch. Twenty past seven. He still had time to stop by the home of Emily and Michael Bryson if he hurried. He figured that eight o'clock was probably the cutoff for knocking on strangers' doors and asking about a missing girl from twenty years ago.

On his way over to Federal Street, Milo's hope began to wane. When he had left Connecticut a little more than twenty-four hours ago, he had been so full of anticipation and excitement. He had expected to drive down to North Carolina, spend an afternoon chatting with the locals, and turn up an appreciative and cooperative Tess Bryson without much trouble. She would in turn contact Freckles, and just like that, Freckles's guilt and uncertainty and pain would be gone. Not only would she discover that her friend was alive, but she would learn that the maps and the planning and the forty dollars that she had lent her friend as a thirteen-year-old had actually done some good. She had helped a young girl escape an abusive and potentially dangerous father and find a new life here in North Carolina.

In discovering that Milo had a hand in this reunion, Freckles might in turn forgive him for watching the tapes, express appreciation and gratitude for his efforts, and move past the possible awkwardness of secrets revealed. Perhaps the two could even find a way to be friends, and maybe, someday, something even more, though Milo could barely admit this secret longing even to himself.

But most important, Freckles would no longer be forced to live with a secret that had plagued her for years. Milo could not envision a better gift. Though it was impossible to rid himself of his own secrets, he found himself in the unique position to do so for Freckles, and he couldn't begin to imagine the joy and the sense of relief that she would feel on realizing that she was free from her burden. Though hardly a believer in fate, Milo believed that he, more than almost anyone else in the world, could understand Freckles's circumstance, and that perhaps it was for this reason that he had found the video camera and the tapes. Perhaps he could do for Freckles what no one could ever do for him. Unable to rid himself of his life of secrecy, perhaps the best he could ever do was save someone else from a similar fate.

Perhaps this would be enough.

But with half of his potential contacts now scratched off his list, Milo was depending on Emily and Michael Bryson to save the day, and he was beginning to realize how unlikely and unrealistic this expectation might be. Tess Bryson had disappeared twenty years ago, and even if she had come to Chisholm, North Carolina, the odds that she was still in town were minuscule. If alive, she would be about thirty-two years old today. She could be anywhere, doing anything. What could he have been thinking?

He was beginning to think that this trip had more to do with his getting away from Christine and from Connecticut and less to do with some wistful, near impossible undertaking. Perhaps this had been an opportunity to take a vacation from his problems and find some excitement by living out a fantasy that offered no hope of success.

Perhaps he had needed this distance in order to come to terms with the end of his marriage.

Still, he decided to finish the job. Complete his due diligence. Even if he was likely to fail, he thought that he owed it to Freckles to at least try. So with a forced smile, Milo arrived at 107 Federal Street, a white and green ranch with an overgrown lawn and a sagging garage, hoping against hope that the solution to his dilemma lay behind a front door that still sported a plastic Christmas wreath.

Emily and Michael Bryson turned out to be a half-ton of peculiarity. They were considerably less nervous than Kelly Plante, but Milo thought that the couple had little to be nervous about. Given their enormous girth, he wondered if a bullet could even penetrate the layers of fat surrounding their theoretical muscle. Emily Bryson was the largest woman Milo had ever seen. *Round* was the best word to describe her, as her torso seemed to lack any specificity of dimension. Beginning around her ears and ending around her knees, her body was composed of opposing parabolas of fatty tissue, expanding to her midsection before narrowing off at either end, thus eliminating any possibility of a neck, waist, or thighs. In fact, she looked more like one of Milo's Weebles than an actual human being, much more so than Pete at the bar, and by the time he was able to leave her home, Milo found himself half-wanting to jam her in a door frame and watch her pop. She wore a pair of denim shorts and a pink sweatshirt that were somehow too big for a woman who looked as though she could wear a tent, and her feet were dirty and bare. Her face was red and streaked with sweat, and she breathed like a racehorse having sex.

Nevertheless, she also possessed a radiant smile and a surprising spring in her step, both of which were in full force as she herded Milo into her kitchen before he could even tell the woman his name. Seconds later, he found himself sitting at a cluttered table in an impossibly cluttered kitchen, being served biscuits on a paper plate.

Milo was stunned at the sheer volume of items in the

kitchen, and from his brief view into what might have been a living room or dining room, he noted that this was not the only space in the home that the Brysons had filled. The countertops were piled high with magazines, newspapers, empty cans and jars, pots and pans, bowls filled with nails and screws, the plastic lids to water bottles, keys, and other assorted items. Boxes and baskets were piled alongside the walls of the room, and random pieces of furniture, including a rolltop desk, several lamps, and a baby changing table were pushed into the corners, covered in dust. It was a wonder, Milo thought, that the kitchen hadn't collapsed into the basement long ago.

Milo attempted to introduce himself and explain his situation, but every time he tried to get her attention, Emily Bryson began moving again, first to the refrigerator, where she poured Milo more than a pint of milk into what appeared to be a pickle jar, and then to the stove, where she began frying sausage links and mushrooms in a cast iron skillet. "Just gimme two shakes and I'll have some of this ready for you, mister."

"Please, call me Milo," he asked for the third time. "If I could just have a minute to explain—"

"You like grits?"

"Huh?"

"Do you like grits?" she repeated. "I still got some from this morning."

"Mrs. Bryson, I just ate dinner. I'm really not hungry."

"I know. I know. That's why I'm not going overboard. But mister, this is what we do in the South. We feed our guests." Then, without taking her eyes off the sausage already sizzling in the pan, she shouted, "Michael!"

From somewhere down a hallway lined with boxes, stacks of newspapers, and books, someone, presumably Michael Bryson, shouted, "Coming!"

Moments later, he emerged, his enormous frame rubbing up

against the piles of detritus on either side of the hallway, causing the bundles of newspapers and stacks of books to teeter as he passed. Michael Bryson, a little over five feet tall, was smaller than his wife, but only in height. The man's dimensions were so askew that Milo could not even ascribe a Weeble-like description to his body. While also spherical in nature, he resembled more of a two-layered snowman propped up on a pair of tree stumps, his small head perched atop an enormous, ovoid body. He had a shock of curly red hair and a complexion to match. Like his wife, he was sweating and breathing heavily as he pushed through the door frame and into the kitchen.

"Michael Bryson," he said, sounding as if his tongue were getting in the way of his words. "Nice to meet you." He thrust his right hand out to Milo, who shook it while marveling at its size. It was like shaking a Christmas Day ham.

"Hi, I'm Milo. I was just explaining the reason for my visit to your wife."

"Did you want grits or not, Milo?" she asked, removing sausage links from the skillet with a pair of tongs.

"No, thanks, Mrs. Bryson. I really am full already. The biscuits were great."

"Sausage is coming right up. I fried some up for you too, Michael."

Milo turned his attention back to Mr. Bryson, who had taken a seat at the end of the table. Because of his girth, his stomach was pressing against the table's edge even though he was sitting nearly two feet from it. Though Milo had no appetite, he was suddenly curious to see how Michael Bryson would manage to eat with his mouth so far from the table. "Mr. Bryson, I came from Connecticut looking for an old friend of mine from grade school, and I was hoping that you might know her. Her last name is Bryson."

"You hear that, Emmy? We've got a carpetbagger in our midst. A Yankee, for goodness' sakes! Shut the doors and board up the windows!" The man barely finished his sentence before bursting into a fit of laughter, his tongue still obstructing his giggles. "No offense, Milo," he finally managed. "Just a little southern humor."

"That's right," Emily Bryson added. "Good food and better hospitality. That's what we're known for here."   .

"Right," said Milo. "That's great. And thank you so much. But you see, I'm wondering if you know of my friend. She would've come to Chisholm about twenty years ago. Her name is Tess. Tess Bryson."

"Tess Bryson," Michael Bryson repeated, appearing to search his memory banks for a match.

"You have a second cousin named Bessie," Emily Bryson said. "Isn't that right, Michael?"

"Sure do. But she lived in West Virginia. Grew up there, I think. Maybe Virginia, but I don't think she's ever lived up north. Probably never been farther north than Baltimore, if I had to guess."

"And besides," Emily Bryson said as she added six sausage links and a spoonful of fried mushroom to Milo's plate. "Her name's Bessie. Not Tess."

"That's true," Michael Bryson agreed. "But you know, Milo, there is a Tess living over on Harris Road, I think. Isn't there, honey? Tess Dailey? Or Bailey?"

For a moment, Milo's hopes soared. Perhaps Tess Bryson had changed her last name, or maybe she had married and taken on her husband's last name.

"You fool," Emily Bryson said. "That was Tally Bailey, and she died five years ago."

"Really?"

"Michael. We went to the funeral. Don't you remember?"

This quality of discussion went on for another thirty minutes, during which time Milo consumed a total of three biscuits, ten sausage links, and two servings of fried mushrooms. He watched as Michael Bryson turned himself and his chair sideways, facing away from his plate, allowing him to sidle up to the table on his left side, where the distance from his plate was reduced to just under a foot. From this position, he was able to lean over his plate and shovel sausage, mushrooms, and grits into his mouth (appearing to hold his breath while doing so) before retracting to an upright position in order to chew and swallow. Between his own bites, Milo also managed to interject the rest of his story between the ongoing litany of non sequiturs, finally wrapping up by passing his phone number to a greasy-fingered Emily Bryson, who immediately placed it under a magnet on the refrigerator. The thought that his phone number would be here long after he had left made him want to retrieve it immediately. He felt as if he were leaving a wounded man behind on the battlefield.

Milo was then subjected to another fifteen minutes of suggestions and recommendations from the Brysons, which ranged from putting an ad in the county's *Rare Reminder* to hiring a crop duster to fly over Chisholm with a banner that included Tess Bryson's name and his phone number. All the while, Milo shook his head in mock appreciation while searching for an opening that would allow him to leave.

With great effort, Milo finally extracted himself from the Brysons' home just after nine, toting a bag of biscuits and a Tupperware container of gravy in his hands, courtesy of Emily Bryson. All he wanted to do was find the motel that Macy had told him about, pay for a room, and close his eyes for the next ten hours. He had lost all hope of finding Tess Bryson. Kelly Plante had proven to be a dead end, and despite the sausage and ample string of suggestions that they provided, Michael and Emily Bryson had been equally unhelpful. He could look into the Bryson family that Kelly Plante had mentioned earlier that evening, but since it was likely that none of them lived in town anymore and he had no definite address, he suspected that finding even a scrap of information on them would be impossible.

Since he had no other means of finding her and no ideas about how to proceed, his mission had sadly come to an end. He would need to leave Chisholm by the next afternoon if he had any hope of making it back to Connecticut in time for his visit with Edith Marchand on Saturday. Maybe once he was back in Connecticut, he would hire a private investigator to locate Tess Bryson. He was feeling more and more foolish for even embarking on this pipe dream of a journey.

chapter 26

Milo was certain that the Do Not Disturb sign was hanging off the door to his motel room, and besides, it was seven A.M. Even though this was hardly a five-star inn, he doubted that the cleaning crew of the Pinecrest Motor Lodge began their work this early in the morning, sign or no sign. And yet there it was again. A knocking on his motel room door.

Milo knew that there were people in the world who would shout at the closed door from the confines of their bed, ordering the disturber to take a hike or hit the road, and though Milo sometimes wished that he were one of these people, he was not. His distaste for confrontation and his genuine desire to be liked kept him from shouting at even unseen strangers. Instead, he stumbled to the door in his stocking feet, trying to adjust his eyes to the light creeping in from the edges of the thick brown curtains.

The woman standing at the door was a slender brunette wearing glasses, an Orioles cap, and a floral scarf wrapped tightly around her neck. A sweater stretched from her shoulders down to her knees, where dark leggings took over and canvas sneakers completed the outfit. Emblazoned across the chest of the sweater was a red-eyed tabby cat slurping down the hindquarters and tail of a doomed mouse. Knit in bursts of oranges and yellows and reds, the sweater was the most garish piece of clothing that Milo had ever seen. He couldn't help but stare at it a moment before raising his gaze and meeting the woman's eyes, which were round, large, and hazel.

"Milo?" she asked.

He was surprised to hear his name spoken from this stranger, but realization quickly dawned as she repeated herself.

"Are you Milo Slade?" she asked again. Her voice had a hint of a southern accent, but nothing close to that of Emily or Michael Bryson, or the man who had handed him his room key late the night before.

"Yes," he said, staring in astonishment. "I'm Milo."

"You're a friend of Cassidy Glenn?"

"Huh?" He was still so stunned by this woman's appearance that he could not answer.

"Cassidy Glenn. You know her?"

"Yes," he managed. "I know her, I know Cassidy." He nearly held his breath as he asked the next question. "Are you Tess Bryson?"

"No. I'm Emma. But I'm a friend of Tess's. She sent me here to see you."

Milo had expected the sky to open up with her response, revealing the sun in all its glory, accompanied by a thousand angels, all singing in harmony. Perhaps this would've happened had this woman been Tess Bryson, but she was not. Nevertheless, a rush of adrenaline shot through his body with her response. He was standing in front of a woman who knew Tess Bryson. Someone who claimed to be a friend of Tess Bryson's. Someone who had spoken with Tess Bryson in the past twenty-four hours.

Tess Bryson.

He had found her.

"Tess Bryson? You know her?" Milo asked. "She's here in Chisholm? How did you know that I was looking for her?"

"Hold on, Milo. I get to ask the questions first. That's the way this works, okay?"

"Sure. Go ahead."

"Not here. Let's get some breakfast. Why don't you get dressed and meet me somewhere. Have you eaten anywhere in town yet?"

"Yes," Milo said. "I had dinner at the Town Chef. On Main Street."

"Good. I know the place. I'll meet you in fifteen minutes. All right?"

"Sure," he said. "Fifteen minutes."

As Milo brushed his teeth and pulled on jeans and a T-shirt, he tried to imagine how this woman could have known that he was here. Not only in Chisholm, but at the Pinecrest Motor Lodge. Room 14. He had left his name and phone number with Kelly Plante and Emily and Michael Bryson, but even he didn't know the name of the motel until he arrived late the night before, after his visits to their homes. How could this woman have found him so fast?

Then it dawned on him. Macy, the waitress at the Town Chef. The one who had recommended the motel in the first place and therefore knew where he was staying. Like the Brysons, she also knew that Milo was looking for Tess, and since Kelly Plante and Emily and Michael Bryson had all seemed genuinely befuddled by Milo's questions, and none of them knew where Milo was staying, it must have been Macy who had led this woman to him. Feeling defeated and dejected just hours before, he now wondered if his original plan had worked after all. Pull into town, find the right person to ask a few questions, and locate his target. It wasn't exactly how he had envisioned things, but it was close.

As he locked the motel door and walked across the parking lot to his car, Milo wondered what hoops he might have to jump through in order to meet Tess Bryson. What questions might this representative ask? How might he convince her of his sincerity?

When he arrived in the parking lot of the Town Chef, Milo scanned the dozen or so cars parked there, hoping to catch a glimpse of a woman, possibly Tess Bryson, sitting behind the wheel, waiting for the signal that Milo's credentials checked out. Not surprisingly, all of the cars appeared to be empty. If Tess Bryson was cautious enough to send a friend in her place to establish contact and ascertain the truth, he didn't think there was much of a chance that she would be foolish enough to be sitting in the parking lot when he arrived. But he also didn't think that she would be very far, either.

In stark contrast to the previous evening, the Town Chef was alive and jumping on this warm spring morning. All but one or two stools were occupied by men and women who were most certainly diner regulars, based on the ease with which they all sat in relative silence. No need for small talk among this group. Many of the booths were also occupied by customers, sitting in pairs, threesomes, and one loud gaggle of old ladies along the back wall. Macy had been replaced by a team of three fast-moving, fast-talking women who were scurrying about the diner like mice, delivering food, refilling coffee, and pounding on the keys of the cash register in a uniform rhythm that bespoke of many years together. There was a buzz in the restaurant this morning, the sound of people chatting about the coming day, accompanied by the clinging of dishes, the dinging of pots and pans, and the clanking of plates and silverware. The way a diner is supposed to sound, Milo thought.

He spotted Emma almost immediately, sitting in the same booth that he had occupied the afternoon before. Sipping coffee from an oversize mug, she motioned him over.

"Hi again," Milo said, immediately feeling like an idiot. Why could he never open a conversation like a normal person?

"Hi," Emma said, the greeting sounding more like a question. "I ordered you a cup." She pointed to an identical mug of coffee set in front of Milo.

"Thanks, but I don't drink coffee."

"No?"

"Afraid not," Milo said. "I don't drink any adult drinks. No coffee, no tea, no wine. Pretty much no alcohol at all except for the occasional beer. I'm basically a soda and juice man. It's actually a bone of contention between me and my wife."

"Really? How so?"

Milo hesitated but then took a deep breath. He didn't see any reason not to tell the truth, to himself and to Emma. Yesterday, while sitting in this very same booth, he had told Officer Eblen that his marriage was over. He could certainly tell this woman a little bit about the reasons why. "Well, my wife says it would be nice if we could have a cup of coffee together at Starbucks, or share a bottle of wine at dinner, or even some tea with dessert. But I just don't like the stuff. She thinks . . . I don't know. She thinks it's sort of juvenile, I guess. And I think she wishes that I could be more of an adult at times. More of a man."

"And a cup of coffee might do that?"

"She seems to think so," Milo said, trying without success to find a way to gently change the subject. As much as he might be willing to share a bit of his life with Emma, this wasn't why he had come to North Carolina. "But I think it's more about image than anything else. When we go to a nice restaurant, she'll order a martini or a glass of wine and I'll order a Coke. I guess it just doesn't complete the picture for her. I swear that she cringes every time I order."

"No marriage is perfect. Right?"

"Nope," Milo agreed. "That's probably why my wife and I

are separated. Maybe we were foolishly expecting perfection but never found it."

"Oh. I'm sorry."

"It's all right. And we're not divorced yet, so there's still hope," Milo lied. "But that's not why we're here. Right?"

"Are you hoping that it works out? Your marriage, I mean."

Milo paused for a moment, wondering how to answer the question, looking for a way to turn the discussion to Tess Bryson. Finally he surrendered, hoping that his willingness to answer Emma's questions honestly and candidly would pay dividends later. "Sometimes I do. Or I did, until recently. I don't know. Sometimes I wish that we could go back to how things used to be, before we started having trouble. I know that I wasn't the happiest guy in the world, but things were set back then. Everything was in its place. And even though we could've been happier, we weren't miserable either. So yes, there are days when I hope that we can work things out."

"And there are days when you don't?"

"Yes," Milo said, resignation tainting his voice. "There are days when I'd love to make a clean break from Christine. More days like that than not, to be honest. Most days, I suspect. And it's looking like that's where we are headed. But you never know what might happen. Besides, I assume that my marital problems aren't the reason we're here. Right?"

"That's true," Emma said, sitting up and assuming a more serious disposition. "I'm sorry if I made you uncomfortable. I have that way about me. Always asking questions without thinking about how they might make someone feel. I should've been a newspaper reporter. I guess that's why Tess chose me to speak to you."

"So how does this work?" Milo asked.

"I ask and you answer. Then I report back to Tess. Then she decides what happens next. Okay?"

"Fair enough," Milo said, hoping it would be.

"I have to tell you that Tess was shocked to hear Cassidy's name after so many years. Can you tell me how you know her?"

"Sure, but let's order first. It's a complicated story."

A woman who introduced herself as Nancy came by a moment later to take their orders. Though the woman had about a dozen pencils protruding from the tight bun of hair atop her head, she committed their orders to memory before scooping up their menus and leaving the table. Emma then excused herself to use the restroom, and Milo readied himself to tell the story that this woman wanted to hear.

He hoped it would be enough.

"You're staring at my sweater. Right?" Emma had resumed her position in the booth opposite him, and it was true. As she returned from the restroom, he had been staring.

"Yeah. I'm sorry. It's just different. What's the deal, if you don't mind my asking?"

"I was at a bad sweater party last night. My friend Taryn hosts it every year. We all spend the year hunting down the most atrocious sweaters possible. You know. Thrift shops. Craft fairs. One of my friends checks the lost and found at every restaurant and movie theater she goes to and has found a couple dandies. Then we show the sweaters off at the party. Taryn lives about four hours south of here, so when I got the call to come and meet you, I had to drive straight through the night. I got in around five A.M. and grabbed a couple hours of sleep in my car outside your motel room. I didn't want to knock on your door too early."

"Did you have the best sweater at the party? Or the worst, I mean?"

"It was pretty good. Top three, I'd say. But my friend Sandy had a sweater with an elephant and a pygmy rhinoceros having sex under the Eiffel Tower. That was the best. But she cheated.

She took up knitting last year and made it herself. Paid someone a hundred and fifty bucks to design the pattern for her."

"She takes this bad sweater stuff seriously," Milo said.

"Sandy takes everything seriously."

"What do you do with the sweaters after the party?"

"Actually, I keep on wearing them. A couple of my friends give me theirs to wear too. I kind of like them, as kooky as they are. And I get some of the funniest looks from people."

Milo couldn't help but marvel over how different this woman was from his wife. Perhaps it was because Christine worked in the corporate world, or maybe it had something to do with living in Connecticut, but she insisted on looking her best at all times, regardless of the situation. Even a sunrise visit to the Quaker Diner or a late-night run to Carvel for an ice cream sundae required a ten-minute visit to the mirror to ensure that every lock of hair was in place and her makeup was *even*, whatever the hell that meant. Milo often wished that Christine could be one of those women who could toss on a T-shirt, a pair of sweatpants, and a baseball cap and head out the door, perhaps even willing to grab a couple hours' sleep in her car before knocking on a strange man's motel room door, but sweatpants and baseball caps were noticeably absent from her extensive wardrobe.

Maybe if she had owned a baseball cap or was less concerned about Milo's choice of drink or had worried a little less about what others might think of her panic attacks, he wouldn't have felt the need to be so vigilant about hiding his demands from her. And perhaps this was why he already felt more at ease with this woman, complete with an Orioles cap, a hungry cat, and a dying mouse.

"I think the waitress gave you one of those funny looks when she took our order," Milo said.

"I think so. But let's get back to the subject of Cassidy, if you don't mind. Can you tell me how you know her? And how you found out about her and Tess?"

Milo had decided long before he'd even left Connecticut that if he found Tess Bryson, he would be completely honest with her. If he was right and she had run away to escape an abusive father, then she was unlikely to be the trusting sort, especially when it came to strange men. If he attempted to falsify or even embellish his relationship with Freckles and was caught in a lie, he might lose his chance to convince Tess to call her old friend. Sticking to the truth would be the easiest and the safest strategy, and so this is what he did. Beginning with his discovery of the camera on the bench on an afternoon that seemed eons ago, Milo told his story with as much detail as he could muster, leaving out only those parts of the tapes that he thought Freckles would want to remain secret. Her love for hospital food. Her involvement in exposing Sherry Ferroni's first period. The blame she placed on herself for Meera's death. But he kept in the rest, including his decision to continue to watch the tapes, the story of Tess Bryson's disappearance, and the means by which he was able to locate Cassidy and Tess and learn the fate of Tess's father.

Emma remained nearly silent throughout the story, only asking for clarification when Milo accidentally referred to Cassidy as Freckles. She reacted very little to the story, which made sense, Milo thought, since she didn't play a role in it. But the lack of any reaction to the events that Milo was describing made it difficult for him to press on. He couldn't help but wonder if he was boring the woman, or if she didn't believe his story, or if she found his decision to watch the tapes reprehensible and was simply counting the seconds until she could get up and leave, offering Milo no hope in finding Tess. Then he'd be left trying to convince Freckles that he, the man who had taken her video camera from a park bench and listened to her deepest, darkest secrets,

268

had found a woman five hundred miles away who claimed to know Tess Bryson but refused to allow her to be contacted.

Not exactly compelling.

Plates of eggs, pancakes, and bacon arrived in the middle of the story, but both Milo and Emma left the food untouched until he was done speaking. After describing the events of the last twenty-four hours, including his fruitless visits to the Brysons and Kelly Plante, Milo raised his fork and knife and began cutting his pancakes into smaller squares, waiting for Emma to respond.

After a moment, she did. "Why did you come all this way, Milo? I mean, you don't even know Cassidy. Not really. What made you think that this was your job? What made you think that this was any of your business?"

"I don't know," Milo said, not anticipating this sort of question. "It's not like I listed the pros and the cons. For twenty years, this girl has blamed herself for the disappearance and death of her best friend. But after I found out about Tess's father and realized that she may have disappeared for a reason, I thought that there was a chance that she was still alive and well. Cassidy has been carrying around this secret for most of her life. Hell, she still thinks that Sean Bryson was treated unfairly when Tess disappeared. She's got this enormous burden on her shoulders and I had a chance to get rid of it for her. It was just what I had to do. I felt like it was the responsibility that I took on when I decided to keep watching the tapes."

There was more that Milo could have said, but he hoped that that would be enough. Saying more would've meant exposing his secrets to this stranger, and this was not something he wanted to do.

Had he the courage, he might have spoken to Emma about secrets, and how he finally understood the debilitating nature of living a secret life. He could've explained that even if a person appeared to be living a normal life to outsiders, someone with a secret like his or Cassidy's or even Tess Bryson's operated behind a veil of constant fear and shame, and it lingered over everything the person said or did. For people living with secrets, Milo knew that nothing was what it appeared to be. Happiness was a shallow, falsified state of being that was adopted only for the sake of others. For the sake of normality. Milo thought that this was what Cassidy was living with on a daily basis. If so, how could anyone allow it to continue?

Or he could've told Emma about how Cassidy had entered his life just when he was feeling the most alone, and how even though her revelations were meant to remain private, he couldn't help but admire the courage that she demonstrated in committing them to tape. He could've talked about the bond that he felt with Cassidy, a connection that was indescribably strong despite its improbability, and how he sometimes thought that she might be the only person in the world who was capable of truly understanding him and the inexplicable demands placed upon him. His secrets. Though it wasn't a full-blown crush, he could've spoken about the affection that he felt for Cassidy Glenn, and how there was little in the world that he would not have done to secure and defend her happiness.

Milo said none of these things. He took two more bites of his pancakes, waiting for Emma to speak, but when the silence grew more protracted than he could stand, he finally spoke again. "Look, all I want is to convince Tess to call Cassidy and tell her that she's okay. Alive and well. That the plan had worked and that Cassidy has nothing to feel guilty about. No need for details. No need for a location or a secret identity. I don't even need to meet Tess. If you could just call her and explain things, or just take Cassidy's phone number to her. I'm sure that when she hears this story, when she hears how much Cassidy has been suffering, and for how long, she'll be willing to make the call. Please, can you just do that for me?"

"I'm afraid not," Emma said with abject finality.

"Please," Milo said, frantically searching for some other means of coercion. "Just take the number and go." He held the slip of paper out for Emma, shaking it when she failed to reach for it. "Please. I don't care if I never meet Tess. Just give her the number. Tell her to call. Call from a pay phone. Use a stranger's cell phone. Whatever. Please, just take the number and convince her to call."

"Relax, Milo. I don't need the number. I've decided to go back to Connecticut with you."

"What?"

"Milo, I'm Tess Bryson."

chapter 27

The euphoria that Milo should have felt on learning that he was sitting across from Tess Bryson was immediately tempered by her declaration that she was returning to Connecticut with him. Once the shock of the moment had passed and the two had eaten a little food, Milo addressed his concern.

"I don't understand. Why don't you just call?"

"I haven't been back north since I ran away as a kid. I missed my mother's funeral and haven't even visited her grave. It's time for me to go back, Milo. And now I have a reason to go."

"But I could just give you Cassidy's address and you could drive up whenever you wanted? Wouldn't that be more convenient for you?" The truth was that Milo did not want to be trapped inside a car with Tess Bryson for more than twenty-four hours, with no telling which demand might suddenly light up and force him to start smashing Weebles or tossing a bowling ball or singing karaoke.

"There's no time like the present. And besides, I think I need to go now. And go with you. Just the thought of New England scares the shit out of me, even with my father in jail. I'm not sure that I could go alone even if I wanted to. And besides, you deserve some credit. Making the effort to reunite me and Cassidy was above and beyond the call of duty. I want you with me when I knock on her door."

"What about your job? You can't just up and leave. Can you?"

"Actually, I can. I'm a writer. I'm working on a book right now, but my deadline is four months away, and I've got two weeks' worth of columns written for emergencies like this. Taking a few days off is no big deal. And besides, this is important. Even if my deadline were tomorrow, I think I'd still be going. This is something I've waited a long time to do. Today is the day."

"Okay, but what about your car? And clothing and stuff. You'll have to drive home to pack, and I really can't wait for you. You said you live four hours away. That's eight hours round trip. I've got to be on the road by noon if I hope to get back by tomorrow afternoon. And I need to. I have clients waiting for me."

"Don't worry. I can drop my car off at Kelly's house and borrow some things from her. No big deal. And I'll rent a car or take the train home."

"Kelly?" Milo asked.

"Yes, Kelly. You met her last night. She's the one who told me that you were here. She's my cousin."

"I can't believe it. Are you related to the Brysons too? Emily and Michael?"

"As far as I know, I'm not. We're probably related in some distant way, but it's not like I have a lot of family left to keep track of these things."

A thought then occurred to Milo. "But how did Kelly know where to find me? I never told her where I was staying."

"She followed you. She knows my story, so when you came asking for Tess Bryson, she knew that you were either the real deal or someone working for my father. He's sent people to look for me before. But since he's in prison, we doubted that. Besides, you didn't seem like the type."

"God, I had no idea that she knew you. She's one hell of an actress."

"It's just practice. She's had people knock on her door looking for me before, so she knew what to do."

"So what name do you use now?" Milo asked. "Tess or Emma?"

"Emma," she said. "I changed my name when I got down here. I'm Emma Keck now. Have been for twenty years."

"How does that work? I mean, how does a thirteen-year-old kid change her name?"

"There are people who do that kind of stuff. Name changes. Social Security numbers. Birth certificates. It's not exactly legal, but it's doable. But it wasn't me. My uncle and aunt arranged everything. I can explain it if you want, but not now. We have a lot of driving ahead of us. Plenty of time to talk about it then. Okay?"

"Sure." And with that single word, Milo resigned himself to his fate. He would be returning to Connecticut on schedule, mission accomplished, but with an unexpected passenger. Tess Bryson, now Emma Keck, would be sitting alongside him for the journey home.

He prayed that his demands would for once remain at bay.

Kelly Plante was much kinder during Milo's second visit. While Emma ransacked her cousin's closets for clothing and rummaged through her bathroom for toiletries, Milo resumed his position from the previous evening on the porch alongside Kelly. This visit began with a brief hug, followed by an offer of lemonade and repeated words of appreciation for making the effort to find her cousin.

"I tried to get Emma to go back home for her mother's funeral, but she just couldn't do it. I even offered to go along for support. So it's wonderful to see her so enthusiastic about making the trip now. This is a big step for her, Milo. I can't thank you enough."

"Did Emma's mother know where she was all this time?"

"Her mother knew that Emma was alive and well, but that was all she knew. It was safer that way. For a long time, Emma's father suspected that she might be down here with her aunt and uncle. He even hired a private investigator to come around and ask some questions, but I was only a few years older than Emma at the time, so I had no idea what was going on. About ten years ago, another guy came around asking questions again, and this time he knocked on my door. I was living in an apartment on Chestnut Hill Road at the time. I knew Emma's story by then but handled that man just like I was supposed to. Just like Emma taught me. "

"You had me fooled."

"I'm glad," Kelly Plante said. "But I handled you differently than the investigators that her father sent. They knew who I was. You didn't. I never had to admit to even knowing Emma. I know it sounds strange, but lying about this stuff is a lot easier for me than telling the truth."

Milo understood this sentiment perfectly. He had decided long ago that lying was easier than the truth, though he was now beginning to doubt that decision. "Like I said, you had me fooled."

"Good. I don't ever want to mess things up for Emma. But to be honest, you were easy, Milo. Nice guys are always easy to fool. That's how I knew that you were one of the good guys."

Emma appeared a moment later with a brown grocery bag in each hand. She had taken off her sweater and was now wearing a simple gray T-shirt and a pair of worn jeans.

"They look good on you," Kelly said, referencing the pants.

"Yeah. They're a little short, but I don't think Cassidy is gonna care."

"Nope. She's just going to be happy to see you."

Kelly and Emma exchanged goodbyes, and a minute later, Milo found himself encased within his Honda Civic with the woman he had come to North Carolina to find. He could never have imagined how much trouble his success might bring.

"Ready to go?" he asked.

"Yup. Let's get moving before I change my mind."

"Are you sure you want to do this?"

"I do. And thank you, Milo. I know I never asked if you would mind taking me with you. I was afraid that if I did, you might say no. And this might be my one and only chance to go back home. Massachusetts, Connecticut, any place north of the Mason-Dixon Line, are like giant black holes in my mind. Every time I've tried to go back, I've frozen up. Chickened out. But this time I'm not going back for myself. I'm going back for Cassidy. Had I known how she felt, I might have gone back a long time ago. I don't know. Maybe it still would've been impossible. But this time I'm going with you. With someone else behind the wheel, it'll be tougher to chicken out."

"It's my pleasure, Emma," Milo said, and even with his fear and uncertainty about the miles ahead, he meant it.

They had been on the road for about half an hour when Emma began asking questions about his personal life, and even though she had warned him of this predilection of hers, the frankness of her questions had still caught him off guard. Added to this was Milo's difficulty in remembering to refer to her as Emma rather than Tess, which only elevated his level of stress. He had already made the mistake once before, as they were exiting the diner earlier that morning, and Emma's immediate and pointed reaction had placed the fear of making the same mistake again in the forefront of his mind. She had stopped Milo in his tracks in the middle of the handicapped parking spot and warned him about making the mistake again. "I'm Emma now. Okay? Even if I could be Tess, I wouldn't. That girl is in my past. Do you understand?"

He did, and expressed as much, but even now, the use of the new name felt awkward and clunky. In an effort to alleviate its foreign feel, he had tried to use it as often as possible during the first few miles.

"Let me know when you need to stop at a restroom, Emma."

"Are you hungry, Emma?"

"Would you like to listen to some music, Emma?"

"Emma was the name of my Aunt Emma, Emma."

Though he knew that he would always think of her as Tess Bryson, he was relatively certain that the calculated explosion of Emmas in the last thirty minutes had ingrained the new name in his mind.

One fear, albeit minor, alleviated.

Milo's greatest concern was that the close quarters of the Honda and the constant fear that one of his demands, and an especially difficult one, such as karaoke or bowling or even the popping of ice cubes from a tray, would precipitate a string of demands from the U-boat captain manning the gauges. In the past, Milo had found that his demands increased in frequency and intensity in times of stress, and particularly when his stress revolved around the possible onset of a demand. In short, to fear the demands made them more likely to appear. And though he had learned to effectively postpone most of them until he was in a position to satisfy their call, a situation in which the demands began piling one atop another made it almost impossible for him to manage any of them at one time, bringing the Point of No Return in dangerous proximity. Milo thought of it as trying to hold back a flood. If it was a trickle or even a stream of water, he knew that he could dam it up or divert the flow for a short period of time, but once that trickle turned into a torrent, there was no holding any of it back. Unless he found a way to distract himself from the possibility of mounting demands and reduce his stress level, the next forty-eight hours might be bad.

"So you're separated from you wife, huh? How did that happen?"

"Excuse me?" Milo asked. "How did it happen?"

"I'm not asking which moving company you chose, Milo. I'm wondering what happened to the marriage. What's the problem?"

"Oh," Milo said, startled by the question. "I guess it's a lot of things. It's hard to say that there's just one problem."

"Really? I don't know about that."

"What do you mean? You don't believe me?"

"It's not that I don't believe you. It's just that I think you've probably got it wrong."

"How would you know?" Milo asked, finding himself both angry at Emma's statement and curious about her possible explanation.

"I just do. I've had plenty of friends who have gone through divorce, and the one thing that I've learned is that most divorces can be distilled down to a single problem. The list of possible problems is long, but in the end, it can usually be summed up in one word."

"Well, I don't know if I agree with you. And even if I did, I wouldn't know what word to choose," Milo said, already hunting for one as he spoke.

"Okay, let me try," Emma said with a level of enthusiasm that made Milo uncomfortable. "Did you cheat on your wife?"

"No."

"Did she cheat on you?"

The question brought up images of Thick-Neck Phil sitting in his Jeep, eyes hidden behind sunglasses, but again Milo answered in the negative.

"Who asked for the divorce?"

"We're not divorced," Milo shot back. "We're separated."

Even though he was wavering between trying to hold on to his marriage and giving up entirely (with giving up having taken a commanding lead), he found himself suddenly and inexplicably defensive when confronted with Emma's assumption that he and Christine had already divorced.

"Sorry. Separated, then. Who asked for the separation?"

"Christine did, but when I left, she was upset. She didn't expect me to find an apartment and sign a lease."

"What did she expect?"

"She was looking for a break. A couple weeks apart. But I guess she did too good a job convincing me that we needed to make a clean split, because I went full-on with my plans when all she wanted me to do was take a sleeping bag over to a friend's house for a while."

"Not a lot of communication going on between the two of you, huh?"

"I guess not," Milo admitted. "It had gotten . . . I don't know. Abrasive between us. Like sandpaper on sandpaper."

"But she brought up the separation first. Right?"

"Yes." Even though Milo wasn't comfortable with the personal nature of Emma's questions, he knew that the conversation was keeping his mind off of other things. Things he was trying not to think about.

"And you would've never left if she hadn't brought it up first. Right?"

"Yes."

"Okay," Emma said in a *now we're getting somewhere* tone. "So your wife had the problem, then. Was it money?"

"No. I mean, we're not rich, but we were doing fine, and we never fought about money if that's what you mean."

"Did she abuse drugs or alcohol?"

"No."

"Did you?"

"Would you be driving to Connecticut with me if you thought I did?" Milo asked, jumping at the opportunity to break her rhythm.

"Good point. Was she bored?"

"What do you mean, was she bored?"

"The fact that you didn't answer no probably means that she was. Did you guys run out of things to talk about? Did life get too routine for her? Did she start changing her behavior in any way?"

Yes, yes, yes! Milo wanted to scream. *Yes, we ran out of things to say, but only because she stopped trying. Yes, she changed her behavior. She started exercising as if it were a religion. She started going to happy hour on Thursdays and Fridays and staying out later than normal. Now she's hanging out with Thick-Neck Phil from work and riding around in Jeep convertibles. Yes! Yes! Yes!*

Instead, Milo said, "Yes. There were changes in her behavior."

"New hobbies? New clothes? New friends? Staying out late?"

"Some of those things," Milo admitted, wondering how this woman could possibly be reading his mind. He had become so enthralled by her line of questioning that he had missed his exit onto Interstate 40 and was now doubling back.

"Well, there you go. Your wife is bored, my friend. Some people call it the seven-year itch. Some call it a midlife crisis. But it all amounts to the same thing: boredom. One word. Told you."

Milo didn't know what to say. There was certainly truth in what Emma had said. Christine did seem bored, no longer finding enjoyment in the television, the movies, the afternoons spent at the town pool, and the occasional games of hearts and setback that filled much of their leisure time. In addition to the exercise regimen and the drinks after work, she had started filling her weekends with more and more community service. She had even begun taking an art class at the University of Hartford and had talked about looking into community theater. Milo hadn't thought anything of it at the time, but in light of Emma's questioning, it seemed as if Christine might have been pulling away from Milo in more ways than he had originally imagined. Could it really have been as simple as that? Could the entire separation amount to nothing more than Christine's being bored with their marriage, bored with her husband, and bored with her life? It seemed so utterly impossible for so much to boil down to so little, but maybe it was true. Whereas Milo found happiness in his relatively simple life—the time he spent with clients, the evenings in front of the television, his Wednesday nights with the guys, and an occasional movie or ball game—maybe Christine wanted more. Maybe she had decided that she needed the kind of man who would sit at the bar on a Friday night and drink martinis. The kind of man who rode motorcycles instead of mopeds. The kind of man who didn't spend his time playing Dungeons & Dragons in the basement of a friend's home and who didn't have to answer requests for adult diapers and Viagra at all hours. Perhaps in the end, he simply couldn't measure up to what she had expected. What she had wanted.

Could it really have been this simple?

He also couldn't figure out how this virtual stranger had managed to diagnose the flaws in his marriage when a professional like Dr. Teagan had not.

"But hey," Emma added in a noticeably more cheerful voice. "That doesn't mean it's your fault, Milo. I'm not saying that you're boring. I'm just saying that your wife is bored. She's bored with her life. And since you're such a large part of it, you can't help but end up with the short end of the stick."

"I guess," Milo said, flipping on his blinker to exit the highway and turn around.

"Seriously. This isn't an indictment of you. It's just the way things are. The two of you were probably incompatible to begin with."

"How can you say that? You don't even know Christine. And you barely know me."

"Maybe I'm wrong, but in my experience, these things are much simpler than people make them out to be. Like I said, divorce can usually be explained in one word. Boredom. Dissatisfaction. Addiction. Incompatibility. You choose the word, but it all means the same thing."

Milo was silent for the next several miles, annoyed with Emma for her presumptuousness, her arrogance, but mostly for her keen insight. And as if she were continuing to read his mind, Emma remained silent as well, allowing Milo to consider all that had been said. Perhaps she was right. He had spent the last five years, including three years of marriage, trying to impress Christine whenever possible, attempting to put forth an image that did not exactly match his personality. He had spent a great deal of time trying to be a cooler, trendier, less nerdy version of himself. Maybe in the end, he had simply failed in his ruse. Perhaps Christine had ultimately seen right through him.

"Maybe you're right," he finally said. "Maybe me and Christine weren't right for each other."

What Milo didn't add was his fear that no one would be right for a man whose life was ruled by the urgent need to do strange, unexplainable things, a man who enjoyed reading books with Edith Marchand and living vicariously through his Dungeons & Dragons characters. Perhaps he had known all along that he and Christine were not right for each other, but afraid of being alone for the rest of his life, he had lived his life like someone else, a man who better fit Christine's expectations, but perhaps never enough so. "Maybe . . ." he added, thinking about the lawyers in Christine's firm and Thick-Neck Phil in particular. "Maybe I just wasn't cool enough for her."

"Don't think of it like that. It doesn't mean that there's anything wrong with you. This is just the way these things some-

times work. I have a theory. A woman has two choices only of
men: the ones who stopped maturing around the age of ten or
eleven and the ones who stopped maturing when they were nine-
teen or twenty. The ten- and eleven-year-olds aren't as cool in the
traditional sense of the word, so maybe that's what you're talking
about when you say you weren't cool enough. These are the
geeky guys. The ones that play video games and listen to weird
indie bands and watch *The Simpsons* and *Buffy the Vampire
Slayer*. They read comic books and walk around in sweatpants
and become musicians and teachers and computer programmers.
You know who I mean, right? These are the guys who think that
The Matrix is the best movie ever made and spend a year learning to speak Klingon."

Milo cringed, remembering the afternoon that he and Andy
spent speaking English in object-verb-subject order, the gram-
matical structure of the Klingon language.

Twinkie want you?
Ping pong play us.
Klingon like I!

"The nineteen- and twenty-year-olds," Emma continued,
"are the ones who become the lawyers and bankers of the world.
They wear the thousand-dollar suits, drink the microbrews, and
go to the gym at lunch. They drive sports cars and take power
naps and play golf on the weekends and marry the prom queen.
You know the type. And based on the car we're in now, I'm guess-
ing you're not it. Am I right?"

"I don't think everything is as simple as you make it seem,"
Milo said, deciding to take a stand against Emma's brash absolu-
tion. "It's pretty narrow-minded to think that every guy in the
world would fit neatly into one of your categories. How would
you feel if I did the same for women?"

"Oh, I have categories for women too, and I can tell you all about them later on, but for now, just tell me. Do you fit into the ten- and eleven-year-old category?"

"Well, I don't speak Klingon and I'm not a musician or a teacher, if that's what you mean."

"Milo, I'm not trying to insult you. I'm not saying that those ten- and eleven-year-old men have anything wrong with them. As painful as it is for me to admit, considering the men I seem to always choose, I believe that the ten- and eleven-year-olds make better husbands. They tend to be loyal, they're better with children, and they're just easier to get along with. The nineteen- and twenty-year-olds have bigger houses and better retirement plans, but most of them, unless they're ultra-religious, never finish sowing their wild oats, and they're more complicated in general to deal with. Gimme a geek any day. But not every woman is as smart as I am. Some care about the house and the car and the well-dressed man. Some want a nanny and a vacation home on the beach and the admiring friends. Maybe your wife is one of them and finally realized it."

Again, Milo said nothing. Part of him wanted to reject Emma's ever-condensing, ever-delineating notions of marriage and men, but there was truth in what she said, even if she wasn't entirely correct.

More important, he was suddenly in need of a sealed jar of Smuckers. Milo didn't know how many of these jars were needed to satisfy the current demand, but if he didn't get to one soon, he worried that this might be just the tip of the iceberg.

chapter 28

"Okay. Your turn. Tell me what it was like to run away."

The two were sitting in a booth at a McDonald's off Inter-state 95, just over the Virginia line. Milo had ordered a double cheeseburger, fries, and a vanilla shake, and Emma was attempting to swallow a mouthful of Big Mac. Thirty-two ounces of Coca-Cola stood in front of her, her fingers laced around the cup, ready to wash down the *two all-beef patties special sauce lettuce cheese* once there was room inside her mouth. Milo had never seen a woman stuff so much food into her mouth at one time, and he couldn't help but admire the size of the bite. Emma grinned in response to his request, held up a hand in a silent plea for patience, and continued to chew and swallow the food with visible effort.

After parking the Honda and entering the restaurant, Milo had told Emma that he had forgotten his wallet inside the car so that he could access the trunk and retrieve two jars of grape jelly. He placed the jars into his coat pockets, one in each, and reen-tered the restaurant, making a beeline for the bathroom before Emma could see his bugling pockets. Once inside the privacy of a stall, he spent about a minute opening the jars, hoping that they would be enough to satisfy the demand.

Thankfully, they were. After resealing the jars, Milo placed them on the floor and left them there, wondering what the stall's next occupant would think upon seeing two full jars of grape jelly alongside the toilet.

"I used to run away all the time when I was a kid," Emma said, still chewing on the remaining mouthful of sandwich. "There were probably times when I ran away once a week. Whenever things got tough at home, my solution was to leave. I guess all those times running away were dress rehearsals for the big one. I'd hide under the bridge at Getchell's Stream or up in our tree house until my parents would finally get around to looking for me. But I never went too far, so they'd always find a way to track me down."

"But they never found you once you made it to Chisholm. Right?"

"Nope. That was the plan. When I was hiding in the tree house, I knew they'd eventually find me. A tree house isn't much of a hiding spot when your parents know about it. But Chisholm was the real deal. When I decided to head for North Carolina, I knew that there was no turning back."

"Why Chisholm?" Milo asked. "Was it the only place outside of Massachusetts that you had family?"

"No. I chose it because my Aunt Kaleigh and Uncle Owen lived there. I knew that if I showed up at their door, they would take care of me no matter what."

"You didn't think they'd call your parents?"

"No, I didn't. The last time we had come to visit, the summer before I ran away, my aunt had said something to me. Something odd. Like she knew about my father and what he was doing. What he was trying to do. We were in the kitchen, drying the dinner dishes together. Everyone else was outside in the front yard, playing Whiffle ball. She was telling me stories about when she was a a little kid, and then she just stopped talking. All of a sudden. Right in the middle of a sentence. Then she put down the dish cloth and grabbed my arm, real hard, almost to the point of hurting me, and she pulled me close. She said, 'If you ever need a place to go, just call us, Tessie, and Uncle Owen and me will be there lickety-split.' *Lickety-split.* That's just how she said it. I think it was her way of telling me that she knew what was going on and wanted to help. So that's what gave me the idea. Only I did one better. They didn't need to come to me. I made a plan to come to them. I knew that if they came to Blackstone, my father would have me back in a month. But if I disappeared . . . if I went to North Carolina and just disappeared, he might never find me. Six months later, I did."

"I don't understand. Your mom didn't know where you were going?"

"Nope. She didn't even know that I was safe for a long time. I didn't want her to know. I know it sounds terrible, but she just let things happen, Milo. She knew what was going on and did nothing. She was afraid of my father and couldn't stand up to him. Couldn't say no. I was thirteen years old, and even then I knew I couldn't trust her."

"So how did she find out?"

"Auntie Kaleigh started to get worried. I had been gone for almost a year and I guess my mom was pretty depressed. Blaming herself for me disappearing. Thinking the worst. Probably just like Cassidy, now that I think of it. Auntie Kaleigh got worried that Mom might become so depressed that she might try to do something to herself, so she convinced me to send a letter to the doctor's office where she worked. No return address. No phone number. Just a typed-up note without even my signature. Uncle Owen drove all night and mailed it from Daytona just in case there was a way to trace the postage mark. I told Mom that I was safe and happy and never planned on coming home. I told her not to worry and that it wasn't her fault. I told her that I was with people who were taking care of me and who cared. Then I told her to burn the letter and never to tell Dad about it. I don't know if she listened, but probably not. Some guy came to Chisholm a couple months after I sent it, knocking on my aunt and uncle's door and asking questions. He said he was a private investigator working for my mom and dad. Then another guy showed up about two years after that, and then another a few years later. They knocked on even more doors, asking the same kinds of questions. Kelly thought that you might be another one of those guys, but when I heard that you mentioned Cassidy, I knew you were for real."

"So you didn't live with your aunt and uncle when you got here?"

"God, no. I knew I couldn't live with them, because I'd eventually be found, but I thought that they might find a place to hide me, and they did. They had friends who lived about twenty miles south of here who owned a farm. Uncle Paul and Aunt Kim. They weren't really related to me, but that's what I called them. They grew sweet potatoes and cucumbers and Christmas trees. They had four kids already, and they took me in and raised me like their own. What's one more, right?"

"And what? They adopted you?" Milo asked. "How did that work?"

"Like I told you before, there are ways of getting a new name. New social security number. New birth certificate. New everything. I don't know how it was done exactly, and it's probably very different today, but that's how I became Emma Keck. Niece of Paul and Kim Keck. I know it cost my aunt and uncle, my real aunt and uncle, I mean, Kaleigh and Owen, a lot of money. Probably most of their savings. Not to mention Uncle Paul and Auntie Kim. Taking in somebody else's kid couldn't have been easy or cheap. We had to invent a brand-new life for me. I had to learn lots of new stuff, fake stuff about a dead mother in Minnesota and a deadbeat dad and a year of foster care. My brothers and sisters—that's how I came to think of Paul and Kim's kids—they had to learn it too. Just in case someone asked them about me. Kelly knew the story too. She's Auntie Kaleigh and Uncle Owen's daughter. She's a couple years younger than I am, but she was home the night that I showed up on their doorstep, so they had to tell her too. They all knew my story and helped me stay hidden. After college, I tried to pay Uncle Paul and Auntie Kim back, but they would never take a dime. So about four years ago, after I sold my second book, I bought them a new tractor and had it delivered on their front lawn one Sunday morning. I figured the one thing you can't return is a tractor, no matter how much you might want to. You can't imagine their faces, finding this huge John Deere sitting on their front grass at sunrise. It was great."

"And you never went back to Blackstone? Never went back north at all?"

"Nope. My therapist has tried to get me to go for years, but I just couldn't. Even when I got news that my mom had died, I couldn't bring myself to go. There was nothing there for me. No reason to deal with all that bullshit ever again. Until now." Emma stuffed the rest of the sandwich, an amount larger than her first bite, into her mouth and began a full minute of laborious chewing. Finally, she had cleared enough room to apologize. "Sorry. I've always been a lousy eater. In my house, you had to eat fast or you didn't get seconds. Five kids on a farmer's income."

Milo excused himself from the table to use the restroom. He wanted to try to use the restroom before leaving, but he also wanted to delay their departure as long as possible, dreading their return to the stifling confines of the Honda. Inside the restaurant, things had gone well. Feeling less enclosed and considerably less vulnerable, Milo had been able to relax and chat with Emma without fear of any demands arising. And even if one did, he wasn't worried that the demand could not be met without informing Emma of his condition. The freedom and the mobility of the outside world, the world beyond the plastic and steel enclosure of the Honda, gave him confidence that all of the problem-solving strategies that he had developed over the years could be utilized in the event that a demand arose. Once he was trapped within the car, however, all of his experience and preparation would be useless. Regardless of his skill, there was no way that he could open jars of jelly, crush Weebles, or peel the price tags off books while simultaneously driving alongside a woman he barely knew. Once they were back inside the car, everything would be considerably more difficult.

As he returned to their booth, Emma rose, piling the detritus from their meal onto the plastic tray. She appeared ready to leave. Though he knew that he could only delay their departure by minutes, Milo couldn't resist trying, if only for a few more moments of relaxed conversation. "Have you ever noticed how much water a urinal uses to flush?" he asked, hoping the question might return Emma to her seat.

"I don't use a lot of urinals, Milo. I know you haven't seen me naked, but I don't have a penis. Makes it hard for me to pee into a wall-mounted toilet."

"Right." Even without the aid of a mirror, Milo knew that he was blushing.

"But I'll bite. How much does it use? Why do you ask?" She hadn't returned to her seat, but at least she had stopped moving for the moment.

"Oh. Well, a urinal has this information written on top. Most of them do, anyway. And they all say the same thing: one gallon per flush. Not in words, but they all say 'one gpf.' Gallon per flush. Does that seem odd to you?"

"The initials, you mean?"

"No, not the initials. The gallons per flush part."

"Milo, I told you. I don't have a lot of urinal experience, so I have no idea what you're talking about."

"But you don't need experience to find this odd. Think about it this way. Of all the amounts of water to possibly choose, what are the odds that one gallon is the perfect amount to clear the average urinal? What if the thing flushed eight-tenths of a gallon instead? Or nine-tenths of a gallon? Am I expected to believe that nine-tenths isn't enough, but one gallon is just right?"

"Okay," Emma said. "But what's your point?"

"With every environmentalist in the world telling us to conserve water, warning us that we only have so much fresh water on the earth, don't you think it's shameful that the urinal companies would choose an arbitrary amount of water to flush their toilets instead of figuring out the exact amount needed?"

"I guess. This really bothers you, huh?"

"It does. But not because of the wasted water. I mean, I'm not happy about the waste, but I don't understand why it doesn't bother other people too."

"I guess that in the grand scheme of things, it isn't such a big deal to people."

"That's what Christine says, but I disagree. Think of all those millions of flushes every day. Each one of them is probably wasting a little bit of water each time, and that adds up quick."

"Okay. Fair enough."

"And another thing. Why am I always hearing that we have only so much fresh water on the earth, and when it's gone, it's gone forever? What about all the salt water that evaporates from the ocean and falls on the land as fresh water? Isn't brand-new fresh water being created all the time?"

"This kind of stuff drives your wife a little crazy, huh?"

"No, it doesn't, and that's the problem. She thinks I get all worked up over these silly little things, but they aren't silly."

"That's what I meant," Emma said. "She doesn't understand why you get so upset about things like this. Right?"

"Exactly. A few months ago we were at dinner with a few of her coworkers, and I came back to the table after using the restroom and told them about the one gallon per flush thing. And the evaporation stuff. I thought it went fine, but on the way home, she asked me why I couldn't just enjoy a peaceful dinner without complaining about toilets and the water cycle. But that's the kind of stuff I'm interested in. Not toilets, exactly, but stuff other people don't notice. You know?"

"Sure. But from Christine's point of view, she might think that the dinner table isn't the place to be talking about urinals, especially if you're out with her friends. Her coworkers, even."

Milo didn't know what to say. In the car, it seemed as if Emma had taken his side of the marital dispute, and that had brought him both relief and satisfaction beyond measure, particularly after he realized how frustratingly insightful she could be. But now it appeared that she was standing alongside Christine, making the same kind of arguments that his wife would make. In fact, she had just sounded eerily like Christine. Milo wondered if his attempt to delay their departure with his urinal observation had just cost him Emma's allegiance.

"Don't get me wrong, Milo. I'm not bothered by it, if that's what you're worried about. We're done eating anyway, and McDonald's is hardly fine dining. In fact, I think you might be right about this urinal thing. One gallon does seem suspicious. I'm just saying that if you were out with your wife's coworkers, she's probably hoping that you'll make a good impression on them, and talking about urinals at the dinner table, as insightful as your observation may be, might not make the impression that she was hoping for." She waited a moment for Milo to speak before adding, "Just something to think about. Okay?"

"Sure," said Milo, feeling torn between Emma's frustrating yet seemingly sensible position and his desire to find someone who would allow him to simply be himself. Throughout his entire life, he had been forced to hide so much of himself from the world, so much so that his desire to reveal the parts that he did not need to hide was enormous. He didn't want to pretend to be a wine-drinking cosmopolitan who refrained from urinal talk at the table. If he couldn't share his mastery of "99 Luftballons" or his need to pop ice cubes from their trays, he wanted to at least be himself in the other facets of his life, in the parts that he had hoped were somewhat normal. But maybe he was wrong. Maybe his need to smash Weebles and peel price tags and trick people into saying words that thundered away in his head was just the tip of the iceberg, one group of oddities piled upon others that he had not been sensible enough to hide.

It occurred to Milo that perhaps Christine had finally gotten sick and tired of all of Milo's strangeness. Maybe in the end, it hadn't mattered if Milo hid his incessant demands from Christine, because his entire life was nothing but an enormous, pulsating mass of oddity and strangeness and abnormality. While he had been focused on keeping his inexplicable demands a secret, perhaps he had failed to realize that he was odd and strange even without the demands, and that his relationship with Christine never had a real chance.

It unnerved Milo to think that perhaps he was no different from Louis the Porn Fiend or Michael and Emily Bryson or Arthur Friedman or Eugene or even Linda the pancake saleswoman. Just like him, these people were imbued with qualities that made them different, sometimes outright bizarre. Even relatively normal people like Edith Marchand had their quirks and eccentricities. Yet these were people willing to live their lives out in the open and share their differences with the world. These were not people burdened with secrets like Milo was, and in many ways, Milo admired them for their honesty and courage. But as hard as he tried, he could never imagine sharing his life with all its strangeness and peculiarity the way they had.

He was simply not that brave.

And when he tried to share the little things, like contemplations on urinal flow, it always seemed to backfire.

"Are you ready to go?" Emma asked, moving past him to dump her tray full of trash into the bin.

"Sure," Milo said, suddenly fearful about what else he might say to her, concerned that the next revelation might be stranger than the last.

By the time they had doubled back onto Interstate 95, the need to bowl a strike had lit up in his head like noontime sun and his fear of not being able to satisfy it was blossoming. Milo also sensed that this was just the first in what would soon become a six-car pileup of demands that he would not be able to control.

chapter 29

Bowling was a bad place to begin.

With the discovery of the twenty-four-hour bowling lane in Vernon, Milo had rarely needed to put off fulfilling this demand, so for reasons that he did not fully understand, it was more difficult for him to quiet the need now. Had a word like *conflagration* or *placebo* lit up in his head, he would have been better equipped at stemming its tide, particularly if a solution was found and only required time to enact. But the need to bowl a strike was so often immediately satisfied that it demanded the same now.

Also, it would be difficult to explain to Emma why he suddenly wanted to go bowling, since he had explained how he needed to be back in Connecticut by midafternoon the following day. Half an hour after leaving McDonald's, Emma had broached the subject of their evening plans, suggesting that they stop and sleep whenever Milo felt the need to rest. He had been relieved, fearing that she might want to drive straight through the night in shifts. Luckily she, like Milo, did not think that driving overnight was the safest idea, even with two of them shouldering the load. Though the decision over sharing a room had not yet been raised, Milo guessed that Emma would want her own room, which was fine by him. The privacy might permit him the opportunity to go out bowling, provided that he could find a lane that was open.

"Where do you think you might want to stop?" Emma asked. "It's your choice. Okay?"

Milo told her that he'd drive until he was tired and then stop at the next hotel, though he had a specific place in mind.

The jelly jars in the trunk began calling to him (he suspected that two jars would not be nearly enough this time) about fifteen minutes after the demand for bowling had made its appearance, and this was followed closely by something new: the desperate need to let the air out of his tires. He could only guess that the demand arose after driving by a motorist experiencing car trouble, but no specific incident came to mind. The demand was also connected with the sudden realization that the majority of the air in the Honda's tires was more than five years old, and though it made no sense to him, this seemed entirely too old to be driving long distances.

As Milo had feared, these three demands began echoing in his brain, feeding off one another, making his attempts to hold them off ineffectual. The added stress of the mounting demands only served to heighten their intensity and potentially bring on others, and Milo knew that if he didn't find a way to satisfy them soon, his ability to think clearly and even drive effectively might be compromised.

It appeared that the U-boat captain was flooding all tubes, ready for an all-out assault.

There were mechanisms that Milo had developed in order to keep his demands at bay, but even these were impossible while trapped in the confines of the Honda. Small pressure releases were often enough to stay the demands temporarily, things such as the snapping and unsnapping the buttons on his jacket or jeans, the popping of a sheet or two of bubble wrap, or the inflating and deflating of a balloon (he kept a supply of them in the glove compartment). But without the proper jacket, a supply of bubble wrap, or a means of explaining his balloon procedure to

Emma, Milo's only option was to begin snapping and unsnapping the snap that closed his jeans around his waist, and he doubted that this action would go unnoticed. Had he known that he would be carrying a passenger, he might have worn one of his multi-snap jackets or carried a supply of bubble wrap in a coat pocket in order to surreptitiously pop, but unprepared as he was, his jacket closed with a zipper and bubble wrap was not among the items that he had packed.

Without these pressure-release strategies, things became steadily worse.

Emma had begun to ask him questions about his job, but, no longer able to focus clearly on the driving and the conversation simultaneously, Milo attempted to turn the conversation back toward Emma and get her speaking instead. He asked her questions about her writing career, discovering that she was a romance novelist as well as an advice columnist for her local newspaper and several online publications. Though Milo was intrigued by her profession, he knew that follow-up questions in this realm would lead to less of a narrative on Emma's part, so he put them off in favor of subjects that would promote more long-form answers.

He asked Emma about her trip to North Carolina so many years ago, and here she offered up a story that carried him and his immutable demands for miles.

Milo had envisioned her hitchhiking her way to North Carolina, climbing into the cabs of trucks and into the backs of pickup trucks on her way south, but this proved not to be the case.

"Milo, I was thirteen, but I wasn't an idiot. And besides, when you grow up with a father who is a monster, you don't trust very many men. Even Uncle Owen and Uncle Paul made me nervous for a long time. Hell, I didn't even start dating until after college, and that was after a shitload of therapy. I wasn't about to climb into a truck with some strange man. Besides, if I was going to hitchhike, why would I spend all that time planning with Cassidy?"

Milo conceded the point and encouraged her to continue, busy as he was with waging a silent war in his head, and losing badly.

Instead of hitchhiking, Emma (Tess at the time) had walked, following a route of secondary roads that she and Cassidy had mapped out, avoiding highways for fear of the police or something worse. It took her a week to make it to Baltimore, one day ahead of schedule, where she used the allowance that she had saved, along with Cassidy's forty dollars, to buy an Amtrak ticket to Alexandria. From there she returned to the road, where she tented in public campgrounds and in wooded areas just off the road as she made her way south. She ate at fast food restaurants and roadside vegetable stands, but mostly from the supply of candy bars, beef jerky, and dried fruit that she had packed for the trip. She filled a two-liter Coke bottle with water at every public restroom she could find and drank as much water as possible.

"The two-liter bottle was actually a bad idea. I can't remember if it was mine or Cassidy's, but I should've sprung for a canteen. It was impossible to fill the thing in restroom sinks because it was so tall and the sinks were so shallow. I ended up using a Pepsi can to transfer the water from the tap to the bottle. What a pain in the ass."

Thanks to their planning, Emma knew the location of many public campgrounds, but her inability to gauge the walking time between them caused her to spend many a night off the side of the road in a copse of nondescript forest.

"I wasn't ready for rain, either, and for two straight days, it poured like nobody's business. I had no raincoat, so I was soaked for the entire time. This was just after I crossed the North Carolina–Virginia border, I think. I remember that I was so wet that I didn't dare go into McDonald's or Arby's for fear of being reported to the police. I was shivering and cold and a complete mess. Even my tent was soaked through. It's a miracle that I didn't catch pneumonia."

Emma explained that she eventually found shelter by pitching her tent under pine trees or stopping beneath bridges when the rain became especially bad. One night in Virginia, she slept in the toolshed of an abandoned farmhouse.

"It wasn't easy," she told Milo. "It was hard. Harder than I had expected. God, I was only thirteen. I was tired and cold and scared the whole way. But the darkest, coldest, hungriest nights on the road were better than any night in my house with my father. That's what kept me going."

Twenty-three days after leaving Blackstone, Massachusetts, she arrived on the doorstep of Aunt Kaleigh and Uncle Owen. "I was tired and dirty and I had lost about fifteen pounds, but I remember seeing my aunt's face in that doorway and knowing that she knew exactly why I was there. I didn't have to say a word. She just took me in her arms and I cried and cried and cried. I cried for my mother, because I knew that I would probably never see her again, but mostly I cried out of happiness. I knew I would finally be safe."

"You must have been one tough kid," Milo said with genuine awe.

"You'd be surprised at how tough a father like mine can make someone. After fighting him off for four or five years, locking yourself in the bathroom and hiding under your bed and running away, you'd be tough too."

Milo continued to be stunned at Emma's willingness to confide in him about her relationship with her father. Though she knew that Milo was aware of her father's criminal history and had accurately surmised the reason for her disappearance, she was willing and able to talk about him without hesitation or emotion, rather than leaving the dynamics of the relationship like some unmentioned elephant in the room, as he thought most would.

"So you remember Cassidy well?"

"Absolutely," Emma said. "We were great friends back then. It was hard for me to be close to anyone with everything that was going on at home, but I was as close to Cassidy as I could be to anyone at that time. I don't think I could've made it to Chisholm without her. Her and those maps. I'm surprised she didn't end up becoming a geographer. Or a travel agent. It breaks my heart to think that she's blamed herself for all these years."

"She'll be happy to see you," Milo said, shamelessly envisioning himself as the hero of the reunion, the one who brought them together.

"I hope so."

Karaoke struck Milo about an hour south of the nation's capital. On top of bowling, the pressure seals, and the need to deflate the Honda's tires, this demand hit him like a freight train. The impossibility to satisfy it (what were the chances of him finding a karaoke bar in Virginia or Maryland?), combined with its sheer intensity, made it almost too much for Milo to bear. He knew that once he arrived at the hotel, the demands of the jelly jars could be satisfied with ease, and even the tires could be deflated without much trouble (though inflating them would be another story entirely). But the bowling, he knew, would be problematic, and the karaoke would likely prove impossible. If so, that meant that these two dueling demands would continue to ring out in his head for the remainder of the trip, increasing his level of tension, elevating the pressure, and strengthening the vise on his mind, which would likely lead to still more demands on him. He was trapped in a vicious circle that would only become worse with each mile.

Fifteen minutes later, Emma told Milo that she needed to pee. Considering that it had become exceedingly difficult to drive with the physical pain that his demands were now causing, he was thrilled with the opportunity to exit the highway and attempt to satisfy at least one of them.

And that's when—in the throes of opening his fifth jar under the sodium glow of a parking lot florescent at a Burger King just south of Washington, D.C., along Interstate 95—the unthinkable happened, the moment that Milo had been avoiding for almost his entire life: Emma had come back to the car, and he had been discovered. In the midst of satisfying a demand, one in a pile of demands that were beginning to tear him apart, Milo could not stop. As she opened the passenger door, Emma paused for a moment, staring at the four opened jars of Smucker's grape jelly on her seat and the one currently clutched in Milo's hands, before asking "Uh . . . what's this?

Surrendering to the pain and pressure of the demands and the impossible circumstances at hand, Milo decided that the time for secrets had come to an end.

"Just give me a minute and I'll explain everything," Milo said, then turned the lid on the jar, absorbed the satisfying pop of the pressure seal, and sighed heavily.

chapter 30

Milo knew three things:

First, during the twenty-five minutes that he spent explaining his condition to Emma, she had remained silent, only nodding when appropriate but never interrupting. Perhaps his opening statement (*I'm going to tell you something that I've never told anyone else in my life*) aptly conveyed the difficulty that he might have in relaying his story and for this reason she allowed him to proceed without disruption.

Second, the process of telling his secret, one that he had held sacred since the age of eight, had alleviated some of the pressure that was building inside, although it in no way satisfied any of the demands that continued to occupy his mind.

Third, Christine had called him three times during his twenty-five-minute monologue, judging by the repeated interruption of the "Take a Chance on Me" ring tone that he had assigned his wife long ago (knowing if she was calling, she would never hear his choice of song).

The irony of the situation was also not lost on him. After keeping his demands from his parents, his friends, and his wife, he was finally telling his secret to a woman who lived under an assumed identity and had many secrets of her own.

He began by opening the remaining four jars of jelly, all in

Emma's presence, which proved to be both awkward and embarrassing for him. Despite his attempts to dampen his physical reaction to the popping of each pressure seal, he was unable to hold back the sigh of relief and body shudder that came with each one. Emma had not reacted to the fifth jar, which he had opened while she was still standing outside the Honda, but she was sitting beside him when he had opened the sixth, having moved the opened jars to the backseat. The infinitesimal hiss and audible pop of the seal forced a soft whine from Milo's nose, and his arms and upper torso nearly convulsed in relief.

Relief and embarrassment, satisfaction and shame, washed over him all at once. As the pressure of the demands decreased with the opening of the jar, the mortification associated with carrying out the process in the presence of a witness began to replace the space in his mind that the demand had occupied.

Emma would say later that she had tried not to laugh, but to Milo, it seemed as if no effort had been made at all. As his body shuddered in relief, the silence of the car was broken by a snort from Emma, the kind of swallowed-up laugh that escapes a person's nose and eventually forces open the mouth. "Sorry," she said. "But what the hell is going on?"

Before he spoke, Milo took a deep breath and checked to see if the demand that had been searing his brain for hours was gone. As he had expected, it was not. Among the pileup of demands still ravaging his mind, the pressure of the pressure seals remained, grinding on in the form of a mind-numbing headache among the echoing clutter.

"Just give me a minute," Milo snapped, and immediately regretted doing so. "Sorry. It's just that I've got to get these jars open first. Then I can explain. Okay?"

"Oh," Emma said, reaching for and grabbing a jar from Milo's lap before he could stop her. In seconds, she was holding the jar in her left hand, her right hand positioned on the lid, ready to open.

"No!" he shouted, his voice sounding enormous in the confines of the automobile. Emma flinched at the sudden boom of
his voice, releasing the jelly jar, which struck the edge of the up-
holstered seat, reversed rotation, and then struck the carpeted
floor between Emma's legs with a thud. Milo released the jar in
his own hands and lunged for it, and as he did so, the jars in his
lap, including the one that had just been in his hand, clanked together, glass on glass, before tumbling to the floor between his
own legs in a series of successive thuds. Attempting to avoid the
gearshift, which was set in a console between the two front seats,
Milo veered slightly right in his lunge and found himself a moment later fumbling with his right hand for the jar between
Emma's legs while his face was planted squarely in her crotch.

"Milo, can you get your nose out of my vagina?" Emma
asked in a surprisingly serene voice, offering some assistance by
gripping the back of his hair and lifting. Thankfully, his right
hand had found and latched on to the jar just before his left hand
gained hold of the steering wheel and he yanked his body back to
its original position.

"Sorry," Milo said, cradling the recovered jar in both hands
now. "It was——"

"Awkward?" Emma suggested.

"I was going to say unintentional."

"Great," Emma said, smiling now. "First guy that close to
my vagina in months and he got there by mistake."

Milo returned the smile, feeling slightly more relaxed despite the awkwardness of the situation. "Sorry. But can you just
wait one minute? I've got to open these jars, and it has to be me
who opens them."

"Sure," Emma said, her response lacking even a hint of sar-
casm. Though Milo wasn't certain, he thought he detected understanding and acceptance in that single syllable.

As he opened each of the remaining jars, the pressure of the demand lessened, but his physical reaction to the hiss and pop did not. A shudder, a sigh, and an exhalation of breath that he didn't even realize he was holding all accompanied each turn of the lid. And each time, Emma could not help but snort or even giggle as his response. Though he would've thought that her reaction would engender even more embarrassment and shame in him, the contrary seemed to be taking place. Her amused laughter did not sound mean or judgmental in any way. Simply amused and perhaps even a little affectionate. Oddly enough, Emma's reactions helped Milo to relax a bit and tell his story with greater ease.

"I'm going to tell you something that I've never told anyone else in my life," he said once all nine jars of jelly had been resealed and moved to the backseat. "Sit back and relax, because we won't be moving anytime soon. This is going to take a while. And I guess I'll start at the beginning. With the juice boxes and the model airplanes and *loquacious*. But I think I'll begin with Jimbo Powers's birthday party and the balloons first. That red balloon."

Milo told his story in chronological order, moving from the demands of childhood to those that plagued him as an adult. He described the repeating demands in detail, the pressure seals, the Weebles, the ice cube trays, and the like, explaining their origins when possible and the strategies by which he managed to satisfy them all. He described some of the one-hit wonders that had arisen over the years as well, those demands that would mysteriously appear, never to be seen again. The smashing of lightbulbs. The need to dial 911 from the pay phone inside the New Haven train station. The demand to flush every toilet in the ladies' room at the now defunct Hartford Civic Center, a demand that had required attendance at three Whalers games and the risk of arrest and imprisonment each time.

He told Emma about Jenny's bar and the twenty-four-hour bowling alley in Vernon and his recent removal of price tags from Bibles at his local Borders Books and Music. He told her about his need to watch certain movies over and over again and his sincere belief that in time, their endings would change, if only once. He even told her about the image of the U-boat captain that he had assigned to the purveyor of his demands, and how he had come to hate the submariner. He described how he managed to conceal these demands from his friends, his family, and especially his wife, creating a life that revolved around secrecy and subterfuge, and how he had begun to realize that this, more than any boredom that Christine might be feeling, was the primary cause of the demise of their marriage.

"As much as I'd like to think that Christine is to blame for our problems, I think I've always known that I deserve a lot of the blame too. Instead of being a good husband, I've spent most of my time being a liar and a sneak. I'm not cheating on her or using drugs, but it amounts to the same thing in some ways."

He finished his story with the litany of demands currently plaguing him, leaving off the pressure seals, since that one had thankfully been satisfied.

"So I need to bowl a strike, which wouldn't be hard if I could find a bowling alley. I could probably find one using the GPS."

"Okay," Emma said. He couldn't tell if her response was sincere or patronizing, but he continued.

"And I've got this new one. God, I feel like an idiot for even saying this, but I've got to let the air out of the tires. Replace it with fresh air."

"The air in these tires?" Emma asked, motioning to the corners of the car with a quick twirl of her index finger.

"Yeah. These tires. God, I hope these tires are enough," Milo said, suddenly realizing that they might not be.

"Me too," Emma said, grinning. "Otherwise you're going to piss off a whole bunch of people."

"Yeah," Milo said, suddenly concerned about a demand that he had considered relatively benign moments ago.

"Anything else?"

"Yeah. One more thing, but this will probably have to wait. I need to sing at a karaoke bar."

Emma smiled, one that could have easily developed into a laugh, but this time, she held back.

"And it can't just be any song. It's got to be 'Ninety-Nine Luftballons.' The song by Nena from the 1980s." Milo paused for a moment before adding, "The German version. But I have the CD if we can find a place."

"Is that it?" Emma asked.

"Yes," Milo said. "I mean, I'm sure there's stuff I forgot to tell, but considering I've never told a soul anything about this, I think I did pretty good. That's it."

With those final words, Milo sighed. His story was complete. He'd been as honest and as forthright as he could possibly be, and he marveled at how the number of people on the planet who knew his secret had suddenly doubled. He wasn't sure if this was the end of the world for him or the just the beginning.

Unsure of what to do next, Milo remained silent, determined to wait for Emma to respond. He began counting in his head, ticking the seconds that passed in order to avoid filling the void with his own words. He had said enough, he thought. More than he had ever said before, and he was ready to wait and listen. He had reached the number thirty-eight when Emma finally spoke.

"So where should we start? The tires, maybe?"

"What?"

"The tires. We've got to let the air out. Right? It seems the easiest to do, as long as we can find a gas station with free air. And as long as our four tires are enough."

"You don't need to do this, Emma. This isn't your—"

"Stop." She raised her hand with the misplaced authority of a crossing guard, halting him midsentence. "Look, Milo. I'm not going to pretend that I'm not a little stunned by what you just told me. Stunned and a little sad for you and even a little impressed. And I have a million questions, if you're willing to answer them. But either way, we're in this thing together. At least as far as Connecticut is concerned. So let's get this done and get moving. Okay?"

"I can wait until we find a hotel, if you'd like. I can handle it myself."

"C'mon, Milo. Do you really think that I haven't noticed the changes in you in the last few hours? The way you've been gripping the steering wheel like you're trying to tear it off. The way you can barely sit still in your seat, like you've got ants in your pants. You've nearly sweated through your shirt, for God's sake. I was starting to think that you were on something. I'm kind of glad to find out it isn't drugs. It's not quite what I expected, but at least you haven't been shooting up in the men's room every time we stop. If we're going to make it to Cassidy, you need to do these things. Right?"

"Yes. I'm sorry, but yeah. I really do."

"Don't be sorry. You said it yourself: You don't have any control over what or where or how these demands hit you. Right? So how could it be your fault?"

Milo shrugged. Though she was right, a lifetime of assuming responsibility, accepting blame, and feeling shame was difficult to relinquish.

"Look, Milo. I'm the last person in the world who is going to pass judgment on you or tell you how to live. But you realize that this thing you have could probably be treated. Right? You don't have to live with it if you don't want to. These demands that you have, they can probably be managed with some counseling and maybe some medication."

Milo had considered the possibility of treatment many times, especially as he had gotten older, and he knew that there was therapy and even medication for people with certain mental disorders.

But he did not believe that his condition was like any other. He had seen movies and read about people with obsessive-compulsive disorder: the need to count things or clean things or check the stove fifty times to make sure that it had been turned off. But his condition was something more than simply having to obsessively count the letters in people's names (his had nine, unless you counted his middle name; then it rose to sixteen) or storing the iron in the trunk of a car in order to ensure that it was turned off (which Milo had admittedly done once or twice before). In his mind, his condition was more insidious and more sophisticated than simple OCD. It involved the interplay between Milo's arbitrary, incongruous demands and his strategic, creative problem solving, going beyond simple compulsive need and obsessive fulfillment. Milo's circumstances demanded intelligence, ingenuity, and flexibility. He doubted that any doctor would be equipped to deal with this rarified condition, and his inability to share his secret with anyone, including a doctor, because of the potential embarrassment that it might bring had always prevented him from finding out.

But more important, Milo knew in his heart that there was no way to subdue, cure, quarantine, or remove this pervasive part of him. His condition had become an integral component of his very existence, insinuating its way into every muscle and tissue and organ of his body. It was as vital and as omnipresent as blood cells or bone marrow. Milo could imagine Dr. McCoy positioned over his body in sick bay, warning Captain Kirk, "Removing the demands might kill him, Jim."

"Look, Milo, I'm not saying that you need to see a doctor or change one damn thing about yourself. You're sitting next to a girl who has refused to confront her own fears for more than twenty years. My therapist says that I have post-traumatic stress disorder. It's why I haven't had a good night's sleep for literally my entire life. I go to bed late and wake up early just to avoid being in bed any longer than necessary. I sleep with the lights on and the bedroom door locked. I can't remember a night when I didn't wake up from the same goddamn nightmare with my sheets soaked with sweat. It's why I couldn't go to my mother's funeral and why I start to shake just thinking about how close we are to Connecticut already. My therapist tells me that I need to desensitize myself to all the stuff that happened to me when I was a kid. I have to talk about it and write about it and think about it until it isn't so . . . I dunno. Awful, I guess. But I can't. Twenty years later and I can't, and even if I could, I think she's nuts to suggest that it could ever go away. That it could ever stop being awful. My mom is dead and my dad is in prison and still I'm stuck in a corner like a frightened mouse. So I'm the last person on earth who's going to tell you to go see a doctor and get yourself fixed. I just want you to know that you can, if you want to."

Milo was silent for a moment, thinking first about all that Emma had shared about herself, and then standing in awe of her acceptance of his insanity. What could you say to a person who had heard your deepest, darkest secret and declared you to be fine just the way you were?

"Okay, then" was all that he could manage.

"So we start with the tires?"

"Sounds good."

It took almost thirty minutes for them to empty and refill all four tires, only after determining what specifically needed to be done. They had found a Mobil station less than a mile down the road from the Burger King, complete with free air behind the pumps. Initially Milo began letting the air out of the right rear tire, so with nothing else to do, Emma moved to do the same on the left. He had thought nothing of her offer to help at first, but on hearing the hiss of air from her tire, Milo realized that it was the release of air that was required of him and that Emma's releasing of the air would not satisfy his own demand. After he explained this to her, comparing it to her attempt to open the jelly jar (and feeling incredibly foolish while doing so), Emma took the air hose and waited for the first tire to be empty. Then, as Milo moved to the next, she proceeded to fill the first with what Milo thought of as gloriously fresh air.

"So you kept this from Christine for all this time, huh?" She had to shout to be heard above the roar of the air pump and the hiss of air issuing forth from Milo's tire. Her volume made Milo uneasy, fearful that others might hear.

"Yup. I've kept it from everyone. You're literally the only one who knows."

"That must've been hard."

"It was," Milo said, also shouting. "But you'd be surprised how you can arrange your life around just about anything. Once I started working for myself, things got much easier. I have the freedom during the day to meet clients and handle any demand that might come up. When I was working for the nursing home and punching a clock every day, things were tough, but that's when I worked on some of the strategies to hold off the demands a bit. Like the balloons and the bubble wrap that I told you about."

"And you don't think Christine ever suspected anything?"

"I think she knew that I was a little odd. Maybe not until we were well into the relationship, but she figured it out eventually. Like watching the same movies over and over again. That's got to be strange in her eyes. Did I tell you about that already?"

"Yeah. *Star Wars*. Right?"

"Yeah. There are others too. *Butch Cassidy and the Sundance Kid* was a problem for me recently."

"Was that a coincidence?" Emma asked, screwing the cap on a tire and moving on to another.

"Was what a coincidence?"

"Cassidy and *Butch Cassidy*? Just a coincidence, or did your mind make it happen?"

"God, I have no idea. I never even thought of it. I can't believe I didn't notice. Wow. I wonder if that happens more often than I realize."

"So anyway, you said that Christine probably thinks you're a little odd, but that's it? She really doesn't know?"

"Nope. She knows about the movies, but she has no idea that I'm waiting to see if the ending changes. And she thinks that my attention to little things like the urinals is weird too. But she has no idea about the bowling and the ice cubes or even the karaoke. She's never even been with me to karaoke, and I've probably performed five hundred times. Oh. That reminds me. That was her calling back in the Burger King parking lot."

"The Abba ring tone?" Emma asked with a grin.

"Don't be mean."

Milo retrieved the phone from his pocket and looked at the list of missed calls on the display screen. Five in all, three from the parking lot and two others, three and five hours ago. All from Christine. "She called a while ago too. I must not have had any service." Milo finished with the final tire, the satisfying hiss of air reducing the pressure in his mind another degree, before he stepped away from the noise of the air pump in order to listen to the messages.

Though she had called five times, Christine had left just one message. He pressed the button that activated the voice mail and listened.

Three minutes later, he placed the phone back in his coat pocket and returned to the Honda.

"What's wrong?" Emma asked. "Are you crying?"

"No," Milo lied. "But I think I just got divorced."

chapter 31

Hi. Milo? This is Christine. I've been trying to call you all day. I'm sorry. I hate to do this on the phone, but I don't want you to be surprised by a knock on your door, and you're not picking up your phone. Listen, I just don't think this is going to work out, and I think you probably know it too. I don't think it's anybody's fault. We're just not right together, and I think you know that too. If we want to get a divorce, we'll have to wait six months from the time we file the papers, and it's what I want, Milo. I hope you understand.

So I spoke to Josh at my firm and he agreed to do it for us pro bono, if that's all right with you. Fifty-fifty for everything, and you can keep Puggles. We can talk about the details later. But I wanted to let you know that I filed the papers today. You're going to get served by a sheriff, but it's totally routine. I'm not looking to screw you at all, and I hope we can stay friends afterward. Our marriage might be lousy, but I always thought that our friendship was just fine. I just don't want to wait six months to finally make a decision and then have to wait another six months for it to be official. I think it's better that we move on as

*soon as we can. But I asked Josh to make sure that
you get served at your apartment, because I thought
that would be easier. I didn't want some guy serving
you when you're with a client or at Andy's house. But
like I said, it's just routine. Okay? Don't freak out or
think I'm suing you or anything. Okay? This is just
how it's done. Call me when you get this message, just
so I won't worry. Okay? Bye.*

"Did your wife just ask for a divorce through voice mail?" Emma asked, handing the phone back over to Milo.

"I think so," Milo said, staring at his sneakers. He had taken a seat on the curb beside the air pump, waiting for Emma to finish listening to the message.

"Goddamn it. That takes some serious balls. Don't you dare erase that message, because no one's ever going to believe it."

Milo still couldn't believe it himself. He didn't know how divorces were traditionally requested by spouses, but he couldn't believe that this life-changing moment had taken place over voice mail. For the rest of his life, whenever he thought about Christine and their divorce, his mind would return to this oil-stained slice of pavement in Virginia, to the hum of the arching, overhead lights illuminating the station and the Doppler whine of eighteen-wheelers on the interstate, and to the Honda, with its four newly inflated tires. He would think back on this moment, listening to a recording of his wife of three years as she spoke of routine warrants and fifty-fifty splits, effectively ending their relationship, as he stared at an Asian woman pump gas into her station wagon and unabashedly adjust her bra. He hadn't expected this news to come wrapped up in a ribbon, but he never envisioned receiving it at a gas station via a recording either.

"I'm sorry, Milo. I really am." Emma had taken a seat beside him on the curb and had wrapped her arm over his shoulder.

"This kind of news is hard enough without it coming by voice mail. It's just unbelievable."

"Yeah. I still can't believe it. I mean, I knew that it was going to eventually happen, and to be honest, I sort of wanted it to happen too. I think. But I never thought it would come so soon. I mean, we've only been in counseling for a couple weeks."

"But it's for the best?"

"Probably. I mean, it wasn't great between Christine and me, but so much of my life was settled with her. We had the house, friends, the 401(k)s. I liked her parents and she tolerated my mom. We had the holiday schedules all worked out: Thanksgiving and Christmas Eve with her family and Christmas Day and Easter with mine. I just had the floors refinished last spring, and we were going to do replacement windows in July or August. I know it sounds like little stuff, but it adds up. It's what makes a life, and it's just hard to believe that it's all over. I feel like I'm hitting the reset switch. Starting my life over after so much was settled."

What Milo didn't add was his doubt that he would ever find a woman again who would be interested in him, and more important, a woman from whom he could conceal so much. Neither did he think he wanted to do so. While he couldn't imagine sharing his secret with any future bride, he also wasn't sure if he wanted to invest the effort and energy in doing so again, especially when it could all end so quickly.

And then Milo realized that he was sitting next to the one person in the world with whom he could share this concern, the one person who knew his secret and didn't think of him as dangerous or insane. For once, he would be able to share his feelings with someone without lying or omitting or altering facts. For the first time since that day on the school bus when *loquacious* took up residence in his mind and lies and fabrications were required to exist, Milo could just be himself with another human being.

He waited a moment, considering how he might phrase his

next sentence, and then he discarded forethought and nuance and took a deep breath. "I'm afraid that I'll never find anyone else like Christine," he said, still staring at his sneakers.

"Well, I hope not," Emma said, rising from the curb as if to imbue her words with authority. "I don't know your wife, but it's clear that you two weren't a good match, Milo. You need to find someone entirely different next time."

"No, I mean, I don't think I'll find anyone else at all. Christine might have been my one chance."

"Why would you say that?"

"It's just true," Milo said, rising from the curb in fear of appearing too pathetic.

"But why?"

"Look, Emma, I'm not the coolest guy in the world. I've got a dog named Skywalker and I play Dungeons and Dragons every Wednesday night with guys from a comic book store. I'm a hospice nurse who delivers Viagra to old men and rakes his client's carpet. I don't have many friends, I don't handle new situations well, and on top of it all, I sing karaoke and smash Weebles and have another two dozen jelly jars rolling around in my trunk because some inner force compels me to do things that I don't want to do. Finding Christine was a fucking miracle, and keeping all of my insanity hidden from her was an impossibility on top of a miracle. What are the odds of me finding that again?"

"You play Dungeons and Dragons?" Emma asked, a grin forming on the corners of her mouth.

"What?"

"I'm just kidding. Look, I could tell you not to worry, and that you'll find someone else, but frankly, I don't know. You're right. You've got some stuff going on that not every woman is going to embrace. But I'm willing to bet all the money in my wallet that the trouble with your marriage had more to do with you than it did with Christine."

316

"How can you say that? You have no idea what my marriage was like."

"I know that you were never honest with Christine. She never knew who you really were. Sure, she just dumped you on voice mail, and she sounds like a complete bitch, but maybe being married to a stranger for three years will do that to a woman."

"A stranger?"

"Yes, Milo. A stranger. You probably expended more energy keeping secrets from your wife than you did opening up to her and letting her know who you really are. What do you expect from her? Is it a surprise that there's no passion in your marriage? That you have nothing to talk about? That she's bored? She's married to a guy who can't share half of his day with her."

"So it's all my fault, then?"

"Don't get pissy with me. Asking for a divorce on voice mail is an awful thing to do, and I have no doubt that Christine is a piece of work. I've got no love for the woman, and I have no doubt in my mind that you're too good for her. But I also know that she married a man who hid the truth from her from day one. She had no clue about who she was really marrying, and that sucks for any woman. And it was pretty selfish of you."

"Pretty harsh for an advice columnist. Don't you think?"

"Bullshit," Emma shot back with a smile. "That's why my column is going to get syndicated. I don't screw around."

"So then what advice do you have for me?" Though he tried to sound flippant, Milo wanted to know the answer to this question more than any other.

"You? That's simple. If you're going to get into a relationship again, be honest this time."

"Easy for you to say. You've got secrets too, you know."

"I know," Emma said. "That's why I don't date. Until I get myself together, I'm not good for anybody, and I know it. I've got about half a dozen bad relationships to prove it. And even though

I bitch about my therapist and his desensitizing bullshit, I'm on my way north. Aren't I?"

"Well, a trip to New England isn't nearly as embarrassing as telling a woman who you barely know that you have to let the air out of your tires because some——"

"You told *me*."

"Not everyone is as *enlightened as you*."

"Thanks." She smiled again, this time a warm, friendly smile that Milo returned in kind.

"One more thing. Like I said before, I wouldn't tell you to change a thing about your life. Be yourself if that's what you want. But if you're embarrassed by these demands, and you said that you were, then maybe you should think about doing something about them. If you've got to keep them a secret from the people you love, then maybe you have a problem after all. But that's not my call. That's yours. Love yourself or fix yourself. Okay?"

The image of Louis the Porn Fiend, a.k.a. Hot Potato, entered Milo's mind. As perverse as that man had been, Louis had not been ashamed of or embarrassed about his predilections in the least. He was a man whose living room was designed to watch pornography, and he made no bones about it. And he thought about the Brysons, Emily and Michael, two enormous human beings who had shown no signs of self-conciousness as they piled enormous quantities of food onto their table and encouraged their unexpected guest to join in. He thought about Arthur Friedman and his unabashed affection for Internet pornography and Viagra-assisted masturbation. He thought about Edith Marchand and the carpet raking and Grace Bedford and her necklace of baby teeth and marveled at their willingness to share their oddities with the world. Milo wondered again if he could ever be as honest or as unabashed about his secret life, if he could share the demands of his U-boat captain with his friends or future dates or even a stranger knocking on the door. He had always been simultaneously disgusted and impressed with Louis's courage and honesty. He had found the Brysons to be both warm and repulsive at the same time, a combination of hospitality and excess that he both admired and abhorred.

Perhaps he worried that others would feel the same about him if he was to be so open about his own secrets.

"Okay," Milo said, knowing that no decision would be made in the parking lot of this gas station. Some of what Emma said had hurt, and he suspected that much of what she said would echo in his mind for days, but for the first time in his life, Milo had been completely honest with someone, and he suspected that it had also been the first time someone was able to be completely honest with him. "By the way," he said. "How much money is in your wallet anyway?"

"None," Emma said with a grin. "I never carry cash. I live and die by the credit card. But I was still right."

"I know you think you were." This time Milo smiled first.

"So what's next?" Emma asked, turning toward the car.

"I don't know. I guess the sheriff will leave the papers in my mailbox. Or he'll keep nosing around my apartment until I come home. I'm not sure how this stuff works."

"Not that. I mean with you. What's next? Bowling or karaoke?"

"Oh. Well, I'm not sure if we could even find karaoke, but the GPS should tell us where the nearest bowling alley is."

"How are you feeling?" Emma asked.

"I'm okay. Letting the air out of the tires helped a lot. There's still a lot of pressure to bowl and sing. It's hard to explain. It's not really a voice in my head. It's more of a force. A throb. But talking about it, out in the open like this, has helped, I think."

"Good. Then let's get going. We'll need to find a hotel soon too."

"I have a place in mind. It's less than an hour from here, but it's nice." Milo paused a moment, and then added, "Actually, I stayed there on the way down, so it's familiar to me. That some-times helps keep the demands away. Routines and familiarity. In the spirit of being honest, I thought I'd tell you."

"Okay. And if another demand pops into your head, you'll tell me?"

"Sure."

The bowling alley, an AMF center that Milo was pleased to see was modern and clean (some bowling alleys, in Milo's estimation, were more like an apology for the adjacent bar than an actual sporting venue), was less than three miles from the hotel where Milo hoped to stay for the night. Emma had not bowled since she was a kid and therefore proceeded to roll gutter ball after gutter ball down the lane, much to Milo's amusement.

At last he had found something at which she did not excel.

While hardly a professional bowler, the constant demands for strikes over the years had afforded Milo a great deal of practice, and he could often score well above two hundred on most days. On this evening, he beat Emma 258 to 34, his largest margin of victory ever. Had the computerized scoring device not continued to display the disparity in their performance on the television screen over their heads, Milo might have stopped keeping score altogether. He didn't have the heart to tell her that it was proba-bly more difficult to score a 34 than it was to score a 258.

Though it was not the first time that Milo had bowled with a partner as the demand for a strike pounded away in his head, it was the first time that his partner was aware of the demand, and this unexpectedly added to the pressure. It was as if his sub-mariner at the controls knew that he had an audience and wanted to make the most of this unusual moment. Not only was the demand for a strike in need of satisfaction, but now Emma was waiting anxiously for the satisfaction as well. Thankfully, Milo managed his strike on the first ball, causing Emma to leap from the plastic bench and embrace him in the middle of the lane while he attempted to savor the release associated with the toppling of ten short white pins.

"That's amazing," she shouted, loud enough to cause the pair of overweight women in the next lane to stare. "How long does it usually take you to get a strike?"

"Actually, I can usually get it on the first or second ball. It's getting to the alley that is sometimes the problem."

"Oh."

Milo watched in amusement as Emma attempted to subtly retract her excitement, slowly returning her arms to her sides and casually stepping back toward the bench, much in the way a man who has tripped attempts to incorporate the stumble into his natural gait, hoping that no one else has noticed.

As if to confirm his claim, Milo bowled four strikes in row before finally missing with a miserable seven-ten split that he failed to pick up for a spare.

After hot dogs and root beer, they made their way to the same hotel where Milo had watched *Butch Cassidy and the Sundance Kid* with Lily and Eugene just two days before, parking in the same spot that he'd had on his first visit. It seemed as if weeks had passed since then.

As they entered the lobby and passed by the movie kiosk that had attracted his attention during his last stay, Milo turned to Emma midstride and said, "I'll pay for your room. No arguments." Even as he was saying the words, he couldn't get over how easy it was to discuss sleeping arrangements now that he was no longer hiding anything from her. Just a few hours ago, those two sentences would've required planning and precision and would have been laden with anxiety and uncertainty. Now they had come without a second thought or the least of concern.

"Actually, how about one room and two beds?" Emma asked.

"Really?"

"I told you that I don't sleep very well. I sleep even worse when I'm not in my own bed in my own apartment. If I have any shot at getting some rest tonight, it'll only happen if I'm not alone."

"Are you sure?"

"Milo, I'm not making a pass at you. You're a Star Wars geek who plays Dungeons and Dragons, for God's sake. And you're still married, at least for the next six months if your wife is correct. Not to mention that I don't date, and even if I did, I wouldn't be sleeping with you after just one day together. What kind of girl do you think I am? I just have a hard time sleeping in a strange place. If you are in the room, it might make it a little easier, okay?"

"Sure. But enough about the D and D. Okay? You're not funny."

"Sorry, Frodo."

"Still not funny."

"I think so."

"Can't you find something else to do besides make fun of me?" Milo asked, though secretly he was enjoying the banter very much.

"I need to use the bathroom," she said. "Can you check us in?"

Emma turned and made her way past the hotel desk and into the restaurant on the far side of the lobby. Milo approached the high counter and waited for an employee to appear from the doorway behind the counter, hoping that it might be Lily.

It was not.

Milo handed his credit card to an African American man named Nigel and waited as the man, whose name badge declared him an assistant manager trainee, processed the transaction while somehow managing to repeat Milo every step of the way without ever making any eye contact.

"Hi, I'd like to get a room for the night."

"You'd like to get a room for the night," Nigel said, already pounding away at the keyboard. "A single, sir?"

"No, I need two beds."

"You need two beds," Nigel repeated, pounding away again.

Nigel eventually handed Milo two card keys to open the room, recorded his request for a six A.M. wake-up call in the computer, and asked if there were any bags to bring up to the room.

"We're all set," Milo said. "I can handle it."

"You're all set. Very good. Thank you, Mr. Slade."

As Milo turned to see if Emma had returned from the restroom, he felt a thundering clap on his back that nearly knocked him off his feet. "Hey! Movie man! You're back!"

Eugene was standing before him, wearing the same blue coveralls and red bandanna from two days ago.

"Eugene!" Milo said with genuine enthusiasm, reaching out to shake his hand. Eugene brushed it aside and wrapped his arms around Milo in an embrace that nearly lifted him from the ground.

"What you doing back here, man?" the large man asked with excitement.

"I'm on my way home," Milo explained. "I needed to stop for the night."

"Who's this?" It was Emma, approaching the two men from across the lobby.

"Eugene," Milo said. "This is Emma. Emma, this is Eugene."

"You didn't have a girl the first time you were here, did you?" Eugene asked.

"No," Milo said. "Emma's going back to Connecticut with me."

Eugene offered Milo a less-than-conspiratorial wink.

"We're just friends," Milo said.

"*Right.*" He winked again, in an even more obvious manner than he had the first time. Emma winked back, causing Eugene to furrow his brow and stare her down for a moment.

"Hey, is Lily here?" Milo asked.

"No, not tonight. She's off tonight."

"Too bad. I was hoping to say hello."

"Yeah, she liked you, man."

"*She did?*" Emma asked. "Who's Lily?"

"Just someone who works here," Milo said.

"And she likes Milo?" Emma asked, directing the question at Eugene.

"Yeah. She said that he . . . what's your name again?"

"Milo."

"Yeah," Eugene repeated. "She said that Milo was a nice guy."

"And that means she likes him?" Emma asked.

"Probably," Eugene said. "Lily hates just about every guy she meets. If she says you're nice, you're already better than most of them."

"And you thought that no one would be interested in you," Emma said, smiling.

"Sure," said Milo. "The girl barely knows me, lives more than five hours from my home, and said that I was nice. Lots of potential there."

"Maybe not this girl," Emma said. "But sometimes it's just nice to know that someone's interested. It gives you hope that it'll happen again."

"You don't know that?" Eugene asked.

"I know—it's sad, isn't it, Eugene?" Emma asked. "But he's a Dungeons and Dragons nerd, so what do you expect?"

"A what?"

"Never mind," Emma said. "Milo, I think I've got a solution to your karaoke problem."

"You found a place?" Milo asked. Even though his karaoke demand continued to pound away in his mind, it was the last of the demands that had threatened to topple him from earlier in the day, and it was one that he was accustomed to delaying whenever necessary. Unlike Vernon Lanes or the availability of jelly jars, Jenny's was not open twenty-four hours and was therefore not available to him at all hours, so he often had to delay the satisfaction. He had also not performed anywhere but Jenny's in more than five years, and the possibility of a new venue instantly raised his anxiety level.

"Sort of. Do you have the CD?"

"It's in the car."

"Go get it. I'll wait for you here."

Emma's solution was Hooligan's, the hotel's restaurant and bar where she had just gone to find a restroom. Though the establishment was not equipped for karaoke (no karaoke player or screen to project the words of the song that was being sung), there was a small stage and sound system set up for live entertainment on the weekends. Just twenty minutes before closing, the place was nearly empty, with a couple of businessmen nursing drinks at the bar and a family of four occupying a booth near the stage. Emma had gotten the manager to agree to allow Milo to sing one song, claiming that it was their anniversary. She had said that five years ago on this very night, she had heard Milo sing onstage in a karaoke bar and had instantly fallen in love. She told the manager, a man with a handlebar mustache and overgrown eyebrows who looked like he should have been herding cattle rather than managing a restaurant, that Milo had planned on reenacting the scene for her tonight, but they were surprised and disappointed to discover that the bar where they had met was no longer in business. She asked if he could sing just one song, and the manager, who asked Emma to call him William, had agreed.

"All set," William said to Milo, pointing at the stage. "The microphone is on. Gina will press play when you point to her. Okay?"

"Thanks," Emma said. "This means a lot."

"No problem," he said, though Milo thought he should've tipped a ten-gallon hat and said, *Don't mention it, miss. It ain't nothing.*

"Emma," Milo said once William had returned to his position behind the bar. "I don't need to do this. I can probably make it until tomorrow. This isn't like the jelly or the ice cubes. I can usually hold this one off for a while."

"But why should you? It's all set up. Now go on. Let's hear it. What's the song again?"

" 'Ninety-nine Luftballons.' But I sing the original. In German. You won't understand the words. God, this is embarrassing."

"Oh, yeah. A girl sang that song, right?"

"Yes. Her name's Nena. She's German. She sang it in English too, but I have to sing the German version."

"Are you going to sing it like a girl?" Emma asked, unable to hold back the broad smile that was nearly dividing her face in two. "Do you try to sound like her? With a high voice and all?"

"You suck. You know that? You really do."

"Whatever. Just shut up and sing."

As Milo removed the microphone from the stand and looked out into the restaurant, he could see that the two businessmen and the family of four had all turned in order to face the stage and watch his performance. Sitting just three feet from the edge of the stage, in chairs that had been dragged over from a nearby table, were Emma and Eugene, staring up at him and hardly blinking. Though Milo would've loved to walk off the stage and head for his room, proximity to satisfaction once again had its grip on him, making any hope of turning back impossible. Though he knew that he could've held off this demand for another twenty-four hours without much difficulty, now that he was on the stage, ready to perform, he was nearly bursting with the pressure and anticipation of relief.

It wasn't until Emma and Eugene began dancing that he finally relaxed and allowed himself to enjoy this odd and unforgettable moment.

chapter 32

"How are you feeling?" They had just passed over the George Washington Bridge and would be entering Connecticut in less than an hour depending on traffic, and Milo knew that the closer they got to her home state, the more difficult the trip might become for Emma.

"I'm fine. Seriously. Stop asking."

The ride from Maryland to New York had been surprisingly uneventful. They had stopped at McDonald's for breakfast and had otherwise not left the interstate. Milo's mind had been quiet all morning, the U-boat captain perhaps having gone silent, deep in enemy waters, allowing for conversation to flow between the two of them. They had spoken about their careers, with Emma detailing the plots of both of her novels and Milo describing some of his more interesting clients, including Edith Marchand, whom he hoped to see later that afternoon. Emma was highly entertained with the stories of these old people, and laughed when Milo told about Arthur Friedman's addiction to Internet porn and his need for Viagra, and Grace Bedford's necklace of baby teeth.

"Is she some kind of witch?" Emma asked between giggles.

"No, she's just an old lady with an herb garden who needs some company and an occasional foot massage. Actually, I looked the baby teeth thing up and found that it was actually common for people to do that sort of thing years ago."

"Disgusting."

"I know, but you have to wonder where all those baby teeth go after parents take them from underneath their kids' pillows. Right? What do you do? Throw them away?"

"You sure as hell don't wear them around your neck."

As the sun rose high into the clear blue morning sky, conversation had dwindled for a while, which was okay with Milo. Ordinarily he would've felt the pressure to maintain a conversation, searching for topics of interest and a means to sustain the dialogue, but with Emma, he was able to simply sit beside her and drive. Without his secret to protect, his life had suddenly become easier and more relaxed, at least around her. For once, he was perfectly at ease with himself and whatever that submariner might have planned.

It was almost noon. They had crossed over the Hudson River about an hour before, and Emma had been silent for most of that time. Unable to see her face, Milo had started to wonder if she was taking a nap. The traffic had been heavier than he expected, and he was beginning to worry that he wouldn't make it to Edith's house by three. He was considering calling and warning her that there was a chance he would miss his scheduled appointment when Emma finally broke the silence with a question that was almost asked in a whisper. "Do you think that I sort of ruined Cassidy's life? Don't lie."

"What? No. Of course not."

"You said yourself that she's been thinking about me for a long time. Ever since I disappeared. That she talked about it on the videotapes. She's spent her whole life thinking that she was responsible for my disappearance and death. That's got to weigh pretty heavily on a person."

"Sure. But it doesn't mean that you ruined her life."

"No, but it didn't make her life any easier."

"Look, Emma. You had no idea what was going to happen. You were thirteen years old. Do you really think that she's going to blame you for not calling from North Carolina to tell her that you were okay?"

"I don't know. Maybe. How would you know? You talk like you know her, but you've never even met her, Milo. You can't predict what she'll say when she sees me."

"You're worried about how Cassidy's going to react?"

"Maybe," she said, her tone negating the uncertainty of the word. "I think I have a reason to be." There was anger in Emma's voice now, but Milo knew that it was not directed at him. Like the anger that he sometimes experienced from clients who could no longer do the things they once loved, this was self-directed, so Milo knew better than to respond in kind.

"Emma, she's going to be thrilled to see you. I promise."

"How can you know that?"

"I watched the tapes. You'd be surprised how much you can learn by watching and listening to a person's diary."

"And you'd probably be surprised by how much you didn't learn."

"True," Milo admitted. "But she didn't hold back on those tapes. There came a time when I felt awful for watching them and listening to her secrets, but I didn't stop until she said her name. I know it wasn't entirely unselfish of me to keep on watching. I wanted to. It was . . . I dunno. Fascinating. Thrilling. If I had brought them on this trip, I don't think I could've resisted popping in another tape and watching some more. But as soon as I found her, I stopped and put the camera away. Then I came and found you."

"You like her, don't you?"

"Don't be stupid. Like you said, I don't even really know her."

"Yeah, but you like her just the same. Right?"

"I like her as a person," Milo said. "I liked her enough to try to find you and help her out. But you said it yourself: You can't get to know someone through a videotape."

"I didn't say that."

"Well, you should've."

The two sat quietly for a few minutes, a silent truce as Milo considered all that had been said and assumed that Emma was doing the same. She was right that he liked Freckles, but he also knew that he wasn't going to admit this to Emma. Falling for a girl whom he had only seen on a videotape was possibly more bizarre than singing "99 Luftballons" in a bar in Maryland while Eugene and Emma danced and threatened to charge the stage.

And then Milo realized that he could admit his fondness for Freckles, that this was Emma, keeper of all of his secrets, and that the old habits of cover and concealment and misdirection were not required in her presence. She already knew all about his strangeness and had accepted him for who he was. Did he really think that admitting to a crush on a woman whom he had never really met would be a deal breaker for Emma? And even if it might be, he should admit to it anyway, because this was the one time in his life when he did not need to withhold or lie about a thing, and he wasn't about to mess it up. But before he could admit to anything, Emma spoke.

"Why do you like working with old people?"

"What kind of question is that?"

"Just answer it. Why do you like working with your clients?"

"I don't know," Milo said, suddenly wondering himself. "I just get along with them, I guess. I think I'm able to sympathize with their situations. I don't know. I think I just like them."

"They don't hide much from you, do they?" Emma asked.

"What?"

"The old people. Like the Viagra man, or the lady who has you rake her carpet. They don't keep a lot of secrets from you. Do they?"

"I don't know. I guess not. Why?"

"I've got this old lady living in the apartment underneath me, and she doesn't play any games either. She hangs her bras and underwear out on the line and leaves her teeth out during the day sometimes and tells me that I look sad when no one else ever will. She even carries her adult diapers from the car to her apartment without ever trying to hide them. She's too old, I guess, to fool around. She must figure that she is who she is and that's not going to change. I bet that's why you like them. The old people. They don't keep many secrets. They show you who they really are."

"Who knows? Maybe Mr. Friedman killed the neighborhood cats when he was a kid. Maybe Edith cheated on her dead husband. Maybe Mrs. Bedford's husband is buried in her herb garden underneath the mint. How can you ever know what someone is hiding?"

"You can't, but I bet that with old people, you can come pretty close, assuming you're not spending time with cat killers or ax murderers."

"So what? What's your point?"

"That's why you like Cassidy. I mean, she's probably pretty, but she doesn't have any secrets either. She didn't intend on telling you about me and whatever other secrets she shared, but she did. She's got nothing to hide. That's why you like her."

"You're unbelievable, Emma," Milo said. "I don't think I've ever met a person more certain of herself than you. You're right. I like Freckles. Cassidy, I mean. And I'd probably never admit it to anyone but you. But it has nothing to do with all that bullshit about secrets. She's a pretty girl with a great smile and she seems smart and kind and a little wounded, and I'm a sucker for a damsel in distress. That's all it is. Okay?"

"If you say so."

Milo sighed. "You know what, Emma? I think we're going to be great friends, but part of me is very happy that you live in North Carolina. I don't think that I could stand you all year round."

"Not too many people can," Emma said with a smile.

To Milo's surprise, there was no discernible change in Emma as they passed over the New York–Connecticut border and into Fairfield County. He wanted to think that all of Emma's talk about New England being a black hole was bullshit, but he knew that it was not. This was simply another instance of Emma handling a difficult situation better than most would. Even though there might be a battle between the present and the past raging in her head, she continued to smile as the wind blew through her hair and she breathed in the smells of the Connecticut shoreline.

"If we go straight to Edith's house, I can make it on time," Milo said. "Would you mind coming with me before we go to see Cassidy? I haven't seen Edith in almost a week, and I don't ever go this long without stopping by. Is that okay?"

"Sure. Cassidy's waited twenty years to see me. She can wait a couple hours more."

Milo thought that Emma could wait a couple more hours as well.

At a quarter after three, Milo and Emma pulled into the driveway of Edith Marchand of Stancliff Road in Glastonbury. He had never been late for an appointment with Edith before, and he had half expected her to be standing on her front stoop, waiting for his arrival.

"I'll be less than an hour. Okay?"

"What?"

"I won't be more than hour," he repeated.

"Milo, I'm going inside with you."

"No, you're not. She's not expecting you. This is *my job*, Emma. I never bring visitors with me."

"Milo, I am going inside with you or we are leaving. I'm not going to sit in this car for an hour waiting for you."

"Emma, I can't let you—"

Edith's voice interrupted midsentence. She was standing on her stoop, just seconds after Milo had expected her to be there, and she was shouting his name. "Milo! Is something wrong?"

"Please just wait here," Milo pleaded.

Instead of waiting, Emma opened the door to the Honda and climbed out. "Hello!" she shouted. "I'm Emma, a friend of Milo's. Do you mind if I join you today?"

"Not at all, dear," Edith said, louder than Milo thought she was capable of. "Good Lord, why are you two just sitting out there? Come on in."

Emma stuck her head back into the car and flashed Milo a sarcastic grin before slamming the door shut and turning up the walkway toward the stoop. "I'm sorry, but Milo never told me your name."

"It's Edith, dear. Come on in. Milo, are you coming?"

He was sitting in the Honda, the engine still running.

Fifteen minutes later Milo was serving tea to Edith and Emma and preparing to rake the living room rug.

"So let me guess," Edith said, directing her question at Emma. "You are the young lady from the videotape. Am I correct?"

Milo attempted to answer, but Emma spoke first.

"Actually, no. I'm an old friend of the woman on the tape. We're going to see her later this afternoon."

"Oh, that's too bad."

"Why's that?" Emma asked, lifting her feet to allow Milo to rake beneath them.

"Yeah, why's that?" Milo asked.

"I don't mean to tell secrets, but Milo has a crush on the girl on that videotape, and I was hoping that she was you. I like you."

"He does?" Emma asked, nudging Milo with her foot. "Really?"

"Yes, he does, and don't let him tell you otherwise. But he's still married and needs to decide on things with that wife of his first before chasing some girl he's never even met before."

"I'm standing right here," Milo said. "Could you please not talk about me like I'm invisible?"

"I wasn't," Edith said. "You know how I feel. But Emma, if things don't work out between Milo and his wife, I want you to know that he's a fine catch."

"Oh, really? Why do you say that?"

"Well," said Edith, leaning forward in her chair, "he is just a nice man, and I'm sure I don't have to tell you how hard that is to find sometimes."

"No, you don't," Emma said.

"It's a shame too," Edith said. "I have a son named Tony, and I love that boy dearly, but he can't go fifteen minutes without rolling his eyes at me or telling me that I'm doing something wrong or that I'm foolish or just plain silly. Milo has never once looked at me like that. I know that raking this carpet may seem foolish to a lot of people, my son included, but I like the way it looks when he's done, and Milo's never once made me feel foolish for asking him to do it. Even the first time. When you can say what's on your mind without always having to worry if someone thinks of you as a fool, you've found a real catch."

"You make a good argument, Edith. I'm afraid that Milo and I are probably just going to be friends, but I'll pass on the good word to Cassidy."

"You wait until he's settled things with his wife. No need confusing things with another woman. Okay, Milo?"

"Yes, Edith. I know."

"I told you so," Emma said once they were back in the car and on the way to Cassidy's house.

"What?"

"Never mind."

"Hey, thanks for not telling Edith about Christine's call. I'll tell her that we're getting divorced, but I'll do it on a day when I have more time to sit around and listen to her scold me."

"No problem. How long before we get to Cassidy's? My Connecticut geography is a little rusty. Cassidy may live here now, but remember, I never did."

"Less than thirty minutes. Why?"

"I have to think about what I'll say to her. What I'll say first, I mean."

"Just introduce yourself," Milo said. "She'll probably do the rest."

"Yeah, like kick me in the shin or slug me."

"You'll be fine."

It was four thirty when Milo and Emma knocked on Cassidy's front door. He couldn't believe it. After all this time, he was about to reunite these two women and finally put a part of Cassidy's mind at ease. All the hours of watching tapes and researching backgrounds and driving to and from North Carolina had led him to this moment. He would finally meet Cassidy Glenn, a.k.a. Freckles, the girl that had propelled him on his journey. And because he was standing beside Emma, soon to be introduced as Tess, he felt more relaxed than he ever could have imagined.

No one answered on the first knock, so Milo knocked a second time and then rang the doorbell when that proved fruitless.

They waited another minute, unwilling to accept that after they had come all this way, she might not be home.

Finally, they had no choice but to accept defeat.

"So we wait?" Emma asked.

"No. I think I may know where she is. But I want to swing by my apartment first."

The sun was low in the sky as Milo and Emma crossed the wide expanse of grass at Mill Pond Park in the direction of the crowd gathered along the north end of the field. Practice was under way on the baseball diamond to their left. Round, hairy coaches shouted commands to small, pale boys wearing gloves twice the size of their hands. The wide path around the pond was peppered with people in spring jackets and sneakers, pushing strollers, holding hands, and jogging in circles. Above the crowd to the north, kites fluttered in the late-afternoon breeze, rising and diving at the command of their owners. Small children were running beneath them, their arms waving, their laughter carried on the wind to where Milo and Emma were now standing.

"There she is," Milo said, pointing to Cassidy, who was talking to a short, thin Indian man while examining a yellow and red striped kite in his hands. She was wearing a green polka-dotted shirt and jeans, and her hair was tucked into a pink baseball cap.

"Look at her," Emma said in a hush. "She's all grown up."

"You are too," Milo said.

They stood, staring for a moment longer in silence, watching as Cassidy continued her conversation with the man.

Finally, Emma took a deep breath and sighed. "So I guess this is it, huh? We should go?"

"No," Milo said. "You should go. I'm going to leave."

"What?"

"I'm going to leave you two and go. But please, give this to her for me." He held out the nylon camera bag that he had found three weeks ago under a park bench beneath a dying elm. "The camera and all the tapes are inside."

"Milo, don't be stupid. You're coming. You didn't spend all that time and energy finding me to quit now. If I'm going to be brave enough to walk over there, you are too."

"It's not about being brave," Milo said. "It just took me this long to realize that this whole thing isn't about me. I thought that by knowing all of Cassidy's secrets, I had some kind of connection with her. I thought I could ride in on a white horse and be her hero. But she doesn't even know me, and she sure as hell doesn't need to see me today. She may never need to see me, and if that's the way she wants it, that's okay with me. If I knew that someone had watched my video diary and learned all my secrets, I'm not sure if I would want to meet them either. But she needs to see you, Emma. She needs to see that Tess Bryson is alive and well and know that what she did twenty years ago was good. That she's the hero. This is about the two of you, Emma. Not me."

Emma opened her mouth and then closed it again in what seemed to Milo as a preempted rebuttal. Then she reached up, placed her hands on his shoulders, and drew him close. "I can't believe that a nerd who plays Dungeons and Dragons could say something so sweet."

"Look who's talking. You still sleep with the lights on."

"Low blow, Milo."

The two stood in the thick grass for a moment longer, smiling at each other, before Emma finally spoke. "Thank you, Milo. But this isn't goodbye, right?"

"Hell, no. And if you need a ride to the train station or a place to sleep tonight, just call me. Okay?"

"All right. But I'm still going to tell her what a catch you are. I don't care what you say."

"Save it for later. You have too much catching up to do. And Emma, thank you."

"For what? My splendid company?"

Milo thought for a moment, unsure how to condense so much into such a small space. Then he smiled again. "For catching me with the jelly," he said. "And everything that came after that. You'll never know how much it's meant to me."

"I have that affect on people," Emma said, returning the smile.

The two embraced as the sun began to mingle among the trees that lined the edge of the park, and then Emma turned and began walking slowly toward Cassidy, shuffling her feet through the carpet of green. Milo began walking in the opposite direction but stopped after a moment and looked back. He looked on as Emma approached Cassidy from behind, tapped her lightly on the shoulder, and waited for her childhood friend to turn. Too far away to hear their words, he watched as Emma spoke first, taking pleasure in the unusual timidity and uncertainty in her posture. Then he smiled as Cassidy's hands flew up to her face, cupping her mouth to muffle a scream that just managed to reach Milo's ears. Emma spoke again, for longer than Milo would have expected, as Cassidy stood frozen in place, staring at her friend, before reaching out and embracing Emma with all her might. The two were still clutching each other a minute later when Milo finally turned and headed back across the field to his car, the demands of life already reasserting themselves in his mind.

He was late in picking up his dog.

epilogue

Unsure of what she preferred, Milo had purchased nine different kinds of candy, ranging from Twizzlers to Whoppers to the pink Canada Mints, which, much to Milo's dismay, were not actually manufactured in Canada. He had stuffed them all into a brown paper bag, which was sitting between his feet and ready to go as soon as she arrived. This was his first date since he and Christine had negotiated the details of their divorce four weeks before, and even though they would have to wait six more weeks for it to be official, Milo had decided that it was time to return to the dating scene.

Emma's prodding had certainly helped.

Thick-Neck Phil had already moved in with Christine and was assisting with the refinance and eventual buyout of Milo's interest in the home, even though his soon-to-be-ex-wife had assured Milo repeatedly that nothing had happened between the two of them until well after the divorce papers had been served. Milo had his doubts but was surprised to find that he no longer cared. Though the thought of all of those wasted hours pulling rosebushes around the house and refinishing the wood floors still bothered him more than it should, the settlement, which had proved to be sizable, more than made up for the bloodied hands and bruised knees.

Emma had offered to drive up to assist in the plans for this first date, but Milo knew better than to accept her offer. The two had spoken at least once a week over the phone since their drive up from North Carolina, and last month she had spent the weekend in Connecticut playing a two-day Dungeons & Dragons marathon after losing a bet with Milo over a Red Sox–Yankees game in mid-April.

It turned out that Emma enjoyed wagering a great deal.

Though Milo and his friends did not typically dress up for their Dungeons & Dragons adventures (with the exception of Cushman), they had made an exception for the special occasion and donned the outfits of a dwarf, an elf, and a Paladin. For Emma, they purchased a wizard's robe and matching hat, tall and pointed and covered in stars, which she grudgingly wore for most of the first day. Even under an agreement that she would play enthusiastically and by the rules, she had made Cushman look like a saint. Still, by the end of the weekend, Andy, Danny, and Cushman had all fallen in love with her.

Milo knew better.

He had also spoken to Cassidy over the phone and had met her once for coffee at her insistence (though he'd ordered an apple juice and water). As he feared, the conversation between the two of them had been strained and awkward. It was understandable. Though Cassidy had expressed great appreciation for his bringing her and Emma together (the two were speaking over the phone almost as much as he and Emma were), she was also talking to the man who had taken her camera and tapes from a park bench, watched them despite their obvious private nature, and knew secrets about her past that she had not shared with anyone in her life.

Milo certainly understood if Cassidy's feelings regarding him were mixed, or if she felt uncomfortable in his presence.

"I don't understand why you aren't taking her to a real movie theater," Eugene said, reaching in and grabbing another handful of popcorn from the bag on Milo's lap.

"This is where we watched our first movie together, so I thought it would be a nice place to come back to the same place for our date."

"In the break room?"

"Yeah. You don't think she'll like it?"

"I know I wouldn't," Eugene said.

"Well, I'm going to take her out to dinner after the movie, if that makes you feel better."

"Only if you don't sing to her. You're just lucky that she wasn't working that night when you got on the stage. Damn, that shit was funny."

Milo had called Lily about a month after his stay in the Ramada, and they had been speaking over the phone two or three times a week since then, exchanging texts and e-mails as well. Milo didn't really think that a relationship with a five-hour commute was going to work, but Emma had persuaded him to give it a try. "You can't expect the first girl you meet after Christine to be the one, so let Lily be your rebound girl. Be nice, have a good time, and get laid."

No wonder her advice column had been syndicated in more than a dozen markets.

By maintaining a buffer zone of more than three hundred miles, Milo had also been able to avoid telling Lily the truth about his condition, which was something he had hoped to do with future women. So far Emma was still the only person who knew about the jelly jars, the bowling, and the replacing of air in the Honda's tires, which had unfortunately become a regular item on the U-boat captain's list. But if things went well with Lily, he hoped to tell her soon.

Maybe.

He had also thought about seeking help to try to reduce the

influence of the demands on his life, as Emma had suggested and continued to suggest, but so far he hadn't done this either. Since he was living alone and could easily satisfy the demands quickly, he wondered if it wouldn't be easier just to continue with the way he was living rather than talk to someone who ultimately might not be able to help him.

What Milo had done was continue to recite the poem that he had extracted from the *Highlights* magazine in Dr. Teagan's office, attempting to apply Nurse Mancuso's advice to his demands by *not scratching* when one arose. He was beginning on a small scale, attempting to ignore the demand for ice cubes by deliberately diverting his attention to other things, including and especially the poem. He had even gone bowling and sung at Jenny's when the demand for ice had arisen, thinking that perhaps he could find a way to substitute one of these demands for another, hoping that this substitution might begin the process of gaining more control over them. Sort of like scratching around an itch instead on top of it, as Nurse Mancuso might suggest. Though this new strategy hadn't met with any success yet, he was still trying.

The door to the break room opened and Lily entered, wearing a short black dress and heels. "Wow, you look great," Eugene said before Milo could say the same.

"Are you staying?" Lily asked, with the beginnings of a grin.

"Don't worry, Lil. I told Milo that I'd stand in the hall and guard the door so you won't be bothered. Unless you want me to stay."

"I love you, Eugene, but how about letting me and Milo watch this one alone, okay?"

"Sure. No problem. I seen it already anyway. And I won't spoil it for you like you did to me last time."

Eugene rose to leave and Lily moved in to take his place on the bench.

"You be a gentleman," Eugene warned as he stood in the doorway.

"We're in the break room, Eugene. Even if I wanted to make a move, what could I do?"

"You have no idea the stuff that's happened on that table," Eugene said.

"That's right. I forgot."

Eugene switched off the lights and shut the door, leaving Milo and Lily alone on the bench under the glow of the wall-mounted television screen.

"What are we watching?" Lily asked.

"*Thelma and Louise*. Have you seen it before?"

"No. Have you?"

"Yes. It's great," Milo said. "Not as good as *Butch Cassidy and the Sundance Kid*, but it's close."

"Doesn't it have a sad ending too?"

"I'm not sure," Milo said. "Things might change at any time. Let's find out."